*While that talisman exists I cannot hope to vanquish either Caitin or the Kingdoms. He holds the one part, his woman the other. Their love binds them as one, uniting the stone. While they, together, possess the cursed thing the balance is weighted in the Lady's favour. I must wrest both parts from them.*

'The woman,' Taws said quickly, 'she will be his weakness: he hers. Separate them, let the one be bait for the other, the talisman the ransom for the captive's life.'

*It had occurred to me,* responded Ashar with massive contempt. *Indeed, I have begun my move. And this time I shall not be thwarted.*

*Also by Angus Wells in Sphere Books*
THE FIRST BOOK OF THE KINGDOMS:
WRATH OF ASHAR

THE SECOND BOOK OF THE KINGDOMS:
THE USURPER

# THE THIRD BOOK OF THE KINGDOMS:
# THE WAY BENEATH

## Angus Wells

ORBIT

An Orbit Book

First published in Great Britain in Orbit by
Sphere Books Ltd 1990

ISBN 0 7474 0263 9

Typeset by Selectmove Ltd, London
Reproduced, printed and bound in Great Britain by
BPCC Hazell Books
Aylesbury, Bucks, England
Member of BPCC Ltd.

Sphere Books Ltd
A Division of
Macdonald & Co (Publishers) Ltd
Orbit House
1 New Fetter Lane
London EC4A 1AR
A member of Maxwell Macmillan Pergamon Publishing Corporation

*For Colin Murray, the right way round at last.*

# Prologue

HE had not known pain until now; that sensation had been the preserve of mortal flesh and he had not thought to experience it. Nor had he anticipated a second defeat, yet that had come and with it such exquisite pain his preternatural senses exploded in disorder. Vision was gone; taste, smell, hearing lost; touch became an abstract, consumed beneath the raw wash of agony. His universe, his very being, was suffering, the pain overriding all save the one remaining sensation: fear. Fear was a permanent thing for all who served Ashar; more so for him, who was created of and by the god, who was so wholly Ashar's creature.

And fear possessed him now. He felt it in the deepest channels of his unnatural being, gripping him with a strength that slowly overcame the pain, relegating that anguish to a secondary status in his returning awareness.

He had failed his master again.

The once at the Lozin Gate, where the might of the Horde he had raised to bring Ashar's will to the Three Kingdoms broke against the determination of a single manling, and now again when that same weak creation of flesh and blood had stood against him, aided by no more than a weaker woman.

*And the talisman*, said a voice that was not a voice but a crescendo of agony within him.

He opened his eyes and saw only fire. Ashar's fire, that had sustained him and now seared him. He screamed, knowing the fury of his master, and the fire abated a fraction, enough that he could assess his situation, order his memories, sense the emptiness inside him.

'The talisman?' he asked in a voice that quavered, no longer confident.

*Kyrie's talisman!* The god spat the words as if even mention of the Lady's name was distasteful.

'She gave them power?' He saw a fragment of hope, a faint glimmer of optimism that glinted dimly through the threatening flames.

1

*Estrevan gave them the stones; the two halves of the talisman. With those they defeated you.*

He shuddered afresh. Had his eyes been capable of producing tears he would have wept, but they could not and instead he said, 'Kedryn was blind.'

*Kedryn regained his sight,* the god responded, *he entered the netherworld with the woman and found the one you used to take his eyes. Borsus gave him back his sight.*

'Borsus?' Disbelief was in his reply. 'Borsus was my man. How might he aid Kedryn Caitin?'

*Did I create so feeble a creature?* The utter contempt stung him with a fiery lash. *Do you know that all is a balance? That for each move of mine there is a countermove she* – again the single word was spat out – *may take? It is decreed so by a power greater even than mine, and that allowed the one they call the Chosen to gain back his lost sight. I had thought to outmanoeuvre her; thought that your suborning of the one called Hattim Sethiyan must win me the game, but it did not. You failed me, Taws.*

He felt resentment then, and the god's knowledge of it brought pain afresh to the embodiment of his creation. He screamed, knowing the ululation was as music to his master and might thus placate the god. After what was either a little while or an eternity the anguish eased and he spoke again, fearfully, knowing that he pleaded for his very existence.

'I did not know he penetrated the netherworld. I did not know he had regained his sight. I did not know he possessed the half of the talisman, the woman the other.'

*And I could not warn you,* said the god. *She is strong in the Kingdoms – stronger now for your defeat – and I could only trust in you to do my will there.*

'As I did,' Taws moaned, cringing as the flames that surrounded him burned brighter. 'Had I but known of the talismans I could have taken measures against their power.'

*You had knowledge of the ones whose souls you drank,* countered Ashar, *You had Kedryn Caitin and the woman called Wynett within your grasp.*

Taws groaned, remembering the blue light, the quintessence of all he opposed, that had struck against him and quelled his own hellish fire. 'I could not fight against the joined strength of the two halves,' he gasped.

*No,* Ashar agreed, *you could not. That power was too great, but it has shown me two things.*

There was a pause that the cringing form of the mage took as hopeful until the god spoke again.

*While that talisman exists I cannot hope to vanquish either Caitin or the Kingdoms. He holds the one part, his woman the other. Their love binds them as one, uniting the stone. While they, together, possess the cursed thing the balance is weighted in the Lady's favour. I must wrest both parts from them.*

'The woman,' Taws said quickly, 'she will be his weakness; he hers. Separate them, let the one be bait for the other, the talisman the ransom for the captive's life.'

*It had occurred to me*, responded Ashar with massive contempt. *Indeed, I have begun my move. And this time I shall not be thwarted.*

Taws smiled then, his fleshless lips stretching despite the pain of Ashar's fires. He asked, 'What part do I play, Master?'

*You have no part*, answered the god, *you have outlived your usefulness and I have no further need of you. What I do now, I do alone. Now Kedryn Caitin shall face me.*

The smile upon Taws's mantis features became a rictus of inexpressible agony as the flames burned higher, brighter, becoming all that he knew, the core of his being until that gift of Ashar was taken back.

\*

Within the farthest reaches of the Beltrevan Caroc hunters trembled as flame lit the night sky, its brilliance dimming the light of the spring stars, midnight becoming as noonday in high summer. It seemed a rift was opened in the very skin of the world to give access to Ashar's fire, the roiling column stretching to the heavens, its outwash rendering the mightiest trees to pale ash that blew on the hellish wind, that awful gusting felling timber in a great corona about the central pyre. Birds roasted in the branches and small animals upon the ground, burrowing creatures died in their holes while others fled in stark terror from the conflagration, forest bulls running alongside the great cats, wolves pacing them, companions in fear with the deer that bounded, wide-eyed and oblivious of the predators, all unified in their desire to escape that ghastly holocaust.

No men were seriously harmed, for none ventured near that place where first, so legend had it, Ashar had brought the Messenger into the world. It was a place both sacred and cursed, for the Messenger had promised much and led the tribes of the Beltrevan down into defeat. Now, with peace agreed and the world turned on its head with a Kingdomer *hef-Alador* by swordright, it was deemed best to steer well clear. Consequently only a few suffered hurt, a handful struck by storm-tossed branches, some by charging bulls, a scattering burnt by the more natural fire that followed the initial eruption. Most hurried to the more hospitable regions of the forest, wishing only to get themselves well clear of the raging flames, not wishing to know whether Ashar expressed his anger or lamented his defeat. That was something for the shamans to debate, and they would not come together until the time of the summer Gathering; honest warriors, having tasted the ashes of vanquishment, preferred now to go about their human business and leave the arguments of the gods to the deities.

\*

In High Fort, the chatelain Rycol was summoned from his dinner table to observe a most curious phenomenon. It was an event without precedence and drew a sizeable crowd of onlookers, doubtless on the Keshi side of the Idre, too.

The serjeant sent by the captain of the watch to inform Rycol did not believe it was the work of the woodlanders for it moved down the river and there was no sign of human participation in its coming. In any event, it came too swiftly for the great booms to be swung out and was, in the serjeant's breathtaken opinion, too large for even the booms to halt. Alarmed, Rycol set down his eating implements, pushed back his chair, and hurried from the dining hall, bellowing orders as he went. Consequently, in addition to those merely interested in the sight, it was also seen by a large part of the garrison as soldiers manned the ramparts with readied bows and the artillerymen realigned their catapults and mangonels. Rycol and those with him had the better view, for they rushed to the quayside where sight of the river was unobstructed.

The night was light, the moon full, its radiance offsetting the shadows cast by the bulking walls of the river canyon so that the surface of the Idre shone like velvet spun with webs of silver. Winter's snows were long melted, though the run-off from the forest country to the north still raised the level of the river, sending her hurrying swiftly southwards like some watery lover anxious to meet her paramour. The floodtides of early spring were ended and Rycol had counted on the great waterway lowering gradually from his walls, the races ceasing to permit a resumption of normal river traffic. What he saw brought a frown of misapprehension to his lean features, for he had never seen its like before.

From the north came a surging wall of water, foam lining the crest, creamed by the moon's light, the waves that buffeted the rocky walls confining the river filling the night with angry sound. Rycol's warning shout was lost beneath the liquid cacophany, though fortunately the sight alone was sufficient to send the observers darting back from the riverside. Fortunate because the surge overlapped the banks, spilling waves knee-high across the flagstones, drenching boots and dress hems, toppling several of the less agile on their rumps. The fort's boats were tossed like corks, three filling and sinking, two others hurled ashore by the sheer force of the wave. Rycol heard it slap the stones and felt the wash over his feet, heard the fishing boats and ferry craft of the town below his citadel crash together and against the docksides, heard the shouts of alarm that rang from his own people. He doubted what he saw, for he thought that within the wave he discerned a shape, the behemoth outline of a massive creature that swam the Idre, creating the unnatural wave with the speed of its bulky passage. He shook his head, staring into the darkness as lights abruptly burned in the town, the folk there rushing to assess the damage. He could not have seen what he thought he saw: no such creature existed; it must surely have been a trick of the light, wave and moon combining to fool his eyes.

He turned to his wife and saw her stooping to wring the soaked skirts of her gown. 'Did you see it?' he asked.

'How might I miss it?' demanded Marga, her tone somewhat irked. 'I am drenched.'

'What did you see?' he wondered.

Marga let fall her skirts and looked at her husband, frowning. 'I saw a wave. A great floodtide wave. What else?'

'Nothing,' said Rycol, shaking his head, wondering if age began to cloud his vision.

'Nothing would not put that look on your face,' Marga said. 'Tell me what you saw – or think you saw.'

Rycol turned to stare at the river, its surface still marked by the swell-torn aftermath, but settling now, smoothing, so that the silvery meshing of moonlight again set a patchwork patterning on the darkness. Wavelets still slapped against the quay, but their susurration was the small irritation of disturbed water rather than the furious roaring of that mighty wave.

'I thought,' he said slowly, taking her arm to escort her over the slippery flags, 'that something moved within the wave. A shape – I am not certain, it was so far out – huge.'

'A log?' she suggested. 'Disturbed by the river?'

'No.' Again he shook his head. 'It was too large. I thought it created the wave.'

'There is nothing that big in the Idre,' Marga retorted pragmatically.

'No,' Rycol agreed, 'it was probably a trick of the light.'

Thoughts of dark magic crossed his mind and were dismissed. Kedryn and Wynett had defeated the Messenger, *mehdri* had brought word from Andurel of their victory over Taws, and with the mage gone, the usurper Hattim Sethiyan slain, the Kingdoms knew peace from Ashar's fell machinations. Not magic then, he decided, merely some natural occurrence. A late spring tide, a melting of snow from the mountains that bound the Beltrevan to the north, perhaps some log jam higher up the river; no more than that and an imagination rendered excessively fertile by the events of the past months.

'Probably.' His wife's voice brought him back from his musings. 'But meanwhile I am wet and the night is chill; shall we find dry footwear and a fire?'

'Aye,' he nodded, and gave orders for the watch to stand down.

His doubts, however, lingered and the signallers in the great towers were ordered to send word across the water to Low Fort, from which Fengrif, the Keshi commander, returned his surmise that some snowy plateau must have slipped to create a tidal wave. Discreet questioning of his men revealed a similar opinion, and even those who, like Rycol, had thought they saw something could not be sure what. The next day he made a personal inspection of the town, taking the opportunity to question the folk there. They concurred with the majority of the garrison that the phenomenon was of natural origin and that whilst several boats had been wrecked when the wash drove them against the wharves neither Ashar nor the woodlanders could be held responsible. Finally he allowed himself to be convinced and inscribed only a brief mention of the occurrence in the log he kept, not bothering to send word downriver to Andurel.

*

Gerat, Paramount Sister of Estrevan, closed the leathern covers of the book she held and set the slim volume on the simple oak table before her. The spring sunlight that filled the tower room shone on the worn bindings, lightening the blue so that it assumed a shade to match the colour of the gown she wore. She stroked the smooth surface as though reluctant to give up its touch, assessing the thoughts that filled her mind, seeking to impose order on them.

Alaria had warned of so much and explained so little, that often enough in terms of parable or near-rhyme so that certain understanding was become a nebulous thing, like the half-remembered images of a fading dream. Yet that had been her intent, surely, for the visions granted her by the Lady were dream-like, and even with Alaria's talent for prognostication not clear indications of the path to be taken, but rather suggestions, warnings, hints. That was the way of the Lady – to allow always the freedom of self-determination – and the very basis of the Sisterhood's philosophy. To define a clear path was to define the actions required, the way to be taken, and thus to limit the freedom of choice that was the essence of the Sisters' faith. The Lady Yrla Belvanne had quit Estrevan of her own free will, under no coercion to go into Tamur where she had met Bedyr Caitin and become his wife. That had been a matching of hearts that had produced Kedryn Caitin, the Chosen One foretold by Alaria. And Kedryn, a stripling then, barely come to his manhood, might without any loss of honour have refused to face Niloc Yarrum in single combat. Yet he had chosen to do battle with the leader of the Horde and thus halted the foresters' invasion at the very portals of the Three Kingdoms, forging afterwards a peace with the barbarians that was unprecedented in living or written memory.

And Wynett, Gerat thought, she was committed to the way of the Lady, dedicated to the celibacy that ensured the continuance of her healing talent, yet she had gone willingly into the Beltrevan with Kedryn. Gone farther with him, into the regions of the netherworld, where together they had won back his sight and Wynett had seen her destiny lay not in sole duty to the Lady, but in love of Kedryn. Without that choice made they would not have celebrated the love that bound them, uniting the two parts of Kyrie's talisman that it might stand against the power of Ashar's Messenger and overcome his magicks to restore unity to the Kingdoms.

All those choices had been made and the Messenger defeated, Ashar's workings thwarted that peace might reign, the Kingdoms secure.

Is it then, Gerat wondered, ended? Is the Text fulfilled? She relinquished her touch on the book and rose to cross the small

7

chamber to the closest window, raising eyes of a startlingly clear blue to the sky. Larks swooped there, pursuing the insectile bounty the warmth of spring raised above the city, darting shapes against the heat-hazed heavens. Far, far off the Gadrizels were a blur across the eastern horizon, darkening even as she watched as the sun continued its westerly path towards its setting. She let her gaze move slowly over the plain that ran from the foothills of the mountain range to the walls of the city, seeing less with her eyes than with her inner knowledge the burgeoning pasture lands and the farms that dotted the fertile champaign. The senses that had made her Paramount Sister welcomed the emotions she felt emanating from those simple homesteads where farmers were content to till their fields and husband their animals, yielding slowly as her eyes moved closer, looking down to encompass the rooftops and avenues of the city men called sacred, to the busier emotions of the inhabitants. Here she could feel the pleasure of merchants at a fair-struck bargain, and the delight of clients in their purchases; the anticipation of good food prepared in a comfortable home; the warmth of companionship; above all, the peace that was an aura of almost physical intensity about the central buildings of the Sisterhood, the very core of Estrevan, the focal point of the city's growth and being.

Perhaps, she mused, we have too much peace. Perhaps we live too far from the daily workings of the Kingdoms. Yet Sisters inhabited Tamur and Kesh and Ust-Galich; teachers and hospitallers, those gifted with the sending powers and the far-sight, the prognosticators. Bethany governed the college in Andurel, and in all the towns of the Kingdoms there were others bringing Kyrie's word and the succour of their individual talents, and through them Estrevan was made aware of the worldly happenings of mankind. And was it not important that one place should stand apart? A place where those who sought it might find peace? They did not have to come – that, too, was a choice made freely, both by those laymen and women who came, and by those who sought to develop latent talents in service of the Lady. Without them – without the tranquillity Estrevan bestowed – would it have been possible to interpret Alaria's Text? To inform those needed in the Kingdom's defence of the choices that lay before them? Without Estrevan would the Messenger have been defeated?

Perhaps I ponder over much, she told herself. What is done is done and cannot be turned back; Taws is gone and Kedryn wed to Wynett, as best I know hailed king. Young, admittedly, but of unquestionable integrity, and gifted with wisdom. He has Wynett to advise him, and his father, too, and Bedyr Caitin is a good man. And I have done all I can to see the way Alaria foretold and guide his steps along that path.

So why, she asked herself as she turned from the window to look westwards to a sun preparing to go down in a blaze of golden glory, do these nagging doubts linger still?

Why am I not sure it has ended?

# Chapter One

KEDRYN Caitin, Prince of Tamur and ruler-elect of the Three Kingdoms, stared moodily from a tower of the White Palace over the lawns surrounding the monarch's residence to the rooftops of Andurel. Set as it was atop a hill, the palace commanded the finest view possible of the island city, and the height of the tower on which he stood granted him a perspective few save the birds wheeling overhead might enjoy. To the south, looking past the cascades that foamed and rumbled down steep steps of time-carved stone, he could discern the borders of Ust-Galich; to the northeast, beyond the Vortigen, the sweeping grasslands of Kesh; northwest lay his homeland of Tamur, separated from Kesh by the great sun-silvered ribbon of the Idre. He could discern boats upon the waterway, fishing craft and ferries and traders, and when he turned his gaze around to the southwest he could see the last remnants of the Galichian army winding ant-like in the distance down the portage that ran alongside the cascades. Below him the city spread in jewel-like brilliance over the slopes of the eyots that afforded it support, as if it sprang from the surface of the river herself, webworks of bridges arching between the juts of stone, the roofs of vari-coloured tile reflecting the early morning sun in myriad hues, the parks and gardens budding green with the promise of spring, crocuses and snowdrops splashing the lawns with bright colours, the avenues like arteries spreading from the heart that was the White Palace.

A heart that must beat to the drumming of a king, the cadence held by the man who occupied the High Throne, resident in this wondrous place.

His eyes turned again to the western banks of the Idre, towards Tamur, misty at this early hour, and his heart swelled with love of that hardy land, and the fear that he might not again know her. The wind coming off the river swept strands of long brown hair across his face and he reached to push them clear, aware that his eyes moistened and not sure whether that

10

was caused by the breeze or the inevitability that sat heavy on his soul.

Below him he could hear the shouts of the masons repairing the throne room ravaged by the magical duel with Taws, the pounding of their hammers and the steady creaking of the windlasses reminding him of those same sounds in High Fort, after the defeat of the Horde, that memory in turn bringing more, a sense of time rushing, bearing him forwards as helplessly as a twig carried on the race of a floodtide. It seemed so short a time since he had ridden out from Caitin Hold a boy, not yet blooded, eager to face barbarian blades and win his manhood, and now he stood atop the palace the folk of the Kingdoms assumed was his, expecting him to take the medallion worn by poor, dead Darr and govern them. They awaited his coronation, he knew, for he was wedded to Darr's elder daughter and he was the Chosen One, he had banished Taws, and Hattim Sethiyan was dead, and all declared him the rightful heir to the High Throne. His father, Bedyr, and his mother, Yrla, both voiced their support, as did Jarl of Kesh, even the Galichians, now repentant of their dead lord's usurpation. All seemed confident of his ability to assume the medallion of regal office; all save him.

He stared across the rooftops to the harbour area, knowing that Galen Sadreth's *Vashti* lay at anchor there, and wondered if the bluff river captain would agree to take him on board and bring him home again to Tamur, or lend his voice to the chorus that proclaimed him bound by right and duty to accept the throne. It seemed they could none of them see any other choice for him, not his parents or his closest friends. Tepshen Lahl, whose council he had valued since first the ageless easterner had versed him in swordcraft, spoke of obligations that could not be avoided; Brannoc, in whose wolfshead love of freedom he had hoped to find a sympathetic ear, could only shrug and say that he saw no other choice. Even Wynett lent her support, pointing out that the occupant of the High Throne unified the Kingdoms and that without a king they must again descend into chaos, and as he had fought so hard to prevent that very disruption how could he now turn his back.

Yet he doubted his ability to assume such responsibility. Tamur, yes, he could govern that kingdom in the fullness of time, when Bedyr finally went to join their ancestors, but that was long years off and he would have time to grow into the role, time to learn the arts of governance, to learn from his father. And Tamur was but one kingdom. To assume the leadership of the Three Kingdoms was a task so vast it frightened him as no physical threat could. He did not, no matter what was said of him, consider himself a diplomat, and whoever sat in the White Palace must be that above all else. To juggle the interests of Tamur and Kesh and Ust-Galich, to balance the desires of three lords, to avoid offence or favouritism, that was a task to try any man. It was little wonder Darr had seemed so aged, his hair greyed before its time, with that great weight of cares upon him every day.

He sniffed, scenting the many perfumes of Andurel, bread hot from the ovens, and fish, grass becoming lush now that the sun shone strong, the flinty odour of stone new-cut, horse smells from the stables below, the oil of tended weapons, and the scents mingled with the panorama below him and reminded him that he must soon decide ... what? What choice did he really have? Could he refuse the medallion, leave the Kingdoms to find a new monarch? Watch petty rivalries spring up, perhaps to erupt into civil war?

No, said the voice of his conscience, sounding like Bedyr and Tepshen and Wynett, Yrla and Brannoc and Jarl, You were prepared to give your life for the Kingdoms when you thought that meant only dying, now it means living and you must still give it.

Living here, he thought, bound to Andurel as surely as any prisoner is bound to his cell. Living daily with the endless problems of governance. Living not my life, but the king's, living as a symbol.

He shuddered at the thought and at the seemingly-inevitable fate decreed for him, reaching unconsciously for the blue stone hung about his neck as apology and blasphemous anger at the destiny the Lady imposed upon him mingled in his troubled mind.

That stone, Kyrie's talisman, had brought him here, for without it he could not have survived the descent into the netherworld, or defeated Taws; not without that and Wynett, who wore the other half. Without it he would have remained blinded by the ensorcelled sword that took his sight; would have died at Taws's hand. Without it, Wynett might not have come to that decision for which he was so grateful, and thence to his bed and her place as his wife. And yet, for all those reasons, it was the talisman that placed him here, now, staring over the land that expected him to rule it.

And as he touched it calm descended upon him. His anguish faded, a clarity of perception wiping the frown from his handsome features, replacing the dour set of his wide mouth with a smile. He nodded to the sky, seeing in a flash of comprehension a path he might successfully take, a path that would be for the lasting benefit of the Three Kingdoms, and also one that would satisfy him.

It was not yet absolutely clear – he would need to ponder it a while, prepare it for presentation, consider all the arguments against it and the responses he would make to those arguments – but it was there, revealing itself to him just as the Idre became clearer as the sun burned off the last of the morning mist, and his smile grew broader as he perceived the first steps along that route.

'You seem mightily pleased.'

He turned at the sound of Wynett's voice, seeing her emerge from the little roundhouse that granted egress to the tower. Her hair blew loose in the wind, gold as the sun itself, and the cornflower blue of her eyes shone bright as she studied him. His eyes drank in the sight of her, delighting in the way the soft, blue overrobe she wore outlined the supple contours of her body, then saw her shiver in the early morning chill and opened his arms that she might draw close, folding his heavier robe about her as she leant back against him and he buried his face in her hair, luxuriating in the sweet, beloved scent of it.

'I am,' he said softly, then laughed, hugging her, saying again, louder, 'I am.'

Wynett craned her head back to brush lips against his cheek, feeling the stubble of his unshaved beard, pleased at this change of heart, for during the past few days she had grown concerned for the man she loved. 'Do you share it?' she murmured.

Kedryn loosened his grip upon her to touch the stone she wore between the swell of her breasts, smiling still as he said, 'The Lady works in mysterious ways.'

'Indeed?' Wynett's tone mocked surprise. 'And I, so long sworn to her service, had not realised that. Did you rise so early to consider these weighty matters?'

Kedryn laughed, bussing her gently on the neck. 'I could not sleep,' he murmured, 'for thinking of what is expected of me.'

Wynett's smile stilled a fraction and she reached to take his hands, cupping them. 'Is it so hard to accept? I am resolved to it.'

'You were born a king's daughter,' Kedryn's voice grew solemn, though his smile became mischievous, 'And you chose servitude to the Lady. I was born a mere prince and thought to live out my days as little more; this notion of kingship sits heavy on my shoulders.'

13

'They are broad enough.' Wynett's fingers traced the outline of his biceps, squeezing gently at the hard muscle. 'And I accepted a life other than the one I expected. Can you not do the same?'

Kedryn drew her closer, holding her that she could not turn to see the amusement in his eyes as he said solemnly, 'I am accustomed to the open places of Tamur, not the walls of a palace. Have I not done my duty by the Lady that I may enjoy freedom? Are we to be confined in Andurel, unable to go where we would?'

'There is none other the Kingdoms will accept as monarch,' Wynett retorted, voicing an argument he knew he would hear again, for he had already heard it so many times before. 'By birthright and marriage right; by what you have done, you have earned the throne. Who else might take it?'

'Jarl's Kemm?' he asked innocently.

Wynett snorted. 'Kemm is a good man, but not even his own father considers him a suitable candidate to the High Throne. No, my love, there is none other.'

'What if I were to refuse?' he asked in the same ingenuous tone.

'You cannot!' Wynett pinched his forearm. 'Would you plunge this land of ours back into chaos? The Kingdoms *must* have a king, and you are the only candidate acceptable to all.'

'Why?' he asked bluntly. 'Why must there be a king?'

Wynett wriggled in his arms then, forcing him to loose his grip enough that she could turn to face him, looking into eyes that he rapidly made earnest, though not without some effort.

'Do you jest with me? The king symbolises the unity of the Three Kingdoms, binding them that they act in concert. Think back, Kedryn! When the Horde was raised what might have happened had you not slain Niloc Yarrum and the woodlanders come down through the Lozin Gate to find not the massed armies of the Kingdoms, but only Tamur, or Tamur and Kesh? What if Ust-Galich had refused to fight? Without a king in the White Palace that might have happened! Without a king in Andurel the Kingdoms are no more than three fiefdoms, each separate, going about their own business, isolated, and so prey to outside influence.

'Corwyn saw that when he imposed unity on the warring territories, and every king since has seen it. A king is *needed*!'

Kedryn could no longer keep the merriment from his eyes and smiled at her, cupping her face as streamers of blonde hair caressed his cheeks, feeling his love for her swell as that calm that emanated from the talisman filled him.

'You speak as my father speaks,' he said. 'And my mother. And Jarl. And Tepshen. Even Sister Bethany has said as much.'

'Because it is the truth,' Wynett insisted.

'It is the truth that without the unity imposed by Andurel – by the White Palace – the Kingdoms might well fall back into chaos,' he agreed. 'But what power does the king really have? He is little more than a symbol and his wishes may be opposed by the lords of the Kingdoms – your father was loath to command Hattim Sethiyan to war for fear he might refuse. Hattim was hungry for the throne not because he sought the good of the Kingdoms, but from vanity, pride, a lust for power, a desire to aggrandise Ust-Galich.'

'Hattim was a vain and prideful man,' Wynett countered, frowning now at the smile Kedryn wore, the disparity between his earnest tone and merry expression confusing her. 'You are not like him.'

'No,' Kedryn allowed, 'but after we are dead, what then? Shall princes vie for the hand of our eldest daughter? Shall ambitions rise again? The Kingdoms want me, now, because some quirk of fate set me in the right place at the right time; because I – with you beside me – was able to defeat Taws. When I am dead, who shall succeed me?'

'Is it such morbid thought that caused you such pleasure?' Wynett's eyes narrowed, the blue clouding. 'When I found you here you were smiling as though all cares were gone. I had thought you resolved to acceptance.'

Kedryn stroked her cheeks, smooth beneath his touch, his own face becoming serious. 'I looked out at all this,' he said, one arm sweeping out to encompass the panorama below them, 'and I felt dread. As a songbird seeing a cage open before it must feel dread. I wondered what it was the Lady had brought me to, and then I touched this.' His hand clasped the talisman again. 'This stone that brought us together, and banished Taws, and brought me here, and I felt . . . calm. I saw a way.'

He paused, frowning afresh, not yet quite sure how to put into words what had come to him in that moment of revelation. Wynett waited, confident of both her husband and the stone's power.

'You speak of unity,' he went on at last, 'as does my father, and all those I trust. You say there must be some central symbol to which the Three Kingdoms may look for guidance; some power of government in Andurel.'

'Aye,' murmured his wife as he paused again, marshalling his thoughts.

15

'And I agree,' Kedryn continued, 'but whilst that symbol is one man – the occupant of the White Palace – the opportunity for ambition exists. Darr was a fair man, but Hattim was not; and had Hattim retained the throne, even without Taws's aid, he might well have wrought immense harm to Tamur and Kesh, to the Kingdoms. One man might impose his own unity on the Kingdoms, rendering them not free domains, but his personal fiefdom. He might establish an empire such as Tepshen speaks of in his homeland.'

'That is the very reason your father and Jarl sought to create a council,' said Wynett. 'That Hattim's power might be bounded.'

'Aye!' Kedryn's smile spread wide across his tanned face, his brown eyes alight now with excitement. 'And that is the way I saw when I held the talisman. The way, I believe, the Lady showed me.'

'What way?' asked Wynett. 'I do not see it.'

'It is so simple,' Kedryn grinned. 'Let the council be established! Let it comprise men of Tamur and Kesh and Ust-Galich! Let those men be elected, not by hereditary right, or might, or precedent, but freely that they speak for their people. Let them sit in the White Palace! Let them promulgate the laws, determine tariffs, settle disputes. Let them call the Kingdoms to war if we must fight again. Let their tenure be limited – one year? Three? I am not sure, but if their seats are placed beneath them by the voices of their people there will be no one man able to outweigh the rest and the threat of ambition is removed.'

Wynett stared at him with solemn eyes. 'It is a revolutionary thought,' she said slowly. 'Would it find acceptance?'

'Do you favour it?' he asked. '*You*, whom I trust above all?'

Wynett pursed her lips, touching her own half of the talisman as if seeking guidance there, then nodded: 'Aye, I do.'

'It would free us,' Kedryn said excitedly. 'We should be able to travel as we wish, knowing the Kingdoms were in loyal hands.'

'Aye,' Wynett agreed, 'but the others . . . Your father, Jarl . . . will they accept it?'

Kedryn's smile grew again, 'They want me king, do they not? As king may I not issue proclamations? As king might I not divest myself of power?'

'Speak first to Bethany,' Wynett suggested. 'With her support you are more likely to persuade them. It is, after all, a notion that defies tradition.'

Kedryn nodded, 'I will. And to Estrevan, if necessary. Does your sister not wish to retire to the Sacred City? It would be seemly that she be escorted, and as king and queen, equally seemly that we pay our respects to the Sisterhood. Were we to travel with Ashrivelle, that would be an excellent opportunity for the council to establish itself – to demonstrate that king and queen need not be caged in Andurel.'

'Estrevan!' Wynett grew radiant at the thought. 'It has been so long since I was there; I had scarce dared think I might see that place again.'

'Shall you change your mind?' Kedryn slid his arms about her shoulders, a tremor of alarm damping the fire of his excitement. 'Shall you regret what you have given up?'

Wynett saw the fear in his eyes and lifted her arms about his neck, drawing his face close. 'No' she said firmly, 'and you are foolish to ask it. I made a choice and that choice was blessed by the Lady: I have no regrets, nor shall have. Do you not know how I love you, husband?'

Her hands tightened on his neck, bringing his face down as her lips confirmed her words, and Kedryn felt all doubts flee, holding her as the breeze freshened, warming, and the sun shone brilliant over the city.

*

'Do you grow soft with this fine living?'

Tepshen Lahl turned the downswing of Kedryn's *kabah*, deflecting the long wooden practice sword off to the side as his own blade continued on an arc that ended, thudding, against his opponent's ribs. Had Kedryn not been wearing the padded tunic, and the blades been steel, his side would have opened, the combat final. As it was he grunted at the force of the blow, knowing he would be bruised and in need of Wynett's herbs ere long: Tepshen was a hard taskmaster, and in the matter of swordplay allowed no respect for friendship or status to interfere with his teaching.

'Again, and this time pretend you know how to use a blade.'

Kedryn grinned, backing away as he adjusted his grip on the hilt, studying his friend as the easterner assumed a defensive stance, the fulvous skin of the high-cheekboned face visible behind the bars of the practice mask unmarked by sweat, his slanted eyes impassive. He was a head shorter than the Tamurin and as unmarked by the

17

passing years as a carved statue, his pigtailed hair jet, gleaming with oil, his breathing even despite a good hour's hard work in the combat arena. Exactly how old he was Kedryn had no clear idea, knowing only that the *kyo* had ridden from the east to swear allegiance to Tamur whilst he was still a child. Since that day he had become what he called *ahn-dio* to the youthful prince, a father not of blood relation, he put it, a guardian and a friend and a true companion. It was Tepshen Lahl had taught Kedryn the art of the sword, and the hand-to-hand style of fighting favoured in the empire he had fled, outlawed by an upstart and vengeful ruler, finding refuge and an adopted home in the hard, wild hills of Tamur, where the pride and the sense of honour of the mountain folk matched his own. No man might ask for a more loyal comrade, and Kedryn was grateful for the swordmaster's friendship.

Though that fact might not have been apparent to any who did not know them, for Kedryn's mouth opened in a snarling yell at the easterner's words and he hurled himself forwards, kabah lifting as though he intended to smash the blade through the wicker mask guarding the smaller man's head and crush the skull beneath.

Tepshen stepped sideways as the sword came down, his own moving to block and cut, but Kedryn turned in mid-stroke, shifting the direction of his swing without lessening its momentum so that his sword moved over the kyo's, landing hard against Tepshen's forearms. The blow slowed the easterner and Kedryn whirled away even as he thrust forwards, his stroke reversing to hack against the padding over Tepshen's back.

Tepshen gasped at the force of it, his feet describing an intricate pattern as he sought to move out of range and turn to counter the attack Kedryn pressed home. The kabah clashed together, then both men were swinging away, returning, trading blow for blow until the kyo's blade struck Kedryn's neck where the high collar of the protective tunic masked the vulnerable flesh beneath and Kedryn's landed in a side-swing against the padded midriff.

'Enough.'

Tepshen grounded his kabah, bowing from the waist. Kedryn followed suit, then pulled off one heavy glove so that he could unlace the latchings of the basketwork helmet and wipe a hand across his sweat-beaded forehead.

'Perhaps you are not gone soft, after all,' Tepshen allowed, a faint approximation of a smile stretching his pale lips. 'Though on that last cut we should both have died.'

'You are still the finest swordsman in the Kingdoms,' Kedryn declared loyally.

'I have an equal.' This time Tepshen's smile was open, a rare occurrence, and Kedryn felt a flush of pleasure at the compliment: such praise was well worth a few bruises. He smiled back, essaying a deep, formal bow as Tepshen had shown it done in the sunrise land from which he came.

'Do you anticipate further warfare, or merely enjoy drubbing one another?'

The question came from the palisade surrounding the practice ground, where a man lounged casually on the tiered seats as if enjoying the noonday sun. He was a swarthy figure, his skin tanned dark as aged bark, his height closer to Kedryn's than Tepshen Lahl's, his eyes laughing. His hair was black and dressed in braids decorated with bright feathers and pieces of shell that tinkled slightly as he vaulted the wall and came towards them, his gait loose-limbed. The necklet of beadwork and the silver hoop suspended from his left ear combined with the rings on his right hand and the ornaments in his hair to give him a barbaric appearance at variance with the fashionable crimson silk tunic and loose-fitting breeks he wore. Indeed, looking at his face it was difficult to discern whether he was of the Kingdoms or the forests, for he seemed a mixture of Tamurin and Keshi and barbarian; which, indeed, he was.

'You might benefit from such practice,' Tepshen answered mildly.

'It looks far too arduous,' grinned the dark man. 'I prefer to watch, idling like some noble in the sun.'

'Does the Warden of the Forests laze away his time, Brannoc?' asked Kedryn.

'My Lord,' Brannoc mocked an elaborate bow, white teeth gleaming against swart skin, 'I deem it my duty to watch over the future king lest this eastern barbarian harm you.'

Tepshen Lahl grunted amusement at the badinage and Kedryn grinned, thinking that since he had come back to Andurel to face Taws and Hattim these two had seldom been far from his side, appointing themselves his guardians despite the presence of Royal Guardsmen and the assurances of the Galichians that their loyalty was unswerving now that their dead lord had been revealed as a puppet of Ashar's Messenger. He wondered how they would take his proposals, firmed now that he had discussed them at length with Wynett; wondered more how his father would take them. Soon, he knew, he must put them to Bedyr, and to Jarl of Kesh, both lords anxious to resolve the matter of the High Throne and establish him finally and incontrovertibly as king. It was necessary to settle it soon, he knew, for until that was done Ust-Galich remained lordless and it was needful that the southern kingdom have a ruler confirmed lest internecine rivalry lead to disruption. Yet he wanted, as Wynett had suggested, to speak first with Bethany, whose support as Paramount Sister of the Sorority College would be invaluable. Today, he decided, abruptly. The rites of purification over which Bethany presided were done, the White Palace cleared of all taint of Taws's fell magic, so there was no longer reason to delay.

'Then you had best come with us to the baths,' he declared, 'for I shall visit Sister Bethany this noon and I'd lief wash this sweat from me.'

Brannoc nodded amiably and fell into step beside them as they ambled across the sun-warmed sand to the low entrance that led to the bathing pools. The passageway was cool, their boots ringing on the tiles of its floor, announcing their approach to the servants who waited discreetly within the subterranean chambers. The thick-padded practice armour was swiftly removed and with Brannoc joining them, they plunged into the steaming water of the first great tub. It was large enough to accept a full squad of guardsmen, but to Kedryn's pleasure, none were there at this time of day and he was able to relax without the pressure of knowing every polite enquiry veiled the one burning question: when will you announce your coronation. Instead, he could float in the heated water, talking idly with his companions of nothing in particular.

He lay there until his stomach reminded him that he had not eaten since shortly after dawn, and rose to cross the patterned tiles to a second pool, where he soaped himself vigorously before plunging into a tub of cool water fed from the same springs that filled the others, but unheated, rising from that to accept the towel offered by a waiting servant. He dried himself and walked to the robing room where he dressed in a shirt of white linen surmounted with a sleeveless tunic of soft leather, bearing on back and chest the fist of Tamur. The breeks he pulled on were of matching hide, worked supple, fitting snug into the high boots presented him by Andurel's finest cobbler. Indeed, all the clothes he now wore were of the finest materials, provided in quantity by the craftsmen of the island city in honour of their saviour and king-to-be. He had never owned so many clothes, nor anticipated such modish apparel, being more used to the plain garb of a Tamurin warrior, and after finding his wardrobes filled with robes and surcoats and tunics cut in all the latest fashions had requested of the tailors outfits in the style to which he was accustomed.

Tepshen Lahl drew on similar garb, though where Kedryn wore only the Tamurin dirk that was the custom of his people, the kyo belted a swordbelt about his waist, the ornately lacquered sheath containing the long, slightly curved sword that was the sole physical reminder of his homeland. Brannoc, like Kedryn, had forgone his customary Keshi sabre, but a blade was sheathed on his waist, and to his left forearm, hidden beneath the billow of his sleeve, he strapped a throwing knife.

'Do you anticipate treachery?' Kedryn asked, grinning.

'Honest men need not fear the blade,' returned Tepshen.

'And I do not feel dressed without a weapon or two,' Brannoc added. 'A relic of my wolfshead days, mayhap.'

Kedryn laughed at their caution and hung the blue stone of the talisman about his neck, letting his shirt cover the now-familiar jewel.

'We go to eat and visit Sister Bethany,' he chuckled. 'Not to war.'

'I had rather be prepared than find myself in need of steel,' Tepshen returned, his face solemn as ever.

Kedryn shook his head, still chuckling, and made towards the exit and the corridor that would take them into the palace. He was not yet so accustomed to the place that he could easily find his way through the labyrinthine interior and several times halted to ask directions of servants or soldiers until at last he found the dining hall, the appetising smells of roasted meats and fresh-cooked vegetables quickening his steps as he approached.

The hall was no larger than Caitin Hold's own dining room, for like his home, the White Palace was built as much a fortress as residence, but its appointments were far grander, prompting thoughts of gilded cages. Great windows of coloured glass filled the hall with patterns of swirling spring sunlight that danced over the rich-polished boards of the floor, sparking off the golden sconces set into the stone walls and the elaborate chandeliers suspended on gilded chains from the high ceiling. Tapestries covered most of the stone, some ancient banners, others merely decorative, hanging between niches in which stood busts and pieces of sculpture, reminding him that Andurel was an artistic centre as well as seat of government. Even the long tables and the high-backed chairs were of ornate design, contrasting with the simpler styles of Tamur, and the implements set upon the tables, and the goblets of artfully-worked crystal, spoke of wealth. To many, Kedryn knew, this must seem a prize well worth the price of freedom's loss, but he was Tamurin and set store on his ability to come and go as he pleased; an ability denied the occupant of this fabulous place.

Flanked by Tepshen Lahl and Brannoc he made his way down the hall, nodding greetings as he went, to the dais at the far end, facing the minstrel's gallery that stood above the door. There a smaller table faced the rest, the diners all seated on the one side, one chair left empty as custom dictated until a new king be crowned to take Darr's place. To the left of that vacant seat stood his own chair, Wynett already settled beside it, her wheaten hair bound up now, her gown pale green, the talisman the only ornament she wore or, Kedryn thought as he smiled at her, needed. To her left sat the nobility of Kesh, the hawk-nosed Jarl, dressed in the sable robe that was the customary garment of the horsemen, the chest marked with an equine head, silver on green. On his left, her gown a rainbow, sat Arlynne, his wife, then Kemm, his son, a plumper version of his father, his features amiable where Jarl's were naturally stern. To the right of the empty chair sat Bedyr Caitin, straight-backed, his features an older mirror of his son's, lean and proud, almost austere, save for the smile that spread his wide mouth and the laughter that shone in his brown eyes as he turned from some sally of the woman at his elbow to greet Kedryn. He wore a surcoat of dark blue, the fist of Tamur on the breast, his hair, like Kedryn's long and brown, but streaked now with grey, a colour that had not yet touched his wife's raven tresses. Yrla Belvanne na Caitin seemed to her son ageless as Tepshen Lahl, her lovely oval face unlined, her eyes a grey that matched the silken sheen of her gown, the hand that touched her husband's smooth and delicate as that of a woman half her years. Kedryn bowed to them all and took his place, Brannoc and Tepshen finding seats to Yrla's right.

'I shall have need of your healing skills,' he said to Wynett, quickly, hoping to forestall the questions he knew the others were impatient to ask, 'Tepshen has delivered more than one bruise.'

'I am at your service,' she answered, the twinkle in her eyes telling him she understood.

Arlynne leant forwards to speak past her husband's stocky frame, her gaze curious. 'Do you then retain your talents, Wynett? I thought them lost with your . . .' She broke off, suppressing a giggle as Jarl glared at her, '. . . marriage.'

Wynett smiled happily, unabashed by the Keshi queen's forthright manner. 'They are reduced, Arlynne. I can no longer sense injury, or magic, nor apply my mind to speed the healing process, but I retain my knowledge of medicine. I can still mix remedies; and what I was taught in Estrevan remains with me.'

Arlynne nodded thoughtfully, the bangles hung about her wrists jangling as she adjusted the voluminous sleeves of her gown, cheerfully ignoring her husband's impatience as she said, 'And you consider it a bargain well made?'

'Oh, yes,' Wynett replied as Jarl gasped. 'How could I not, with so handsome a husband?'

Jarl snorted, ringed fingers drumming for an instant against the table, a signal his wife seemed to recognise, for she smiled and closed her mouth.

'Forgive me,' said the lord of Kesh, 'I have no doubt the Lady blesses this happy union, but there are more pressing matters at hand.' He looked along the table, seeking support from Bedyr. 'Are there not, my friend?'

Bedyr nodded, turning serious eyes towards his son.

'Have you thought on it, Kedryn?'

Kedryn nodded, his face grave as he answered his father's stare. 'I have. Long and hard, and I will give you my answer soon.'

It felt strange to prevaricate, for they had no secrets and always in the past Kedryn had sought his father's advice, trusting to Bedyr's wisdom to guide him. It was, perhaps, a mark of his growing maturity that in this matter he was determined to make his own decision, unwilling to discuss his stratagem with any but Wynett. In a way he was afraid to present it openly, here at the dining table, for he was not certain of Bedyr's reaction, knowing his father's loyalty to Darr had been unswerving, and that Bedyr had not seen any alternative to his acceptance of the High Throne.

'How soon is soon?' Bedyr asked. 'The Kingdoms wait on your announcement, and Ust-Galich must have a lord ere long.'

Kedryn nodded, seeing further opportunity to delay a direct answer. 'Do you favour any particular candidate? In that I shall be guided entirely by you.'

'Chadyn Hymet was acceptable to all,' said Bedyr, 'until Hattim poisoned him. But even so, that elevation renders his line the most suitable. We,' his gaze took in Yrla and the Keshi, 'have discussed the matter and feel Chadyn's eldest son, Gerryl, should receive your nomination.'

'The king's nomination,' Jarl corrected. 'Which may be given only *after* the coronation.'

'Indeed,' Kedryn smiled placatingly at the green-eyed Keshi. 'And that shall not be long, Jarl. You have my word on it.'

'How long?' asked Jarl, bluntly.

'I would speak with Sister Bethany,' Kedryn said. 'Once I have eaten. I must ask the guidance of the Sisterhood, but I shall set a date then. Mayhap tonight.'

'Excellent,' Jarl growled. 'The sooner we settle this matter the better.'

'It will be settled,' Kedryn promised, wondering how so traditional a lord as Jarl would take his unprecedented proposal.

'The Sisterhood supports you,' Bedyr murmured, knowing his son too well to miss the equivocation in his response. 'There is no question but that Estrevan will give full blessing.'

Kedryn toyed with his goblet, lowering his voice as he looked to his father. 'There is something I would ask Bethany; a thing that must affect my decision. I crave your patience, Father, but in this I must be sure of my own mind, and until I have spoken with Bethany I cannot be sure.'

Bedyr frowned slightly, studying his son as though seeing him for the first time in a new light. Beyond him, Yrla smiled quizzically and set a hand upon his. 'Our son is grown, Bedyr. A man now, and as a man he must be allowed to act as such.'

Kedryn smiled his thanks as Bedyr nodded and said, 'So be it. The High Throne is oft a lonely seat and it is well you learn early to decide of your own mind.'

There was a hint of sadness in his tone, and Kedryn recognised it, sharing it: this was a new beginning, the departure of the child from the family, the first steps along the road to true maturity. He put a hand upon his father's shoulder and said, 'You were ever my guide, and I thank you for that.'

'And shall be still whenever you ask it,' promised Bedyr, cheering.

'Aye.' Kedryn's grip tightened in gratitude. 'I know that.'

'So,' Bedyr raised his voice that Jarl might hear, 'Hopefully we shall firm the future of the Kingdoms tonight.'

'Good,' declared the Lord of Kesh bluntly, 'now shall we eat?'

Kedryn grinned, realising that the servants hovering about the kitchen doors waited on him to give the signal to bring out the food. No such protocol existed in Caitin Hold and had he delayed so long there the cooks would doubtless have emerged to tell him he allowed their work to go cold, or some warrior complained that his stomach went empty. It seemed the duties of kingship were already placed upon him and it firmed his decision the more as he raised his hand, indicating the great platters should be brought out.

Conversation faltered then, the assembled company falling on the roasts with hearty appetite. Kedryn ate with a will, his own hunger keened by the morning spent on the practice ground and the knowledge that, whatever opposition his proposals might find, he would soon resolve the problem that had nagged at him since first he realised he was expected to spend his life in Andurel.

Beside him Wynett murmured, 'Tonight?' too low for any save Kedryn to hear.

'Aye,' he whispered back, 'I can delay no longer. And my father and Jarl are right – the Galichian question must be settled.'

'It is not that that will prompt discord,' Wynett returned. 'It will be your proposal of a council.'

'I know,' he smiled, taking her hand as he caught Arlynne's conspiratorial glance, letting the dark-haired Keshi woman think they exchanged lovers' pleasantries, 'but hopefully Bethany will stand with me on that.'

'She may seek the guidance of Estrevan before she decides,' warned Wynett. 'Mayhap she will feel this a matter beyond her sole discretion.'

'There is not enough time', he said. 'Even using the senders and the mehdri, that would take too long. No – like me, Bethany must decide now.'

'You sound,' Wynett smiled, 'just like a king.'

'And you,' Kedryn countered, 'look just like a queen.'

'Thank you, my lord,' she laughed, looking then less regal, but rather what she was: a young woman in love.

They finished eating and Kedryn rose, anxious to consult with Bethany, bidding the others remain if they wished as he left the hall with Tepshen Lahl and Brannoc at his back.

They walked to the stables located in the outer courtyard of the palace and selected three horses, fine, strong-limbed Keshi stallions brought across the Vortigen by Kemm when he crossed with his men to lend support to Kedryn in the confusion following Hattim's death. There had been little fighting, for the Galichians were in confusion, horrified to learn their lord had leagued himself with Ashar's Messenger, but sufficient of the southerners had stood firm against Kedryn that he had been thankful for the sabres of the black-robed horsemen, trusting them more than the demoralised palace guard. Now all opposition was ended, either on sword's edge or in banishment, and the Galichians who remained were sworn with binding oaths to loyalty, declaring fealty to the king-elect.

Kedryn waited as the ostlers saddled the beasts, smiling his refusal of the watch captain's suggestion that a squadron of cavalry escort him to the Sisters' College and ignoring the perplexed officer's arguments that the king – or king-elect – always travelled with a guard of honour.

'They will find you a mightily strange king,' Brannoc remarked lightly as they cantered down the wide avenue leading from the palace to the city below. 'They are accustomed to protocol here – to ritual – and you break their rules.'

'Aye,' chuckled Kedryn, wondering how Brannoc himself would take his pending announcements, 'but they will have to get used to me. A king who cannot travel freely in his own capital must surely be doing something wrong.'

'You have a point,' acknowledged the former outlaw, 'but customs are hard things to break.'

'But not inviolate,' Kedryn said.

'Custom binds,' offered Tepshen, 'it is the mortar of tradition.'

'Is tradition always right?' asked Kedryn.

The easterner turned in his saddle to stare curiously at the younger man, his gaze shrewd. 'You plan something,' he stated flatly.

'Aye, I do.' Kedryn nodded. 'This visit to the College determines it. Tonight, when I speak with my father and Jarl, I would have you both there, and have you both speak freely. I would hear your opinions of what I plan.'

Tepshen nodded back. Brannoc said, 'I know no other way to speak,' though his dark eyes were alight with curiosity.

Kedryn chose to ignore it, thankful that Brannoc curbed the questions that were obviously tormenting him. He rode in silence for a while, studying the still unfamiliar sights of the great city that waited for him to assume its governance. There was no other metropolis in all the Kingdoms so large as Andurel, perhaps none other in all the world, and he was not yet accustomed to so close a press of buildings. Nowhere in Tamur was there a settlement a man could not walk through within a matter of hours – far less in most – whilst Andurel was a maze that would take days to explore, a place of alleyways and avenues, arching bridges and winding stairways all lined with houses, shops, taverns and a myriad other unfamiliar emporiums. Parks and gardens provided open space, but to one raised in the open country of the western kingdom the city had a claustrophobic feel, the more so for the thought that he was expected to make it his home.

He smiled politely as folk cried greetings, waving in answer to their encomiums, staring about him with what he felt sure they must interpret as the wide-eyed wonder of some country bumpkin marvelling at the glories of their fabulous city. Balconies overhung his passage as he turned his mount off the avenue in what he hoped was the right direction, the narrowing of the visible sky emphasising the vague discomfort he felt at being so hemmed in by brick and mortar, albeit brick and mortar wrought in marvellous designs, covered often in coloured tiles, or painted bright, with trailing plants hanging from baskets of intricate patterns.

Then the road entered a broad square and he saw the College of the Sisterhood before him. The flags of the square were a dark blue, like deep water, so that the building that housed the Sisters of Andurel seemed to float at its centre, a cube of pale azure stone surmounted by a gently-angled roof of snowy white that was a land-bound match of the clouds drifting overhead. Balconies ran the lengths of the walls, their wood painted the blue of Estrevan, as was the open doorway facing him. He walked the Keshi stallion towards the portico, aware of the clatter the animal's hooves made in the stillness that seemed to surround the College, a calm centre in the bustle of the city.

At the gate he dismounted, Tepshen Lahl and Brannoc following suit, and waited, unsure of what protocols appertained. It was a brief wait, for a Sister appeared, smiling, and without formality asked what she might do for them.

'I would speak with Sister Bethany,' Kedryn said, 'if that is possible.'

'She expects you,' smiled the Sister. 'Do you see her alone, or with your companions?'

Kedryn looked apologetically to his friends. 'Alone. Will you wait here?'

'There is a more comfortable chamber in which to wait,' said the Sister, and clapped her hands, two younger women appearing on the summons to escort Tepshen and Brannoc away, one taking the reins of Kedryn's mount.

'Please,' said the first Sister, 'Bethany's chambers are this way.'

Kedryn followed her down a low-roofed passage that opened onto an inner courtyard, revealing the College as a hollow rectangle, the interior given over to gardens redolent of medicinal herbs, though later in the year the flowers budding in the carefully-tended beds and the profusion of shrubs would doubtless fill the air with different scents. Fountains played gently as the blue-robed woman paced the pathway leading through the gardens to the far side of the rectangle. There a wide stone stairway ran up to a balcony overlooking a well, the sound of the water trickling over smooth stone restful as bird-song. Kedryn's guide halted before a plain wood door and tapped twice. From within, a voice bade them enter and the Sister thrust the door open, gesturing for Kedryn to go in.

The room was lit by the afternoon sun that entered through a wide window in the farther wall, outlining the figure of a tall woman, her hair prematurely white, the eyes that studied Kedryn hazel, and hawk-keen. He bowed, recognising the Paramount Sister, second only to Gerat of Estrevan.

'Sister Bethany, thank you for granting me audience.'

Bethany smiled, the expression transforming her narrow face, banishing its natural severity. 'I anticipated your coming, Prince Kedryn. I imagine there is much you wish to discuss.'

She gestured at a chair set before the simple, book-littered table and Kedryn sank into it, not particularly surprised to find it far more comfortable than its somewhat stark outlines suggested. Bethany seated herself across from him and folded her hands, waiting for him to speak.

Kedryn cleared his throat, not sure where he should begin and choosing preamble: 'You have done with the purification?'

'The rituals are finished,' Bethany nodded. 'There remains no trace of the Messenger.'

There was something in her tone that prompted a doubt in Kedryn's mind and he asked, 'Taws is dead?'

'I do not know.' Bethany's gaze was direct. 'He is gone from here, but whether such as he *can* be killed I have no way of knowing.'

'The talisman . . .' Kedryn touched the blue stone through his shirt, 'Surely that destroyed him.'

'His physical manifestation, yes,' Bethany nodded. 'But that form was a creation of Ashar's will, and whilst the mad god exists, so does his will. So perhaps Taws lives on in some other form.'

'Do you say my task is not yet done?'

Kedryn frowned, an ugly prickling of unwonted anticipation running down his spine.

'I am not sure exactly what your task is,' Bethany replied evenly. 'My own interpretation of Alaria's Text – and, it would seem, that of my Sisters in Estrevan – is that you have fulfilled the prophecies outlined therein. But each step we take must surely lead to another, so mayhap there is more you must yet do. Your ascension to the High Throne, for example, appears a logical step. One that is needful if the Kingdoms are to be truly united.'

'You echo my father,' Kedryn murmured.

'I echo all Andurel,' smiled Bethany, 'and all the Kingdoms. But you are not happy with that.'

It was a statement, not a question, and Kedryn found himself nodding in reflexive answer. 'You read me well,' he smiled.

'I am trained to it,' said Bethany, mildly. 'Do you have some alternative proposal?'

'Aye!' Kedryn's nod became emphatic. 'This morning I stood upon the highest of the palace's towers and looked out over the city and thought of all I must forgo if I accept the High Throne. I found the prospect . . . daunting. Then I held the talisman in my hand and . . . I am sure . . . I felt that an answer was given me.'

He broke off, shrugging, no longer certain of his words. Bethany smiled gently and said, 'The Lady may well have spoken through the stone. It has, after all, remarkable properties.'

'Indeed,' said Kedryn, his voice gaining enthusiasm, 'but I am not sure how that answer will be taken.'

'What was it?' asked Bethany. 'Outline it and I will tell you if you have my support, or not. That is what you seek, is it not?'

'Aye,' Kedryn smiled, marvelling at her perspicacity. 'It seemed to me that the king is a symbol, a rallying point, more than he is a real power. Oh, he deals with the minutiae of government – tariffs, trade agreements, that sort of thing – but all important decisions are taken in concert with the lords of the Kingdoms, without whose support the king is, effectively, powerless.'

'You have the grasp of it,' agreed Bethany. 'But there is still a need for a king in the White Palace, and it is important that he should not be an absolute ruler. No one man should be able to impose his will on the Three Kingdoms.'

'Exactly,' said Kedryn, his voice earnest as the expression that reminded Bethany of his father, 'and to that end I propose the formation of a council.'

He studied the Sister's angular face, seeking to read it, but finding only attention so that he went on swiftly, 'A council such as was proposed to hold Hattim Sethiyan in check, but greater – a council that would truly represent the Kingdoms. Not individual lordlings, but all the people. A council that would be elected by the folk of the Kingdoms so that whomsoever sat on it would speak truly with the voice of his kingdom. The members would advise their lords, and they would sit not in perpetuity but agreed periods. They would promulgate the laws, govern. Then no single man could ever hope to impose his will; there would be no more opportunity for ambition such as Hattim showed – no further chance for Ashar to suborn some lord to become usurper.'

He halted, as much to catch his breath as to give Bethany a chance to reply, though the Sister took the opportunity.

'This came to you as you held the talisman?'

'Aye,' he nodded.

'Jarl of Kesh will not accept it lightly. Your father may have reservations.'

'I know that,' Kedryn said. 'But you, what do you think?'

Bethany watched him for long moments, her face calm, unreadable. Then she smiled: 'I think it a most revolutionary suggestion.'

Kedryn's enthusiasm faltered, his brown eyes clouding.

'And a most excellent idea,' continued Bethany. 'One that shall have my full support.'

Kedryn's spirit soared, as would a caged bird's seeing the door left open that it might once again reach the open sky.

# Chapter Two

WHILST spring brought a warmth to Andurel that would not yet have touched the more northerly reaches of the Kingdoms the breeze blowing off the Idre grew chill with the setting of the sun and so the windows of the chamber were closed, though not shuttered, the thick glass diffusing the wan silver moonlight shed by the half-girthed orb. It mingled with the citrine radiance of the candles and the rutilant glow of the fire burning in the stone-mantled hearth to fill the room with shifting patterns of warm light that, in a way, reflected a luminous parallel of the arguments that echoed, not always softly, off the panelled walls.

Kedryn had chosen this room for several reasons, not least among them the fact that it was not one used much by King Darr. He had no wish to remind his wife of her father's unpleasant fate and so had generally taken occupance of quarters that were not associated with the deceased monarch even though Wynett appeared reconciled to his demise. Further, he felt that his avoidance of such chambers served to emphasise that he did not simply assume a continuance of tradition – one of the prime points under debate – but was, in every way, his own man. Additionally, this chamber was large enough to house all those he wished present around the central table, and so they had been able to eat there, sequestered from the ever-present ears in the great dining hall. Finally, the walls were solid stone beneath the veneer of panelling and the only entrance from an outer chamber, beyond which guards were posted to ensure privacy. Now the last remnants of dinner were cleared away and those present able to speak freely.

They did; and forcefully.

Bedyr sat with Yrla beside him towards one end of the table, a goblet of ruby Galichian wine untouched by his right hand, his handsome face set in grave lines as he listened attentively to the harsh voice of Jarl, Yrla's a match in solemnity. The Keshi's wife, Arlynne, occupied a cushioned chair beside the hearth, her dark

31

eyes enigmatic as her husband voiced his opposition. Kemm, their son, sat facing the Tamurin couple, his plump features creased in a frown as he watched his father pace back and forth before the fire. Wynett's face was calm at the table's end, Tepshen Lahl impassive on her left, Brannoc grinning quizzically to her right. At the far end, Sister Bethany was an equal focus of tranquillity, her hands clasped before her as if in prayer. Kedryn perched on the ledge of an embrasure, moonlight pearling his brown hair as he listened to the Lord of Kesh, his features shadowed by the stone.

Jarl was all black robe and rubicund feature, his green eyes flashing as he spoke, seeming to draw light from the flames.

'It is madness, Kedryn! It flies in the face of all precedent.'

'Corwyn flew in the face of precedent when he imposed unity on three warring lands,' Kedryn responded evenly, eyes and teeth white against the obfuscation of his face. 'Would you say he did wrong?'

Jarl's right hand chopped a dismissive gesture, thumb ring sparkling. 'You play with words – you know I do not say that. I say that Corwyn gave us peace and that what you propose will likely destroy all that has been built since then.'

'How so?' asked Kedryn. 'I do not propose dissolution, but a different form of government. A form I believe likely to create far greater unity.'

'*You believe*,' barked Jarl, 'but you do not *know*. Why change what has worked for generations?'

'Because the world turns and we must turn with it,' Kedryn said, stroking absently at his shirtfront, as though seeking inspiration from the blue stone that hung beneath the linen. 'Simply because a thing has existed for generations is no reason to reject a better alternative when such arises.'

Jarl made a sound deep in his throat that was the vocal equivalent of his gesture. 'You think it better; I do not.'

'Did you think that when Hattim Sethiyan stood at the foot of the High Throne?'

Kedryn's voice was mild, eliciting a furious glare from the hot-tempered Keshi. 'Again you play with words.'

'I intend no offence, but you welcomed a council then,' Kedryn pressed. 'Why not now?'

'Because you are not Hattim Sethiyan!' snapped Jarl. 'Because I trust you.'

'Thank you,' Kedryn smiled, seeking to mollify the bow-legged man's anger. 'But after me – do you not think the circumstances might again arise whereby an ambitious lord might seek to elevate himself?'

'Not whilst the council of lords exists,' said Jarl.

'Or,' said Kedryn before the Keshi had a chance to continue, 'whilst the council I propose exists. It would forestall any such ambition. It would contain any monarch whose personal desires might run against the good of the Kingdoms. It is, after all, nothing more than an extension of what you yourself proposed.'

Jarl threw up his hands, the sleeves of his black robe swirling dramatically, and glowered at his wife as if willing her to support his arguments. 'What do you have to say to all this?'

Arlynne arranged a fold of her rainbow gown and fixed her husband with an even stare. 'I say that much of what Kedryn proposes is eminently sensible,' she answered. 'There are niceties that must be ironed out, but in essence I find myself in agreement.'

'Blood of the Lady!' Jarl turned towards Bethany, 'Forgive me, Sister, but I see the Kingdoms fall apart.'

'Do you, my Lord of Kesh?' Bethany's voice was mild as her gaze. 'Why do you see it so?'

Jarl stared at her as if unable to credit the words he heard. His mouth hung open a moment, then snapped shut. 'Do you then support this . . . heresy?'

'I do not see it as heresy,' Bethany returned, studying Jarl with what looked to Kedryn like mild amusement. 'Rather, I believe I detect the Lady's hand in Kedryn's decision. He has told us how he came by the notion, and I can find little fault in it. Consequently, I support him.'

Jarl gazed at her with the same disbelief he had turned on his wife, spinning to seek support from Bedyr.

'And you, old friend, how do you see this?'

Bedyr turned his goblet between his palms, his even gaze travelling from Jarl's suffused features to Kedryn's, then back. 'I find the notion shocking, but I also find it hard to fault Kedryn's reasoning.' His tone was thoughtful and he paused before continuing as if weighing all that had been said, both pro and con, throughout the long hours of debate. 'Given the turmoil of recent months, I cannot argue against the establishment of a council; as Kedryn has pointed out, it was the first thought in our minds when it seemed Hattim must assume the throne. Therefore I find I must ask myself if the shock I feel is merely that of one long accustomed to a particular way of thinking faced with the unexpected, the unfamiliar. I am not yet convinced, but I find merit in much of what Kedryn suggests.'

'Am I alone then?' Jarl gasped. 'Yrla, your judgement has always been sound – what is your opinion?'

Yrla's grey eyes regarded the Keshi's flashing green orbs calmly, one hand smoothing the folds of her russet gown. 'My son has become a man, Jarl, and he has a right to his own way of thinking. Like Bethany, I believe the Lady's hand may be detected in this, and for that reason – and others – I feel we should consider what Kedryn says without anger.'

It was a mild enough admonishment, but it rocked Jarl back on his slippered heels, ending his furious pacing. He tugged at his drooping moustache, mouth pursed, then turned towards the young man lounging in the cut of the window.

'If I seem angry, Kedryn, I ask your forgiveness. I trust you know I feel only friendship towards you. But this notion . . . This I cannot accept – the Kingdoms *must* have a king.'

'They shall,' Kedryn said. 'I do not propose to destroy all you and my father – all here present – have worked to build and nurture. I do not reject the High Throne, but rather seek to ward it against any such as Hattim. Against the machinations of Ashar.'

'Ashar? What has Ashar to do with this?' Jarl asked, frowning his perplexity. 'You and Wynett despatched the Messenger to whatever hell spawned him. That threat is surely ended.'

'Is it?' Kedryn's voice was soft, but the simple question brought a silence to the room that was broken only by the sputtering of the logs burning in the hearth.

'What do you mean?'

It was Bedyr who voiced the question, his eyes locking with his son's, grave as his tone.

Kedryn shrugged, glancing at Wynett and then Bethany. 'I am not sure. Wynett and I saw Taws consumed in fire and heard a . . . voice is perhaps not the right word, but I know no other, that said, "He is mine". Then the Messenger was gone. No trace remained, neither fleshly nor metaphysical; but does that mean he is dead? I am not sure.'

'Bethany?' Bedyr turned to the Paramount Sister, unaware that Yrla had taken his hand, her eyes fearful as they studied her son's calm face. 'What have you to say on this?'

All looked to the Sister, whose composure remained undisturbed as she said, 'Little more than Kedryn, I fear. We of Estrevan believe

34

the Messenger to be Ashar's creation, the embodiment of the god's will rather than a naturally-wrought being, and so not necessarily bound by such laws as govern our existence. It may be that he was, indeed, destroyed – it is to be hoped! – But it may also be that the Lord of Fires took back what was his to send him against us in some other form.'

She paused, turning her hazel eyes on each in turn as the import of her words sank in. 'If that should prove to be the case then once again Kedryn, as the Chosen One foretold in Alaria's Text, will face the threat. And if Kedryn is inextricably bound to Andurel by the duties of kingship he might well find himself torn between responsibilities.'

'There can be no greater responsibility than defending the King-doms against Ashar,' Jarl said softly, wide-eyed.

'Indeed,' Kedryn declared abruptly, seizing the moment, 'and for that reason, also, I seek a freedom greater than that customarily enjoyed by our kings. Do you see it now, Jarl? Were I required to spend all my time in Andurel how might I combat Ashar?'

Jarl nodded thoughtfully, finding a chair, slumping as though this sudden turn of events deflated him, the fire dimming in his eyes.

'Were it necessary that I ride against Ashar,' Kedryn added, 'I should leave behind a council capable of governing. There would be continuation, rather than the chaos likely to foment about an empty throne.'

Bedyr spoke then, his lean face thoughtful, directing his words at his son, though the gist was addressed as much to Jarl. 'You do not reject the High Throne?'

'No!' Kedryn shook his head emphatically. 'I cannot say I wel-come such unanticipated elevation, but I see – and accept – the arguments in favour.' He smiled at Wynett. 'I am wed to the king's daughter and it seems you consider no other acceptable, so I do not reject your wishes in that direction. I seek, rather, to establish a firmer order.'

'And,' smiled his father, 'to allow yourself a little freedom, mayhap?'

Kedryn smiled back, unabashed as he said, 'And that, too.'

'There is another has a say in this,' suggested Yrla, 'and we have not yet heard from her. Wynett? Your part in this is vital, as royal heir and Kedryn's wife, equally because you hold one half of the talisman – do you have comment?'

35

Wynett's blue eyes were brimmed with love as she looked towards Kedryn. 'I believe my husband has only the good of the Kingdoms at heart,' she said firmly. 'And I believe that the Lady guides him in this. I stand with him in this matter.'

Yrla nodded, seeming pleased with the response, saying, 'I cannot fault you; nor Kedryn.'

'Kemm,' said Kedryn, 'you have not yet spoken.'

The heir of Kesh, shrugged, looking uncomfortable to find himself the focus of attention. He glanced at his father and said softly, 'If Kedryn takes the High Throne who may gainsay him? As king he is able to declare for a council.'

'You lend weight to my argument,' Kedryn smiled, ignoring Jarl's snort. 'To prevent such arbitrary declarations I would have this council formed. Not even the king may stand above the Kingdoms' law.'

'You turn a neat phrase,' Jarl grunted, though his tone was milder than before, 'and it seems I am out-argued.'

'Do you then agree?' asked Kedryn.

Jarl shrugged expressively. 'I will not oppose you.'

'There is much to discuss, however,' murmured Bedyr, smiling at the Keshi. 'The formation of this council will require careful thought.'

'I look to you all for advice on that,' Kedryn nodded. 'We must agree the numbers, and the manner in which the councillors be chosen.'

'Aye,' Bedyr agreed. 'There will be those who see such a thing as a means to personal aggrandisement. We shall needs take care to weed such out.'

'That may be done easily enough.' Wynett smiled, glancing at Brannoc. 'Do you recall how once this wolfshead's loyalty was questioned? And how the matter was resolved?'

'By the Lady!' Bedyr chuckled. 'I do; and you have the answer.'

Wynett saw Jarl's frown of incomprehension and said, 'When Kedryn first came to High Fort with Bedyr they required a guide to take them into the Beltrevan, my lord Jarl. Brannoc here was suggested by your own chatelain, Fengrif, but Commander Rycol doubted Brannoc's honesty and so I was called upon to utilise my talent to look into his soul that I might determine his intentions.'

'Which were indisputably honest,' Brannoc muttered.

'Indeed,' Wynnet confirmed, her lovely face mischievous as she added, 'In that respect, at least. But the point is, I was able to discern the innermost loyalties. I am no longer able to exercise such a talent, but there are Sisters in all the Kingdoms capable of the same – let them determine the intentions of the candidates.'

'An excellent suggestion,' Bethany complimented.

'Would you bring the Sisterhood within the political arena?' asked Jarl dubiously.

'Are we not already there?' countered the Paramount Sister. 'We advise the king; you lords seek our guidance; you send your daughters to Estrevan. Wynett speaks sense, Jarl.'

'So be it.' The swarthy Keshi shrugged his resignation and reached for the decanter, filling a goblet. 'I grow old, I think, and mayhap I am too set in my ways. I bow before this onslaught and acquiesce to our new king and his supporters.'

He raised the cup in toast and Kedryn laughed, sliding from the embrasure to take up his own cup.

'To the Kingdoms, Jarl. To the future of the Kingdoms.'

'Aye.' Jarl smiled now, nodding. 'To the Kingdoms.'

Kedryn drank thirstily, grateful the hardest part was done. The night was old and he had, from the befurred feel of his tongue, spent most of it arguing his points, winning slow agreement from one after the other until only Jarl, ever the traditionalist, remained. Now it seemed the Keshi lord was won over and there remained only the practical details to settle. He stretched, flexing muscles he had not realised were so tense, and settled into a chair. Wynett caught his eye, smiling fondly, and he smiled back.

'So when shall you be crowned?'

Jarl's question brought him from his contemplation of the luminous dance the candlelight played in her hair and he shrugged, thinking that he would rather find their bed than spend time in further discussion.

'When think you best?' he asked diplomatically.

'Soon,' replied the Keshi, seeming not at all weary.

'Preparation is necessary,' Bedyr interjected. 'I think it wise that the nobles of the Kingdoms be present when Kedryn announces this council, and it will take time to gather them in.'

'They will form the council,' Kedryn nodded. 'Initially, at least, so they had best be here.'

'Initially?' asked Jarl.

Kedryn nodded again, hoping what he was about to say would not result in further disagreement. 'There is no reason why the council should be limited to those of noble birth. Once it is properly

37

formed I do not see why commoners should not find a place within its ranks.'

Jarl stared at him with hooded eyes, then, to Kedryn's surprise, ducked his head once and said, 'Why not? If we are to upend all tradition, let us do it thoroughly.'

'Mehdri can be despatched on the morrow.' Bedyr glanced to the windows, through which the moon was visibly lower in the sky and corrected himself, 'Today. By the next full moon all needed should be here.'

Kedryn swallowed, thinking of long weeks confined in Andurel, then stifled a sigh that elicited a chuckle from Brannoc. 'I accept whatever date you set.'

'There will be little enough time in which to prepare,' said Arlynne enthusiastically. 'Gowns must be made, the celebrations organised; there will be so much to do.'

Yrla caught her son's eye then, her full lips curved in a sympathetic smile. 'If you are agreeable, Kedryn, I believe Arlynne and I can successfully arrange all such matters.'

'I leave it entirely to you.' Kedryn's response was no less enthusiastic than Arlynne's, whose eyes glowed at the prospect.

'So be it,' Bedyr said, grinning at the relief he saw on Kedryn's face. 'And for now I suggest we have accomplished enough. Shall we find our beds?'

Kedryn nodded eagerly, lifting from his chair, then halting as Wynett coughed. He turned towards her, a question in his eyes. 'There is one matter we should settle swiftly,' she murmured. 'That of my sister.'

'Ashrivelle?' Kedryn's face became apologetic: he had forgotten about Ashrivelle.

'Aye,' Wynett confirmed, her pretty face become serious. 'She remains intent on seeking retreat in Estrevan, but for that she requires the royal permission.'

'It is given,' Kedryn declared. 'Or will be, once I am crowned.'

'And an escort,' Wynett added.

Kedryn stifled the grin that threatened to burst forth: in all the debating he had forgotten both Wynett's sibling and the promise he had made earlier. 'She shall have it,' he declared, 'as befits the queen's sister. Sister Bethany, is it not customary for the king to seek Estrevan's blessing?'

Bethany ducked her head, light glinting on the silver strands, and said, 'It is, though it is not always observed.'

'We shall not let all tradition go,' Kedryn announced. 'After the coronation – and the formation of the council – Wynett and I shall accompany Ashrivelle to the Sacred City.'

Jarl opened his mouth to protest, but before he was able to speak Bethany said, 'A most excellent notion. Let all the folk of the Kingdoms see that Estrevan favours both your ascension and the formation of the council and both shall be the stronger.'

Jarl's protest was still-born, becoming instead a grunt of surrender.

'I will tell her,' said Wynett, her smile radiant.

'And now may we retire?' asked Kedryn.

A chorus of agreement answered the question and they rose to find their respective chambers.

Those occupied by Kedryn and his bride were the closest and they bade the others goodnight at the door, entering a room still warm from the fire banked in the low hearth. Kedryn felt a weariness such as he had not known since the battle with Taws, and at the same time an elation at the successful accomplishment of his scheme. He crossed the darkened room to the sleeping chamber beyond, where two thick candles burned in crystal cases, lending both a mellow light and a pleasant perfume to the welcome sight of their bed. Through the window he could see the moon was almost down, the sky fading into the utter blackness that precedes the dawn. He tugged at the fastenings of his tunic, tossing it carelessly to a chair and fell onto the bed, reaching down to unlace his boots. Wynett loosed her gown and slid the silk over her hips, its rustling attracting his gaze so that he paused in his own undressing to watch her. She was unembarrassed by his attention, becoming, rather, coquettish as she let fall her undergarments and raised her arms to unpin her piled hair, the movement emphasising the swell of her breasts so that his breath caught, his eyes fixed on the enticing curves of her slender body. Naked, she shook her hair loose, letting it fall in golden waves about her pale shoulders, smiling as she saw him watching. He dragged off his boots, kicking them aside as he worked on the fixings of his breeks, stumbling out of them as he hauled his shirt over his head.

'For one who claims no skills in diplomacy you were most eloquent,' she murmured as his feet tangled in the discarded breeks and he fell sideways, head lost in the shirt.

A muffled grunt was her only answer until he struggled free of the garment. He pushed it aside and wriggled farther onto the bed, grinning. 'You think so?'

'Aye,' she said gravely, 'and you must be tired for it.'

'Not too tired,' he answered, reaching for her.

She stepped towards the couch and his hands found her hips, drawing her towards him until her knees met the side and she fell forwards, onto him.

'In fact, not much tired at all,' he whispered throatily, mouth against her neck.

Wynett shuddered deliciously and turned her face down to meet his exploring lips. 'Nor,' she gasped, 'am I.'

*

Derwen Pars had been a fisherman all his life, as had his father and his before him. His earliest memory of the Idre was of lying on a warm blanket nested in a coil of rope, the smell of fish about him, and his father lifting him out over the prow of the boat to dangle above the blue water, gurgling as wavelets splashed his bare feet. More clearly he could recall the first time he had taken active part in his father's venture, nervous that he might fail and delighted when Verran Pars declared him a fisherman born, as they hauled in the net filled with the small silvery blue fish called *pardes*. He had not yet reached his tenth year then, but thereafter he accompanied Verran each day and, once he was deemed old enough, each night the little boat put out.

In thirty years Derwen Pars had come to know the Idre and her bounty as well as any of his calling. He knew her calm and when she was storm-whipped; knew her currents and her moods; when and where the shoals of parde would run, and where to cast a line for the great dark red *savve*. He had seen his father drown when their boat turned turtle in a spring floodtide and refused to let that tragedy deter him from pursuing the only life he knew, or wanted to know. He had taken his father's place then, refurbishing the damaged craft and ignoring his mother's pleas that he seek some safer occupation. Instead, he had become the finest fisherman in Drisse, purchasing a fine, stone-built house large enough to contain both his mother and his new wife, later the three children, none of whom – to his carefully-hidden disappointment – showed any aptitude for the watery life. He had taken each one out on the river and finally agreed to their becoming something other than fisherfolk, which pleased their grandmother, whose tolerance of the river had turned to distinct antipathy after Verran's drowning, and was not altogether to his wife's dislike, for whilst she loved her husband she did not share his regard for the great waterway, and prayed regularly in the little chapel at the centre of the small town that the Lady guard him while he plied his trade.

So far it seemed her prayers were heard, for Derwen was a wealthy man, so successful that he now owned two boats, both new, and employed two hired men to man the larger *Volalle* whilst he preferred to work alone in the *Verrana* that he had named for his father.

On this night, with the half-full moon bright enough in a clear sky, the Idre shining silver as his mother's hair and the *pocheta* running north in shoals large as any he had seen, he had both boats out, the largest of his nets strung between them to catch the succulent fish. Gille Ornan and Festyn Lewal crewed the *Volalle*, drifting her on a sheet anchor as Derwen manouevred the *Verrana* into position with a single stern sweep, spreading the skein wide to enmesh the northbound acquatics. He watched the master line cautiously, shipping his oar and tossing out his own anchor as the heavy cable reached the correct tension, settling on the stern boards as he waited for the fish to come to him. Farther out, and both up- and downriver, he could see the faint outlines of other craft as they positioned their nets, dark bulks against the argent filigree of the water. It would, he calculated, be a profitable night for all of Drisse's rivermen, but he was most confident of his own catch, for he was certain he had picked the best spot – and laid his claim before the rest – to enmesh the heart of the shoal.

Now he could rest for a while, letting the net fill before he sculled the *Verrana* round to meet the *Volalle* and the hard labour of hauling in began. Tomorrow, he thought, after the catch was gutted, he would divide it and take the larger boat over to the Keshi bank, where the horsemen would pay handsomely for such a delicacy. The prospect pleased him and he thought that with the proceeds he would buy his wife the cabinet she admired in Larl Suttoth's workshop. He stretched, flexing muscles only a little wearied by the long row out, and looked up at the moon. Soon; soon they would come to him: it was merely a question of waiting patiently for the Idre to yield up her bounty.

He reached between his outspread legs with one eye still on the bobbing corks of the net and found the waterproof sack that lay there, deftly working the cord loose from the neck and bringing out a slab of pale goat's milk cheese. The big knife he wore sliced a chunk from the slab with the skill of habit, his hand lifting it to his

41

mouth without his eyes moving from the net, and he began to chew, savouring the pungent taste. He cut a second slice and sheathed the knife, replacing the cheese and tugging the drawstrings of the sack tight. He swallowed and drank a mouthful of the thick, dark ale his village brewed, then began to chew on the second morsel of cheese.

Then, abruptly, he choked it down, leaning forwards with his eyes fixed disbelievingly on the corks. They no longer bobbed on the gentle wash of the Idre, but stretched in a taut line, shaping a vee that pointed, not north as it should when the pocheta struck, but south. He cursed softly, thinking that some drifting piece of debris had snagged his net, though he could see nothing that suggested flotsam, and moved amidships to set a hand on the master line. His curse became a grunt of surprise as he felt the line vibrate beneath his fingers, then a cry of amazement as the corks disappeared beneath the surface and the line coiled beneath the thwart ran out with a speed that no shoal of pocheta could produce. Nor any fish he knew of was his final thought before the cable snapped tight against its fastening and he felt the *Verrana* tilt under the pressure, the planks beneath his feet no longer secure footing, but a dangerously angled platform.

Water splashed inboard and Derwen Pars shouted as he felt his craft spilled from under him, the Idre enfolding him in a cold, wet embrace. For an instant panic gripped him and he sucked water into his lungs, icy needles probing his throat and nasal passages as he fought for breath. Then instinct overcame the panic and he was striking for the surface, head plunging into moonlit air, his eyes blinking clear in time to see the *Volalle* spun about and turtled just as his father's boat had gone down so long ago. Save now there was no floodtide to explain the capsizement. With the time-stretched clarity that danger brings he saw Gille Ornan and Festyn Lewal leap from the turning boat into the river and heard through their frightened shouting the twanging snap of the net cable, like some gigantic harp string breaking.

And then raw terror gripped him, freezing him so that his legs ceased their paddling and he was suddenly sunk, the shock of submergement reactivating his body and bringing him back to the surface in time for his eyes to confirm what had so terrified him.

A great dark hulk rose from the water, blacker than the night, a neck thick as a fat man's waist supporting a triangular head on which eyes glowed with an awful fire above a mouth that was all serrated, angular teeth, surrounded by wavering tendrils that seemed possessed of their own life. It rose up and up, the net trailing like a shroud, until it hung above the foundered *Volalle*, seeming for a moment to be suspended in the air, then crashing down to shatter the craft with its bulk. Water swirled, a whirlpool forming as the thing submerged, then the head appeared again and Festyn Lewal screamed once as the cruel teeth fastened about his waist and he went under. Derwen felt his stomach churn as half the man bobbed back to the surface, then was gone into the ghastly maw. He began to swim in the direction of Drisse, but saw that the monster lay between him and the shore and turned his course just as the creature's head swung round, the weirdly-glowing eyes fixing on Gille Ornan, seeming to bathe the unfortunate man in rubescent light. Ornan held a knife in his right hand, and he raised it against the thing as the great head descended. He might as well have struck a pin against a rock, for the jaws gaped and took him in whole, the fangs grinding against his yielding flesh, shaking him as a terrier shakes a rat. The bile that had risen in Derwen's stomach found its way to his mouth as he saw his friend swallowed and he flailed helplessly in the water, choking and spitting.

The leviathan snaked its serpentine neck in his direction and the massive bulk flowed effortlessly beneath the churning waves, the wedge of the skull building a foam crest that cut arrow-straight towards Derwen. Briefly he saw the silver of that crest incarnadined, the blood of his crew darkening the Idre's surface. Then all he saw were the rows of teeth and the pulsing pink throat behind them, the tendrils that stretched out, slimy and grey as putrescent flesh, and the glowing, awful eyes.

The teeth closed and Derwen Pars was gone, the *Verrana* smashed to matchwood as the monster carried the man down, leaving behind only wreckage and oily slicks of blood that drifted south, wavering memories of three lives.

All about was confusion, Derwen's fellow fishermen sculling their craft in close to see what had happened. None were sure, for none had been near, their attention caught only by the screaming, and by the time they arrived there was only floating timber left. Their own catches went forgotten as they quartered the river, lanterns lit and voices hailing the survivors they never found. Finally, as dawn paled the sky and the eastern horizon grew pink, they gave up the search and turned back to Drisse, congregating in their usual waterside tavern to debate who should carry word to the missing men's

43

widows. When that was decided, and all had compared their stories, delegations went to each household with the tragic news. After that they went to the chapel to seek enlightenment of the Sisters there, but as all they were able to tell the Sisters was that they had heard screams and found the wreckage of two boats, no men either live or drowned, the Sisters could shed little light on the strange incident. They recorded it, as was their wont, and prayed for the souls of the dead, but in Drisse it remained a mystery.

*

Brannoc turned back the sleeve of his leaf green shirt with a dramatic flourish and shook the dice in the cup of his dark-skinned hand. They rolled across the polished oak of the table and stuttered to a halt with threes showing on both cubes. White teeth flashed as the dark man grinned, reaching to scoop up the small pile of coins that lay beside a pewter flagon of pale yellow wine.

Tepshen Lahl's face remained enigmatic as he took the dice and threw five, reaching into the pouch on his belt to extract another coin that he tossed towards his companion. Brannoc caught it in mid-air, his grin becoming wider still, until it seemed it must split his face.

'Enough?' he enquired mildly. 'Or do you remain bent on rendering yourself destitute?'

Tepshen grunted and took the flagon, tilting it above his cup to spill the wine brimful into the container. He lifted the cup, not a drop falling from the rim, and drank, his eyes calm on Brannoc's face.

'The best of three,' he challenged as he set the cup down.

'And the stakes?' Brannoc emptied his own cup and filled it afresh.

Tepshen shrugged, dropping coins. Brannoc studied them a moment, then nodded. 'Very well.'

He shook the dice and tossed a seven. Tepshen threw nine, though his expression did not change as the former wolfshead snorted and scooped up the ivory cubes. A three followed and Brannoc laughed, then stopped as the easterner matched it. He threw six and began to chuckle again. Then stopped again as Tepshen rolled two sixes and reached across the table to retrieve what he had bet, his jet eyes glinting as he faced Brannoc and said, 'And what you owe me, barbarian.'

Brannoc shook his head, extracting coins from the stack at his elbow and counting them carefully onto the table.

'That is everything I won from you.'

Tepshen nodded sagely, the corners of his mouth curving slightly as he remarked, 'A battle is not won until the last blow falls.'

'Eastern wisdom?' asked Brannoc lazily, tilting his chair back so that the mid-morning sun shining into the secluded courtyard struck his face, lightening the tan from the colour of aged oak to a more polished sheen.

'Common sense.'

Tepshen rose to his feet, fluid as a cat, and with the same feline grace fastidiously smoothed the loose-cut frontage of his shirt as he stepped from the shadow of the colonnades that supported the tiled roof of the portico spanning one wall of the yard. Sunlight gleamed on his oiled queue, striking blue from the black, though it seemed to meld with his yellow skin as though the flesh absorbed the radiance. He stretched his arms wide, turning slowly around, his eyes travelling casually over the stuccoed walls and the blank rectangles of the windows.

Brannoc scratched at the tangle of dark hair exposed by his open shirtfront, yawning prodigiously, the shells and feathers woven into his hair fluttering with the motion. A faint beading of sweat decorated his brow for it was very warm in the courtyard, the vaulting walls of the palace buildings trapping the heat, the white plaster that covered them reflecting it, even the smooth slabs of granite that formed the floor seeming to radiate it back, and he was more accustomed to the cooler climes of the north. He watched Tepshen Lahl execute one economic circle, seeing how the dropping arms fell close to the swordbelt about the kyo's waist, the left thumb hooking instinctively over the scabbard of the longsword, resting against the guard where it might instantly loose the blade from the retaining sheath.

'He is safe enough here,' he smiled. 'And if I guess aright, still abed.'

Tepshen ducked his head once in acknowledgement, but his hand remained close to his sword as he returned to his chair.

'Do you ever relax?' Brannoc added as the smaller man sat down.

'I am.' Tepshen's smile was fleeting, not from disapproval, but rather because he seldom smiled, his wide-cheeked face being of a naturally solemn set.

Unlike Brannoc's, which was mobile and given easily to the laughter that now rang from his wide mouth, startling the sparrows that hopped about the table into flight.

'Perhaps we are too relaxed,' he ventured, more for the sake of making conversation to fill the empty afternoon than any real belief in his words. Besides, he found it amusing to bait the easterner a little, fascinated by Tepshen's stoic attitude to whatever crossed his path. He knew himself to be volatile, and the differences in their attitudes intrigued him. Tepshen Lahl intrigued him, he thought as he waited for the sallow-featured man to reply – or not, for Tepshen did not always deign to answer what he considered frivolous – and the fact that he counted this enigmatic easterner his friend was a source of wonder. There was a kinship of spirit he knew; that had been recognised between them when first they met in High Fort, when Bedyr Caitin sought his guidance into the Beltrevan. Neither gave his friendship easily, but once given it was a lasting loyalty, and in those early days he had known that Tepshen would not hesitate to kill him had he proved false. Nor, having witnessed the kyo's skill with a blade, did he doubt that he would be the loser in the fight: he was adept at swordwork – better than almost any – but Tepshen Lahl was a master and Brannoc doubted there was anyone, save perhaps Kedryn himself, who could best the man.

It had been that perilous journey into the forests that had first forged their friendship, for it was during that trip he had recognised his own loyalty to Kedryn, and that in itself was strange, for the Prince of Tamur had been little more than a boy then and Brannoc had considered him at first to be more liability than asset. That opinion had altered radically over the ensuing months until the halfbreed's regard for Kedryn was scarcely less than the easterner's. It was as though the young man exercised some power of which he was scarcely aware, for whilst he was definitely a likeable fellow he did nothing to ingratiate himself, save, it occurred to Brannoc, *be* himself. Yet he had felt drawn to Kedryn, and when Bedyr had come asking his help in finding the blinded youth in the vastness of the northern woodlands he had not hesitated; nor when Kedryn, his sight regained, had announced his intention of sailing south to Andurel to combat the Messenger had it occurred to Brannoc to do anything but go with him. Thinking about it now, cloistered comfortably in a yard of the White Palace with the spring sun warm on his face and swallows twittering overhead, a flagon of fine Galichian wine to hand, it seemed a trifle odd that he had so readily sailed into the teeth of Ashar's wrath. At the time it had seemed only natural, yet Brannoc was, by nature, a cautious man. That was, he decided, the effect Kedryn had on people, and mayhap

Tepshen had recognised the spell and seen in Brannoc a kindred spirit, for it was without question that Tepshen would lay down his life for the young man.

Whatever, the halfbreed thought, the cause is not important; the friendship is.

'Too much comfort softens a man.'

The kyo's voice interrupted Brannoc's musings and he cocked his head a little, anticipating some further extrapolation. When none was offered he asked, 'Do you think we grow soft? Would you rather we had war?'

Tepshen shook his head, and for a moment Brannoc wondered if he saw doubt in the dark eyes.

'No, not war. But Kedryn has kingly concerns to occupy him. You and I, though, we are neither diplomats nor courtiers. We have no place in this peaceful city.'

Brannoc shrugged expressively, his heavy brows drawing together. 'After Kedryn takes the High Throne we shall be free. And I have the impression our young king-to-be has little intention of spending more time than he need here. Has he not established the notion of that? With this council formed he seems bent on travelling to Estrevan.'

'And I shall go with him,' nodded Tepshen.

'Mayhap I, too,' murmured Brannoc, thinking suddenly that he would be mightily loath to part from this company of friends.

'You are appointed Warden of the Forests,' said the kyo.

Brannoc shrugged again. 'A reward for services rendered. With the Messenger gone and Niloc Yarrum dead this past year, the tribes return to their old ways, though with less love for Ashar after the Horde's defeat. They offer no threat and my old wolfshead comrades will know what transpires beyond the Lozins. Should aught stir there, I should hear. Or word go to Rycol and Fengrif.'

'It remains a duty,' said Tepshen.

'Aye,' Brannoc agreed, 'but in definition it is surely a duty to the Kingdoms. To ward them. And how better to ward them than by warding their king?'

'You think some danger threatens this proposed journey?' Tepshen asked.

'Who knows?' grinned Brannoc. 'Kedryn himself, and Sister Bethany, seem doubtful that Ashar will give up the game easily, so mayhap hazard does lie in wait. In which case I would be there. Would you have me trust Kedryn's safety to your blade alone?'

'No,' said the kyo, and this time his smile was clearly visible.

*

In another part of the White Palace a similar conversation occupied four others concerned with both Kedryn and the welfare of the Kingdoms. Here there was more space, the buildings set farther apart and the ground between planted to form lawns on which shrubs and small, decorative trees put forth buds eager to drink in the sunlight and unburden themselves of their weight of flowers. The centre was given over to a long avenue at one end of which stood a butt, its white cloth cover painted with concentric circles of gold, green, blue and black, at the other the lords of Tamur and Kesh with their wives, all holding bows.

Bedyr Caitin's was the great longbow of the Tamurin, a length of supple yew near tall as its wielder, and the cords of muscle along his right arm stood out as he drew back the string, sighting down the clothyard shaft. He loosed the string and smiled his appreciation as the arrow flew true, the blunt practice head imbedding deep in the straw beneath the bull.

'Well shot,' applauded Jarl of Kesh, turning back the sleeves of his customary black robe as he took his place on the firing mark.

His bow was shorter than Bedyr's and constructed of overlapping layers of horn and bone, deeply curved: the bow of a horseman. A frown of concentration creased his swarthy features as he sighted, followed by a grunt as his shaft struck the target three fingers' width clear of the bull.

He stepped aside to allow Yrla her shot, smiling as she brushed a loosened tendril of raven hair from her eyes, voicing his approval as her smaller version of the longbow sent its missile to the edge of the gold.

'This talk of Ashar,' he murmured as his own wife moved to fire, 'what credence do you give it?'

Bedyr shrugged, rustling the linen of his brown shirt. 'Kedryn and Wynett were the only ones to see the Messenger at the last,' he replied softly, studying the dark-haired Keshi woman as she gritted her teeth and inexpertly drew back her bowstring, 'and it seems they cannot say for sure he died. Bethany appears equivocal.'

He paused as Arlynne squealed her disappointment, pointing to where her arrow vibrated against the outer circle of blue.

'Hold your left arm straighter, Arlynne. And loose your breath slowly with the shaft.'

'Bethany could find no trace of magic remaining,' Jarl said.

'No.' Bedyr selected an arrow from the quiver racked beside him and nocked the shaft to the string. 'But nor . . .' he drew, right thumb touching his cheek, '. . . is she prepared to say . . .' he loosed the arrow, '. . . that he is dead.'

The long oak shaft drove deep into the target, so close to its predecessor that both arrows rattled an unmelodic tune.

'Then is it wise that Kedryn should depart Andurel?'

Jarl set arrow to string, bending the shortbow as he raised it. This time he hit closer to the mark, just on the edge of the gold.

'Might Estrevan not shed more light on Bethany's doubts?' asked Yrla as she took her place.

'If these doubts are founded in truth,' Jarl replied as she fired, 'then surely the king's place is here.'

Yrla's shot hit the bull slightly left of centre. Arlynne said, 'Did you learn this in Estrevan?'

'No,' Yrla smiled, the expression rendering her girlish, 'this comes of marrying a Tamurin.'

Arlynne giggled and missed the target completely.

'Not necessarily,' Yrla said, resuming her conversation with Jarl, her face serious again. 'With this council of Kedryn's formed there will be less need for the king to remain in Andurel. And as he pointed out, the greater duty is the defence of the Kingdoms. If Estrevan is able to clarify the situation, then the journey will be well worthwhile.'

'You did not argue against it last night,' Bedyr said.

Jarl shrugged expansively. 'Last night I was won over by Kedryn's eloquence. There is something about your son that elicits support, but since then I have had time to ponder it.'

'You find these proposed departures from tradition hard to accept,' said Arlynne. 'Surely if these notions came to Kedryn through the talisman, it is the Lady's wish he travel to the Sacred City.'

'I will accept that the idea for the council was inspired,' Jarl allowed, somewhat grudgingly, for he knew his wife spoke the truth, 'but this desire to visit Estrevan stems, I suspect, more from Wynett, and Kedryn's desire to retain his freedom.'

'You doubt their motives?' Bedyr asked.

'No.' Jarl shook his head, setting his bow down as he moved to the table that held a decanter of wine, beads of moisture glistening on the facets of crystal. He poured a goblet, raising the decanter questioningly to the others, pouring when they nodded. 'I believe they are sincere, but I am not sure of the wisdom of departing the White Palace so soon after the coronation.'

'I believe they may be persuaded to remain a while,' said Yrla, accepting the delicate glass the Keshi held towards her. 'At least until we see the council settled firmly in place.'

Bedyr braced his longbow against his knee, bending the wood until he had the string slipped loose. He set it carefully against the stand holding his quiver and moved to the table, his handsome face serious.

'I think Kedryn is set on this,' he murmured, taking a goblet. 'I do not think he will be dissuaded.'

'But surely,' Yrla suggested, 'he will not depart before he knows the council may function successfully.'

Bedyr grinned somewhat ruefully. 'Kedryn is a man now, and king besides – or will be soon – and he has already shown us that he has a mind of his own. As for the council – well, he has outlined its nature and the nucleus exists already. If he feels he may leave the governance of the Kingdoms in safe hands, what reason is there for him to delay?'

'The nucleus?' Jarl asked dubiously, a glimmer of suspicion in his hooded green eyes.

Bedyr's grin grew wider and perhaps more rueful as he nodded. 'Do you not see it, old friend?'

'You mean,' Jarl gasped, setting down his goblet, 'us?'

'He has not said it,' Bedyr returned, 'but is it not the obvious choice?'

Arlynne clapped her hands, the bracelets that covered her plump wrists jangling, a smile wreathing her pretty face. 'We shall stay in Andurel? That is wonderful!'

'No!' Jarl snapped. 'It is not wonderful. Kesh needs me.'

'It will be an excellent lesson for Kemm,' his wife retorted. 'He must take your place one day and this will be a chance for him to rule without your hand guiding all he does.'

Jarl's face clouded, his heavy brows drawing together. He chewed for a while on the trailing ends of his moustache, teeth grinding furiously.

'It cannot be,' he said at last.

'Would you refuse what you ask of Kedryn?' demanded Bedyr, smiling at the Keshi's obvious discomfort.

'He is – will be – the king,' said Jarl desperately.

'And as such,' said Yrla, joining her husband in support of their son, 'you would have him remain here. Surely, Jarl, if you find a short sojourn so distasteful, you must see Kedryn's point of view.'

'I had thought his eloquence stemmed from the talisman,' muttered the bow-legged man, 'but I perceive I was wrong – it was inherited.'

Yrla laughed, Bedyr joining her as he clapped a hand to Jarl's shoulder. 'I have no great desire to stay longer,' he declared cheerfully, 'but if Kedryn's mind is made up, be it by the Lady or his own desire, I do not believe he will allow himself thwarted.'

'And should Ashar offer further threat, then it is only wise to seek the advice of Estrevan,' added Yrla.

'But . . .' Jarl spluttered, seeing himself backed into a corner.

'But he will travel knowing loyal friends occupy the palace,' Bedyr finished for him. 'Men wise in the ways of the Kingdoms, Jarl. Men experienced in governance. Men like you.'

'I would lief see Kesh again,' Jarl declared plaintively.

'You will,' said Arlynne, gleefully unsympathetic. 'In time.'

Jarl glowered at her for a moment, then his expression shifted slowly to one of resignation. He shrugged, sighing, spreading his ringed hands wide as he allowed a smile to split his fleshy lips, his eyes locked on Bedyr and Yrla.

'What is it about your son,' he wondered, 'that enables him to command such loyalty?'

'He is the Chosen One,' Yrla said with simple pride.

# Chapter Three

TAWS had failed him – and paid the price of failure – but there remained value in what his creature had learnt of the ways of the cursed followers of his enemy, and that knowledge he would put to use. The souls Taws had drunk all yielded up their little tidbits, their little scraps of learning, and each soul – condemned by the manner of its owner's death to wander the domains of the netherworld – was now his to draw upon, each one a source of further information that he might utilise in the formation of his trap. And this time he would rely on no agency other than himself: this time he would conquer! Not through strength of arms, for the Lady (he did not vocalise her name but rather conjured an image of enmity and hatred) had thwarted that design; nor through such subtleties as his minion had sought to employ in seducing Hattim Sethiyan, for again her stratagems had proven too adept. No, this time he would strike directly at the living embodiment of her challenge to his power.

He chuckled at the thought, the sound roiling like malign thunder through the ethereal realm of his domain, its forlorn inhabitants cringing at the echoes, for Ashar's laughter seldom presaged aught but further suffering. This time no fallible human agency would fail him, nor a creature of his own making; this time the agency of his attack would be a force so elemental as to be insuperable, impervious to defeat for it was unthinking, guided only by his will and the task he had imposed upon it. Already it was freed, questing for its prey, and he needed only obtain a little more knowledge from those luckless souls Taws had sent into the limbo to guide it to its quarry.

Thought was as deed to such as he and in the instant of conception so he stood upon the ash-grey strand that was one boundary of the netherworld, a luminous being in human form, for it pleased him to appear so, and being a god he was able to assume what shape best pleased him. He looked about him, not for want of orientation but rather for the pleasure of contemplation, studying the ugly, seething surface of the bleak mere, the sunless sky above,

52

filled with the fluttering things it had been his amusement to create, and he smiled, enjoying the joyless panorama, drinking in the fetid atmosphere, redolent of lost hope, savoury with despair.

He turned as he issued a summons to stare towards the shifting mist that banked the recesses of the miserable shoreline. The mist twisted and turned as though alive, columns of reddish grey shaping and dissipating, and from its depths came a slow, foot-dragging figure. Ashar studied it, savouring the irrevocable dejection that slumped the shoulders, twisted the once-proud mouth, sat like wasted ambition in the dulled eyes as the slow-moving feet brought it ever closer, each step leaving a smouldering print indented in the immaterial matter of the strand.

*You are unhappy?*

He made his tone conversational for it ever amused him to toy with such as this, knowing it dared not question his majesty.

'Is that not your wish?' asked Hattim Sethiyan, his voice dull as the scene, as empty of optimism.

Ashar chuckled, sending ripples over the surface of the lake, and said, *Will Kedryn Caitin be king in your place?*

Hattim nodded, lank strands of toneless hair falling unnoticed across his downcast eyes. 'He is wed to Wynett and she is Darr's elder daughter.'

*And after he is crowned in your place? What then?*

Shoulders that hunched as though in anticipation of pain hunched further in a shrug that rustled the drab material cladding Hattim, drawing it crackling from the bleeding wound between his shoulders, dislodging maggots that fell writhing to the ground.

*Come,* urged the god, *you were king once, albeit briefly, you know what protocols appertain.*

Lips still fleshy despite their absence of blood thinned, pursing, and for a moment Ashar wondered idly if he should have the pleasure of punishing rebellion, then Hattim sighed and said, 'It is customary for the new-crowned king to seek the blessing of the Sisterhood, so he may well journey to Estrevan.'

*And how,* Ashar demanded in the same smooth tone, *would he travel to that accursed place?*

'The Idre,' Hattim grunted, coughing as a maggot found its way into his throat, spitting it out, 'he would travel up the river. Likely to Gennyf and then overland to Caitin Hold; thence to the Morfah Pass and on to the city.'

*And would his pretty little queen accompany him?*

Again Hattim nodded. 'By custom, aye. And likely eager to see Estrevan once more.'

*And she, too, wears the blue stone?*

'When last I saw them,' Hattim confirmed, 'both wore the talismans.'

Ashar nodded in turn, eyes that seemed to open on reeking furnaces thoughtful.

*So be it. You may leave me.*

The shade that was now Hattim shifted reluctantly, risking a glance at that face he dared not observe directly. 'Shall I be freed of this?'

He gestured at his surroundings and Ashar chuckled afresh, shaking his head. *Never. This is what you chose when you failed me.*

'I?' Despair lent Hattim courage, though his voice emerged a thin, wailing cry. 'It was not I, but Taws who failed you.'

*No matter*, Ashar returned cheerfully. *This is your lot for all eternity.*

Tears formed in the lustreless eyes of the shade, running slow down the hollowed cheeks. The shoulders slumped deeper than before and Hattim Sethiyan turned about, walking back into the shifting mist that folded about him in a grey cloak of despondency. Ashar watched him go, the taste of despair delicious to his godly senses, then issued another summons, this one met with a degree of resistance that the god quelled with a thought, bringing the one he required slowly as Hattim from the swirling mist. There was less enjoyment to be had from this confrontation, for Darr lacked the Galichian's pride, that overweening ambition that lent such a delightful tang to Hattim's despond, and the god knew that the shade of the former king retained a faith in the Lady that succoured his ghost in this place of lost hope. Sometime he would spend more time with Darr, teach the inferior creature who was the true master, but for now he needed only information. He beckoned, the motion forcing Darr's shade closer until it stood before him, the shimmering shape of the god towering above the slighter frame of the once-mortal man.

*I have spoken with Hattim Sethiyan. He tells me Kedryn Caitin stands where once you stood.*

Had he expected regret he would have found disappointment, for Darr nodded and said, 'Kedryn will make a fine king.'

*He has your daughter for his wife*, Ashar remarked. *The one sworn to serve my enemy. It seems her vows of fealty meant little to her when*

54

*the chance to rut with that upstart presented itself. Clearly the Lady* (he
forced the word out) *means less to her than a man's prick. Even now he
likely paws her body; or she his. Doubtless they couple like beasts on heat
and she drinks his lust with avid lips.*

'Wynett is his wife? I had not known that. They are happy then.'

Ashar contained the rage that boiled with Darr's mild acceptance,
the eyes he had assumed incandescent as he studied the frail form
before him, unable to prevent the retort, *Not for long.*

Orbs bleached of colour, but not of defiance, answered the god's
glare. Darr said, 'Then Kedryn must have defeated your minion. As
the Lady will defeat you.'

Ashar's rage became uncontainable. His mouth opened, spitting
fire, and Darr's shade was wreathed in flame, red light filling the
grey air with its fury, a scream of agony climbing from within the
pyre. In time, before the shade was destroyed and thus beyond
suffering, the god called back his unholy fire, a gesture restoring
the charred shape to some semblance of normality.

*No*, he snarled, *she will not. It is Kedryn Caitin and your daughter
who stand between me and victory and I shall have them both. And you
will help me in that conquest.*

'I will not,' Darr said with simple dignity.

*You will not?* Ashar snapped, then modified his tone. *But I will
offer you a choice. Aid me and you shall be freed of this place. I will set
you amongst the privileged. Refuse and you shall see your daughter join you
here. And Kedryn Caitin, too, knowing that you brought them to this.*

A lucid arm swept out, encompassing all that mournful place.
Darr did not follow the gesture, but shook his head. 'You are a god
of liars and cheats and I will have no truck with you.'

*Then you shall have no choice*, Ashar barked, his anger seeming to
burn against the mist so that it glowed and trembled. *I will have it
from you against your will.*

Hands of fire gripped Darr's shoulders, lifting him so that he
hung above the ashen ground, the god's furnace gaze transfixing
him, dragging from him the knowledge Ashar sought. It was if
immaterial pincers plucked pieces from his very soul, and he writhed
at the agony of it, his moaning bringing a smile to the god's mouth.

*So*, Ashar intoned when he was done, releasing his grip to let Darr
fall shuddering to the seething strand, *I have it. Go.*

The shade that was Darr rose unsteadily, compelled by the god's
will, and shuffled back towards the mist that extended tendrils as
if in welcome. Ashar watched him, promising later vengeance, and

55

turned himself, stepping proudly to the edge of the canescent lough, where he stooped to dabble a hand in the viscous liquid, fervid eyes concentrated on the surface as his mouth moved in silent speech.

When he was done he rose and disappeared, that place where he had stood shimmering for a while with baleful red light as the tattered grey wings of the bat-like creatures fluttered anxiously, their piping voices raised in reedy chorus.

*

In Estrevan Paramount Sister Gerat felt an unseasonally cool wind brush chill fingers over her face and wondered if the prickling sensation dancing like tiny needles over her skin was a product of the building storm or something else.

There was, undoubtedly, a storm building. To the east a band of livid sky hid the bulk of the Lozins, massive banks of black cumulus hanging above, moving ponderously westwards as if in pursuit of the azure that dominated that part of the heavens. Billows of white fought briefly with the black, and were engulfed, or sent scudding and streaming from the celestial combat as their darker opponents took the victory. The wind grew stronger, tainted with the odour of rain, and across the underbelly of the great cloud mass flashed shafts of brilliant light. Unconsciously Gerat counted off the pauses between lightning and the ensuing peels of thunder, remembering how she had done the same as a child, calculating the arrival of the storm. She smiled, the expression a mingling of amusement and apprehension, and felt the first droplets of rain touch her cheeks. Within moments the droplets had become a downpour and she retreated from the balcony of her chamber, stepping back into the room as globules of water lashed the stone outside, splashing over the sill to rest translucent on the polished boards of the floor. The chamber grew dim as the storm settled over the city, lit only by the dancing tendrils of levin that stalked the rooftops as if some air-borne behemoth trod on insectile legs above Estrevan. She felt her hair stand up as the world became a shadow show, all darkness and brilliance, alternating, great racking booms echoing against her eardrums as the rain beat a manic tattoo upon the stones of the balcony and the droplets shining on the floor became a pool of light-shimmered effulgence.

And then it was gone, sweeping westwards, the canescence to the east brightening to welcome blue, white cloud repossessing the sky, sailing in alabaster billows across a cerulean backdrop that mirrored the re-emergent sun.

Gerat stood at the threshold of the balcony, studying the sparkle of rain on the rooftops, unaware that her slippers rested in the puddle left by the storm. Equally unaware as she turned away that she left a trail of dark footprints across the rosewood boards, leading from the portal to the desk on which sat Alaria's Text and several other volumes of carefully-bound parchment. She settled herself in the high-backed chair, smoothing strands of glossy black hair into place with an absent-minded gesture as she returned to her studies, not quite sure what it was she sought in the ancient volumes.

The Text she now knew almost by heart, able to quote Alaria's enigmatic words with a facility to match Sister Lavia's, but what intrigued her was its possible correlation with other, mostly earlier, writings of the Sorority's visionaries. Those of Sister Qualle were of particular interest, plucked from the oldest shelves of the library by the diligence of the acolytes she had entrusted with the research. She turned the pages of that tome now, wondering who had scribed for the illiterate Sister, and what they had made of her seemingly meaningless ramblings. The original document had long crumbled into dust and what she held was a copy of a copy, and thus possibly subject to alterations, but even so it seemed to her that Sister Qualle had preceded Alaria in her warning of Ashar's interventions in the affairs of the Kingdoms. Lavia, she knew, disagreed, as did Jara, and by common consent those two were the finest antique scholars in living memory; yet she was unable to rid herself of that doubt that nagged at the edges of her mind, that conviction that the fight was not ended with the Messenger's defeat but merely held in abeyance.

She turned the ancient pages carefully, smoothing each one as sunlight filled her chamber again, the slightly musty odour of the vellum joined now by the fresher perfume of rain-washed air, the inking seeming to glow in the radiance of the afternoon. A frown drew lines across her forehead as she studied the archaic language, her lips shaping words no longer in common usage, her blue gaze darkening as she found the passage she wanted – or had hoped not to find, she was not sure which.

She read it slowly, then again, faster, and then a third time slowly, each time the meaning remained unchanged and her frown grew deeper. She pushed the tome aside and reached for Alaria's Text, her long index finger tracing a passage already marked with the indentation of her nail, then returned to Qualle's words.

The sun still shone when finally she looked up, and the sky was still blue, but Gerat's gaze was sombre and sighted not on the heavens but on the words burning within her mind. For long moments she sat staring blindly at the rectangle framed by the balcony door, then she rose to her feet, pacing across the chamber to throw open the door and call for an acolyte.

A gangly girl in a pale blue gown answered the Paramount Sister's summons, listening carefully to her instructions before scurrying like an eager puppy to do her bidding. Gerat returned to her desk and once more read Qualle's words, then closed both that and Alaria's Text, folding the two books against her bosom as she quit the chamber and made her way through the corridors to a room furnished with a single large table and five plain chairs. Two walls were of blank stone, the others windowed so that sunlight filled the recesses, burnishing the oak of the table's top to a lustrous glow. It fell on the straw-coloured hair of the young woman who sat facing the door, lending a honeyed glow to her tanned skin, and on the untidy brown strands of the homely woman seated beside her.

Gerat nodded a greeting and said, 'Porelle, Reena – thank you for coming so swiftly.'

'Your summons had the ring of urgency,' Porelle answered, curiosity in her light brown eyes.

Reena pointed to the books Gerat carried. 'You study the Text again, Sister?'

'And Qualle's,' Gerat confirmed. 'But shall we await Lavia and Jara? I would have them hear what I need say.'

Reena nodded, glancing at Porelle, who shaped a little moue with her rosebud mouth, her expression dubious. Reena smoothed her blue gown, content to wait.

She did not have long, for the door opened to admit two older women, one silver-haired, her face creased as a winter apple, age stooping her shoulders, the other stood straighter, though the grey that predominated in her dark hair suggested she was only a little younger. 'What is it?' she asked without preamble, seating herself across the table from Porelle and Reena.

Gerat waited until the older Sister was settled in a chair and sat down herself at the table's head.

'We are the council of Estrevan,' she began, interrupted by the silver-headed woman, who turned age-dimmed eyes towards the two volumes resting on the oak and asked, 'Is that Qualle's book?'

'It is, Jara,' Gerat nodded, 'and I have been reading it.'

'It is of little but historical interest.' Jara's tone was dismissive. 'What meaning it might have had is dissipated by age.'

'Mayhap,' Gerat allowed.

'There is no *mayhap* to it,' said Jara firmly.

'Let our Sister finish,' suggested Lavia. 'I see concern in her eyes, and she would not have summoned us so urgently were this not a matter of some importance.'

Gerat smiled her thanks and opened Qualle's book to the page she had earlier studied. 'I would ask you all to read this,' she said. 'Or perhaps you, Lavia? Your tongue accommodates the old language better than most.'

Lavia nodded her agreement and took the book, reading aloud.

'I do not understand,' Porelle said when she was finished. 'What is so urgent?'

'Do you not see a meaning here?' Gerat asked.

'It parallels Alaria's Text,' Porelle allowed, 'but the prophecies set out there are fulfilled, surely?'

Reena murmured agreement. 'The Messenger is defeated and soon Kedryn Caitin will assume the High Throne. How does that passage go? Jara, you have it, do you not?'

Jara closed her watery eyes a moment, then grunted softly and said aloud, '*The Chosen One shall take the seat, his queen beside, and peace shall reign.*'

'*I saw the conqueror defeated,*' Lavia quoted from Qualle's manuscript, '*and he was driven into fire and I saw him no more.*'

'Read on,' urged Gerat, 'The latter part.'

Lavia's brow creased as she studied the page. '*And I saw he who was raised up go down into the earth where dwell the worms of corruption, and yet they could not overcome him for his purpose was high and I saw the love of his fellows sustained him that he be not forgotten, nor those he loved. And I saw that he brought them to her love, for such was the strength with which she vested him that not death himself could overcome, neither his worms, not his sundry minions that dwell beneath.*'

'Do you see it now?' Gerat demanded.

Porelle shook her blonde head, her expression confused. Reena said, 'Surely it refers to Kedryn's death. But that is long away.'

'It has a certain merit as poetry,' said Jara, 'but I do not think it has the relevance of Alaria's work – and as Porelle has said, the terms of her prophecy are fulfilled.'

'There is something else,' Gerat reached across the table to bring the book closer, her eyes scanning the ornate lettering. 'Listen:

*And I saw that what he had fashioned for his deathly purpose was his undoing, for that which he had fashioned he had imbued with his own strength, that death himself might be slain, should life and death be joined.'*

'The meaning is unclear,' Lavia suggested, studying Gerat's face, 'and Qualle's sanity has been questioned by scholars.'

'She was mad,' Jara said bluntly.

'Surely it is a poetic assumption,' said Reena, encouraged by a nod from Porelle. 'I am not a scholar such as my Sisters, but it seems to say that the Lady's salvation awaits us all.'

'It refers to death in the masculine,' said Gerat earnestly. 'Nothing else I have read does that.'

'Archaic custom,' said Jara. 'Lavia, what is your opinion?'

'It was custom,' Lavia agreed. 'How else do you read it, Gerat?'

'I believe Qualle used the masculine because she spoke of Ashar,' said the Paramount Sister.

Frowns of doubt and incomprehension met the announcement. Jara snorted, 'Nonsense.'

'I do not see it,' said Lavia, though her tone was, like her expression, less certain.

'Tell us your doubt,' asked Porelle.

'I believe Qualle warns of Ashar's meddling,' said Gerat slowly. 'I believe that Kedryn faces some further test before his task as the Chosen One is done.'

'But what?' Reena demanded. 'Alaria's Text is obscure enough, but this . . .' she paused, shaking her head, dislodging fresh tendrils of untidy hair, '. . . this defeats interpretation.'

'Mayhap,' Gerat said wearily, 'but I feel there is more. I cannot rid myself of the feeling.'

'Your talent extends towards clairvoyance,' Lavia murmured, 'Are you certain of your doubts?'

'No.' Gerat shook her head. 'They are no more than that – doubts.'

'What would you have us do?' Porelle asked pragmatically, glancing at her companions as she asked, 'Does any here claim understanding of Qualle's words?'

Negatives answered her question and she went on, 'Then I do not see what action we might take, Gerat. Warn Kedryn? Of what? Ashar's Messenger is defeated and soon Kedryn will be crowned. There is peace in the Beltrevan and it seems the tribes turn from Ashar, weakening his power. Within the Kingdoms he is reviled, and he cannot cross the Lozin barrier. Of what should we warn the Chosen One? That Ashar is his enemy? He knows that. That he will one day die? He knows that, too.

'What would you have us do?'

'I had hoped that one of you might enlighten me,' Gerat responded without rancour. 'I had hoped that one of you might read in these words what I believe I find there.'

'We cannot,' said Porelle gently. 'I find nothing there save old poetry.'

'Likely dictated by a mad woman,' nodded Jara. 'You know that Qualle died before she took her final vows? The title of Sister is an honorific.'

'I know I cannot rid myself of this doubt,' Gerat said. Then, 'Reena, what have you to say?'

'I echo Porelle,' answered the homely woman. 'I cannot believe this is anything of much importance.'

'Lavia?' asked Gerat.

Lavia pursed her lips, staring for a while at her intertwined fingers before turning towards the Paramount Sister. 'I am doubtful of Qualle's validity, but wary of your doubt, Sister. I place little faith in the book – more in you. Do you have some plan in mind?'

Gerat sighed, wondering again if what she felt was nothing more than paranoia. 'I believe that these words should be transcribed and delivered to Kedryn,' she said at last. 'I believe they refer to his future and should be communicated to him.'

'That can be done easily enough,' said Lavia.

'I believe also that I should communicate them,' Gerat said.

Shocked silence greeted the announcement, broken by Porelle.

'You are the Paramount Sister of Estrevan. The Paramount Sister does not leave the city.'

'Besides,' Reena added, 'will Kedryn not come here? By custom the new king comes to seek the blessing of the Lady in the Lady's city. You may communicate your fears then.'

Gerat shook her head. 'I cannot explain it, but I feel that will be too late. Kedryn must know before he journeys here.'

'It is against all precedent,' said Jara in a disapproving tone. 'Against all custom.'

'And based on a feeling you cannot even explain,' said Porelle.

'Let one of us go,' suggested Lavia. 'I have visited Caitin Hold before – I could meet Kedryn there.'

'No.' A note of authority edged Gerat's voice. 'These are my doubts and may become clearer to me as time passes. If I am right and some threat stands betwixt Kedryn and Estrevan, mayhap I shall feel it clearer when I meet him. But whether I be right or wrong, I feel I must alert him as swiftly as I may. And the swiftest way is for me to go to him.'

'Your mind is made up,' Lavia said softly.

'It is,' Gerat nodded, realising quite suddenly that she had been working towards this decision for some time. 'I shall leave Estrevan in your hands and depart as soon I may.'

\*

Kedryn let slip a slow sigh and stretched back in his chair as another lengthy round of discussion ended, the westering sun bright on his face, dust motes floating with balletic grace in the beams that found their way through the tall windows of the council chamber. He studied them idly, thinking that it was far harder to see through his plan than he had anticipated. It had seemed so simple when first it came to him, and he had succeeded in persuading the others of its worth easily enough, but he had not foreseen the endless debating necessary to its precise formulation. That a council should be formed and assume the bulk of regal powers was agreed, but the membership of that first council had to be settled, and the extent of its powers, and the duties remaining to the king, and a myriad other intricate matters of protocol that left his head swirling and his mouth dry. Honest battle, he thought wryly, was less trying than this diplomatic game.

He reached for the decanter occupying a space amongst the litter of papers and filled a goblet with wine, grateful for the support of his parents in persuading a still somewhat reluctant Jarl that he should depart for Estrevan on the first full moon after his coronation, that thought reminding him that he must first suffer the interminable ceremonies that Arlynne and his mother planned to mark his enthronement. It seemed nothing was simple in Andurel, and that all must be accompanied by banquets and balls and receptions of one kind or another, each one requiring his attendance, and each attendance requiring some fresh outfit of the restricting formal regalia the two women had explained were *de rigueur* for such occasions. Even Wynett had joined them in this, and he had found no support from Bedyr, who was himself acquiring a wardrobe that would have elicited laughter in the halls of Caitin Hold.

His home seemed far away in that moment and he suffered a pang of homesickness that he stifled with a long draught of the chilled wine and the silent promise that the full moon should see him on the Idre, bound for Caitin Hold. He would sail up-river as far as Gennyf then strike overland to Caitin Hold, stay awhile there and then ride on to the Morfah Pass and Estrevan. After that, he knew, he must return to Andurel, but by then the council should have proven itself workable and he would be able to depart again, perhaps to visit Kesh, or even travel south into Ust-Galich.

The contemplation of such journeying cheered him and he realised it was less the absence from his homeland that he regretted than the notion of finding himself imprisoned in the White Palace. The sombre expression that had clouded his youthful features faded behind a smile and he glanced about the room. Bedyr and Jarl were locked in discussion of some formal point, whilst Arlynne was holding forth to Yrla on the choice of music she felt appropriate to the banquet that would follow the coronation; Tepshen Lahl and Brannoc were engaged in debate on the merits of eastern longsword and Keshi sabre, and Wynett had already excused herself, explaining that she wished to visit Ashrivelle. Sister Bethany was rising to leave, and Kedryn rose to meet her at the door, motioning for Tepshen and Brannoc, still following him like mismatched watchdogs, to remain behind.

'Sister,' he said quietly, 'there is something I would discuss with you.'

Bethany smiled, nodding, and was about to return to the table when Kedryn took her elbow, discreetly propelling her through the door as he murmured, 'In private.'

'Of course.' Bethany's keen eyes studied his face, alight with interest. 'I am at your command.'

Kedryn smiled his thanks and led her to a smaller room, where comfortable chairs were ranged before an empty hearth, a small table on which stood a bowl of sugared sweetmeats between them. He ushered the Sister to a chair and closed the door, his expression becoming serious again as he took a place facing her. Bethany waited expectantly, sunlight glinting on her silvered hair.

Kedryn said, 'I would ask you about possession,' the statement bringing a frown to the Sister's angular features.

'Possession?' she queried.

'Aye,' he nodded, marshalling half-formed thoughts. 'The Messenger possessed Sister Thera, did he not? I saw her become him when I confronted Hattim Sethiyan.'

Bethany ducked her head in agreement. 'The Usurper had me under guard when you entered Andurel,' she reminded, 'but that is what I have heard. Eye-witnesses told me of the transformation.'

'So what happened to Thera?' Kedryn asked.

Bethany shrugged helplessly. 'I cannot say for sure. I believe that the Messenger must have entered Andurel by dint of some gramarye and taken possession of poor Thera by the same thaumaturgical means, but what was, or is, her ultimate fate I cannot say.'

'When I went into the netherworld with Wynett,' Kedryn said slowly, 'I met the shade of the warrior who took my sight. It seemed he was condemned to wander in that limbo. At least until he gave me back my vision, for then I saw him whole again and he . . . disappeared. If Thera was tainted by the Messenger's evil, might she, too, be condemned to that?'

'Mayhap,' Bethany allowed, 'or perhaps her faith in the Lady translated her elsewhere. I cannot believe she succumbed willingly to Ashar's minion. I must admit that I have troubled myself less with thoughts of the afterlife than with the betterment of what we have now, but the teachings of the Lady tell us that those who believe – and seek to practice her work – shall enjoy serenity in whatever follows this mortal span.'

'And Darr,' Kedryn asked thoughtfully, 'did you not attend him at his death?'

'After,' Bethany said, frowning her incomprehension. 'I was summoned to the palace after his death. Why?'

Kedryn gestured placatingly and asked, 'Was he killed by natural causes? Or by Hattim? Or the Messenger?'

'It seemed by natural cause,' Bethany murmured, 'but I thought I detected the taint of fell sorcery before Hattim had me removed. And then poor Darr's body was burned as is the custom here, so I could not ascertain the cause.'

'Were you to decide it,' Kedryn asked, 'which would you say?'

'You ask me to choose between the bursting of his heart, some poison, or magic?' Bethany pursed her lips, staring at Kedryn's solemn face. 'And I cannot tell you for sure, but I would opt for magic.'

'Another victim of the Messenger.' Kedryn's voice was soft, but edged with anger. 'How many others, I wonder? And are they condemned to the same limbo as held Borsus?'

'That is not a thing I can answer,' Bethany told him, her eyes widening as she began to perceive the drift of his interrogation. 'You may well find Estrevan better suited than I to resolve such matters.'

Kedryn nodded without speaking and the Sister added, 'Should Estrevan furnish you with answers, what can you do?'

'I went into the netherworld once before,' he said, very quietly.

'No!' Bethany leant forwards, her voice urgent as the hand that gripped Kedryn's wrist. 'You must not! Chosen One you may be, but you are still mortal. You would chance too much.'

'The talisman protected me then – why not again?' Kedryn fingered the blue jewel that hung about his neck.

'Then it was necessary that you regained your sight,' Bethany retorted, her voice harshened by anxiety. 'Alaria's Text spoke of that descent, and without your sight you could not have defeated the Messenger or Hattim. Do not seek to meddle now, Kedryn! The dead are dead, and if they inhabit that limbo you visited, it is through the agency of a power greater than we may understand.'

'Darr was Wynett's father,' he responded, 'and though she does not speak of it, I know she mourns his passing.'

'As she would mourn yours, should you essay so foolhardy a venture,' Bethany said fiercely. 'And remember that she went with you then, wearing her half of the talisman, your defenses strengthened by that joining. Would you take her to that place again? Better, I think, to place your trust in the Lady and leave her to succour the dead.'

'I would not ask Wynett to repeat that journey, yet I am reluctant to ignore such a plight.' Kedryn smiled thinly, recalling that dismal place.

'You have other duties now,' Bethany reminded him. 'You are to be crowned king, and even with this council of yours you will still be needed here. Would you ignore your responsibilities to the living?'

'No.' Kedryn shook his head. 'I would not. But I would still know Darr's fate.'

'Then ask Estrevan,' urged Bethany. 'Gerat is Paramount Sister there and she is versed in such matters. There are scholars there who will advise you better than I am able – listen to them!'

'I had not intended to attempt such a venture without the guidance of the Sisterhood,' Kedryn murmured reassuringly. 'But I would set Wynett's mind at rest.'

'Wynett is mayhap better able to understand – to accept – fate than you,' suggested the silver-haired woman. 'Do not take too much upon yourself.'

'No,' he assured her, 'I shall not. In any event, it was the shamans of the Drott who gave me entry before and mayhap they would not agree again.'

'Whether they would or not,' said Bethany, 'I should counsel against it. That limbo is Ashar's kingdom, and not a place for living flesh.'

'No, it is not.' Memory sent a shudder through Kedryn's body.

'Then you will not act without the blessing of Estrevan?' asked the Sister.

'My word on it,' Kedryn told her, smiling now, 'and in return yours that you will not mention this conversation to Wynett, or any others here – they are already stirred enough by my notions.'

'None here shall know of it from me,' Bethany promised.

'Thank you.' Kedryn rose to his feet. 'And now I had best find Wynett.'

Bethany nodded and followed him to the door. There he left her, going in search of his bride, and she, mightily troubled, returned to the College, where she penned a report of the conversation and her fear that he might risk so foolhardy a venture. She had not, she told herself as she sealed the wax with the emblem of the Sisterhood, promised not to reveal his thoughts to Estrevan, only to those present in Andurel. She summoned a mehdri, entrusting the rider with the missive, instructing him that he was to deliver it into the hand of Gerat herself and no other, and watched the man depart, hurrying towards the docks. Gerat would dissuade Kedryn: Gerat was too sensible to bless such a wild adventure.

\*

Tarn Lemal had no great love of night-sailing, but his task was urgent and he anticipated a bounty if he dispensed it with alacrity, so he shouted for the *Vendrelle's* single squaresheet to stay up as the sun went down and overrode the objections of his crew. That was not too difficult as only three men rode the pitching boards with Tarn, and they were his brothers and so would divide the bounty equally with the captain. They grumbled a little, but Tarn's assurance of reward quelled that and they settled to their task without further argument.

It was a fine night, the first quarter of the moon that would see Kedryn Caitin crowned king riding graceful as a sabre's curve in a sky filled with stars. Rafts of underlit cloud were drifting in from the east, but the wind that propelled the barque hung steady behind them, billowing the pale green sail to send the *Vendrelle* swift and smooth over the silver-traced surface of the Idre, her crimson-painted prow cutting a vee-shaped swathe that hung milky foam on the ripples of her passage. Tarn lounged on the sternboards, the tiller in the crook of his arm, his eyes studying the dark water ahead. Nathan was crouched in the lookout position at the bow, his own eyes fixed warily on the river, ready to shout warning of flotsam or reefs, and Harl and Dervin were settling to sleep on the canvas-wrapped cargo that filled the scuppers.

That was an added benefit. A hold filled with early fruit from Ust-Galich would fetch a fine price in Bayard, and the message Tarn carried for Xendral, the Keshi *landril*, should earn the bounty he had promised himself and his brothers. The Lady alone knew how many boats, how many mehdri, were bringing word to the nobles of the Three Kingdoms of the impending coronation, or how grateful Xendral might be to receive his summons so swiftly. Tarn had already received payment from the White Palace for carrying the document that now sat snug between his shirt and leathern jerkin, but there was never harm in hoping for more and so he had kept the *Vendrelle* moving through three nights now, docking only briefly to sample the thick, sweet beer the Keshis brewed and snatch a hurried meal when his brothers became overly insistent. Otherwise they had sailed relentlessly northwards, holding to midstream, where the wind blew stronger and there were fewer vessels to impede their passage.

Aye, Tarn thought, we should reach Bayard by late morning. The fruit can be off-loaded and I can leave Nathan to negotiate the sale for he's skilful enough to command the best price, while I take this message to Xendral. He patted his chest, hearing the stiff parchment rustle comfortingly, the sound equating in his mind with the clatter of coins falling into his palm.

It augured well for rivermen such as the Lemal brothers that the reign of this new king should commence with so profitable a journey, not only in terms of the pecuniary rewards, but also in

67

the honour to be won from carrying his summons. Tarn smiled at the thought, seeing himself as a royal messenger, even though his employment had come not from Kedryn Caitin himself, but a palace orderly who had appeared with a bag well-stuffed with coin and in urgent need of honest boatmen willing to supplement the ranks of the mehdri, who were overstretched by the sheer numbers of notables deemed worthy of invitation. The Lady knew it could do no harm to gather the gentry of the Kingdoms to Andurel, for the past months had left the land confused and the folk would be reassured to have word of their new king from the lips of other than passing traders. The war with the barbarians had been bad enough, but to find that followed by alarming rumours of King Darr's death and the assumption of Hattim Sethiyan, aided, it was said, by Ashar's foul magicks, produced a state of near-panic in the far-flung reaches of the Kingdoms. No doubt Xendral would set his people's minds at rest before travelling south, and doubtless return with further comfort for them after Kedryn had assumed the High Throne.

Tarn nodded complacently, thinking that with the Chosen One in the White Palace the Three Kingdoms must surely enjoy a time of peace and prosperity that would benefit all.

Then his peace of mind was disrupted by a shout from Nathan and he rose to his feet, gripping the tiller in both his powerful hands as his eyes strained to follow his brothers' pointing finger.

'Ware flotsam!' Nathan bellowed, the shout waking Harl and Dervin. 'Hard aport!'

Tarn put the tiller over and the *Vendrelle* swung leftwards, Harl and Dervin cursing as the motion rolled them from the stacked cargo into the scuppers.

'Blood of the Lady!' Tarn heard his brother shout from the prow, then echoed the oath as he saw the object Nathan had spotted. He was not sure what it was – could not be for it seemed to have no distinct shape – seeing only the vast bulk of green tinged blue black that humped from the water on his right. A floating hulk? A turtled vessel? He was not certain. No eyots were charted on this part of the river, yet the *Vendrelle* might have beached on that indistinct mass. Or grounded and sunk had he not acted so promptly! Anger stoked his tongue as he shouted at Nathan.

'Do you sleep up there, brother? How could you miss that?'

'It was not there!' Nathan's answer was tinged with disbelief and more than a little fear. 'I swear it on the Lady – it was not there!'

Tarn snorted, turning about as the *Vendrelle* passed the thing to study it. It was, without doubt, curious, for it seemed not to reflect the stars or the moon that lit the night sky well enough, and he knew Nathan to be the keenest-eyed of them all. He opened his mouth to say, 'It must have been,' but the words became a gargle of incredulity as he saw the shape slide beneath the water, leaving behind a swirling pool of light-speckled disturbance.

'What goes?' Harl demanded surlily. 'Do you deny us sleep?'

'Starboard and astern!' Tarn bellowed. 'Mark the river! What do you see?'

Harl scampered over the cargo to peer downriver, shaking his head. Dervin, who had landed in the scuppers beneath his brother, struggled upright cursing with all the fluency of a born riverman. Harl called, 'I see nothing.'

Tarn screamed, 'Dervin! Beware!'

Dervin looked to the stern, the rank terror that he saw etched on Tarn's features communicating so that his mouth gaped open and he turned slowly about to follow the direction of his brother's bulging eyes, his own growing to great owlish circles as he found himself staring into a vast, fang-edged maw about which writhed greasy tendrils seemingly equipped with a life of their own. His jaw dropped and he staggered back, stark fear slowing his movements as he raised ineffectual hands against a creature of nightmarish delineament.

Tarn reacted faster: he hauled the tiller over, sending the barque hard to starboard, trusting in his brothers' riverblood to lay hands to lines and hold their position as the *Vendrelle* leant perilously over, knowing only that he must bring his craft away from that awful leviathan.

The barque was a dancer, built for speed, and she responded eagerly, surging away from the creature as if her insensate boards knew the peril that threatened. But the monster was faster still and Tarn saw a massive, wedge-shaped head thrust forwards on serpentine neck to snatch Dervin from his place. For an instant he saw one huge, red-orbed eye, but then he could see nothing save the kicking legs of his brother as the jaws closed and cut off Dervin's scream.

Blood spurted in thick gushes from between the oily-looking lips, visible only in the moonlight and the fluorescence of the river, for the skin of the thing seemed to absorb light, only the glowing eyes and the jagged ivory fangs clearly discernible. Tarn heard a ghastly crunching sound, and Dervin's legs disappeared into the maw.

'Lady preserve us!' he heard Nathan yell and screamed back, 'Set the foresail!' hoping they might outrun whatever demon the Idre had conjured up to assail them.

He crouched by the tiller, unaware of the liquid that fear sent spilling into his breeks as he mouthed a prayer that the Lady grant them the speed to outpace the creature, instinct governing his actions as he put his helm over in a desperate attempt to reach the too-distant shore. At the prow, Nathan hauled the sheets that brought the triangular foresail to position and forced his trembling fingers to lash them fast. Then he snatched a knife from his belt and flailed the blade wildly at the head swooping towards him. The whetted edge hacked against a tendril as effectively as if he sought to carve granite, and the writhing, vermicular thing fastened about his arm, others securing his legs so that he found himself lifted from the deck of the barque and swung aloft, for all the world like some tidbit the monster dangled above its hideous mouth. Tarn screamed imprecations as he saw that the behemoth paced his craft as easily as a Keshi charger might pace a plough horse, then closed his eyes, unwilling to witness his brother's descent into that gaping pit of teeth.

Unlike Dervin, Nathan did not scream as the leviathan released its tentacular grip and dropped him between its rows of serrated fangs. Harl, however, did, and flung himself into the Idre, striking for the far shore with a strength born of pure terror. He was gone before Tarn opened his eyes, unaware that he was now alone.

He swam furiously, easing his pace only when straining lungs warned his near-mad mind that he would weaken too rapidly should he continue at such speed, and that the fury of his actions might attract the beast. He turned onto his back, frog-kicking in the direction of Kesh with his gaze fixed on the two shapes outlined against the river. One was clear enough, the pale green sails near-luminous in the starry night; the other was a blur, a hulking darkness that seemed formless, immaterial, save that he had witnessed its very material solidity. He saw it swallow Dervin and arch its undulating neck, the wedge of the head driving hard into the water, seeming to drag the great, indistinct bulk of the body behind it. For an instant he thought that it was gone, Tarn and the *Vendrelle* safe, and he opened his mouth to shout, to call his brother back to pick him up. Then his mouth snapped shut, cutting off the cry, for blackness loomed from the river ahead of the barque, an enormous, impossible blackness that climbed up and up until it hid the stars like some vast storm cloud.

It came down directly onto the *Vendrelle*, snapping both masts as if they were no more than sticks of kindling, splintering the sturdy planks, sending Tarn screaming into the air as the vessel broke in two. For long, fear-filled moments, Harl watched the behemoth flail amongst the wreckage, hearing the sound of its teeth on oak boards, the mighty splashing of its flukes, the whiplash crack of a tail that rose and fell in sparkling sprays, then he turned on his face again and began to swim with a strength he had not known he possessed, intent only on putting as much distance between himself and the leviathan as possible.

While his brother swam, Tarn Lemal found himself tossed helplessly in the midst of the creature's destructive fury. The sundering of his barque had thrown him high in the air, still clutching the tiller, which the sheer force of that awful descent had torn loose from its mountings, and he clung to the painted wood as he saw the *Vendrelle* reduced to splintered, fang-marked chunks of random timber. He did not attempt to swim clear, for he knew that he could not escape that ghastly thing, and hoped that it would vent its rage on his vessel, forgetting his presence.

It did not. Instead, it smashed the barque with dreadful deliberation and then sunk its bulk beneath the tossing water leaving only the triangular head above the surface, rubescent eyes swinging back and forth as the tendrils surrounding its maw twitched and wavered like the heads of serpents aroused by some unexpected sound. Tarn found himself staring into its eyes, seeing the water around him pinked by its gaze, as if the blood of his brothers coloured the river. He said, 'Oh, Lady, spare me,' as the head came down, the jaws stretching wide, and then he felt only the mercifully brief agony of the teeth that drove like swordblades into his soft flesh so that he was dead before the Idre could fill his lungs as the leviathan carried him under.

Harl saw none of this, for he was swimming for the eastern bank, his mind no longer coherent, focused on the single purpose: to reach land and never set foot on boat again.

It was long past dawn before he came to the Keshi shore, and the herdsmen who found him were not at first certain whether he was a man or some river fish, for what they saw on the sandy beach was a thing that kicked and stroked, dragging itself over the land. And when they came closer and sought to lift him to his feet he screamed aloud and began to writhe like a worm, seeking to burrow into the sand. Finally they decided to strike him into unconsciousness, for that appeared the only way they might hold him still long enough to get him on a horse and bring him to their camp, and when he awoke they had to bind him and force food and drink between his shuddering lips, which they did before lashing him afresh across a gelding's back and bringing him to Bayard, where there were Sisters who might know how to cure his madness.

The Sisters nursed Harl Lemal back to health, but they could not ascertain what had happened on the river that night for he would not – or could not – speak of it, and when he was strong enough he quit Bayard and made his way on foot deep into Kesh, where he found whatever employment he could, which was mostly of the lowest sort as he would not allow water near him and his smell offended folk.

# Chapter Four

'WHEN I am king I shall set a precedent of informality,' Kedryn vowed, the statement prompting a look of alarm from the four tailors and several apprentices busy measuring him for yet another formal robe, this one a long, wide-shouldered affair that was, as best he remembered, to be worn at the banquet honouring Gerryl Hymet of Ust-Galich. He was not certain, knowing for sure only that Yrla had warned him to hold himself ready for the fitting, overriding his objections with a maternal authority that took little account of his newly-elevated status.

'It does not please you, Prince Kedryn?'

Alarm rang in the chief tailor's voice and Kedryn sought to assuage it with a smile, fingering the heavy green silk as he shook his head and said, 'It is a most excellent garment, my friend, and the problem lies with me, not in your work. I am more accustomed to plain Tamurin wear.'

Consoled, the tailor smiled thinly, adjusting a pin in the white border. 'Doubtless plain wear is suitable enough in the north, Prince, but for the king . . .'

He allowed the sentence to tail away, considering his point made. Brannoc grinned over his head and said, 'It is a most impressive robe, Kedryn. You look decidedly regal,' his tone elaborately sincere.

Kedryn answered with a rueful grin that brought a deep chuckle from the halfbreed, who had cheerfully availed himself of the tailors to produce a selection of dandified garments that contrasted vividly with his customary garb of mottled leathers. Today he wore a shirt of black linen edged with pale blue beneath a tunic of apple green silk, belted tight so that the waist flared above close-fitting breeks of white seamed with green to match the jerkin, the same colour decorating the tops of his black boots.

'Had I your taste for the exotic,' Kedryn replied sarcastically, 'mayhap I should feel easier about all this.'

He emphasised the statement with a shrug that rustled the robe and brought a disapproving tutting from the tailor.

Unabashed, Brannoc turned to Tepshen Lahl to ask, 'Does he not look magnificent? Or would, did he not affect so surly an expression.'

Tepshen, dressed in a loose-fitting robe of yellow slit at the sides to free his ever-present blade, studied Kedryn with a calmly critical eye and nodded. 'He looks a king.'

'Is kingship measured by the cloth?' the young man demanded, raising his arms on a murmured instruction to allow the tailor to adjust the hang of the robe.

'By some,' Tepshen informed him. 'And it does no harm to look the part for those who cannot see beyond the cloth.'

'It is said that clothes make the man,' the chief tailor murmured sagely, echoed by Brannoc's gleeful, 'Exactly!'

Realising he would find no support from his friends Kedryn fell into silence, suffering the tailor to finish his work without further disturbance.

'It will be ready in two days, Prince Kedryn,' the man said, easing the garment from Kedryn's broad shoulders and handing it reverentially to an underling. 'Now, for the banquet in honour of Lord Jarl and his retinue I have prepared this.'

Kedryn groaned as yet another outfit appeared. 'Must I . . .' he began, interrupted by Tepshen.

'You must. Your mother gave us clear instructions.'

'We are to see that you complete your wardrobe,' Brannoc added, casually swinging his feet onto the low table before his chair. 'We are to remain with you, here in this room, until all is settled.'

Kedryn glanced at Tepshen, who nodded solemn agreement and poured himself a cup of wine.

'In honour of Kesh,' the tailor intoned, 'I have sought to emulate the style of the horse lords. If you will, Prince?'

He held up a long robe of black silk, trimmed with silver, the tripartite crown of Andurel gleaming on the left breast, the clenched fist of Tamur on the right, both sewn in gold against a crimson background ringed with a silver band that matched the edgings of the garment. Kedryn sighed and allowed it to be eased over his shoulders.

'I think,' the tailor said, more to himself than to his living dummy, 'a belt of silver links. Breeks and shirt of black will produce a most dramatic effect.'

'And match his scowl,' Brannoc chortled.

'I shall be wreathed in smiles,' retorted Kedryn. 'On that I have already received my mother's instruction.'

'Please,' asked the tailor, pushing Kedryn straight so that he might measure the hem.

'How many more?' the king-to-be asked helplessly.

'One, Prince.' The tailor spoke around a mouthful of pins. 'Your coronation robe.'

Kedryn grunted, thinking that if he remained silent and still this ordeal would be over the sooner. He held himself rigid as the tailor fussed about the black robe, pinning here, marking with chalk there, until he was satisfied and eased the thing off. 'Now,' he announced proudly, 'my masterpiece.'

He clapped his hands and two apprentices brought forward a surcoat of silk so white it shone in the morning light, like snow under a new-risen sun. Gold gleamed along the edges and where the crown of Andurel stood upon the chest and back. The tailor clapped again and a shirt of gold linen appeared, and breeks of white silk, finally boots of purest doe hide, white as the breeks, but trimmed with more gold. Kedryn stripped dutifully and drew the shirt over his head, the snug trousers over his legs. The tailor knelt to fit the boots, then rose and like a man performing some religious ceremony, adjusted the surcoat. It hung loose and the tailor placed a golden belt about Kedryn's waist, a sheath of white satin embroidered with gold thread latched on the left side.

'I believe it is customary for Tamurin to wear the dirk,' he murmured regretfully, 'though the hang would be the better without. There is no chance you might forgo the knife?'

'No,' Kedryn said firmly.

'Try it,' Brannoc grinned, swinging from his lounging position to scoop up Kedryn's dirk and toss it to the young man. The tailor winced as the long, straight-bladed knife whirled through the air, his relief clearly visible as Kedryn caught it and slid the razor-edged weapon into the ornate scabbard.

'Umm.' He studied the hang of his creation, then glanced at Tepshen. 'I think ... perhaps a slash here, in the style of your friend.' He touched Kedryn's hip, indicating where he would place a cut to allow free access to the dirk. 'This is absolutely necessary?'

'Absolutely,' said Kedryn solemnly.

75

'Very well.' The tailor made a note and walked slowly around Kedryn, smoothing the surcoat. 'I suppose it will lend a certain . . . contrast.'

'You will not wear your sword?' Brannoc asked innocently.

The tailor gasped, his face crumpling until Kedryn shook his head and replied with an equal solemnity, 'I think not on this occasion.'

The tailor sighed noisy relief. 'Then save for these few small adjustments I am done, Prince. I shall return in two days with the finished garments.'

'Thank you.' Kedryn let him ease off the surcoat and stripped out of the remaining articles. 'You have done well.'

'I have done my best,' the tailor nodded, folding the coronation robes with infinite care. 'I believe you will cut a fine figure.'

Kedryn was too busy climbing into his more familiar outfit of less splendid breeks and tunic to reply and the tailor took this as dismissal, exiting with a bow, his underlings scurrying about him, laden with their wares.

'The sooner all this is done,' Kedryn remarked as he laced his boots, 'the better. These formal robes sit heavy.'

'But your majesty looked splendid,' smiled Brannoc, simpering.

'His majesty contemplates suggesting to his council that the Warden of the Forests be despatched to take inventory of the woodland tribes,' Kedryn grunted. 'A headcount of the children born since Niloc Yarrum fell, perhaps. Followed by a count of livestock. Pigs and goats in particular.'

Brannoc aped alarm, spreading his arms wide as he exaggerated a sweeping bow. 'If your humble servant has offended, majesty, I crave your regal forgiveness.'

'I may change my mind,' Kedryn grinned.

'It will not be long,' said Tepshen. 'The moon draws close to full, and the city fills already with incomers.'

'Do I not know it?' Kedryn went to the table, helping himself to wine. 'How many feasts have I attended already?'

'It is as well to gain their support,' the kyo remarked.

Kedryn nodded. 'I know, old friend, but the eating!' He rubbed his flat stomach.

'A few more days,' Brannoc grinned, 'and you will be crowned. Then you shall see your council formed and soon we'll be Estrevan bound.'

'We?' Kedryn asked. 'Do you then intend to accompany me to the sacred city?'

Brannoc nodded. 'With your permission.'

'That you have, and gladly given,' Kedryn told him, 'but I had thought you would return to the Beltrevan.'

The former wolfshead shrugged. 'The forests will not go away, and I have never seen Estrevan.'

'And you, Tepshen?' Kedryn smiled at the pig-tailed easterner. 'Do you accompany us, or return to Tamur? Or remain here?'

Tepshen Lahl looked at the young man as though he had suggested something outlandish. 'I go with you,' he said flatly. 'I have discussed this with your father and we are agreed I remain at your side.'

'I could not ask for better companions,' Kedryn declared earnestly, 'and I thank you both.'

'There is no need for thanks,' said the kyo. 'It is our wish.'

'And,' Brannoc murmured, 'you have in the past brought a certain degree of excitement to our lives.'

'Hopefully that is ended,' Kedryn smiled. 'I trust my reign will be marked with peace.'

'It will certainly be marked with high fashion,' the halfbreed responded.

'Aye,' Kedryn chuckled, 'for a little while at least. But after Estrevan I have a notion to attempt one more . . .' he paused, his laughter dying as his features grew serious, '. . . one more quest.'

His two comrades watched him as he frowned, sensing a most uncharacteristic indecision. He toyed with his goblet, studying the play of light on the crystal facets, turning the cup between his hands.

Finally he said, 'I tell you this because you are true companions, but I ask your confidence, for I would have it go no farther lest it raise false hopes.'

'It will not,' Tepshen Lahl promised.

'No word,' Brannoc confirmed.

'The manner of Darr's dying troubles me,' Kedryn went on, his voice low, 'and that of Sister Thera. I have spoken with Bethany, but she cannot offer enlightenment and suggests I seek it of the Paramount sister, Gerat, in Estrevan.'

'I had thought you sought her blessing,' murmured Brannoc when Kedryn lapsed silent again. Tepshen Lahl said nothing.

'There is that; but more,' Kedryn nodded. 'It irks me that the father of Wynett might wander the netherworld as did the shade of Borsus. I would also ask of Gerat what may be done to remedy that.'

'Ashar does not willingly relinquish his playthings,' Brannoc said warily.

'Do you think to enter that place again?' Tepshen demanded, fixing Kedryn with his jet stare.

'Mayhap,' nodded the young man. 'If Gerat believes that by so doing I might bring Darr to the Lady.'

'You cannot know he is there,' Brannoc said.

'No,' agreed Kedryn. 'But if he is . . .'

'You would risk too much,' said Tepshen, unaware that he echoed Bethany's warning. 'When you made that journey before, Wynett was with you, uniting the two parts of the talisman. Would you risk both king and queen? Risk depriving the Kingdoms of their new-found monarchs?'

'Is this why you form the council?' asked Brannoc.

Kedryn shook his head, unconsciously touching the blue stone that hung about his neck. 'That notion came to me through the talisman. This came later, and though I have sought the guidance of the stone I have felt no further enlightenment. I have promised Bethany that I shall abide by Gerat's advice in this – but if she deems it propitious that I attempt such a venture I would ask you to stand beside Wynett as you have stood by me.'

'If such is your future quest,' Tepshen said firmly, 'then I shall take that road with you.'

'And I,' said Brannoc, though a trifle less readily, his right hand shaping the warding gesture of the tribes as he spoke.

'No.' Kedryn shook his head. 'I would not ask that of you. Nor am I certain one not wearing the talisman might survive. What I ask is that you ward my bride until such time as I return. Or not.

'Besides, if Gerat should say me nay, I shall not attempt it.'

'This is not a thing to attempt alone,' Tepshen declared. 'Nor to decide alone. Wynett should have a say.'

'No!' Kedryn spoke fiercely. 'Wynett hides it well, but I am sure her father's death troubles her – I would not raise false hopes. Nor fears that may prove groundless. I am bound by my promise to take Gerat's word on this, and until I have that there is no point to alarming Wynett. Therefore I ask that you say nothing to her – nor any other – of this.'

He studied their faces almost defiantly until they both nodded and gave their words afresh, then he smiled and said, 'It may come to nothing, but I would set my own mind at rest.'

'What brings you to this idea?' asked Tepshen. 'Your place is with the living, not roaming the halls of the dead.'

Kedryn shrugged, uncertain of the answer. Exactly when the notion had come to him he was not sure. It had not been there when first he spoke with Wynett of his desire to form the council, nor had she spoken much of her father or the manner of his dying. It seemed that she had steeled herself to acceptance of Darr's untimely end and did not allow herself to contemplate the possibility that the Messenger had condemned him to the netherworld. As with Bethany, her concerns were more for the living than the dead and the whirlwind rapidity of events since their triumph over Taws had swept her along just as they carried Kedryn. He had asked her what she would have him do in memory of Darr and her response had been to suggest no more than a simple service – which Bethany had already carried out – after which she had made no further mention of the dead king, her manner prompting Kedryn to avoid discussion of his demise.

Perhaps it had been Ashrivelle who put the idea in his mind, for her grief manifested itself in copious weeping and self-accusation, the younger sister declaring herself responsible, blaming herself for her potion-induced infatuation with Hattim Sethiyan. Both Wynett and Kedryn had sought to dissuade her from such inwardly directed reproaches, but Ashrivelle remained adamant, imposing upon herself a virtual banishment that kept her to her own quarters despite the blandishments of her sibling or Kedryn, or even Bethany, who – in the name of the Lady – had absolved her from guilt.

It was with the intention of expunging that notional culpability that Ashrivelle declared herself for Estrevan and a life of service to the Lady, and perhaps it had been her threnodies that awakened the idea in Kedryn. He was not sure, and could only shrug in answer to Tepshen's question.

'It may well come to nothing. Gerat may well give me the same advice, in which case debating it now is fruitless. Let us forget it until I have spoken with the Paramount Sister.'

He smiled afresh as he said it, setting down his goblet to glance around the chamber. 'And let us remove awhile from the palace – I begin to feel caged by these luxurious walls.'

Both the kyo and Brannoc were ready enough to accept the suggestion and Kedryn led the way from the room into the winding corridors.

'Where do we go?' asked Brannoc as he slung his swordbelt across his chest, the well-worn leather contrasting dully with the splendour of his new garments.

'The waterfront,' Kedryn declared impulsively. 'Let us find Galen Sadreth.'

They made for the palace stables, where Kedryn once again threw the Royal Guard into confusion by refusing an escort, overcoming the fastidious objections of the watch captain by pointing out that two swordsmen of Brannoc's and Tepshen's quality were surely bodyguard enough. Leaving the officer muttering behind them, they mounted and rode out through the palace gates.

The day was cooler than of late and Kedryn availed himself of a cloak that served both to fend off the wind blowing from the river and disguise him sufficiently that they succeeded in reaching the harbour area with a minimum of fuss. There he was able to move unnoticed, for the quarter was marked by a refreshing degree of informality, and busy besides. As Tepshen had remarked, folk were already arriving for the coronation and the docks were packed with boats disembarking Tamurin and Keshi from the farther reaches of the Three Kingdoms. The sky had become overcast, a threat of rain redolent in the moist air, mingling with the odours of fish and fruit and people that hung about the warehouses. Bustle was everywhere, stevedores manhandling cargo from the vessels bobbing on the swell as captains bellowed instructions and merchants screamed offers and counter-offers, the harbour officials adding their own cries to the cheerful tumult, and more than one man cursing the horsemen who pushed amongst the throng.

'By the Lady!' complained one red-faced exciseman. 'Do you know no better than to bring animals here? Are you too good to walk like the rest of us?'

Kedryn saw Tepshen Lahl about to respond and gestured the easterner to remain silent. 'Forgive us,' he smiled, 'we seek Galen Sadreth.'

The official craned his head back to peer up at the tall young man on the massive Keshi charger, the irritation writ fierce on his ruddy features dissolving as recognition dawned.

'You are ...' he stared doubtfully, confused by the absence of escort for one so exalted, '... are you not Prince Kedryn?'

Kedryn nodded, 'But I would not have it voiced abroad, my friend.'

'Sire, forgive me.' The exciseman ducked an obsequious head. 'I had not recognised you. Let me summon an escort to clear a way.'

'No!' Kedryn shook his head quickly. 'I travel incognito. Simply tell me where I may find Galen Sadreth and I shall no longer clutter your harbour.'

'I did not know,' spluttered the embarrassed official. 'I crave your pardon, Sire.'

Kedryn curbed his impatience at this reminder of Andurel's formality: in Tamur the directions would have been given without such rigmarole, and said, 'You have it. And my thanks if you can furnish directions.'

The official nodded vigorously and pointed across the seething dockside. 'You might try *The Grapes*, Prince. Or *The Lantern*. Otherwise you will find the *Vashti* anchored on the farther pier.'

'Thank you,' Kedryn responded, and urged the Keshi warhorse forwards before the man could reveal his identity with his bowing.

'Lady's blood! Get that clubfoot nag out of my way.'

Now Kedryn laughed aloud as a stevedore wide as he was tall and laden with a huge crate pushed past.

'Forgive me, I do not mean to block your path.'

'Then don't,' grunted the sturdy man, adding in a milder tone, 'You'd do better afoot, lad. And offend fewer folk.'

'Sound advice,' Kedryn agreed, and dismounted, leading the horse towards the tavern the exciseman had indicated.

The place had a small courtyard where they were able to leave the animals happily investigating the vines that gave it its name as they went inside, the interior only slightly less crowded than the harbour. The ceiling was low and beamed with smoke-stained oak, a pall of bluish vapour hanging in the body-heated air. The floor, what little of it was visible, was planked and strewn with straw, the walls stone, their whitewash covered with graffiti of remarkable imagination. A massive hearth occupied most of the far wall, the remains of a roast pig impaled on a spit above a bed of cold charcoal. A second wall was fronted by a long counter of stained wood on which stood numerous barrels and sundry mugs, glasses and cups, and the others were hidden behind trestle tables occupied by rivermen and stevedores. Rough tables filled the space between, and a troubadour was attempting vainly to make his *balur* heard above the racket.

Kedryn paused at the entrance, aware of Brannoc slipping his sabre to his side and Tepshen hiking a thumb with seeming casualness over the scabbard of his longsword. He studied the room, feeling, for all its claustrophobic press, more at ease than in the spacious halls of the White Palace, more at home in this noisy, inelegant gathering where men jostled him with cheerful unconcern and the tavern wenches eyed him speculatively.

Close to the hearth he espied a familiar figure, a bald head glistening above gigantic shoulders, hands like hamhocks clutching what appeared to be one whole leg of the spit-roasted pig, a flagon that would undoubtedly contain *evshan* beside an elbow sleeved in garish green. Flanked by Tepshen and Brannoc he forced a way through the throng to confront Galen Sadreth.

The master of the *Vashti* looked up as the three men halted before his table and wiped a hand across his greasy mouth, beaming hugely.

'Well met, Galen,' Kedryn said, adding before the river captain could speak, 'I come incognito.'

'My friends, sit down.' Galen's voice was a stentorian rumble that turned heads on all sides, rising to a bellow as he added for benefit of the closest serving wench, 'Three mugs and a new jug, woman!'

His eyes twinkled beneath overhanging brows, like stars shining from the moon-round of his face. 'It seems you always come incognito, Kedryn. How fare you?'

'Well enough,' Kedryn smiled. 'Though wearied by the formalities of the palace.'

Galen nodded sagely, as if familiar with palace protocols. 'You discover that your new-won fortune brings its own restrictions? Little wonder – responsibility is a hard mistress.' He wiped a hand on a soiled napkin, glancing about to ensure none listened. 'And your bride? How is Wynett?'

'Well,' responded Kedryn. 'And you?'

Galen spread expansive arms, the gesture serving to clear space on either side and simultaneously expose the embroidered frontage of his viridescent tunic. 'I do well, my reputation enhanced by our acquaintance. I have already brought several guests to your,' he lowered his voice to a conspiratorial level, 'forthcoming event.'

'I am delighted to aid you,' grinned Kedryn, stretching long legs beneath the table. 'And I trust you will attend the . . . event.'

'I would not miss it,' said the riverman, looking up as a buxom woman appeared with a flagon and three mugs clutched to her ample bosom. 'My thanks, Bella.'

The woman smiled as he tossed coins on the table, dismissing Kedryn's offer to pay with a wave of one mighty hand and the whisper that few might claim to have bought the new king a mug of evshan. He filled the mugs and raised his in silent toast. Kedryn sipped cautiously, savouring the fiery liquor that was the chosen brew of the rivermen. Brannoc sighed and smacked his lips. 'A pleasant change from all that vintage wine.'

'If the gods drink, they drink evshan,' beamed Galen. 'Health to us all.'

'And prosperity,' added Brannoc.

'That, it would seem from those fine clothes, has come already,' Galen remarked, studying the halfbreed's outfit with some envy. 'Your tailor has improved since last we shared a cup.'

'There are certain advantages to living in the palace,' murmured Brannoc.

'And you wear them well,' chuckled the giant. 'And you, Tepshen? Does the palace suit you?'

Tepshen had seated himself across the table from Kedryn, where he was able to study the room, and his dark eyes flickered sideways, a brief, thin smile curving his lips.

'My place is at Kedryn's side. That suits me well enough.'

Galen clapped a hand to the kyo's shoulder, rocking the easterner forwards. 'Ever loyal, eh? You are fortunate to have such friends, Kedryn.'

'Aye,' the young man nodded, 'I am.'

'So what,' Galen enquired, 'brings you incognito to the harbour?'

'A desire to be myself,' Kedryn shrugged. 'To be free again for a little while.'

'And a great boredom with tailors,' Brannoc chuckled. 'He takes to the fitting of his ceremonial robes like an unbroken stallion to its first taste of the saddle.'

Galen nodded. 'There is much to be said for the life of the common man. But rumour has it our new king already lays plans to free himself. I have heard talk of a council.'

An enquiring eyebrow cocked in Kedryn's direction and he grinned, asking, 'How do you know that?'

'Secrets are hard to keep in a city packed as close as Andurel,' said the captain blandly.

'And how are they received?' Kedryn took another mouthful of evshan.

'Well,' said Galen. 'Folk say that our new king must be a man willing to listen to his people – not that they had complaint of Darr! But they feel the notion of a council affords the common man a greater say in his own destiny.'

Kedryn nodded, smiling, for this was the reaction he had hoped for. 'I intend to announce it after I am crowned,' he said. 'Initially my father and Jarl will preside, but in time I hope to see representatives elected from amongst the folk of the Kingdoms.'

'Bedyr and Jarl?' Galen's bushy brows rose. 'You make it sound as though you will take no part.'

'I go to Estrevan,' Kedryn explained. 'To seek the blessing of the Sisterhood, and deliver Ashrivelle to the sacred city.'

'Poor Ashrivelle,' Galen murmured. 'There are those who name her traitor.'

'Calumny!' snapped Kedryn, his voice fierce. 'What Ashrivelle did was done under the influence of a love potion. She was not responsible for either Hattim's treachery or Darr's death.'

Galen's head ducked in agreement. 'I do not name myself amongst those who say it,' he remarked mildly. 'Merely that it is said.'

'Best not in my hearing,' grunted Kedryn. 'And when you hear such imputations I should mark it a favour were you to correct them.'

'Consider it done,' beamed the riverman. 'But this journey to Estrevan? Might my services be required? The *Vashti* is ever at your beck.'

'I know that, and you have my gratitude for all you have done,' Kedryn replied, 'but this will not be a warrior's mission; rather a royal progress. Wynett accompanies me, and Ashrivelle, and these stalwarts.'

He gestured towards Tepshen and Brannoc, adding apologetically, 'The *Vashti* is built for speed more than comfort, and I suspect the ladies would prefer a cabin.'

'No matter.' Galen dismissed the apology with a smile and a wave of one huge hand. 'There'll be work enough for all honest rivermen when your guests depart. And a larger vessel will afford you room for a guard.'

'A guard?' Kedryn heard something in the captain's voice that chilled his smile a little. 'Why should I need a guard? I had thought to sail as far as Gennyf and travel overland from there, and in Tamur there will be warriors enough to provide escort.'

Galen's broad shoulders lifted in a shrug that threatened to burst the seams of his gaudy tunic. 'Likely you'll not, but . . .'

'But?' Tepshen Lahl's voice cut sword-sharp into the pause, his dark eyes fixing on the riverman's face.

'There is talk,' Galen continued, his moon-face growing serious under the easterner's scrutiny. 'Likely no more than river gossip, and so far unproven, but still . . .'

He paused again, topping his mug, glancing at each man in turn before returning his gaze to Kedryn's face.

'I have heard of craft disappearing with all their crew. No explanation is offered – and these things are prone to exaggeration – but I have heard it said that boats have been found in splinters; destroyed as though struck by a thunderbolt, and their crews gone the Lady alone knows where.'

'Pirates?' asked Brannoc, his swarthy features alert with interest.

'I think not.' Galen shook his head. 'Pirates are not wont to wreck what they have taken, and from what I have heard – which is, I must admit, vague – no cargoes have been offered for sale.'

'How many?' Kedryn asked.

Again the riverman shook his massive head. 'I do not know. I simply repeat what I have heard of waterfront gossip. There is only one such of which I have personal knowledge.' He swallowed evshan and licked his lips. 'I have recently brought a Keshi landril by name of Xendral south from Bayard. That holding stands a little downriver from Gennyf, on the eastern bank, and the landril anticipated a summons to Andurel. I know it for a fact that Tarn Lemal and his brothers sailed under palace commission, and with a cargo of Galichian fruit, for Bayard. But they did not arrive there and the Keshi booked passage with me. The *Vendrelle* has not been seen farther north than Larn – some four day's sail from Bayard – and though I have enquired of fellow captains, none has word nor sight of the *Vendrelle* or the Lemal brothers.'

'Mayhap they grounded,' Kedryn suggested. 'Or sold their cargo elsewhere.'

'Not Tarn,' said Galen. 'He'd know his best profit was to be made the farther north he travelled, and he carried the summons for Xendral, besides. He's a greedy man, but he'd not renege on that undertaking.'

'Might he have encountered some problem?' Kedryn wondered. 'Something that caused him to put ashore so that you passed him on the river?'

'Were that the case,' Galen answered, 'he'd have put in on the Keshi side, and I brought the *Vashti* in close enough to spot any beached craft. There was no sign.'

'A storm?' queried Brannoc.

'There have been no storms,' said the riverman. 'The spring floods are ended and the Idre runs smooth as a compliant woman. Besides, it would take a most powerful storm to sink the *Vendrelle*, and Tarn was an experienced captain – he'd not be caught out by bad weather.'

'Mayhap he sought the western bank,' said Kedryn.

'No.' Galen was positive, emphasising the negative with a further shaking of his head. 'Bayard bound, Tarn would sail closer to Kesh than Tamur. Had he put in for any reason it would be on the Keshi side.'

'I still say it could be pirates,' Brannoc mused.

'You do not know the Idre,' retorted Galen, a trifle sharply, as if he considered the comment critical of his undoubted expertise. 'Were pirates abroad we captains should have word of it; and they'd need dispose of that fruity cargo swiftly – or lose their profit.'

'Mayhap they wanted the boat,' argued Brannoc, refusing to be deterred.

'Too easily recognised,' said the riverman, 'and too hard to hide. No, my wolfshead friend, you must not confuse river craft with horses or trade goods sold beyond the Lozins. What few pirates do dare sail our Idre are minor cut-throats – they might sally forth in dories to ransack a likely vessel, but they'd not take the *Vendrelle*. And of the Lemals' boat there is no sign at all.'

Brannoc grinned easily, bowing his head in acknowledgment of Galen's superior familiarity with the ways of the river. Tepshen demanded, 'What interpretation do you make?'

Galen shrugged again. 'I have no idea. I know only that the *Vendrelle* is gone.'

'And others,' Kedryn murmured.

'Aye. So it would seem from the waterfront gossip. A fishing craft here, a ferry boat there, and no one to say how.'

He drained his mug and tilted the flagon again, emptying it and shouting for more.

'We sail with an escort,' said Tepshen firmly.

'Very well.' Kedryn saw no reason to argue the point. 'Though I doubt any cut-throat would dare attack a royal vessel.'

'It may not be any human agency,' grunted Galen, this time allowing Kedryn to purchase the flagon.

'A monster?' asked the young man dubiously. 'Some mythic beast from the depths of the river?'

'The Idre runs deep,' responded Galen, his smile a trifle defensive. 'Who knows what she holds?'

'Water,' said Brannoc, 'but in the event of her revealing worse secrets I doubt we shall encounter anything that may not be slain by honest steel, or a squad of archers.'

'We shall take no chances,' declared Tepshen. 'The craft that carries us north will bear a full complement of soldiery.'

'As well to take such precautions,' nodded Galen.

'I am well guarded,' grinned Kedryn, refusing to let the riverman's ominous gossip dampen his spirits. 'And now let us talk of more cheerful matters.'

'Aye,' Galen agreed. 'Tell me, Brannoc, does this tailor of yours charge excessively?'

Kedryn chuckled as the halfbreed embarked on a discussion of cloth and cutting with the massive captain, interrupting to suggest that Galen present himself at the emporium in question to request an outfit suitable for an honoured guest and inform the tailor that the bill should be presented to the White Palace.

'And,' he added, eyeing the remains of the roast pork still set before the riverman, 'let us eat. The palace will not miss us for one meal.'

They dined on cold cuts and bread, cheese and fruit, washed down with pale beer and then bade farewell to Galen, retrieving their horses from the courtyard and leading them back through the busy harbour to the wider avenues beyond.

The overcast that hung above the city had solidified into dark rafts of threatening grey as they negotiated the streets, and heavy droplets of rain splattered on the cobbles, freshening the scents of the place. As they climbed the broad roadway leading to the palace gates the sky to the north grew black, the wind strengthening so that the Idre rippled and spat wavelets against the docks, the masts of the craft moored there bobbing and ducking, their pennants snapping in the growing bluster.

'A storm approaches,' Brannoc remarked, easing the hood of his cloak over his braided hair.

'Aye.' Kedryn shivered suddenly, feeling a strange chill. For no reason he could define he clutched the stone about his neck, but it remained cool and hard, as if no more than a jewel worn for ornament.

'The river is full of stories,' murmured Tepshen, noticing the gesture. 'And rivermen love nothing more than to embroider them.'

Kedryn grinned, letting go the talisman, feeling obscurely ashamed, as though Galen's yarns had sparked some indefinable apprehension too childish for a grown man to consider. No doubt the chill was nothing more than the effect of cooling air and the freshened breeze after so warm a commencement of spring. He turned his face to the sky, feeling the rain splash against his skin, and heeled the Keshi stallion to a canter, Tepshen and Brannoc following on either flank.

They cantered towards the White Palace, seeing the clouds above thicken as they approached, the rafts of grey massing to form pitchy thunderheads from which emanated an ominous rumbling, as if some great beast prowled above Andurel, hidden within the nubiferous mantle. The walls of the palace were darkened by the rack and before they reached the gates the rain had become downpour, drumming against their cloaks, splashing about the hooves, and transforming the gutters that sided the avenue into tumbling freshets. Guardsmen in armour silvered brighter by the rain presented halberds to their approach, saluting as they recognised Kedryn and his companions and drawing back beneath the shelter of the arches to allow the trio entry. They slowed as they crossed the wide yard fronting the palace and walked the horses down the covered way that opened on the stable court. Halting beneath the cloisters encircling the open area, they dismounted and gave the animals over to the waiting ostlers, shaking raindrops from their capes as they strode along the colonnaded way, the rain beating fiercely now against the tiled roof.

The rumbling became real thunder as they reached the doors granting ingress to the palace, and a lance of brilliance struck down against the damaged cupola of the throne room.

'It seems likely your coronation will break with precedence in more ways than one,' Brannoc remarked, glancing at the unfinished dome, 'those masons will not be done by the full moon.'

'Nor will there be a throne,' nodded Kedryn, remembering the melted slag to which his duel with Taws had reduced the seat. 'No matter – we shall make do.'

They pushed through the doors and halted to doff their cloaks, their boots leaving glistening prints on the ornate tiles that covered the entry hall. Servants appeared in courteous ambush to take the rain-wet mantles and both Tepshen Lahl and Brannoc paused to ascertain their blades were dry. Kedryn, who wore no sword, waited for them, looking to the high windows, slick now with the sky's outpouring, the light beyond dimmed by the storm so that torches were lit, burning in the golden sconces along the walls.

'Prince Kedryn.' A seneschal came forward, resplendent in the gold and silver robe of his office. 'The Lady Wynett requests that you attend her as soon you may. She is with the Princess Ashrivelle.'

'In the Princess's chambers?' Kedryn asked. 'Is aught amiss?'

In Tamur the servitor would have vouchsafed an opinion; in Andurel the man merely shaped a small gesture with his right hand and said, 'I do not know, Prince. I know only that the lady requests your presence.'

After the cheerful informality of the dockside tavern it was a sharp reminder to Kedryn that the White Palace was greatly different to Caitin Hold and he fought a flash of irritation at the man's bland manner.

'My thanks,' he said, knowing that it sounded somewhat curt, and not caring as he turned towards the stairway that spiralled upwards on the farther side of the hall.

Tepshen and Brannoc fell into step beside him and his good humour returned at their persistence. To the palace servants, he was sure, it must seem that two near-barbarians dogged his every move and it amused him to think of the dignified seneschals and formal major-domos worrying about the two sword-wielders ever in attendance on the king-to-be. Likely they would feel more comfortable with him out of the palace, when their lives might continue in more urbane fashion.

Nonetheless, there were some occasions on which he preferred to be alone, and he paused outside Ashrivelle's door to murmur, 'I do not believe danger threatens within, my friends.'

Tepshen nodded, murmuring his acceptance of the dismissal, but Kedryn noticed that he remained, Brannoc at his side, in the corridor long enough to see that it was Wynett who opened the door.

'Kedryn!' she smiled, turning up her face to brush her lips to his. 'I am glad you have come. Where were you?'

Kedryn set his hands on her shoulders, holding her at arm's length so that he might study her face. It was lovely as ever, but he detected worry in her clear blue eyes and said, 'On the waterfront with Galen Sadreth. What is amiss?'

'Ashrivelle.' Wynett shook her head in frustration, dislodging a strand of blonde hair that he reached to straighten. 'She claims

89

herself unfit to attend the coronation and vows she will remain here until we sail for Estrevan.'

Kedryn glanced about the room. It was an ante-chamber and there was no sign of Wynett's sister. In answer to his scrutiny Wynett said, 'She refuses to leave her bedchamber.'

'What would you have me do?'

Wynett took his hands, drawing him across the room towards the panelled door on the far side. 'I have spent the morning arguing with her. Yrla and Arlynne have both tried to dissuade her, but she remains adamant. I hope that you may change her mind.'

'I can try,' he allowed, not altogether enthusiastic.

Wynett smiled confidently and he basked in the radiance. 'Then do your best,' she murmured, tapping on the rosewood door, raising her voice to call, 'Ashrivelle? Kedryn is here.'

The answer sounded like, 'Go away,' to Kedryn, but Wynett said firmly, 'He wishes to speak with you.'

She opened the door and Kedryn followed her into the chamber. It was spacious, though darkened by the storm outside so that candles had been lit, shadowing the corners, and a fire burned in the stone hearth, lending a somewhat stifling heat to the atmosphere. Dense carpets covered the floor, patterned in designs of blue and grey like the surface of the Idre, their thick piles washing against the feet of a large bed overhung with a canopy of gauzy material, as if a great wave burst overhead. To one side stood a dressing table littered with the cosmetic paraphernalia of a fashionable woman. It occurred to Kedryn that Wynett gave no time to such niceties, nor needed to. He paused just inside the room, embarrassed to see that Ashrivelle lay on the bed clearly wearing no more than the dark green dressing robe she drew over her legs as he smiled at her.

'Ashrivelle,' he said pleasantly, 'may I enter?'

'You are the king,' came the answer, her voice low, as though she had been weeping, 'or soon will be – you may enter where you will.'

He crossed the room, glancing to the tall windows as thunder rumbled and more lightning stalked the sky. Chairs were placed close to the bed as if in vigil and he took one, Wynett seating herself beside him. Ashrivelle turned her face away and he saw that her hair was unkempt, the blonde tresses so much like Wynett's tangled and lank.

'I do not come as a king,' he said, 'rather as a friend.'

90

'Friend? How can you name me your friend?' Ashrivelle's voice was muffled by the silken pillow against which she pressed her face. 'You must surely hate me.'

'That is foolishness,' Wynett said firmly, 'and unworthy of you.'

'I *am* unworthy,' Ashrivelle retorted. 'And clearly foolish.'

'I do not hate you,' Kedryn said. 'Why should I?'

'I am tainted,' was the dramatic response.

'Tainted? How tainted?'

Kedryn looked to Wynett, who shrugged slightly, a frown tugging shallow lines between her finely arched brows.

'I gave myself to Hattim,' Ashrivelle moaned. 'Had I not done that our father would live still. I gave my support to the Usurper!'

The declaration ended on a wail and she dug her face deeper into the pillow, her shoulders trembling beneath the thin silk of her gown.

'Look at me,' Kedryn urged, and when she would not, reached to grasp her shoulder, turning her towards him.

He was shocked by the change in the woman. He had thought her beautiful once, and even now the delineaments of beauty could be seen in her features, but masked by grief and guilt. Her face was very pale and her eyes seemed sunken, ringed by dark halfmoons of shadow, reddened by her weeping. Her cheeks were hollowed and as she stared at him she drew her lower lip between her teeth, gnawing on its fullness. He glanced again at Wynett, reminding himself that they were sisters and that once he had thought optimistically of a liaison with Ashrivelle. Now, although she was the younger of the two, she looked older, aged by the guilt writ large in her staring eyes. Wynett smiled at him nervously, urging him to speak, and he turned towards Ashrivelle.

'Listen to me,' he said slowly. 'Do you believe I would lie to you?'

Reluctantly, she shook her head and he reached to take her hand, holding it firm when she sought to withdraw it from his grasp.

'You are not tainted. I have discussed this with Sister Bethany and she tells me you were fed a love potion. You were not responsible for your infatuation, nor was there any way you could know what you did. The Messenger tricked so many, forcing them to act against their will. The potion he administered to you caused you to do what you did, not your will; and because you did not act of your own volition you cannot be held responsible. There are none here who do hold you responsible, save you yourself!

91

'You had no hand in your father's death – that was,' he paused, aware that he might by chance reveal his doubts before time, 'the work of Hattim Sethiyan and the Messenger. Not you! No guilt attaches to you. Has Bethany not absolved you in the name of the Lady?'

Ashrivelle nodded mutely, sniffling.

'And does not Bethany speak for the Sisterhood?'

Again she nodded, blinking tears now.

'Then surely to assume guilt is to deny the Sisterhood, to deny the Lady. Would you do that?'

Ashrivelle shook her head, her hand no longer seeking to escape his clasp but returning the pressure of his fingers as if she sought to clutch the hope implicit in his words.

'Then do not,' he urged. 'Accept the judgement of the Sisterhood and cast off this guilt.'

'Will others?' she asked doubtfully. 'Do folk not point at me and name me Hattim's doxy?'

'You are not – nor have been – anyone's doxy,' he retorted. 'What folk feel for you is sympathy.'

'I stood beside Hattim when he claimed himself king,' she whispered. 'I supported the Usurper.'

'Because you were held in thrall,' said Kedryn. 'Because you had no choice. There is no guilt in that.'

'Do you absolve me?' she asked.

Kedryn nodded. 'Aye, of course. As does Wynett. As does Bethany.'

'I would have seen you dead,' she murmured wonderingly. 'Hattim would have allowed the Messenger to slay you both and I should have stood by him. I stood by him when he imprisoned your parents.'

'And yet they do not blame you,' he responded. 'They wish only that you should recover. Does Wynett blame you?'

At his side Wynett shook her head, saying gently, 'We are sisters, you and I, and I cannot blame you. As Kedryn has told you – there is no guilt in actions over which you have no control.'

Ashrivelle shifted higher on the pillows and Kedryn felt his face redden as the movement loosened her gown, revealing the swell of pale breasts. He concentrated his gaze on her eyes, hoping it was trust he saw behind the tears.

'Do you truly forgive me?' she asked wanly.

'Aye,' he nodded, 'truly.'

Ashrivelle swallowed and abruptly threw her arms about his neck, sobbing against his shoulder. He felt tears on his skin and stroked her head, turning helplessly to Wynett. She was smiling, both pleased and amused, and for long moments made no move to help him extricate himself. Finally she rose and took her sister by the shoulders, gently pushing her back onto the bed. Kedryn found himself staring at a lissom torso revealed by the rumpled gown. Wynett folded it in place and sat on the bed beside Ashrivelle, stroking her hair.

'There is one thing I shall not forgive,' Kedryn announced, smiling as Ashrivelle turned alarmed eyes towards him. 'Your absence from the coronation. I would have you there as befits my royal sister.'

The alarm faded and she essayed a faint smile. 'As you command.'

'I would not command it,' he said, 'I would ask it.'

'Then,' said Ashrivelle, her smile growing stronger, 'I shall be there.'

# Chapter Five

KEDRYN stared at Wynett and shook his head in wonderment.

'I did not believe you could look lovelier, but you prove me wrong.'

Wynett curtsied, smiling. 'Thank you, my Lord. And you look every inch the king.'

They studied one another as if for the first time, which in a way it was, for neither had been crowned before and this day must, they knew, change their lives. Both were dressed in white, Kedryn's the surcoat, shirt and breeks promised by the tailor, Wynett in matching gown, fitted close about her upper body, with demurely high neck and long sleeves, but flaring over her hips into a voluminous skirt, edged like the neckline and cuffs with gold. Her hair was bound up in a golden snood indistinguishable from the blonde tresses and the talisman suspended between the swell of her breasts seemed to match the blue of her eyes. She stood very straight, her bearing regal, and Kedryn felt dizzied by her beauty.

'I feel distinctly nervous,' he said ruefully, tearing his eyes from the pleasant contemplation of his wife to study his own reflection in the mirror. 'I can scarce recognise myself.'

Indeed, the white robed figure staring back him seemed to bear little resemblance to the casually-dressed young Tamurin he remembered from his infrequent checks of his appearance. His hair was combed to a glossy chestnut, held back by a golden circlet, and the surcoat emphasised the width of his shoulders, its length making him seem taller, whilst his expression seemed that of an older man, poised somewhere between dignity and a massive apprehension.

'A smile would help,' remarked Wynett, her reflection appearing over his shoulder as she put her arms about his waist. 'You look more like a man contemplating execution than a king on his way to coronation.'

Her own expression was deliberately solemn and they both began to laugh.

'I only hope I can remember the correct responses,' he chuckled.

'If not,' Wynett promised, 'I shall prompt you.'

Kedryn turned to face her, holding her close, breathing in the scent of her fresh-washed hair. 'I wish it was done,' he murmured.

'It will be, soon enough,' she replied, turning up her face to kiss him. 'And soon after we'll be on the Idre, bound for Estrevan.'

'Aye.' Kedryn's nod was enthusiastic.

A knocking at their door cut short another kiss and, hand in hand, they went to the portal, opening it to find a cluster of nobles awaiting their presence. Bedyr stood closest, flanked by Yrla, Jarl and Arlynne at their side, Kemm, Tepshen Lahl and Brannoc close behind, beyond them a seeming sea of faces, all beaming. All were resplendent, Bedyr in tawny surcoat, Yrla in a gown of cerise, Jarl in sable robe, with Arlynne a striking rainbow of red and green and yellow. Tepshen and Brannoc, by accident or design, both wore green while the rest offered a kaleidoscope profusion of colours and a murmur of heartfelt approval as the royal pair emerged.

'It is time,' said Bedyr, smiling proudly.

Kedryn nodded, then paused, looking over the throng.

'Where is Ashrivelle?'

The crowd parted and Darr's younger daughter came forward. She remained somewhat nervous, but her features were transformed from their haggard outlines to her previous beauty, albeit aided by cosmetic artifice. She wore a pale blue gown and her hair, like Wynett's, was bound in a snood. Kedryn smiled, taking her hand.

'I am pleased you attend,' he murmured.

Ashrivelle smiled at him. 'Thank you, Kedryn,' she whispered. 'You look magnificent.'

He released her hand and followed Bedyr along the corridor. Beside him, in a voice intended for his ears alone, Wynett murmured, 'I believe you have made a conquest. If you dance with her more than twice I shall grow jealous.'

Kedryn set an arm about her shoulders, the alarm he aped not entirely unfeigned. 'I had forgotten about the dancing.'

Wynett drove an elbow into his ribs and he grunted, adding, 'I think one dance with me will be sufficient for anyone. At least, if they wish to walk the next day.'

Wynett giggled, then composed her features in dignified mien as they reached the wide stairway descending to the great hall, where more dignitaries waited. Kedryn took a deep breath and offered her his arm, proceeding down the staircase with what he trusted was

95

a suitably stately tread. They crossed the hall and went past an honour guard magnificent in burnished silver armour to the portico. Horses waited there, a jet stallion for Kedryn, a snow white mare for Wynett. He helped her onto the mounting box, watching as she settled herself side-saddle on the animal and then swinging limber astride the black. The big horse stamped impatient hooves, sensing the excitement in the air, and Kedryn patted the arching neck as seneschals fussed over the arrangement of his surcoat.

The sun hung golden in a cloudless azure sky as the procession filed through the gates of the White Palace and began the slow journey down the long avenue to the city. A squadron of the Royal Cavalry rode in the van, the sun dazzling on polished helms and breastplates, pennants fluttering from the upright lances, then Kedryn at the head of the main body, Wynett on his left, Bedyr, Yrla, Jarl and Arlynne abreast behind them, then Kemm, riding alongside Ashrivelle, followed closely by Tepshen Lahl and Brannoc, their prominence testimony to their relationship with the king-elect, behind them the nobility of Tamur, Kesh and Ust-Galich, united now in celebration of Kedryn's ascendancy, a second phalanx of guardsmen bringing up the rear.

The avenue was lined with people, and their cheers sent flocks of birds, startled, into the warm air, so that the sky seemed filled with beating wings and the flowers, ribbons and scatterings of coloured paper thrown in cheerful acclaim from all sides.

By custom, the king-to-be was required to promenade the city before presenting himself at the College of the Sisterhood, where the Paramount Sister would give her blessing and join the procession for the return to the palace and the ceremony of crowning. It was a progress that occupied a large part of the day and Kedryn was grateful for the hearty breakfast Wynett had cajoled him into eating as he paraded streets strung with garlands of flowers, folk hanging precariously from balconies and windows to add their shouting to the hubbub echoing over the rooftops. Down through the trading quarter they went, and along the harbour area, past warehouses and taverns, boats from whose masts cheering sailors hung, through streets narrow and wide, past houses large and small, over bridges and through gardens, until Kedryn's head spun with the enormity of Andurel and he realised how little of the great island city he had visited. The muscles of his jaw began to ache with smiling and he thought that his arms had not felt so tired since the days of swordwork on the walls of High Fort, nor his ears so dinned with unrelenting clamour. Beside him Wynett smiled and waved as though accustomed to such public display, but as they followed the glittering armour of the vanguard down an alley so pinched no onlookers awaited them there she turned and sighed and said forlornly, 'I fear my arms shall wither should there be much more of this.'

'I doubt I shall lift a sword again,' he nodded, smiling encouragement. 'Unless you have some potion to restore my strength.'

Wynett was about to reply, but the alley gave way to a square and that was filled with folk whose enthusiasm made further speech impossible, and they readjusted their smiles and set to waving afresh.

The progress took them around all of Adurel's boundary, in a great circle from the harbour to the bridges linking the city with Kesh and on to the Idre cascades leading down into Ust-Galich, then back towards the bank of the Vortigen and again into the maze-like depths of the city. Finally they came to the blue-stoned square of the College, where Bethany stood between the ever-open gates.

The cavalry halted there, forming in two ranks between which Kedryn and Wynett rode until they faced the silver-haired Paramount Sister. Kedryn dismounted, handing his reins to a smiling Sister and moving to help Wynett down. Together they walked across the sun-warmed stones to Bethany, who raised her arms and said, 'I bid you welcome, Kedryn of Tamur, and Wynett of Andurel.'

'I thank you for your welcome,' Kedryn responded, 'and ask that you bless this coronation to which we go in the name of the Lady.'

Two Sisters came forwards to place cushions of blue silk upon the flags and Kedryn and Wynett knelt. Bethany placed a hand on each of their heads and said, 'Go to your coronation with the Lady's blessing, and may she be with you always.'

They rose and turned back to their horses as a roan gelding was brought out for Bethany and the square rang with cheers. Kedryn helped Wynett onto her saddle and mounted the stallion. The vanguard formed again into a phalanx and Bethany took her place directly behind the couple as they rode once around the College and then began the return journey to the White Palace.

The crowds had not diminished and the tumult was no less than when they had descended the avenue. Indeed, it seemed there were even more folk pressing in, for the procession had been collecting a following of walkers all through the city and now they surged through the gardens flanking the esplanade, adding their numbers to those already present until it seemed all Andurel clustered there in joyful besiegement of the palace.

The road was bright with petals and ribbons and paper, a fresh bombardment greeting them as they ascended towards the gates. There, halberdiers raised pikes in salute and palace servants filled the courtyard as Kedryn reined in, grateful that he could now stop waving and allow his arms to drop. Wynett was already dismounted as he turned to her and he took her arm, leading the way into the palace with the shouting of the citizens outside still ringing in his ears.

He was unsure of the time, though his stomach told him the hour was past midday and he hoped it would not rumble as he made his way across the great vestibule to the dining hall, which, the masons having been unable to rebuild the Throne Room in time, was to be used for the ceremony. As he had been told, he strode to the centre of the room and halted, facing the chairs that took the place of the melted thrones. They were on the dais usually reserved for the high table, that removed for the moment so that the carved chairs stood in solitary splendour. Bedyr and Jarl, with Bethany standing tall between them, went to the foot of the dais. Yrla, Arlynne and Ashrivelle moved to the left, Tepshen and Brannoc with Kemm to the right, whilst the rest gathered about the sides. From the corner of his eye Kedryn saw Galen Sadreth towering above the notables, his round face wreathed in smiles, his surcoat a startling crimson. The riverman caught his friend's sidelong glance and winked hugely, threatening to disrupt the solemnity of the occasion by reducing Kedryn to helpless laughter.

Fortunately, Bethany spoke in time to forestall his amusement, commencing the ancient ritual.

'Do you come forward, Kedryn, Prince of Tamur, and Wynett of Andurel.'

They walked towards the dais, halting within arms' length of the trio standing on the lowest step.

'Do you, Kedryn, and you, Wynett, swear loyalty to the Three Kingdoms?' Bedyr intoned.

'Aye,' they said together, 'we do so swear.'

'Do you swear to defend these Kingdoms?' Jarl demanded.

Again they said, 'Aye, we do so swear.'

'Do you swear to defend and uphold the honour of the Lady?' Bethany asked.

'Aye, we do so swear.'

'On what do you swear?'

'We swear this in the name of the Lady and on our honour.'

'Kneel,' Bedyr commanded.

They knelt as Yrla and Arlynne came forward, each bearing a cushion on which rested a medallion of office, silver chains supporting discs of the same metal on which the tripartite crown was raised in gold. Jarl took one and Bedyr the other, handing it to Bethany, who placed it about Kedryn's neck, saying, 'In the name of the Lady, Kedryn, I pronounce you king.'

'In the name of Tamur,' said Bedyr, 'I pronounce you king.'

'In the name of Kesh I pronounce you king,' said Jarl.

He handed the second medallion to Bethany, who hung it about Wynett's neck, pronouncing the same formula, echoed by Bedyr and Jarl.

'Rise,' said the Sister, 'and govern wisely with the Lady's blessing.'

A cheer arose then as they got to their feet and climbed the three steps to the makeshift thrones, stilled by Bedyr's upraised arms. 'Let there be no dissent on this day or any other,' he declared. 'Who speaks for Ust-Galich? Let him come forward.'

Gerryl Hymet stepped from the crowd, his thin face nervous, pale above a surcoat of green and gold.

'Do you speak for Ust-Galich?' Jarl demanded.

'I do,' Hymet said.

'Is there any here who would dispute this man's right?' asked Bedyr.

There was silence and Bedyr added, 'Then do you, Gerryl Hymet, in the name of Ust-Galich declare Kedryn your crowned king, Wynett your queen?'

'In the name of Ust-Galich I pronounce Kedryn our king, Wynett our queen,' said Hymet, his voice high. He cleared his throat, achieving a deeper tone as he added quickly, 'And I do swear my Kingdom's loyalty, in the name of the Lady and upon my honour.'

'Well said,' Jarl approved.

'So do I proclaim Kedryn king,' Bethany announced.

The cheering that Bedyr had stilled rose up now, echoing off the walls. Gerryl Hymet turned to rejoin the Galichian contingent, but Kedryn rose to his feet, beckoning Hymet to stand before the throne.

He placed a hand upon the man's arm and motioned for silence. Curious faces looked towards him and he felt a moment's alarm as he realised that he was about to make his first proclamation as monarch.

'I thank you,' he said firmly, 'and I announce to all here present that from this day Gerryl Hymet be Lord of Ust-Galich.'

Hymet's long face paled further, his adam's apple bobbing in his throat as he swallowed. 'My Lord,' he gasped. 'I do not know what to say.'

'Thank him,' suggested Jarl, his green eyes twinkling.

'I do thank you,' Hymet said earnestly, 'and I swear to serve you well. Ust-Galich is loyal, Lord Kedryn. While I live there will be no more . . .'

He broke off, aware that there were those present who had followed Hattim Sethiyan, a roseate blush suffusing his features. Kedryn smiled and clapped him on the shoulder. 'And I thank you for your pledge,' he declared, 'you have our confidence.'

Hymet smiled then and took Kedryn's hand.

A moment later all was confusion as the gathering clustered about the thrones, the nobles vying to present themselves to the new-crowned pair and swear personal oaths of loyalty. Bedyr clasped his son, murmuring, 'That was well done, Kedryn,' then his place was taken by Yrla, who hugged him with tears in her eyes. Kedryn put an arm about Wynett's shoulder, drawing her close as Jarl and Arlynne added their congratulations. Ashrivelle hugged her sister and planted a moist kiss on Kedryn's cheek. Tepshen Lahl put hands upon their shoulders, nodding without speaking, fierce pride in his dark eyes. Brannoc, grinning hugely, took their hands and said, 'I swear you make the prettiest monarchs these Kingdoms have known.' Nobles pressed in from all sides, adding their felicitations and swearing their loyalty, parting as the vast bulk of Galen Sadreth cut through their ranks like some great ship surging through a flotilla of lesser vessels. 'The Lady bless you both,' he declared, engulfing them within the compass of his massive arms. 'Do we eat soon?'

Kedryn laughed then, for the riverman's blunt question lent a welcome normality to the unreal proceedings and reminded him that he was, indeed, mightily hungry.

'Must we wait?' he asked Wynett. 'Or may we command?'

His new-crowned queen turned a flushed face towards him, her smile for him alone, and said, 'I believe it is arranged, though we have a duty to perform first.'

Kedryn sighed, remembering the protocols Yrla had discussed with him, and moved towards the doors. With his arm still about Wynett's shoulders he crossed the outer hall and the courtyard beyond, their progress greeted with salutes and good wishes from the soldiery on guard. They climbed the narrow steps to the catwalk of the walls, looking out to the avenue and gardens, which were a solid sea of expectant faces. A cheering akin to thunder burst forth as they appeared, dying away as Bethany, her gown of Estrevan blue light as the sky, raised her arms and called out, 'Let all the Kingdoms know we have a king, and that he has a queen. May the Lady bless us all.'

The cheering reverberated afresh. Kedryn and Wynett raised arms heavy from waving to wave again, smiling down on their enthusiastic subjects, who shouted their names and called on the Lady to bless them. It went on and on, Kedryn felt his stomach grumble, reminded of food by Galen's question. Wynett said, 'That does not sound particularly regal,' and Kedryn, still smiling, answered, 'I fear my belly does not know it now belongs to a king.'

The crowd could not hear the exchange, but the expression on Wynett's face as she began to giggle was clear enough and produced a louder chorus of cheers.

Finally, when it seemed to Kedryn he must spend the remainder of the day on the wall, Bedyr suggested that they might decently adjourn to the dining hall and they turned about, descending the stairs with the tumult still ringing in the background.

By now the dining hall was returned to its usual function, the tables replaced and minstrels ready in the gallery. Kedryn seated Wynett and took his own place, amused to see that none moved to raise their glasses until he had lifted his in toast to the woman beside him.

'To my queen,' he murmured.

Wynett smiled and lifted her own goblet: 'To my king.'

They drank, their toasts echoed by all present, and servants trooped from the kitchens with great platters of food.

The feasting saw out the day's light and Kedryn's hunger, and by the time it was ended he wanted nothing more than to retire with Wynett to the privacy of their chambers, but could not for no sooner had the tables been cleared than the minstrels struck up a lively tune and he was reminded that that part of the celebrations he had, perhaps, dreaded the most was arrived.

'They wait on us,' Wynett murmured, indicating the expectant faces turned towards the high table.

Kedryn nodded and whispered, 'I felt more confident when we faced the Messenger.'

'You cannot disappoint them,' Wynett replied, her smile mischievous, and Kedryn sighed and rose to his feet, offering her his hand.

She took it and he led her down to the floor.

'The king is about to look foolish,' he murmured.

'As king you may set a new fashion,' she answered, cheerfully implacable. And Kedryn took her in his arms and began to dance.

They circled the floor once and then, to Kedryn's immense relief, Bedyr brought Yrla down to join them, Jarl and Arlynne close behind, so that he felt less isolated, though nonetheless clumsy. Soon Ashrivelle appeared on Kemm's arm, and then Gerryl Hymet with his red-haired wife, and before long the hall was filled with dancing couples and Kedryn felt his faltering steps were hidden by the press of bodies.

Wynett forced him to remain for what she considered a reasonable time and then agreed that they might resume their seats, though she did not stay long for Brannoc claimed her and showed himself an accomplished dancer. Kedryn found himself alone with Tepshen and Galen Sadreth, the formality of the evening forgotten now. The kyo filled a glass and handed it to the younger man, the hint of a smile on his thin lips.

'So, you are king.'

'Aye,' Kedryn nodded, sipping the wine. 'It feels strange.'

'You bore yourself well,' said Tepshen. 'That matter of Gerryl Hymet was well done.'

'Thank you.' Kedryn smiled, pleased by the rarely-given praise. 'It seemed as well to settle the question swiftly.'

Tepshen ducked his head in confirmation and added solemnly, 'But you should learn to dance.'

Kedryn spluttered wine and Galen bellowed laughter, pounding his goblet against the table. It was as well, Kedryn thought, that Sister Lyassa had declared herself too old to travel to Andurel, for she would surely have had sharper words to say on the matter of his Terpsichorean abilities, having spent so much time with him in Caitin Hold striving to teach him what she deemed the 'courtly arts'. He wiped his mouth, looking over the swirling throng, and experienced a renewal of alarm as he saw Ashrivelle approach.

Her colour was returned and her blue eyes shone, her full lips parted in a smile as she curtsied and asked, 'Will you dance with me, Kedryn?'

Feeling it would be uncouth to refuse, he nodded and escorted her onto the floor. The minstrels had slowed the pace of their tunes as the night grew older and he found himself holding Wynett's sister close, aware of the perfume she wore and the way she gazed at his face. He remembered Wynett's joking comment and wondered how deep it might be rooted in truth.

'I am not very accomplished,' he remarked apologetically.

'I think you do well,' Ashrivelle replied.

Kedryn smiled, suddenly aware that her gown was somewhat less demure than her sister's, revealing a pleasant cleavage that conjured an abrupt picture of her breasts as she had lain despondently on her bed. He felt momentarily confused, aware that his face reddened, and fixed his gaze on her eyes, only to find that was equally disturbing for she looked at him with an expression embarrassingly close to adoration.

'I owe you my gratitude,' she murmured.

'For what?' he asked.

'Your forgiveness,' she said, 'and for persuading me to attend. I find I enjoy myself.'

'I am pleased,' he responded, wondering how long the tune might last before he could decently excuse himself.

Ashrivelle lowered her gaze as if she sensed his discomfort, and he was able to look over her head and find Wynett, willing her to rescue him. His wife smiled over Brannoc's shoulder, and when the music faded came with the halfbreed to lay a proprietorial hand on her husband's arm.

'I claim my lord,' she smiled. 'Brannoc, will you not dance with my sister? Ashrivelle, you will find him a most excellent partner.'

Ashrivelle seemed almost reluctant to relinquish Kedryn's arm, but she allowed Brannoc to lead her away as Wynett moved into Kedryn's grip.

'My sister appeared to enjoy herself,' she said equivocally.

'Thank you for rescuing me,' Kedryn answered.

'Did you need rescuing?' Wynett's finely arched brows rose in amusement.

'I believe you were right.' Kedryn frowned, his voice serious.

'That you have made a conquest?' Wynett laughed, drawing closer as they spun about to brush her lips to his mouth. 'Of course you have – how could any woman resist you?'

'Easily,' he said gallantly, and quite seriously, 'when the only woman I want is you.'

Her own expression grew serious then and she ignored all decorum as she pulled him tight against her and kissed him firmly.

He did not realise they had stopped dancing until the kiss ended and he became aware that they stood within a circle of beaming onlookers who began to clap and cheer and shout their approval as he looked up, his face flushed. Wynett was unabashed and cheerfully led him into the dance again, returning the hall to a swirling mass of colour and laughter.

It went on long into the night and Kedryn felt he had danced sufficient for a lifetime as the sky paled into dawn. Yrla had claimed him, and Arlynne, too, and after them it seemed every woman there sought to circle the floor at least once with the new king. Many of the men, no more enthusiastic than Kedryn, had forsaken the round to settle in conversation, and now slumped, somewhat the worse for wine, at the tables. None, he realised, would leave the hall until he retired and he found Wynett, suggesting that they might decently go to their beds. She was breathless, her face flushed prettily with excitement, but when he spoke to her she yawned, nodding, and he turned to his parents, asking if he might not end the celebration.

'You are the king now,' Bedyr smiled. 'You may end it when you wish.'

Kedryn shook his head, grinning. 'I am not used to such authority,' he murmured.

'You will grow accustomed to it,' his father informed him, the notion mildly alarming to the young man.

'What should I do?' he asked. 'Must I make some kind of announcement?'

Bedyr laughed aloud and Yrla spoke past him. 'You need only retire, Kedryn. No official proclamation is necessary.'

'Good.' Kedryn yawned hugely and rose, extending a hand to Wynett.

'You would not like one more dance?' she asked, her blue eyes shining.

'No,' he said firmly, tugging her upright as she chuckled and leading her towards the doors.

Their departure was marked by a hail of good wishes that slowed their exit and when they finally succeeded in breaking free Kedryn sighed, circling Wynett's waist with his left arm as she rested her blonde head on his shoulder and they followed a lantern-bearing footman towards their chambers. Guards stood before the door and sleepy-eyed servants waited within the ante-chamber. Kedryn dismissed them, happy to be once more alone with his wife. The room was warm, heated by a banked fire, and the windows were shuttered against the dawn chill, the candles burning in the sconces along the walls lending a mellow light that danced in Wynett's golden hair. Kedryn shrugged off his surcoat, tossing it carelessly over a chair, and pulled Wynett close.

'I thought,' she murmured when he finally removed his mouth, 'that you were tired.'

'Of official celebration,' he answered, smiling, leading her towards the bedchamber.

'Does my king command?' she asked as he began to unhook the fastenings of her gown.

'Does my queen object?' he countered, lowering his mouth to her neck as the silk slipped from her shoulders.

'No,' she said huskily. Then, as his hands moved over her hips and his mouth over her breasts, 'Oh, yes.'

\*

Had Gerat been given to cursing, she would have cursed the lack of equestrian skills that denied her the use of swift horse and confined her to the carriage that lumbered with seemingly irrevocable slowness across the high plateau of central Tamur. As it was, she did her best to compose herself to acceptance of so tardy a method of travel and prayed to the Lady that she would be in time. In time for what, she could not exactly define, but the feeling of unease that had gripped her in Estrevan grew as she traversed the highlands of the Geffyn, as though the menace she sensed drew closer with each passing day, and she willed the four animals pulling her carriage to maintain their pace as they hauled their burden along the mountainous trails.

Urgency rendered time meaningless and the Paramount Sister could not say exactly when she had departed the sacred city, overriding the objections of Porelle and the others even though she could not tell them just why she felt it so needful she go. A single acolyte accompanied her, and the driver, a bluffly cheerful man called Wyxx, whose concern was as much for his animals as for the immediacy of the Sister's mission. Blown horses, he told her with phlegmatic calm, would pull no carriage, and unless – no disrespect

105

intended – she could persuade the Lady to propel her vehicle, she must allow him to set their speed.

It had seemed swift enough as they traversed the fertile plain between Estrevan and the Gadrizels, but then they had slowed on the long climb to the Morfah Pass, and beyond that more as they ascended the winding roadways that brought them into the Tamurin heartland. The commander of the Morfah garrison had furnished them with a fresh team, and that had been replaced by another when they reached Caitin Hold, but Gerat knew that if she could only sit a galloper she could make far better time. If she could entrust her mission to a mehdri word would travel faster, but she could do neither, the one because she had no skill with horses, the other because she did not know how to word the message. It did not seem a thing she could put into words: she had tried to explain it to Porelle and Lavia, to Reena and Jara, but could not, so how to word it that a mehdri might carry it to Kedryn? It was impossible and she knew that she must confront the new king herself, no matter what customs were broken by her departure.

Indeed, she was not certain what she would say when she did finally meet him. That there was something in the words of Qualle that seemed to relate to Alaria's Text and that disturbed her? That she sensed a threat? That she felt, in a manner she could not clearly define – let alone express in words – that Kedryn's mission as the Chosen One was not yet done?

It was so nebulous; and yet, she was sure, so urgent.

And the word that had come from Bethany in Andurel, carried by a mehdri who – thank the Lady! – had met her on the road east of the Morfah Pass appeared to relate to her sense of unease. Again, she was not certain how, but that Kedryn contemplated a second descent into the netherworld had a bearing, of that she did feel sure, though not of why such certitude gripped her. She could only trust in the Lady, both to bring her to Kedryn in time and to lend her eloquence. She did not know what she would say to him, though she had read and re-read the transcribed documents she carried in the satchel slung about her shoulders, never letting the pouch out of her sight, as though afraid it might disappear, transported by some fell gramarye to thwart her.

She smiled at the thought, wanly, and let her gaze wander over the landscape unfolding before her as Wyxx jammed a boot against the lever of the brake and close-hauled his traces as the carriage tilted on the steeply-descending trail.

It was a magnificent landscape, all sweeping hillsides thick with timber, dotted here and there with mountain meadows like green pools amongst the trees. A brook ran noisily beside the trail, splashing over stones as it tumbled towards the distant foot of the scarp, the water irridescent in the morning sun. She saw a kingfisher dart, a flash of brilliant colour, across the stream, and when she looked to the blue sweep of sky above, she saw two falcons circling in stately isolation. A pleasing breeze blew, taking the edge off the heat, rustling the burgeoning foliage of the oaks and beeches and ash trees, a sussurant counterpoint to the ever-present birdsong, itself balanced by the clop of hooves and the creaking of the carriage. Wyxx mumbled softly, reassuring the four horses as they moved downwards, his barely-vocalised words a drone like the buzzing of the insects in the warm air. It had been a long time since Gerat had seen Tamur and she had all but forgotten how different it was to the country surrounding Estrevan. A high, hard land that bred a hardy, proud people, majestic in its mountain fastnesses, lovely in its luxuriant forests. Far off, no more than a blur at this distance, she could see the gentler footlands, blue-green in the haze, knowing that she must cross them to reach the Idre, to reach Genyff, where Bethany had said Kedryn would disembark and strike out overland.

'This is the Genyff road?' she asked her driver, knowing the question to be unnecessary, but needing to speak.

'Aye.' Wyxx nodded, not taking his eyes from the horses. 'As I told you yesterday, Sister. And the day before.'

'Forgive me.' Gerat turned eyes that were blue and grey at the same time on the burly wagoner. 'But I am anxious that we should not miss the king.'

'If you told me aright, we shall not,' Wyxx grunted. 'If Kedryn comes ashore at Genyff he'll take this road to Caitin Hold.'

Gerat nodded, then: 'Shall we reach Genyff by the half moon?'

'All being well,' came the complacent answer.

'Can you be sure Kedryn will be there?' Donella, the acolyte, asked, her voice a trifle breathless, for she had no great love of this perilous descent.

Gerat turned on the high driving seat to see the acolyte clutching tenaciously to the carriage sides, her usually-calm face tense, and wished that Donella had told her she had no head for heights before they had departed Estrevan. She smiled reassuringly and said, 'He sails on the first full moon after the coronation. The journey up the Idre will last at least to the half moon, so – aye, we can be reasonably sure.'

'Unless,' said Donella, peering over the carriage side to the flank of tree-covered hillside that swept away on her left, 'we overturn. Or lose a wheel.'

'We'll not spill,' said Wyxx amiably. 'And our wheels are sound. Have I not checked the carriage each night?'

'Have faith, child,' smiled Gerat. Then clutched the woodwork herself as the carriage slewed around a curve, the outer wheels dislodging a tumble of stones that bounced away down the hillside. 'Have faith.'

Wyxx clucked, flicking the reins to drive the horses a little faster, hauling the vehicle clear of the angled section, its surface slippery where the stream had overspilled its bank and run across the trail.

'Nothing to fear,' he said over his shoulder.

Donella did not reply because her eyes were closed tight and her lips were moving in a silent prayer. Nor did Gerat speak because her thoughts had returned to the matter of Qualle's book and the abrupt reminder that their journey was not without a degree of peril prompted her to commence worrying again.

Were her Sisters right in their belief that the book contained no more than the arcane ramblings of a woman whose sanity was, in the most charitable estimate, questionable?

Was their opinon that the prophecies set down by Alaria were all fulfilled correct?

Certainly, they disapproved of her departure from Estrevan. Even Lavia, who would willingly have gone in her place, deemed it unseemly and unwise that the Paramount Sister should quit the city. Yet she could not see any alternative. It was as though some voice she could not properly hear whispered about the outer limits of her perception; as if the partially remembered fragments of a dream lingered in her consciousness. It was an imperative she could not deny, even though she could not explain it, and that in itself was strange, for she was a pragmatic woman, usually able to comprehend and explain her impulses. What she had read in Qualle's book she did not properly understand, yet it seemed some meaning had penetrated her inner consciousness, even taken hold of her, for here she was, perched on the swaying seat of a carriage doing what no Paramount Sister in living memory had done, breaking with all tradition to attempt a rendezvous at which she did not know what she would say.

It did not matter, she decided as the roadway flattened, curving around a spur, what she felt, she felt and the power of that feeling was such that it could come only from the Lady. She knew what she must do and she would do it, even if it meant no more than handing to Kedryn the parchments contained in her satchel.

'Have faith,' she murmured, this time to herself.

'No need to worry,' said Wyxx, misunderstanding her. 'We'll be off the Geffyn in a day or two and the way runs flat from there.'

Gerat smiled, forcing herself to study the magnificent terrain.

\*

'We,' said Kedryn, glancing at Wynett and wondering if he sounded pompous, 'are confident we leave the Kingdoms in good hands. Our council is formed and on it sit men trusted by all. Your loyalty and your wisdom are undoubted, and we have faith that you will govern well.

'You have, after all,' he added softly so that only Wynett heard him, 'more practice than us.'

The men and women gathered in the royal council chamber nodded, only Gerryl Hymet looking as though he doubted the veracity of Kedryn's words. His long face was almost mournful and Jarl clapped him stoutly on the shoulder, saying, 'Fear not, my friend, this matter of governing is not so difficult.'

'You set enough objections to Kemm's appointment,' his wife remarked tartly, prompting a black look from the Lord of Kesh.

'We shall ward your realm,' Bedyr promised gravely. 'Have no fear.'

'I – we – do not,' said Kedryn. 'And after we have visited Estrevan we shall return.'

'You will sojourn a while at Caitin Hold, will you not?' asked Yrla. 'It would be as well were you to attend affairs there before returning.'

Kedryn nodded enthusiastically, smiling his thanks to his mother for making such a delay easier. Yrla smiled back, knowing that her son harboured a longing to see his home again after so long away.

'Then we are done,' said Bedyr. 'The council is formed and the measures of future appointment set in motion. You will ask of Gerat that she issue a fiat instructing her Sisters to attend all those who seek a place?'

'I will,' Kedryn promised.

'Do not be gone too long,' his father smiled. 'You are not alone in your desire to see our homeland.'

'No.' Kedryn shook his head, raising his voice for the benefit of the others. 'I know that you all wish to return to your homes, and I thank you for your aid in this.'

'I am perfectly happy to remain in Andurel,' remarked Arlynne, rearranging the skirts of her latest gown, the movement jangling the array of bracelets she wore.

'As are the merchants of Andurel to have you here,' grunted Jarl, 'though my treasury is less happy.'

Arlynne smiled at her hawk-faced husband and patted his hand. 'You need only breed more of your horses,' she said cheerfully. 'Now that Kedryn has opened trade with the Beltrevan you can find a new market.'

Jarl snorted, but the smile that curved his thick lips suggested that the prospect was not without its attractions.

'So you sail on the morrow,' said Yrla, a note of regret in her voice. 'It seems so soon.'

'Galen tells me the full moon offers the best tide,' Kedryn nodded, feeling himself a little saddened now that departure was so imminent. Confinement in Andurel had been a constraint he had longed to break, but at least it had been a confinement amongst those he loved, and now that he was about to find the freedom he planned for he realised that he would miss his parents and the others he had come to know so well.

'Galen mans your barge?' asked Yrla, as much to dispel the note of sorrow as for any other reason.

'He has agreed to leave his beloved *Vashti* here,' confirmed Kedryn. 'She is to be dry-docked while he captains the barge.'

'It is good to know you will be in safe hands,' Yrla said with maternal concern, glancing to where Tepshen Lahl and Brannoc stood.

'No harm shall come to him whilst I live,' said the kyo.

'With these two champions on guard, you need have no fear.' Bedyr set an arm about his wife's waist. 'And what harm can there be in a journey to Estrevan?'

Kedryn smiled encouragingly, wondering what his father might make of Galen Sadreth's stories of disappeared vessels. He had not mentioned the riverman's gloomy yarn to anyone, and had pressed both Tepshen and Brannoc to silence on the matter, for he could see no reason to cause alarm with so nebulous a tale, and knew that if any present had the slightest suspicion there might be danger in the trip they would argue fervently against his going. And what harm could befall? As Bedyr said, he was guarded by champions, and the barge would carry a squad of Tamurin bowmen together with a complement of warriors, surely safeguard enough against any attack.

'Be of good cheer,' he urged his mother, taking her hands. 'We shall be safe enough, and return soon enough.'

Yrla nodded, essaying a smile that could not entirely hide her regret at having her son taken once more from her. She studied him, seeing Bedyr reflected in Kedryn's tall frame, and told herself it was time she accepted he was a grown man, married and crowned, with his own life to lead. She was too good a mother to deny him that right and she forced a greater cheer than she felt into her expression as she murmured, 'I know, my dear, and you must forgive me these maternal foolishnesses.'

'I do,' Kedryn said, with all his father's gravity.

'He will be safe.' Wynett stood beside them, her own smile confident. 'We shall be well-guarded, and besides – do we not wear the Lady's talismans?'

She touched the blue stone that hung with the medallion of her office about her slender throat and Yrla's expression grew more genuine at the reminder. 'Then mayhap we should attend the dining hall,' she suggested. 'There is the final banquet requires your presence.'

Kedryn groaned at the thought, for it seemed he had done little the past few weeks save eat and dance and talk. There had been banquets in honour of Tamur, and for Kesh, and for Ust-Galich; in honour of Gerryl Hymet; in honour of the Sisterhood; in honour, it seemed, of anyone with the slightest claim to acquaintanceship or royal notice. In that respect alone he looked forward with pleasure to his departure, for he was wearied with the seemingly-endless formalities and longed for the simpler life he anticipated on the journey.

At his side Wynett smiled innocently and said, 'And there will be dancing after.'

Kedryn groaned afresh at the thought.

Nonetheless, he performed his duties with good grace and still succeeded in persuading Wynett from the floor before the hour grew too late, finding their bed in good time, so that they slept soundly and rose not long after dawn, their excitement mounting as they dressed in preparation for departure.

It was another fine day, the sky clear and the sun already warm enough to lift the early chill. Andurel glittered, jewel-like, as they rode their horses to the harbour, a squadron of the Royal Guard trotting proud before them, the Tamurin archers and warriors marching sturdily behind. Bedyr, Yrla, Jarl, Arlynne and Kemm composed the farewell party, and Kedryn rode between Wynett and Ashrivelle, smiling broadly at the folk who greeted them along the way.

They reached the harbour and saw Galen Sadreth awaiting them, decked in a flamboyant tunic of purple, the trident emblem of the river guild on one breast, the tripartite crown on the other. The travellers had chosen simpler garb, Kedryn readily re-assuming his plain tunic and breeks, his sword once more at his side, whilst Wynett and Ashrivelle both wore gowns of practical cut, designed for the relatively close quarters of the barge rather than for the banqueting hall.

'Welcome,' the giant declared heartily. 'By your leave, we sail as soon as we may.'

He stepped forwards to assist Ashrivelle from her saddle, his massive hands spanning her waist to lift her down with no more effort than a normally sized man would expend in playing with a kitten. Kedryn helped Wynett dismount and they said their farewells, exchanging embraces and kisses, and crossing the gangplank to the wide deck of the barge.

Compared with the sleek *Vashti* the craft was huge. Two stout masts lifted from the deck, and a bowsprit thrust from the prow. A poop stood high at the stern, affording Galen a clear view over his command, and down each side ran two series of recessed benches seating forty oarsmen. A cabin filled the centre of the craft, its walls painted a shining gold that glittered in the sunlight. The rails and prow were of Estrevan blue and the gunwales silver, as were the oars that dipped on Galen's order and eased the great vessel from the dockside.

'She's a pretty thing,' said Galen as Kedryn brought his party onto the poopdeck. 'Not my lovely *Vashti*, but she'll do.'

'I am pleased you find her to your liking,' Kedryn grinned, raising a hand in farewell as the barge moved away from the dock.

He watched until the figures standing there grew indistinct against the press of buildings and then turned to escort the women to the cabin. The soldiery were already settled about the deck and before long Wynett and Ashrivelle had the cabin arranged to their liking. It was comfortable as a moderately sized room, equipped with chairs and a brazier, cupboards containing food and drink, and more providing space for their clothes. In a pinch it could be used for sleeping, though their intention was to travel by day's light and find harbourage by night. Kedryn left his wife and her sister there and went to rejoin Galen on the poop, Tepshen and Brannoc with him.

The captain was roaring orders that brought the two lateen sails down to catch the wind, adjusting his tiller as the sheets billowed and the rowers shipped their oars, the barge sailing smooth on the spreading bosom of the river.

'What news of strange happenings?' Kedryn asked.

'No more than I told you,' Galen answered. 'Though since your coronation river traffic has lessened.'

Kedryn gestured to the bowmen, their weapons held in oilskin wraps against the damp, and the sword-bearing warriors. 'With these we should be safe enough,' he remarked.

'Aye,' Galen nodded. 'I doubt there's any would dare attack so well-defended a vessel.'

How wrong they were they discovered as they approached Gennyf.

For three days the wind had blown against them and Galen had tacked his craft against the bluster, finally calling on the rowers to dip their oars as twilight descended over the Idre and the lights of Gennyf beckoned in the distance. Like men answering the call of a siren they bent to their task, the great sweeps rising and falling in disciplined unison, glinting silver in the dying light. The sails were furled and Kedryn went with Wynett to the prow, pointing out the welcoming twinkle of the lights marking the riverside town. There was a stir of activity as all on board readied themselves for the landing, the Tamurin eager to set foot on their own soil again. The sun was gone behind the western horizon leaving only a band of red light across the sky and the half-full moon hung pale in the east, a sundered disc against the filigree stars. The Idre was a ribbon of blue velvet, slapping against the bow, discordant with the steady rhythm of the oars. Kedryn draped an arm about Wynett, hugging her as he studied the growing string of light that marked their destination.

Then his grip tightened as he saw something lift from the water. A chill that had nothing to do with the night wind stung his spine and he was suddenly aware of a tingling sensation where the talisman hung against his chest. He felt Wynett stiffen in the circle of his arm as she raised a hand to clutch her own half of the stone. She said,

'Kedryn! The talisman!' and he glanced swiftly down to see the blue jewel glowing between her clutching fingers.

'The cabin!' he said. But before she could move from his side the shape rose above them, blotting out the stars and the moon, gigantic, indistinct in form, but palpable in the evil that emanated from it. He felt a shock of awful recognition, knowing that he stared at the creature first encountered in the gloomy mere of the netherworld, and roared, 'To me! Ware danger!'

Tepshen Lahl and Brannoc were at his side in the instant and the deck thudded with the pounding feet of archers and swordsmen. Ashrivelle screamed from the cabin and the barge tilted as Galen put his helm over.

The leviathan towered into the night, larger than before, larger than any beast of the mortal world, eyes like great rubescent shields burning with implacable hatred, tendrils writhing about a gaping maw filled with teeth the size of swords. The serpentine neck curved upwards, lunging sideways as the barge responded to Galen's tiller, the jaws encompassing a bowman whole as the vessel slid past the impossible shape. Oars broke upon its body and a fluke tipped with wickedly-curved talons tore a ragged gash in the starboard gunwale. Oarsmen screamed as the great paddle crushed them and Kedryn drew his sword as he saw a volley of arrows rattle against the slimey hide. Rattle and fall away as if the creature were armoured too thick for clothyard shafts to penetrate.

The ugly head thrust towards him and he slashed his blade in a curving arc even as Tepshen and Brannoc raised their own swords in defence.

The kyo screamed, 'Find the cabin!' as his blade bounced from a questing tendril, and Kedryn threw Wynett back, his arm jarring as steel met something that was not flesh, that had no place in the world of men.

He saw Brannoc drive his Keshi sabre at an eye, the lunge deflected by a tendril that dashed the halfbreed bodily to the deck, and then he felt the barge tilt beneath him as a fluke found purchase and drove the craft down into the Idre as if the behemoth sought to clamber on board. More arrows ricochetted uselessly from the slug-like hide as he slid over the planks, scrabbling desperately to his feet as he saw the hellgate mouth open, the hideously blank orbs burning with red purpose. Tepshen hacked again, a great two-handed swing that would have sundered a man, but seemed to have no effect on the beast. A tendril snaked, seemingly of its own volition, about the kyo's waist and tossed him aside, sending him spinning through the air as the maw continued its awful progress towards Kedryn.

He could no longer stand upright, for the barge was taking water, half its starboard planking stove in like matchwood, oarsmen screaming piteously as the tremendous weight smashed down upon them and the taloned flukes raked out their lives. Warriors slid helpless across the canting deck and Kedryn clutched a rope and cut savagely at the descending jaws, his steel smashing against the fangs that snapped shut a handsbreadth from his face. Stinking breath gusted over him, redolent of decay and corruption, and he gagged on its nauseous reek, feeling his feet go out beneath him. He clung to the rope for long, heart-stopping moments as the head drew back, flicking irritably from side to side as the few men still able to wield sword or bow assailed it from both sides, his feet swinging over the water that now welled dangerously close. Then a hand closed on his tunic and he was snatched back, the jaws colliding with the tilted deck, driving into the boards as Galen Sadreth flung him to the temporary safety of the cabin's side, now almost horizontal. He saw Ashrivelle clinging wide-eyed and screaming to the portside gunwale and turned with upraised blade to seek Wynett.

Brannoc was manhandling her across the tilted deck, pushing her to his side, and he took her hand, dragging her onto the cabin.

The head rose again, splintered planking spilling from the jaws, and the furnace eyes swung again towards Kedryn. He heard Galen yell, 'It seeks you!' and saw the riverman hurl himself between the behemoth and its quarry.

A tendril flicked the giant's weight aside as easily as Galen had lifted Ashrivelle from her horse. Then a fluke stove in the roof of the cabin and Kedryn felt himself falling again, toppling towards the anticipatory gape of the hideous maw. He fastened a hand against the ragged edge of the structure and swung his sword at the monster's snout.

Above his head he heard Wynett scream, 'No! you shall not have him!' and screamed himself as he saw her plunge past him, one hand out-thrust in denial, the other clasped about the talisman she wore. Saw her fall between the jaws, and the jaws close about her.

He saw the great head lift, oily lips closed tight, and let go his hold on the cabin, intent on reaching the leviathan, intent on prising the jaws apart even though it meant his death.

T.W.B.—7

He slithered over the jagged wood, sword driving at the snake neck, and felt a tremendous blow against his ribs, hurling him away as pain flared like fire in his side and a far greater pain burned in his soul as the monstrous creature slid from the sinking barge and dove beneath the corpse-littered surface of the Idre.

He gasped, 'Wynett!' and then water filled his mouth and despair filled his heart as darkness closed about him.

# Chapter Six

KEDRYN swam in darkness, a stygian gloom filled with such soul-numbing despair that panic gripped him and he struggled against the insubstantial bonds holding him within that aphotic limbo. Whatever clutched him grew stronger as he fought its retention and his exertions became more desperate, driven by a will that was governed by the single heart-rending memory of Wynett tumbling helpless into the gaping maw of the leviathan. He choked out her name, and realised, less through the conscious processes of his mind than through his body's immanent knowledge of itself, that water did not fill his lungs: he did not drown, nor did fangs rend him: he was alive.

He opened his eyes.

And saw two orbs of blue, clouded with concern, close to his face.

A voice he did not know said, 'Kedryn! Kedryn, be still.'

There was such benign command in that voice that his limbs ceased their struggling without mental instruction, falling not into water, but onto the soft sheets of a bed. He blinked, focusing his gaze, and saw the eyes belonged to a woman of indeterminate age, not young but neither old, her face tanned, her hair a sleek black, shining in the sunlight that filtered through the thick panes of glass above and behind her.

'I am Gerat,' she said, 'Paramount Sister of Estrevan. And you are safe in Gennyf. In the hospice of the Sisters.'

He said, 'Wynett?'

Gerat let go his arms and placed a hand upon his forehead, the gentle pressure forcing him back against the pillows more effectively than any strength. 'Drink this.'

She held a cup to his lips and the tone of her voice, though not an order, compelled obedience. He drank, wincing at the bitter taste, and felt a calm he could not welcome grip him.

'Good.' Gerat smiled thinly and set the cup aside. 'Now listen to me, for my concern is no less than yours, and what I must say to you is not easy for either of us.'

'Wynett?' he repeated, aware that his voice was slurring about a thickened tongue, feeling a lassitude assail his limbs and fighting against it, uselessly.

'Wynett is taken,' Gerat said. 'Lie still! There is nothing you can do for now and you must rest.'

She placed hands against his shoulders as he struggled to rise, her gaze and the inflections of her voice combining with the potion he had drunk to overcome the panic that once more threatened so that he could do no more than allow her to press him back, helpless now as a new-born babe, and as insensately resentful of the cataclysmic disruption of his world.

'You must listen to me,' Gerat repeated. 'If you are to do anything for Wynett you must listen to me. Will you listen to me, Kedryn?'

The urgency of her tone penetrated his anguish and he nodded dumbly, his head heavy, thick with grief.

'Your ribs are cracked,' she said. 'They will mend soon enough, but until they do you must rest. And before they are mended, there is nothing you can do. Now tell me what you saw; tell me what happened.'

'The beast came,' he mumbled, vaguely surprised that he was able to speak and then grateful as his voice gained strength, seemingly from the hand she touched to his lips. 'The beast we saw in the netherworld. It rose from the Idre to attack the barge. It was about to take me, but Wynett . . .' He broke off, tears forming unnoticed in his eyes, coursing down his cheeks. 'Wynett threw herself at it and it took her in my place.'

Gerat reached to brush the tears away, her hand gentle as her eyes. 'Did she wear the talisman?'

'Always,' Kedryn nodded. 'It was in her hand.'

The image was vivid in the eye of his mind, even as he squeezed his lids tight shut on that awful vision.

'Good,' said Gerat, the satisfaction in her voice snapping his eyes open in surprise. 'If that was the case, then mayhap she lives.'

'Lives? How can she live? She fell directly in the mouth of the beast.'

Kedryn stared at the Sister, disbelief etching sharp lines of pain upon his face. Gerat took his hand, her own cool and immensely comforting. 'You above all should know what power there is in the talismans,' she said quietly. 'What happened when first you saw the creature, in the netherworld?'

118

'It threatened us,' he said, his own voice slow, as if afraid to clutch at hope that might prove illusory. 'It rose before us, but when it saw the talismans it drew back.'

Gerat nodded as though this confirmed some hoped-for belief. 'I do not think it can harm one who wears the talisman.'

'It took her in its mouth and carried her under,' Kedryn groaned. 'Can the talisman prevent her from drowning?'

'I am not sure,' said Gerat, 'but I believe the beast can. I do not believe it was Ashar's intention to kill Wynett. You, mayhap, though I suspect he had rather secure the talismans.'

Kedryn frowned a question and the Sister went on, 'I believe Ashar sent the beast into this world in mortal form after you defeated his Messenger because he knows that while you hold Kyrie's stone you remain a threat to his ambitions. Mayhap the leviathan was sent to kill you; mayhap its purpose was to separate you from the talisman, but I do not believe it can harm one who holds the talisman in faith.'

'So where,' asked Kedryn slowly, 'is Wynett?'

'Gone into the netherworld,' said Gerat.

'And good as dead, therefore,' moaned Kedryn, fresh anguish in his eyes, bitterness in his voice.

'Mayhap,' said the Paramount Sister. 'Or mayhap that depends on you. I feel a gathering of destiny's threads – were you not so overcome with grief you might well have wondered what the Paramount Sister of Estrevan does in Gennyf.'

She smiled as confusion clouded his features.

'I have studied Alaria's Text at length, Kedryn. That and other writings from our archives, chief amongst them those of one called Qualle. My fellow Sisters dismiss Qualle as a madwoman, or believe her words irrelevant, but I felt a certainty that compelled me to break with all precedent and come here to meet you. I was not sure until now that the Lady guided me, but these events confirm what at first I felt only as compulsion.

'Along the way I met a mehdri bearing a message from Bethany – that you contemplated a second descent into the netherworld should I confirm your suspicion that Darr, and others, might be saved from the fate to which the Messenger condemned them. Now I wonder if that notion was not placed in your mind by the Lady.' She reached behind him as he nodded thoughtfully, plumping his pillows that he might sit straighter, alert now as he studied her face. 'I will show you transcriptions of Qualle's text when you are better recovered, but for now know that I translate them as a prophecy that you shall descend into the netherworld to confront Ashar himself.'

'To save Wynett?' he gasped.

'That, aye,' confirmed Gerat. 'Or mayhap in taking Wynett Ashar falls unwittingly into a pattern established by the powers that govern even the actions of gods, unknowingly strengthening your determination.'

'If I may save Wynett I will face Ashar,' Kedryn said grimly. 'Face him and slay him if I can.'

Gerat nodded again, smoothing the pale blue skirt of her gown. 'I believe you can save her,' she said, the single sentence igniting the fire of his hope, 'for I do not believe she is dead. I think the talisman protected her from the leviathan, else it would have returned to seek you. As it did not, I believe it must have gone back to that place from whence it came, bearing Wynett with it. Now she will be Ashar's prisoner, but I do not believe the god may harm her whilst she retains the stone. Or that if he can harm her, he will not so long as she serves to bait a trap for you.

'You are the Chosen One, Kedryn, and Ashar knows that you are his enemy, the mortal agent of the Lady.'

'But if the talisman is protection against even Ashar's might, then how could the leviathan harm me?' Kedryn asked.

'You might have drowned,' Gerat told him calmly. 'Or been crushed by the flukes. Had that blow landed a degree harder, your ribs would be stove in now, and you dead.'

'Then how,' Kedryn demanded, quickly lest fear of the answer still his voice, 'can you be sure Wynett lives?'

'You say she held the stone,' said Gerat, 'and that suggests she called upon the Lady. In the face of that power I do not think the beast could close its fangs upon her. I am not sure death *was* the intention, for there is something in Qualle's words that suggests to me the talisman will be the agency of Ashar's defeat and for that reason – for doubtless Ashar knows of the stones and their power – I suspect the god's intention may have been to remove the stones from this world.'

She paused, her eyes clouding and becoming slightly unfocused, as though she grew lost in thoughts that locked together like the pieces of a jigsaw, and when she spoke again her voice was grave. 'Were the stones both brought to the netherworld there would be little on this mortal plane that might stand against the god's future minions. Should he have created another like the Messenger, then that minion would likely prove unstoppable without the talismans. And should Ashar gain possession of them and bend them to his purpose, he would have a key to unlock the magic that holds him beyond the Lozins – he could move freely into the Kingdoms.'

Kedryn frowned, dull dread fastening clammy hands upon his soul. 'How should he obtain them?' he asked slowly. 'Wynett would not relinquish hers to the mad god.'

'Not knowingly,' Gerat agreed, 'but remember that Ashar is the god of lies.'

'And,' Kedryn said softly, his voice dulling as the fire of his hope diminished, 'you cannot be sure Wynett lives.'

'Touch your own stone,' Gerat commanded, 'and tell me what you feel.'

Kedryn raised a leaden arm to fasten a hand about the blue jewel, clutching it within his fist. It tingled against his palm, seeming to vibrate slightly with a strange, crystalline life. He closed his eyes, then opened them as certainty filled him and he said, not knowing how he knew, 'Wynett lives!'

Gerat smiled. 'When you stood on the walls of High Fort with Grania to dispel the gramarye of the Messenger Wynett was with you. Grania recognised what none of us in the Sisterhood then knew: that your destiny was linked to Wynett. That joining created a union deeper than may be easily explained, a union enhanced by the wearing of the talismans. Whilst Wynett lives, her talisman and yours – the two halves of the one original stone – are attuned, and you will always know she lives; as she will know you live. The Lady gives you hope, Kedryn!'

'Aye.' He relinquished his hold on the jewel, his lips curving in a wan smile. 'There *is* hope. And I must go into the netherworld to save my love.'

'To save your love and the Kingdoms, too,' said Gerat. 'But to do that you must be well. Those ribs must mend, and to that end you must sleep. What you may face there will be far worse than any Horde; worse, even, than the Messenger. Ashar will doubtless seek to suborn Wynett.'

'She is no flighty girl to be bought with deceits,' Kedryn protested.

'No,' said Gerat, 'but she will likely find herself in a world where nothing is as it seems, and Ashar is a master of deception. He may seek to win the talisman through treachery rather than force, and Wynett is alone there.'

'I go after her,' he declared, his voice fierce now.

'And that may be what Ashar wants,' Gerat warned. 'It may be that he seeks to entrap you both – to win both talismans.'

'He must kill me first,' said Kedryn, 'and to do that must he not overcome the power of the talisman?'

Gerat nodded and Kedryn asked, 'And you believe the talisman is the means by which *he* may be slain?'

Again the Paramount Sister nodded.

'Then, for both Wynett and the Kingdoms, I must go there.'

'If that is your choice,' Gerat said, 'but it is a mightily hazardous venture you plan.'

'No matter.' Kedryn's mouth set in a firm line. 'He has already wreaked sufficient harm; now let him pay.' The thought prompted another and he asked, 'The others? Tepshen and Brannoc; Ashrivelle; Galen – do they live?'

'They do,' Gerat assured him, 'and like you need to recover. Now, sleep.'

Kedryn began to shake his head, but she placed a hand upon his face, her fingers touching gently on his eyelids so that they came down to enclose him again in darkness, though now the blackness that descended was beneficial, without panic, and he slipped easily into dreamless slumber.

Gerat sat a while beside him, murmuring softly, her voice musical as if she sang a lullaby, which in a way she did, for soon his breathing was deep and regular and she could sense the healing processes commencing in his battered body. She sat like that for long moments, then rose to silently close the shutters, dimming the sunlight so that the simple, white-walled room became a place of restful shadows.

With no more sound than a cat might make, the Paramount Sister crossed to the door and went out, closing the portal behind her before turning to the two men waiting in the chamber outside.

'He sleeps,' she told them. 'His ribs mend, but he needs to sleep.'

Tepshen Lahl nodded, his luteous features grave. Beside him Brannoc wound a finger about a feathered braid and asked, 'How long?'

'He will be healed within the week,' said Gerat. 'In the time it takes your arm to mend.'

'And Wynett?' asked Tepshen.

'I believe she lives,' Gerat murmured, 'for I do not think it was the beast's purpose to slay her.'

Briefly, she recounted the gist of her conversation with Kedryn. Tepshen glanced at Brannoc and said, 'He had spoken with us of his notion of descending a second time into the underworld and I told him he was unwise. Now there will be no stopping him.'

Brannoc smiled grimly, glancing down at the limb strapped across his chest. 'The Lady be praised for your healing talents, Sister. We shall need full use of our swordarms where we go.'

'You would go with him into that place?' Gerat looked from one sober-faced man to the other. They nodded. 'It will not be easy,' she warned. 'Kedryn wears the talisman and that is greater protection than any device I can provide for you.'

'No matter.' Tepshen's voice was flat, stern with resolve. 'Where he goes, I go.'

'*We*,' Brannoc amended.

'So be it.' Gerat smiled approval of their loyalty. 'I shall protect you as best I can. But we shall speak of this later; for now, I must tend the others.'

'How fares Galen?' Tepshen asked.

'Several ribs were broken and the muscles of his shoulder badly torn,' Gerat informed him, 'he must remain here until the next full moon at least.'

The kyo nodded and said, 'I must send a message to Andurel.'

'Wait,' Gerat advised. 'When Kedryn wakes again there will be much we must discuss. Leave the message until then.'

Tepshen thought for a moment, then ducked his head in agreement.

'And now go rest yourselves,' said Gerat, firmly. 'You are neither of you fully recovered.'

The two warriors nodded and turned to follow her into the sunlight of a little courtyard, Tepshen limping, Brannoc holding his damaged arm protectively. She left them there, crossing the plaza to a door on the far side through which she disappeared. They settled on a stone bench mounted against the wall beneath the window of Kedryn's chamber, their movements unusually cautious, for both were severely bruised. The sun was lowering towards the west, angling golden light into the court, and the sky an unsullied blue. The flowers that grew within the yard filled the air with pleasant scents, their brilliant colours vivid against the white of the walls and the pale sandstone of the flags. It was warm, spring fading into summer, the scene suggestive of two men lazing out the end of the day, an impression belied by the tension writ clear on both their faces.

'You do not have to do this,' Tepshen said quietly.

Brannoc glanced at the kyo, his swarthy features quizzical. 'Do I not?' he asked, sounding almost – but not quite – amused.

Tepshen turned from his contemplation of the flowers to fix the halfbreed with a jet stare. For long moments he studied the former wolfshead, then smiled briefly. 'Thank you.'

'I have,' Brannoc paused, seeking the right word, 'a regard for Kedryn. And for you. I would not see either of you risk that place alone when I might aid you.'

'No,' said Tepshen, and then both lapsed into silence.

\*

When next Kedryn woke he judged it to be morning from the angle of the sunlight entering his room and the odours of hot bread that drifted on the warm air. His stomach prodded his memory and he eased upright in the bed, wincing as the movement strained his healing ribs. He felt refreshed, as though he had slept a long time, and glanced around the chamber. It was small and plain, its resemblance to the room he had occupied in High Fort's hospital awaking painful memories of Wynett so that he experienced a rush of impatience and pushed back the sheets, preparatory to rising. Bandages swathed his midriff and a sharp pain lanced his side as he set bare feet to the floor, seeing his clothes folded neatly on a small chest across the room, his sheathed sword resting atop the bundle. He stood up and felt his head swim as if he had been too long abed, placing a hand against the wall as dizziness threatened to topple him. Then the door opened and a familiar voice said, 'Kedryn, I have brought you . . . Oh!'

The sentence cut short on a gasp of embarrassment and he settled back on the bed, tugging the sheets across his naked body as he turned to see Ashrivelle standing just inside the chamber, a cloth-covered tray balanced on her out-thrust arms.

'Forgive me,' she stuttered, 'I did not . . . I thought . . .'

'No matter,' he forced a smile, easing his legs onto the bed and drawing the sheet up. 'Come in.'

Wynett's sister came forward, her pale face pinked with discomposure, and set the tray on the small table beside his couch. She wore a gown of Estrevan blue and her hair was gathered in a simple coif. She reminded him of Wynett and he felt the smile freeze on his face.

'There is bread,' she said, speaking fast in nervous response to her embarrassment, 'and eggs. Butter. A tisane.'

124

'How long have I slept?' he asked.

Ashrivelle looked at him with troubled blue eyes. 'Two days. I was afraid you would die.'

'No.' He shook his head. 'I have too much to do.'

'I have spoken with Gerat.' Ashrivelle settled herself on the single chair. 'She told me what you plan.'

Kedryn reached for the tray, grunting as he twisted so that Ashrivelle was instantly on her feet, bringing the platter to him, settling it solicitously across his thighs. As she stooped her hair brushed his face and he caught its fresh scent: another reminder of Wynett.

'Is it wise?' she asked as he spread butter on new-baked bread.

'What else should I do?' he retorted, the sharpness of his response bringing a flush to her pretty features again so that he modified his tone as he added, 'I am sorry, Ashrivelle, but whilst there is the slightest chance I may save Wynett I have no other choice. *Would* have no other.'

'You love her very much,' she said softly, staring at him in a way that prompted some small degree of discomfort.

'Aye,' he said, 'I do.'

'But you are also king now,' she said slowly, still staring at him.

'And Ashar is still the enemy of the Kingdoms,' he answered, 'and he has taken my wife.'

Ashrivelle nodded, her expression forlorn. 'But should the Kingdoms lose both queen and king . . .'

'They have not!' he snapped fiercely. 'Wynett lives.'

Ashrivelle started back, her eyes widening at the ferocity of his response. She composed herself with obvious difficulty, forming tears glistening on the blue of her gaze as she swallowed, seeming to steel herself to speak again.

'Gerat believes that – and I pray that she is right – but what if she is not?'

'Gerat is Paramount Sister of Estrevan,' Kedryn said, refusing to entertain any doubt, 'and I feel Wynett, here.'

He clutched the talisman, comforted by the faint tingling it imparted, the warmth he felt radiating from the stone.

Again Ashrivelle nodded, but now a hand crept forwards to touch his. 'I would not lose you both,' she whispered. 'I saw the beast and felt its power. I would not see you, too, lost to Ashar.'

Kedryn let go the talisman to fold his hand comfortingly about hers. 'Would you have me abandon Wynett?' he demanded.

'No!' Ashrivelle gasped, both her hands clutching his now. 'Not that! But nor could I bear to lose you, too.'

The face she turned towards him was reminiscent of the adoring expression he had seen during his coronation celebrations and gently he extricated his hands from her grasp, busying them with bread. 'I shall not be lost,' he said. 'The talisman will protect me and I shall bring Wynett from the netherworld. And you are bound for Estrevan, are you not?'

Abashed, Ashrivelle lowered her eyes. 'Aye. Gerat says I may accompany her when she returns.'

'I am pleased for you,' he said.

'But,' she began, then shook her head. 'No . . . I shall not journey to Estrevan until I know you are safe returned.'

Her tone alarmed him and he said, 'You can as easily await our return in Estrevan as here, Ashrivelle.'

'Gerat travels to High Fort,' was her answer. 'She will wait there until you return . . . Or not.'

'Once these ribs are full-mended I travel fast,' he said. 'On horseback I can take the river trail north. You could not keep up.'

'Then we shall follow after.' There was a trace of defiance in her voice. 'Gerat came here by carriage and we shall take that north.'

Kedryn shrugged and forked egg into his mouth. 'As you wish.'

'Not quite,' she murmured, almost too low for him to hear. Then, abruptly, she rose to her feet. 'I shall leave you now. Forgive my . . . weakness.'

Before he could voice a response she was gone, closing the door behind her so that he was left alone with his confusion. And his hunger, he realised as he swallowed egg, and began to consume the breakfast with relish.

He was sipping the last dregs of tisane when the door opened again and Gerat entered, carrying a small satchel of blue leather and accompanied by Tepshen and Brannoc. The kyo's limp was gone and Brannoc's arm was no longer in a sling, though he held it cradled still. Gerat took the chair and the two warriors settled upon the bed.

'How do you feel?' asked the Paramount Sister.

'Rested,' Kedryn answered. 'Though my ribs feel a trifle sore.'

'And will for some days yet,' Gerat nodded, casually removing the bed clothes that she might prod at his damaged side. Kedryn winced as her hands moved over his bandages, but she appeared pleased with her findings for she nodded and said, 'Aye, they heal nicely. You'll be fit enough to sit a horse ere long.'

'And these two?' Kedryn gestured at his companions.

'Mending apace,' Gerat said.

'You'll have companions on the journey,' grinned Brannoc.

'To High Fort,' Kedryn nodded.

'Into the Beltrevan,' Brannoc corrected. 'And beyond.'

Kedryn began to shake his head, but Tepshen fixed him with a solemn look and said, 'We are sworn to ward you. We go with you.'

'There are charms and cantrips fashioned for their protection,' Gerat told him as he started to protest, 'and their minds are made up. I think it no bad thing you travel with such boon companions.'

'Besides,' said Brannoc, 'you are not so well-acquainted with the Beltrevan that you may find Drul's Mound unaided. And as I have told you, the Drott may not take kindly to grave robbers.'

'Grave robbers?' Kedryn frowned. 'Do we go to rob graves?'

Gerat brought the satchel to her knees and fetched parchment out, smoothing the vellum across her knees, her expression serious.

'I have the writings I spoke of, and I have discussed them with Tepshen and Brannoc. Listen.' She began to read: *'And I saw that what he had fashioned for his deathly purpose was his undoing, for that which he had fashioned he had imbued with his own strength, that death himself might be slain, should life and death be joined.'*

'This is the Sister you spoke of?' Kedryn asked. 'Qualle – was that not her name? What does it mean? I do not understand.'

'Nor,' said Gerat, 'did I, until I read the passage to Brannoc.'

She turned to the halfbreed who unconsciously shaped the three-fingered gesture of warding as he cleared his throat and fixed his dark eyes on Kedryn's face.

'There is a legend amongst the Drott,' he said slowly, 'that says when Drul raised the first Horde Ashar gave him a sword.'

'Niloc Yarrum's blade was ensorcelled,' Kedryn interrupted, the confusion in his eyes replaced with interest. 'I felt it when I fought him.'

Brannoc nodded. 'Likely by Taws. The legend has it that Drul's blade was fashioned by the god himself.'

*'What he had fashioned for his deathly purpose,'* Gerat read, *'imbued with his own strength.'*

'And Drul's sword is said to rest with his bones in the mound,' Brannoc added.

*'His undoing,'* Gerat quoted, *'for that which he had fashioned he had imbued with his own strength, that death himself might be slain, should life and death be joined.'*

'I am no wiser,' Kedryn murmured, perplexed.

'The sword is death – Ashar's tool,' Gerat said, 'and the talisman you wear is life. I believe the jointure of the two may fashion the means of Ashar's downfall.'

Kedryn stared at her, a strange calm in his brown eyes. 'You say I must go to Drul's Mound and join sword with talisman?'

'I believe that to be the way of it,' Gerat confirmed, 'if you are to save Wynett. I do not say you *must*.'

'Will the shamans agree?' he wondered, as if the Sister's final sentence had not registered. 'Will even Cord help in such a venture?'

'Likely not,' said Brannoc. 'Hence our grave robbery.'

'We dig up a rusted sword?' Kedryn demanded. 'How, after, do I enter the netherworld.'

'*We*,' Tepshen corrected. 'You shall not dissuade Brannoc and me from accompanying you.'

'We,' Kedryn allowed, 'but my question stands.'

Gerat turned again to the parchment. '*And I saw he who was raised up go down into the earth where dwell the worms of corruption, and yet they could not overcome him for his purpose was high and I saw the love of his fellows sustained him that he be not forgotten, nor those he loved.*' She looked up, her eyes intense as they fastened on Kedryn's. 'I believe Qualle foresaw this and has shown you the way. I believe that if you enter Drul's Mound again, whether through the agency of the woodsfolks' shamans or through your own enterprise, the way beneath will open to you.'

'And Drul's sword – joined with the talisman – may slay Ashar?'

Kedryn's voice was harsh with urgency now, his eyes burning with purpose.

'Aye,' said Gerat, 'I believe that is the meaning.'

Kedryn nodded thoughtfully. 'But if the Drott refuse help how may we obtain the sword? How may we enter the tomb?'

Gerat looked again to Brannoc, who grinned, a trifle nervously, Kedryn thought, and said, 'Until the summer Gathering the Drott will be scattered throughout the northern reaches of the forest. None will come near the mound before the time of the Gathering, so we have time enough to find the place and start digging.'

'In which venture,' Tepshen added, 'three will make better headway than one.'

'Then,' Kedryn said, 'we had best start out as soon as we may.'

'As soon as your ribs are healed,' said Gerat, firmly. 'What you attempt will need a hale body.'

128

'There is no time to waste,' argued the young man.

'No,' Kedryn was not sure whether Gerat's negative was an agreement or a denial of his implicit decision, 'but nor will you accomplish what you intend with cracked ribs – and they cannot heal on horseback. You must curb your impatience a few days longer, lest it jeopardize all chance of success.'

'The Sister speaks truth,' said Tepshen, and Kedryn sighed his frustration as he nodded.

'So be it.'

'A few more days,' Gerat said consolingly. 'And you will ride the faster for it.'

'Ashrivelle spoke of your travelling to High Fort,' he said. 'Was she right?'

'Aye,' confirmed the Paramount Sister, 'we shall ride my carriage north after you – I shall not enter the Beltrevan for I should slow you down, but mayhap I can still aid you.' Her unlined features became serious and her blue eyes travelled from one man to the other, resting at last on Kedryn again, though her next words, were addressed to them all. 'What you attempt is fraught with danger. I do not pretend to know what you may encounter in the netherworld, though I am confident Ashar will seek to destroy you, or entrap you there. This is not a thing to take lightly: think on it before you decide.'

'There is nothing to ponder – you believe Wynett lives, and that Qualle's words suggest I may overcome the god.'

Kedryn's gaze was no less sombre than the woman's and she ducked her head in agreement, saying simply, 'I do.'

'Then there is no other way of it,' he said calmly. 'As soon you deem me hale enough to ride, I – *we* – depart.'

'May the Lady stand with you,' murmured Gerat; then, in businesslike tone, 'Now let me examine those ribs properly. After, you may rise.'

She brought pots of unguent from a compartment of her satchel and peeled the sheets from Kedryn's body, her fingers deft as she unwound the bandages. He saw that his side was coloured from chest to waistline, an angry red merging into purple edged with ugly yellow. Gerat began to smear her ointments over the damaged flesh, their cool welcoming, seeming to seep into the very fibres of his being so that the dull aching eased and ceased. She covered the bruised area with unguent and then wound fresh bandages around him, swathing him, before producing a small cup and a jar of colourless liquid. He drank without protest, anxious now only to allow the Sister to heal him as swiftly as possible so that he might go out to rescue his love.

That he must attempt to battle a god to achieve that aim was a thought he pushed to the hindmost compartments of his mind, for it was so large a thought he feared it might cloy his purpose with its enormity.

Finally Gerat was satisfied, rising from the bed to nod approvingly and tell him that he might now dress and walk a little in the sun.

When this time he stood upright his head remained clear, and though his side pained him he was able to dress with the help of Tepshen and Brannoc, and flanked by them went out into the corridor.

'I would see Galen,' he remarked, then shook his head, muttering a curse as he realised that concern for Wynett had overcome all other thoughts. 'How many died?' he asked.

'Nineteen,' said Tepshen. 'Seven warriors, the rest oarsmen. Fifteen more were injured.'

Kedryn was chagrined. 'The survivors?'

'Our Tamurin I sent home,' said the kyo. 'The rivermen await a southbound vessel.'

'I must send word to Andurel,' Kedryn murmured. 'And order compensation for the families of those slain.'

Tepshen nodded his agreement, but said, 'Your council will not likely approve our venture.'

'No.' Kedryn smiled tightly, the curving of his lips humourless. 'But by the time word reaches the city we shall be long gone.'

'Galen would make a reliable courier,' suggested Brannoc, 'and he will be confined here for some time yet.'

'Aye.' Kedryn smiled his thanks. 'An excellent suggestion. Now let us find him.'

They found the giant river captain in a room farther down the corridor. He dwarfed the bed, his girth thrusting up the sheets in a mound of sunlit white, his ruddy features less than amiable, though he cheered a little as they entered.

'Kedryn!' he cried. 'I am happy to see you on your feet.'

'And I am sorry to see you laid low,' returned the younger man.

Galen shrugged as best he could, his moon-round face darkening as he grumbled, 'I have never lost a vessel before this.'

'You – nor any other – have ever faced such a hazard,' Kedryn said. 'You were not to blame.'

'And Wynett?' Galen spoke the name lowly, afraid of causing grief.

'Gerat believes she lives.' Kedryn eased gingerly onto a chair. 'Once I am healed we go to seek her.'

Disbelief showed in Galen's eyes and Kedryn explained the nature of Gerat's discourse.

'So,' the riverman murmured when he had finished, 'you ride against a god. Would that I might accompany you.'

'I have another task for you,' Kedryn told him, 'if you agree.'

'Of course,' Galen nodded enthusiastically, wincing as the movement shafted pain through his broken bones. 'Whatever you command.'

'I must send word to Andurel,' Kedryn said. 'To my father. I shall prepare the message before we leave, but I would not have it reach the council in time for mehdri to overtake us with dissuasions.'

Galen nodded again, this time more cautiously, and gently patted the mounded sheets. 'These ribs of mine will be some time knitting,' he smiled, 'or so the good Sisters tell me. If you depart within the next few days I doubt I shall be in fit state to journey south for several more. And I shall needs find passage on a passing craft, so you will be into the Beltrevan before Andurel hears the news.'

'Thank you,' Kedryn smiled.

'It is the least I can do,' said Galen. 'Is there nothing more? Would you have me advise Bedyr to march an army north?'

'No.' Kedryn shook his head. 'An army cannot enter where we go, and my father can serve the Kingdoms better in Andurel.'

Unspoken was the thought that should he not return the council would need to choose another king, and it imposed a moment of sombre silence upon them.

Brannoc ended it as though he, like Kedryn, preferred not to dwell upon the less optimistic possibilities: 'Do the Sisters tend you well?'

'Excellently,' Galen answered, 'save for a most curious denial of a riverman's most cherished nourishment.'

Brannoc nodded sagely. 'Fear not – we are permitted to exercise ourselves a little and might well return with evshan.'

'Were that the case,' said Galen with ponderous solemnity, 'and were a flask or two to find its way to my chamber, I should be forever in your debt.'

Brannoc tapped his nose in a conspiratorial gesture and they rose, leaving the heavily-bandaged riverman alone again.

They went into the ward of the little hospital, where Kedryn spoke with the wounded, reassuring them and promising them reparation for their injuries, then found their way into the town.

Summer touched Tamur now and the air was warm, a refreshing breeze blowing off the Idre, the sun shining golden from a near-cloudless sky, where larks darted and sparrows fluttered busily about the rooftops and streets, vying with raucous gulls for the bounty to be found along the waterfront. Gennyf was tiny in comparison with Andurel, but for Tamur it was a settlement of respectable size, both a fishing port and a jumping-off place for the long trail into the heartland. The road to Caitin Hold began here, cutting west and north from the river to cross the lowlands before rising up the scarp of the central plateau to breast the Geffyn and roll on to Kedryn's home. How long might it be before he saw that place again, he wondered as they strolled towards the river. How long before he saw Wynett again? Unconsciously he inserted a hand beneath his shirt, clutching the talisman that he might again experience that reassuring warmth, confident that so long as he could feel that vibrancy hope remained.

'We shall bring her back,' Tepshen murmured, noticing what he did.

'Aye,' said Kedryn, and forced himself to let go the stone.

They walked on across the square surrounding the hospice and found a road that went down between low houses, their stuccoed walls bright in the sun, to the banks of the Idre. The town was quiet, going about its own business, and the informality, after the ceremoniousness of Andurel, was refreshing as the breeze. Those who recognised Kedryn did little more than murmur brief condolences, characteristic of the Tamurin not wishing to intrude upon what they felt was private grief, and he reached the riverside feeling simultaneously more at home than in long weeks and gripped by a terrible impatience to be gone again.

Warehouses faced the river here and they turned to stroll past the looming buildings to where nets were strung out to dry, tended by fishermen whose boats bobbed on the swell, their tanned faces incurious as they glanced at the trio of strangers. Kedryn paused, staring across the river. It shone a silvery blue, tranquil, without any hint of the terrible menace that had so recently risen from its depths. The far bank was lost in the distance, sky and water seeming to merge in a fusion of dazzling azure, while to north and south the great waterway rolled smoothly to the horizons, implacable as fate. There was no sign of the royal barge and Kedryn turned to ask of his companions what had become of the vessel.

'It sank,' said Tepshen, succinctly.

132

'The beast crippled her,' Brannoc expanded. 'Fortunately for us there were fisherfolk out and they brought the survivors off. Had they not come to our aid likely more would have died.'

Kedryn nodded, saying nothing, his eyes fixed on the water. It occurred to him that none of them had suggested taking a boat north, as if it were tacitly understood that they preferred to travel overland, regarding the Idre as potentially dangerous now.

'Let us find a tavern,' he suggested at last, feeling he had seen as much of the river as he wanted; for a long time.

They moved away from the water, turning back into the town, and found a cheerful-looking alehouse with benches and rough-hewn tables set outside in a small courtyard where apple trees flourished white blossoms above the sun-warmed flagstones.

It felt good to sit in the open air, the breeze soft on their skin, and sip the cool ale the serving wench brought them, though the calm exterior each presented was more facade than reality, for each hid private thoughts of the future and their quietude was that of warriors before battle. They drank the dark beer and requested food, eating platters of cold meats and cheese, with bread, and then more beer, speaking little for there seemed little to say. Finally Kedryn felt he could sit no longer and suggested they deliver Galen his evshan and explore the town, purchasing two flasks that were secreted under tunics as they went back to the hospice.

Galen greeted them with more cheerful aspect when they produced the liquor and they sat a while with the riverman, sipping the fierce brew, until a Sister chased them out, confiscating – much to Galen's distress – the flasks that she declared would be kept for him.

'Sister!' he cried dramatically. 'You do not know rivermen! Do you not know that evshan is the finest cure for whatever ails us? We are not like you land-dwellers – we need that balm to fuel us.'

The Sister turned calm eyes on the moon-faced giant, a small smile twitching the corners of her mouth, and said, 'Mayhap you shall be allowed a mug or two after your evening meal, but for now you must sleep. Drink this instead.'

She poured a draught that she held to his lips, ignoring his stricken countenance. Kedryn and the others watched from the doorway, amused at the grief he pantomimed, his eyes rolling as he allowed the diminutive woman to tilt the mug and swallowed with a grimace of distaste. The Sister nodded approvingly and set the cup aside, watching as Galen's lids grew heavy and his eyes closed. Within

133

seconds stentorian rumbles echoed from the walls and the Sister left the room, fixing the three onlookers with a stern gaze.

'You should have sought our permission before bringing him evshan,' she informed them, rank meaningless here in the domain of the Sorority. 'There is no harm in it, but that great tub is likely to drink himself to a state of agitation from sheer boredom. And should so large a man be drunk, we should find it difficult to control him.'

'He is a difficult man to control at the best of times,' Brannoc said solemnly, 'but it was his majesty's wish we bring him the liquor he requested.'

'There are no kings here,' the Sister retorted brusquely, 'only patients in need of care. Now find yourselves something to do.'

Dutifully, they nodded and made themselves scarce, wandering back into the town.

By late afternoon they had explored Gennyf from the waterfront to the smallholdings that bordered the landward perimeters. A stable was found bearing the insignia of the mehdri on its board and they selected three good mounts that the ostler promised to have in prime condition for their departure, together with tack, and with little else to occupy their attention they made their way to the hospice again.

Gerat awaited them, asking them to enter the room set aside for her use.

'You have had the day to think on it,' she declared. 'What is your decision?'

Tepshen stared at her as though he did not understand her words; Brannoc shrugged and said, 'Our decision was made this morning, Sister.'

'Then I should lief begin the preparation of the cantrips,' she announced. 'Kedryn, your presence is not needed and might prove a distraction – will you leave us alone?'

Kedryn nodded, quitting the room as Gerat drew the shutters closed over the windows. He felt no desire to return to his own chamber, nor any wish for company, and so he avoided the more populous quarters of the hospice and found his way once more to the little courtyard.

Although the sun was close to setting the yard remained warm, the wall against which he rested his back pleasantly heated, the still air heavy with the scent of flowers, vibrant with the buzzing of insects. It reminded him of that similar yard in High Fort, where first he had kissed Wynett, and that memory brought a sharp stab of pain so that he felt his teeth grit as he fought against the image that threatened to form in his mind's eye, of the behemoth rising from the river, the great maw gaping as Wynett plunged between the awful teeth. He clasped the talisman, turning his face to the sky, seeking calm in contact with the stone. In some measure it came, for with the touch he felt that certainty that Wynett did still live, and with that resolve descended again, the determination that he would – no matter what the odds – uncover Drul's sword and enter the netherworld to face Ashar. But it was not the all-consuming certitude he had known before; not that overwhelming resolution that had carried him into battle with Niloc Yarrum, nor the unflinching will that had upheld him as he contested with Taws; not even the conviction that had guided him in forming the council. That he would attempt the quest was beyond doubt, but behind that lay a slippery ambiguity, as if not even Kyrie's talisman, not even the Lady herself, could be certain of the outcome. Before it had not occurred to him that he might lose the struggle, the strength of purpose imparted by the blue stone filling him with unimpeachable optimism, but now there existed an element of doubt, as if the stone, Gerat, Qualle's words, showed him a way, but not the outcome.

This time, he thought, struggling against the terrifying scepticism that threatened to assail him, I face a god. They say I am the Chosen One, the only one who may defeat Ashar, but can I? Can even the Lady protect me in the realms of the dead? Does her power extend so far, or do I go into a place where Ashar holds full sway?

He shook his head as if to disperse the unwelcome misgivings, staring blindly at the sky as he mouthed a silent prayer to the Lady, asking her for strength, his fist tight about the jewel, its contours imprinting on his palm.

There can be no doubt, he told himself. Doubt is the father of despair, and despair is to lose all. I will not lose Wynett! I will go into the netherworld and face Ashar and bring her back!

Or I will die in the attempt.

Slowly he relaxed his grip on the talisman, peace returning, and a grim certainty. His eyes focused again and he saw a brace of hawks wheel high above, planing the air currents, outspread wings bearing them majestically across the heavens. He watched them until they were gone from sight beyond the walls of the courtyard and lowered his gaze to see bright butterflies dancing over the flowerbeds, as delicately regal as the birds, and he smiled, wondering if the Lady sent him a sign.

He did not know, but he felt a return of calm, a benison after that threatened upsurge of panic. He would inevitably suffer reminders of Wynett, for everywhere he was about to go he had gone before with her, but those, he told himself, would be memories from which he would draw strength, for each would recall how much they shared and firm his purpose until he had her back.

He watched the butterflies until shadows fell across the yard and they disappeared into the commencing twilight, and when he looked up he saw that the sun was close to setting, the sky to the east already dark. He rose to his feet, stretching his torso cautiously, gratified to feel an easing of the stiffness, knowing that his damaged side mended apace and that soon he could be gone on his way. The sound of a door opening brought him round, unaware that his hand fell in reflex action to the dirk sheathed on his belt, and he saw Tepshen and Brannoc enter the court.

The kyo seemed unchanged, but his mien was naturally solemn and now Brannoc wore a matching expression, as if he had undergone some experience that imposed an unusual gravity on his cheerful features.

'Is Gerat done with you?' Kedryn asked.

Tepshen shook his head: 'Not yet. A day or two more, she says.'

'You appear . . .' Kedryn studied Brannoc, 'changed.'

The halfbreed grinned, his natural good humour returning, though there remained in his dark eyes a faraway look. 'I believe I am,' he said. 'It was an . . . interesting . . . experience.'

He offered no further explanation and Kedryn turned to Tepshen, who shrugged slightly and said, 'I recall nothing of it. Gerat lit scented candles and we sat in near-darkness. She sang and it was as though her voice mesmerised me. It felt like sleep.'

Brannoc nodded and stretched his arms wide. 'I feel stronger,' he murmured. 'As though some power awakens in me.' He turned slowly around, studying the yard. 'It is as though I see more clearly. I feel . . . confident. Is that what your talisman gives you?'

'Certainty? Aye,' Kedryn nodded, 'a sense of surety, a strength of purpose.'

'It is a fine feeling,' Brannoc said. 'It banishes doubt.'

'But it does not banish hunger,' remarked Tepshen.

'No,' agreed the halfbreed, no less solemnly.

They quit the yard in search of food.

\*

In three more days Gerat's ministrations had healed Kedryn's ribs. The bruising disappeared and he was limber as ever, racked now with impatience. The Paramount Sister declared Tepshen and Brannoc readied, protected to the best of her ability, and they determined to leave Gennyf on the morrow. Kedryn prepared messages for Andurel, an official account of his intentions and more personal letters for his parents; Gerat added her own documents and the package was entrusted to Galen. The riverman was still confined to his bed, saddened at the departure of his friends, but hearty in his blessings on their venture. Gerat declared her intention of following them north to High Fort, accompanied by Ashrivelle, and blessed them in the name of the Lady.

'May she stand beside you and ward you from evil,' she intoned. 'May she strengthen you in your purpose and guide you back safe.'

'Amen,' Kedryn said firmly, echoed by his two companions.

They turned to the waiting horses, anxious to be gone.

Then Ashrivelle came forward, laying a nervous hand on Kedryn's arm, worry in her blue eyes as she gazed at him. He had seen little of her since that morning she had surprised him, and her manner then had confused him, as if there were things she wished to say but dared not utter, and so he had avoided her as much as possible, wary of unwanted complications.

Now she stared at him with a mixture of fear and that adoring look he had seen in Andurel and said, 'May the Lady protect you, Kedryn. I would not lose you.'

He smiled at her, masking his impatience, and said, 'My thanks, Ashrivelle.'

'I . . .' she broke off, then swiftly leant forward to brush her lips against his mouth, blushing as she did so and spinning instantly about to retreat into the group of watching Sisters.

Kedryn swung astride his horse, dismissing her from his thoughts as he raised a hand in farewell and drove his heels against the animal's flanks. The gelding sprang forwards, hooves clattering on the cobbles, and Kedryn led the way out of Gennyf, following the ribbon of the Idre northwards, to High Fort and the destiny that waited beyond.

# Chapter Seven

WYNETT woke bathed in sweat, the claws of nightmare still fastened in her dawning consciousness, tenacious as burgeoning insanity. For long, agonising moments she relived the horror of that twilight attack, seeing the leviathan rise from the darkened surface of the Idre, its vast crimson orbs encompassing her gaze so that she could only stare in horror at the monstrosity unleashed from the peaceful river. She saw it strike at Kedryn, saw Tepshen Lahl and Brannoc flung aside like rag dolls tossed by a wilful child. She saw it heave athwart the barge, timbers and men alike crushed beneath its massive bulk. She heard her sister scream and Kedryn roar in outrage and anger. Saw Galen Sadreth snatch Kedryn up, and the giant riverman smashed down. Saw Kedryn sliding helplessly towards the questing maw, and then that ghastly orifice hurtle closer as she floated, time slowed by terror, towards the fangs. She screamed as those wicked teeth closed about her, putrescent breath assailing her nostrils, her world becoming a place of darkness and fetid stink.

And her own screaming brought her to full wakefulness, and she opened her eyes to sunlight and the scent of flowers.

She realised that she clutched the talisman suspended about her throat and that she was naked in the same moment of disbelief. She blinked and drew a hand across her eyes, wiping away the sweat of fear, unconsciously summoning the disciplines imparted by her training with the Sisterhood to impose calm on her trembling body and agitated mind. Was she alive? Or was this the after life promised the followers of the Lady? Could such be so mundane as to include sunlight and flowers and sweat? She stared down at her body, instinctively drawing a sheet of fine, white linen over her breasts, seeing their heaving ease as she calmed, aware that the cloth clung to her, moist with the outpouring of her panic. She closed her eyes and took several deep breaths, then, fear and curiosity mingling, snapped her lids up and looked about her.

She was in a wide bed of pale, honey-coloured wood, its covers a startling white, set in the centre of a spacious, airy chamber, its wall and high ceiling no less immaculate than the sheets, pure as fresh-fallen snow, seamless and unbroken save by the single tall window through which the sunlight entered. The floor, too, was white, though this the pearly lactescence of fine marble, hued with gold where the sun struck, gleaming like the surface of a calm river in mid-summer. To either side of the bed stood fragile tables fashioned of the same pale wood as the couch, each one supporting an alabaster vase filled with a profusion of flowers that lent the chamber its delicate scent. At first she could see no door, but then, facing her, she made out the shape of a portal so finely cut into the dazzling wall that it was almost invisible. She could see no handle with which to open the door.

Confused, she rested back against the pillows, gathering her wits, the talons of the nightmare loosed now, fading back into her memory as she confronted the reality – or, perhaps more properly, the unreality – of her situation.

She squeezed her fist about the talisman and felt its outline dig hard into her palm: whether dead or alive, it seemed she retained physical awareness. She lowered her feet to the floor, vaguely surprised to find the marbled surface pleasantly warm beneath her bare soles, and drew the sheet demurely about her nudity as she crossed to the window.

The casement consisted of a single pane of the purest glass she had seen, finer than anything in Andurel, set within a frame of what appeared to be wood bleached so white as to be indistinguishable from the surrounding wall. There was no obvious catch, but set into the recess at one side were two hinges, so she pressed on the opposite edge and the entire pane swung smoothly outwards. As if summoned by her action, a warm breeze caressed her face, redolent of new-mown grass and apple trees heavy with fruit, refreshing, vivifying as spring water or a fine, chilled wine. She felt the perspiration evaporate from her brow and lips as she leant out, resting her elbows on the embrasure so that she might study what lay beyond.

It was a tranquil scene. She looked down from the height of a high, smooth wall that appeared as cleanly as those of her chamber onto a sweep of lawn boundaried by a sparkling brook. Colour exploded from the verdancy of the grass where beds of flowers broke the smooth spread, scattered in a pleasantly random manner, busy with the darting of small, bright-plumaged birds. Trees trailed gnarled limbs thick with foliage over the water of the brook, and rushes thrust tall leaves upwards to meet the descending branches. Beyond the freshet the trees grew more densely, though not so close as to preclude pleasantly shaded walking, and from her vantage point she could see that the wood was interspersed with little meadows, shining a lush green amongst the darker hues of the timber. Above, the sky was a translucent blue, soft billows of white cloud floating stately across the azure, the sun a huge, golden disc, so bright it was edged with silver.

She craned out, looking to either side, and saw that the lawns and woodlands appeared to surround the white edifice, which gave no sign of battlements or any other defensive structure.

Leaving the window open, for the breeze was most pleasant, she returned her attention to the room.

It was empty of any furniture save the bed and the two tables, and an examination of the walls revealed no hidden cupboards so, with the sheet still draped about her, she approached the door. Like the window it opened at the touch of her hand.

She stepped through into a chamber larger than the other, the ceiling spanned by heavy beams of light wood, seemingly taken from the same source as the material of the bed and tables. The walls were again white, but the floor was planked to match the rafters and spread with rugs woven in subtle patterns of blue and grey and silver, shades of red, green, hints of gold, white and violet, as though the petals of a myriad flowers were scattered over the boards. Two high windows of the same impossibly perfect glass let in sunlight, shining on a hearth in which stood a gleaming golden fire-box piled with logs. Two high-backed chairs stood before the fire, padded with silk that was gold and grey and silver at the same time, between them a low table of smooth-beaten copper on which sat a black lacquered tray holding a decanter of glittering crystal and a single goblet of intricate workmanship. Between the windows, placed so that sunlight should fall on whoever sat before it, was a dressing table and a stool covered with the same delicate fabric as the chairs, and against the wall, to either side of the door, stood high wardrobes. Past them, set within an arched recess, she saw a tub, seemingly constructed of gold, faucets of the same bright metal fashioned in the shape of gaping fishes' heads. Soap and wash-cloths and towels were set on a separate stand beside a sink of pale blue marble. For an instant she thought to go to it and lave herself of the stickiness left by the nightmare, but then she thought that such action must leave her naked, vulnerable, and she ignored the temptation, turning back to her inspection of the room.

She moved slowly to the centre of the chamber, the carpets a delight beneath her bare feet, soft as wool and smooth as silk, and saw that another door faced the inner portal, this one more clearly marked, for there was a handle of gold and a heavy bolt of the same metal. It was drawn back and she crossed quickly to slide it shut, then returned to the alcove and let the sheet fall as she spun the faucets to fill the tub with clean, fresh water that seemed far too tinglingly real to be part of either a dream or death. She bathed swiftly and dried herself, then moved towards the wardrobes, gasping as she opened the first.

It was filled with a profusion of garments such as she had never seen, not in Andurel or any other place, and the second revealed a like plethora of raiment. Magnificent formal gowns hung there, alongside only slightly more mundane apparel, robes and riding clothes, filmy pantaloons such as the women of Ust-Galich favoured, and tunics, blouses, nightwear, cloaks; more costumes, it seemed, than a woman might wear in one lifetime. There were shelves and interior compartments holding underwear, shoes, boots, jewellery, belts, veils, scarves, an incredible cornucopia of trinkets, all wrought with the same delicate workmanship as everything else she had seen in these two unbelievable rooms.

She selected undergarments and a simple gown of blue silk that fastened with tiny, pearly buttons, cinching it with a belt of silver filigree so intricate it wound cord-smooth about her waist, and drew soft boots of darker blue hide, soft as the gown, on her feet.

She was, she decided, alive, for she could not believe such material luxuries existed in death, and that decision led instantly to fresh confusion.

If she did live, then where was she? The leviathan had attacked with the lights of Gennyf in clear sight, but no such place as this existed in that little riverside town, nor – as best she knew – anywhere within the boundaries of the Three Kingdoms. She had plunged into the maw of the beast, of that she was certain, so wherever she was now, presumably the creature had brought her here. And the creature was remembered from her descent into the underworld – so was this the netherworld?

The thought chilled her, despite the pleasant, summery warmth of the chamber and she set her hand to the talisman again, holding

141

the stone tight as she voiced a prayer to the Lady. The stone tingled against her palm, seeming filled with an internal vibration, as if its crystalline structure trembled with a life of its own, but it offered her no answers and she sensed, without knowing how, a suppression of its powers.

She went to the dressing table, settling on the stool to study her face in the mirror hinged above the table's surface. Blue eyes stared back at her, wide with wonder and more than a little fear, and she quelled incipient panic with the ordinary gesture of brushing her long, wheat-blonde hair. Cosmetics were arrayed before her but she ignored them, setting the silver-handled brush down and rising to take a deep, determined breath as she crossed to the outer door and put her hand on the bolt.

However she had come to this mysterious place no harm had so far been offered. Someone – or, she told herself nervously – some *thing* had undressed her and placed her in the bed, but as best she could tell had done no more than that, leaving her to sleep until she woke.

How long after the attack?

And what of Kedryn?

Was he alive? Or dead?

Was he here?

Before trepidation could overcome her she slid the golden bolt back and opened the door.

On a colonnaded balcony that ran around four sides of an interior courtyard scented with the honeysuckle and magnolia and jasmine that clambered up the supporting pillars of pink-shaded marble, spreading over the loggia to form a delightfully shadowed, sweet-perfumed arbour from which she looked down on an atrium of soft yellow flagstones, a fountain of basalt spilling clear water into the surrounding pool at the centre. Benches of the same dark stone were spaced about the yard, and the three sides she could see were flanked by a stoa so thick with climbing flowers it seemed more arboreal than lithic. She halted, confused afresh by this idyllic scene, her sense of unease mounting. She looked up, seeing a series of balconies climbing towards a square of blue sky, then along the vine-hung gallery to left and right. Three doors stood to her left and three to her right and she identified the source of her immediate confusion, stepping back into the chamber she had just vacated. It was unchanged, sunlight still streaming through the tall windows in the left-hand wall. Impossibly: for when she stepped onto the balcony again she confirmed the chamber was flanked on both sides by the doors, presumably opening into more rooms.

She moved to the door on her left and tried the handle. It turned in her grip, the door swinging open to reveal a chamber similar to the other in its dimensions, but tiled in Keshian fashion, the floor a kaleidoscope of geometrically-patterned ceramics, the walls hung with gay tapestries, the ceiling replaced with a great dome of coloured glass that filled the chamber with shifting patterns of multi-hued light. There were no windows and when she touched the wall that must adjoin the chamber she had just vacated it was solid under her hands. The place was empty and she left it, going along the balcony to the door beyond her own room, amazement furrowing two shallow lines upon her brow.

This room was more like hers, though masculine in its appointments, the floor of sturdy boards polished to a reddish sheen, the chairs before the hearth solid wood, the arms and uprights carved with horse heads. An armoire stood against the left-side wall, and flanking it there were two windows, framed in dark wood, affording a view over the lawns.

Perplexed, she returned to the balcony, leaning out over the rail to confirm that the building did, indeed, extend upwards, rendering the glass dome she had seen, like the windows, impossible.

And started as a deep voice called, 'Be careful, Wynett. I would not see you fall.'

She sprang back, instinctively seeking refuge in the dappled shadows of the gallery, a cry of surprise coming unbidden from her lips, and the same voice said, 'Forgive me, I did not mean to startle you.'

It was a vibrant baritone, as confident as it was apologetic, reassuring and commanding, without any hint of threat. Wynett steeled herself and moved to the edge of the balcony again, looking down.

A man stood beside the fountain, his head tilted back as he stared up at her. He reminded her of Kedryn, for his hair was long and brown, glossy in the sunlight, and he was tall and broad-shouldered, his stance stretching the fine linen shirt he wore tight across a hard-muscled chest. Breeks of soft brown hide fit snug on his legs and the resemblance was completed by the high boots upon his feet. She studied his face, seeing wide-set brown eyes, a firm nose, and a mouth parted in a smile that revealed even white teeth

143

in a powerful jaw. He radiated confidence, the hint of laughter in his eyes oddly comforting.

'Come down,' he invited. 'There is wine, and sweetmeats, and I am sure you must be hungry.'

She had not thought of hunger but now she followed his gesturing hand and felt its pangs as she saw a table spread with a cloth of purest white linen stood within the shadow of an arbour, laid with decanters and goblets and food.

'Please,' he urged. 'Come sit and drink with me.'

Wynett nodded, not knowing what else to do, and walked along the balcony until she found a stairway that seemed almost too delicate to support her weight, spiralling down to the courtyard. It was firm enough as she descended for all that it appeared to have no other supports than the stems of the roses that twined about it on either side and she stepped onto the sun-kissed flagstones to find the man awaiting her arrival. He bowed deeply, presenting a smiling face of ruggedly handsome aspect as he offered her his arm and led her decorously towards the table.

Two chairs were set beside the board and he drew one gallantly back, seeing her seated before settling himself across from her.

'Your choice of gown is delightful,' he murmured, raising a decanter of finest crystal to fill a goblet of equally magnificent design with pale wine. 'My compliments on your taste. And, indeed, your beauty.'

He held a goblet towards her. Wynett ignored it, studying him. Light and shade played across his handsome visage, making his expression difficult to read.

'Who are you?' she asked. 'Where am I?'

Amused brown eyes answered her gaze and her question in silence for a moment, then he set the goblet down before her and chuckled, a sound rich as his speaking voice.

'You need not fear me: I mean you no harm.'

'Who are you?' she repeated.

'Your saviour,' he said simply, and sipped the wine, sighing his approval. 'This is most excellent. Please try a little.'

Wynett shook her head and he shrugged, saying, 'Then at least take food. Are you not hungry after your ordeal?'

She was, she realised, though the empty tugging in her stomach was not entirely to do with need of sustenance, but nonetheless amplified by the enticing odours that rose from the array of dishes set on the linen.

'Who are you?' she said again; doggedly.

'Are names so important?' he countered; casually, as if the question was too trivial for consideration. 'Surely they are more a matter of convenience than of definition?'

'Is definition not important?' she asked. 'I say again: who are you?

'One with only your interests at heart,' he returned. 'But if it will ease your mind, then you may call me Eyrik.'

Laughter sparkled in his eyes, urging her to accept him, to answer it, but she shook her head, a slight, dismissive gesture, and said, 'Where am I . . . Eyrik?'

'Safe,' he said solemnly, selecting a tidbit from the selection on the table and popping it into his mouth.

Wynett continued to stare at him, thinking, almost against her will, that he was the most handsome man she had seen since Kedryn. 'Safe where?' she demanded.

'Here.' A hand waved casually to encompass the courtyard, the balconies, the stoa. 'There is nowhere safer. Nothing may harm you here.'

Wynett frowned, confusion growing apace, fuelled by his prevarication, the mild amusement he evinced, as if they played out some courtly game of words. She set a hand upon the talisman, feeling the stone vibrate, warm in her palm.

'Ah, Kyrie's talisman,' he said mildly. 'That helped save you, too.'

'Too?' asked Wynett.

'I had some small part in it.' He smiled modestly, waving a self-deprecatory hand. 'The beast might have taken you . . . elsewhere . . . had I not intervened.'

'You know of the beast!' It was not a question. 'Then do you know of Kedryn? What was his fate?'

Fear burst anew in her breast as she studied his face, almost afraid to hear the answer. Eyrik returned her gaze, his eyes no longer laughing, but filled now with sincerity.

'I am not sure,' he said. 'I believe he lives, but I cannot know for certain.'

The bewilderment that had filled Wynett as she discovered the impossibilities of the sunlit chambers welled up, fear and frustration taking the form of tears that she fought, telling herself that she must keep her wits about her; losing the struggle.

'Please,' Eyrik said solicitously, 'do not cry. You are safe and I promise that I shall do my utmost to discover Kedryn's fate. If it is within my power to re-unite you, I shall do so – even though I envy him your affection.'

This latter was said softly, as though embarrassment intruded upon his confidence, and Wynett blinked back her tears, clutching at the straw of hope.

'You would do that? *Can* you do that?'

Eyrik shrugged, his expression almost bashful. 'I shall try,' he promised. 'You have my word on it.'

Wynett felt oddly reassured, for there was a palpable sincerity in his tone. 'I am confused,' she declared. 'Will you answer my questions?'

Eyrik moved with graceful speed, a tanned hand reaching out to enfold hers, gently, but still forcefully, so that she found her fingers entrapped as he gazed earnestly into her eyes.

'You must forgive me.' His tone was conciliatory, not quite pleading. 'I am so long accustomed to this place that I forget my manners through familiarity, and there are so few visitors. Of course you are confused! Who would not be? Ask me what you will and I shall answer to the best of my ability.'

He let go her hand, lifting his goblet again as she composed herself, seeking to impress order on the myriad questions that danced through her mind.

'Where am I?' she asked.

'In one of the several worlds beyond those known to men,' he said. 'I cannot explain it better than that. The beast brought you to the netherworld, where you might have wandered with those other unfortunate souls had I not intervened.'

'Then am I dead?'

'No!' He shook his head, smiling again. 'You are most definitely alive. Can you not feel it?'

'I am not sure,' she responded. 'I do not know what death feels like.'

'Not this,' he chuckled.

Wynett nodded. 'How were you able to . . . intervene?'

'I have certain powers,' he told her. 'I am of this world, rather than that one you know, and in consequence am able to exert an influence over those creatures of the limbo.'

'Are you . . .' she clutched the talisman again, cold dread deepening her voice, '. . . Ashar?'

She felt relief as he threw back his head and roared laughter: it was an honest sound.

'Does this seem to you Ashar's domain?' he asked as his laughter abated.

Wynett glanced around her. Sunlight fell on the petals of magnolia blossoms, on cheerful roses, on the water sparkling from the fountain. It glinted on his chestnut hair. She shook her head.

'There is much to understand,' Eyrik said, the laughter still echoing in his voice. 'Mayhap too much for my poor capabilities to explain. Better, I think, that you allow me to show you this place; that you explore it at first hand. That will likely lead to a clearer understanding than I may give.'

If he prevaricated he was a master of the art, for his gaze was direct and clear, empty of guile. 'Then how can you determine Kedryn's fate?' she asked.

'This place is . . . different. And as I said, I have certain powers: I place them at your disposal. I give you my word that I shall do my utmost to ascertain what has become of Kedryn and bring him to you.' He paused, adding gallantly, 'Even though I had sooner see you reign here with me.'

'Reign?' she asked.

'You are, undoubtedly, a queen amongst women,' Eyrik declared, raising his goblet in toast. 'But even a queen must eat. Do you now trust me enough to partake of my board?'

He gestured again at the laden table and this time Wynett nodded, selecting roasted meat. The cut was honeyed, sweet and savoury at the same time. She took more, allowing Eyrik to suggest delicacies, each one proving a culinary masterpiece, mouthwatering and satisfying. She sipped the wine he had poured and found it equally excellent, pleasantly chill. She found herself relaxing.

'I do not know how long it may take me,' he murmured as she ate. 'Can you endure to stay a while?'

'Do I have any choice?' A chill that had nothing to do with the coolness of the excellent wine iced her senses.

'Not really,' Eyrik said amiably, leaning back in his chair, the posture drawing his shirt taut across the muscles of his torso, 'we are governed by laws different to those you know, here.'

Wynett frowned and Eyrik was instantly attentive, leaning forwards, his elbows on the table, his eyes fixed on hers. 'What may seem a long time to you may be no time at all in the outside world. Or vice versa. It may be that Kedryn comes tomorrow, though that may be long weeks for him; or his tomorrow may be your year – I cannot tell.'

'Can you not return me?' she asked, as calmly as she was able.

Eyrik went on smiling as he shook his head. 'That I may not do. I am not omnipotent.'

Wynett found a napkin and dabbed at her mouth. 'What are you then?' she wondered.

'Not so different to you,' he said, a hint of melancholy impinging on his smile. 'You might call me another lost soul.'

'That does not answer my question.'

'No.' He shook his head, his expression serious again. 'It does not, but it is an honest answer. Once I was much as you, but . . . fate . . . decreed that I should come to this place, and that I should not leave it. So here I remain, alone.'

He sighed as if describing a destiny regretted, then brightened again, adding, 'But let us speak of more cheerful matters. Your chambers are to your liking?'

'They are magnificent,' Wynett told him, 'though I cannot understand them.'

Eyrik chuckled, and as his head tilted back she saw that flecks of gold danced in the brown of his eyes, tiny motes of brilliance. 'You will grow accustomed to them,' he assured her. 'At first they are a mite bewildering, but – remember – different laws apply here. Now, if you are replete, shall we explore a little? It would give me great pleasure to show you something of my domain.'

Without awaiting a reply he stood up. Wynett saw that he was taller than Kedryn, and although she could not put a precise age on his unlined features, she guessed that he was older. He extended a hand and she found herself, unthinking, accepting it, allowing him to bring her to her feet. Still holding her hand, he set it on his arm, gallant as any courtier as he led her out from the arbour to the centre of the courtyard. He paused beside the fountain and she saw that fishes swam in the surrounding bowl, sleek shapes of gold and red and blue, circling endlessly in the transluscent liquid that spilled from the upper ornamentation, the sound like faraway cymbals carried on the breeze. Designs were carved in the basalt, but she could not make them out, the combination of shallow indentations and sunlight defeating her scrutiny. Eyrik dabbled a casual hand in the water and the fishes scattered.

'Poor, timid things,' he murmured. 'Come.'

Wynett found further questions rise to her lips, but something about Eyrik's manner forestalled them. He seemed so excited at the prospect of escorting her about his *palace*, which was, she decided, the only word, that they died stillborn in the face of his enthusiasm and the fabulous place was sufficient in itself to dazzle her senses so that she remained mute as he thrust open a door that appeared to be carved from a single slab of green-veined marble and ushered her into the hall beyond.

Windows filled three walls, high, narrow bays terminating in pointed arches, the glass in each of a different colour so that the room was filled with rainbow light. The floor was of the same réséda marble as the door, and like the portal appeared to consist of a single vast slab. A walled fire-pit stood at the centre, above it a silver chimney cone suspended on fragile silver chains from a roof arched with sweeping beams of dark wood. Circular tables inlaid with mosaic patterns stood about the chamber, three high-backed golden chairs placed about each one. Wynett stared at the windows and said softly, 'It cannot be.'

'But it is,' said Eyrik. 'Here *anything* can be.'

Wynett dragged her gaze from the fantastic hall to study his face, framing a question, but he smiled and took her across the floor, the pavonine light transforming him to a thing of pure colour, as if the rainbow irridescence took form and walked, the multi-hued brilliance become substance. It assaulted her senses, dizzying her, for it seemed she walked not on material stuff but on air, moving as did the fishes in the basalt pool of the fountain, and she found herself clinging to his supportive arm, needing that contact lest she float away, or fall, and be trapped forever in that whirling, mind-numbing spectrum.

His arm was strong, hard-tendoned beneath the fine material of his shirt, and he strode across the floor as though the cataclysmic aurora had no affect upon him. Wynett was grateful when he thrust open a second door and brought her into a quieter room, pausing again so that she might survey it. She realised she was breathing hard, as though the mad patterning of the rainbow hall leeched air from her lungs, and she staggered.

'I am sorry.' He was solicitous again, his arm encircling her. 'I forget how dazzling that hall can be.'

Wynett leant against him, imposing calm on her disordered senses, barely aware that he held her, or that she rested against his tall frame. When that realisation dawned upon her she straightened, finding her own feet, and his arm fell from her shoulders.

'Mayhap this is more to your liking?'

She nodded silently. The room was smaller, the floor tiled in blue, the walls white, a simple hearth set to one side, a long settle before it. There was a plain oaken table and twelve high chairs at the centre, as though the chamber were a dining room in some rural hold or rustic ostlery, that impression heightened by the unadorned benches that sat against the walls. Though not by the windows, for whilst they were of plain design, simple casements set within rectangular embrasures, they existed where no windows could, again on three walls that, physically, must be interior because Eyrik led her through the chamber to another door, of solid oak like the furniture, and into yet another room.

Now she found herself staring at a vast, high-vaulted chamber that looked to be carved from living rock. The floor was blue-black stone, smooth and curved upwards into the walls as if the whole space had been scooped from a mountainside. There were no windows, the only illumination coming from long lines of dull golden sconces set in serried ranks along the cavernous abutments, each one containing a thick yellow candle that burned with a clear, bright flame that was reflected back from the rock so that fulvous light filled the place. She could not see the roof, for the upper part of the chamber was lost in shadow, though it occurred to her that it must be higher than the stairway she had descended from the balcony, and that each of the rooms was higher than those she had occupied and so must – *should* – extend beyond the upper levels. The concept defied logical explanation, the dimensions of this unreal place seeming ungoverned by physical limitations, and she felt her head reel afresh, assailed by the sheer impossibilities she experienced.

She felt Eyrik's hand upon her elbow, urging her forwards, and allowed him to steer her into the weird, candle-lit sanctum.

It was empty of any furniture save a single massy seat, more throne than chair, that bulked from the floor towards the farther end. Like the walls, it appeared to be one fabric with the cavernous chamber, raised on three broad steps, seamless, the back high, the arms ponderous. Unlike the walls and floor, however, it seemed to reflect no light, for whilst it was of that same blue-black stone it appeared to sit in a darkness of its own, ominous in its huge solidity. Eyrik paused before it, but when Wynett offered no comment, nor made any move towards it, he led her on, past, to a door cut so artfully into the rock that it was invisible until he swung it open.

Wynett looked through to sunlight, seeing the lawns spread before her, and wondered why none of that light entered the chamber. Eyrik bowed, beckoning her on and she passed thankfully into the open air, relieved to find herself once more surrounded by comprehensible sights, the apparent normality of the vista reassuring.

The grass was springy beneath her feet, the sun warm on her face, a breeze refreshing as it rustled her hair. She heard birds singing and the brook she had seen babbling, she could smell apple blossom and when she looked up the sky was a perfect blue, great swells of white cloud spread majestically along the horizon.

'Shall we walk?' Eyrik asked. 'A little of this place can, I know, be daunting.'

'Aye,' Wynett agreed, answering both his question and his statement.

'You will grow accustomed to it,' he smiled. Then added quickly, 'Until Kedryn comes.'

'Are you?' she enquired, confidence returning a little now that she stood in surroundings she could understand.

'Oh, I have had ample time to grow familiar with all this strangeness,' he said cheerfully, offering his arm again.

Wynett ignored it, which seemed not to offend him, for he simply proceeded across the lawns towards the stream, smiling broadly.

'How long have you been here?' she asked.

'I forget,' he said, shrugging. 'Mayhap forever. Time has little meaning here, remember. It is no more important than space, and you have seen how limitless that is.'

'Aye,' Wynett nodded, thinking of the rooms. 'Are you alone?'

'Not now.' He moved in front of her, his smile wide and white, laughter in his eyes as he exaggerated a bow. 'Now that you are here I have all the company a man could want.'

His smile, his manner, something in his look, rendered logical thought difficult. Wynett experienced a sensation similar to that feeling of helpless floating, her concentration evaporating. She steeled herself to retain the thread of her thoughts. '*Are* you a man?' she wondered.

'What else do you think me?' he rejoined, something of his earlier bantering manner returning.

'I am not sure,' she said honestly.

'Observe me,' he urged. 'Do I not speak as a man? Walk as a man? Do I not have arms and legs, a head, a torso? Other parts? Would you prick me to see if red blood flows in my veins?'

'I do not wish to see your blood,' she said, somewhat nervously.

Eyrik laughed, shaking his head, and took her hand, drawing her towards the stream. 'Wynett, Wynett, you must learn to trust me. Did I not save you from the leviathan? Have I not promised to do my utmost to re-unite you with Kedryn?'

'You have so promised,' she allowed.

'Then believe me,' he said earnestly. 'And believe *in* me. All will become clear as time passes.'

Wynett would have spoken more but they had reached the stream and Eyrik indicated the stepping stones that spanned the burbling freshet, saying, 'Be careful, the water is deeper than it seems.'

She looked down, seeing what appeared no more than a pleasant brook, the bottom sandy, streamered with green weeds, the flitting silver shapes of fishes coursing the race.

'Shall I carry you across?' he asked, his voice innocent.

'Thank you, no.' Wynett shook her head, feeling an abrupt surge of alarm at the prospect of being held in those solid arms. 'I believe I may safely cross unaided.'

Eyrik nodded, looking mildly disappointed, and stepped casually onto the first stone. He halted at the centre, waiting for her as if afraid she might falter and fall. Wynett lifted her skirts and set foot on the first slab. It was wide, almost a rectangle, and flat. She could see where it met the sand of the stream bed, yet when she transferred her weight, she felt it move beneath her. It was less a sensation of tilting than of internal movement, as if the stone itself gave way under her. The thought flashed through her mind that the experience of the weird chambers had distorted her sense of balance and she moved swiftly to the second stone. That appeared smaller than the first, though she would have sworn it was the same size when first she saw it, and she stepped hurriedly to the third. That, too, felt less solid than stone should, and as she moved on she experienced a strange sensation of shrinking, of dwindling, for the brook seemed wider, the stones more numerous, stretching before her as though they crossed not a narrow stream, but a small river, which, when she glanced down, did, indeed, appear deeper than it had at first seemed. Dizziness made her halt, arms outstretched as she fought to hold her balance, and she felt a flush of embarrassment and irritation at her weakness.

Then Eyrik had her hand and the brook was no more than that: a rivulet, shallow and little more than a few steps across. She felt his fingers close about hers and the touch seemed to imbue her with strength, clearing her head. The stepping stones became solid again and she allowed him to lead her to the far bank, retrieving her hand as she stared back over the water. It shone silvery blue in the sun, eddies swirling about the bulk of the stones, the bottom knee-deep at best.

'Your gown is wet.'

Eyrik's voice was solicitous and Wynett glanced down, seeing the hem of her skirt banded with darkness where it had fallen into the water as she struggled to maintain her balance.

'No matter,' she murmured, 'it will dry quickly enough.'

'If you are sure?' He was all courteous concern and when she nodded and he took her elbow again she found it impossible to remove her arm from his grip. It was not that he clasped her, though there was, undoubtedly, strength in his fingers, but something in his look and the tone of his voice, as if refusal of contact would hurt and offend, that sapped her will to break the contact. It seemed, anyway, innocent enough and she allowed him to hold her lightly, taking her into the woodland.

There was a path, a band of grass trod short, winding between overhanging trees, moving to left and right so that it was never possible to see more than a few paces ahead, sunlit and picture pretty. Light filtered through the trees to either side, falling in bands striated with blue shadows, dappling the path. Birds sang and insects buzzed and as Wynett looked about she saw a profusion of timber akin to the great forest of the Beltrevan. Oak and ash and birch grew alongside beech and larch, willows edged the stream and tall sycamores thrust towards the sky, here and there sombre pines standing stately, and hawthorn, elderberry, chestnut, foxgloves, harebells and violets growing in the shade: a bosky extravagance that paid no heed to nature's laws. Within a few steps the stream was out of sight and within a few more Wynett felt lost. The path seemed to curve gently, but turns that should, she was certain, have brought them back upon it revealed instead fresh avenues into the wood.

They came to a meadow bright with buttercups, cowslips and red poppies, and she saw rabbits scutter to the cover of a bramble thicket on the farther side; she glanced at the sky, for the presence of the conies suggested a latening of the hour. The sun, however, remained high, seeming to have moved little, if at all, since she had first looked from her bedroom window. It filled the meadow with warm, golden light in which butterflies drifted on fragile wings and fat yellow-banded bees dusted heavy with pollen moved busily from flower to flower.

'Is it not lovely?' asked Eyrik, his voice soft, as though he were afraid to spoil the perfection of the scene with intrusive sound.

'Aye, it is,' Wynett agreed.

He led her to the centre of the meadow, their passage raising clouds of pollen that hung dusty on the still air, bees and butterflies winging from their path, and paused facing the sandy bank pocked with the entrances of burrows. There was a stillness at the centre, as if the wood held his sylvan breath, and Eyrik let go her arm to pluck a flower, presenting the bloom.

Wynett smiled a trifle doubtfully as she accepted the offering; Eyrik smiled and said, 'It matches your eyes.'

She studied the blossom and saw that it was a cornflower, though such would not normally grow in this location.

'Come.' He took her elbow again, bringing her across the meadow to the bank, up which he insisted on helping her even though it was by no means steep. Yet when they reached the top and paused again within the circle of seven pine trees she found she could look back and see the stream and the white bulk of the palace, shimmering as if viewed through heat haze and distance. In all other directions the wood stretched, unbroken save by the little meadows, the variegated shades of green becoming blue as wood and sky merged on the horizons. It seemed large as the Beltrevan.

'How far does this extend?' she asked, thinking that she did little but ply him with questions, and knowing that there were many more to come.

'Far,' he answered vaguely.

'Have you not explored it?'

He shook his head, smiling. 'Not all of it. There is so much, and it will always be here.'

She turned to look up at his face, seeing in his gold-flecked eyes a look as distant as the horizon. His head was cocked slightly to the side, as though he listened for something, attuning his ear to the breeze that would carry sound. She opened her mouth to frame a fresh question, but he caught the movement from the corner of his eye and forestalled her.

'Look.' She followed his extended hand and saw three hawks swoop from the blue, low over the treetops, banking and disappearing amongst the timber. He waited a while as if expecting the birds to reappear, but when they did not he turned, gesturing to the far incline of the ridge. 'Shall we return now?'

Wynett nodded and they descended the slope into a stand of slender, silvery birches. Before the path curved she turned back, glancing at the bank, and saw the seven pines standing like sentinels atop a mound little more than twice a man's height. A cony emerged from a burrow, standing on its hind legs, its long ears erect, its eyes fastened on her as if it studied her with more than animal intelligence. Then the path turned into the birches and the creature was hidden, the mound and the bramble thicket and the pines all lost behind the slim trunks.

She began to count the twists and turns, convinced that the trail wound like a maze through the wood, as inexplicable as the dimensions of the building, finding a leftward curve, or a swing to the right, where her senses told her it must recross itself, wondering how far into the timber they had penetrated, but unable to guage time because the sun appeared unmoving, shining resolutely through the overlaying latticework of branches. Perhaps, she thought, no night fell on this strange place; or perhaps it fell when Eyrik decreed it should. She was about to enquire when the path straightened and she saw the willows that marked its meeting with the brook.

They emerged at the stepping stones and Wynett frowned, convinced, for all the meanderings, that their way must have taken them some distance from the ford. She looked across the brook and saw the wall of the palace, apparently from the same vantage point.

'May I?'

She turned to find Eyrik offering his hand and this time took it without argument, allowing him to lead her over the stones, which remained solid.

'It is a wondrous place,' he remarked as they reached the bank and began to walk across the lawn, 'but a little confusing until you are accustomed to its nature.'

Wynett assumed that he spoke of the wood and wondered if it was a warning she heard. 'An easy place in which to lose yourself,' she replied.

'Aye.' Eyrik nodded solemnly. 'You are, of course, free to come and go as you please, but for the moment I suggest you rely on my guidance.'

'I shall,' she said, the agreement eliciting a satisfied smile.

There was an indefinable element in his expression and without knowing exactly what it was, or why it should have such an effect, she felt a flash of irritation. She became aware that she still held the flower he had given her and let it fall from her grasp. If Eyrik noticed

155

he said nothing, merely continuing to smile as he took her across the grass towards the looming white wall.

She assumed they approached the same door from which they had come, but when he swung the portal open she saw, not entirely to her surprise, and somewhat to her relief, that the chamber beyond was not that vaulted, candle-lit hall, but another, low-ceilinged and wider than it was long. Nor was she surprised to find when he closed the door that windows marched along the wall where none had shown outside. She looked through them and saw the sun was westering – if compass points had any meaning in this place – settling close to the horizon, the woodland already shadowy, the gallery-like chamber lit with mellow, red-gold light. Plush benches stood across from the windows, as if placed to catch the sunset, interspersed with alcoves in which stood slim silver pedestals, each one supporting a vase of dark green glass filled with flowers. The floor was of tessellated marble, pink and gold that emphasised the radiance of the setting sun, and the walls seemed imbued with a coral tint.

'It is very pretty,' Eyrik murmured absently, 'but there are finer views I shall show you.'

Wynett offered no comment and followed him silently across the mosaic floor to a door of pink-hued wood.

This opened on the smallest room she had seen since awakening, and the only one to possess neither windows or any visible source of light. At first she did not realise that, for the chamber was filled with a shifting, shimmering blue luminescence that made her think of mountain pools, or the calmer reaches of the Idre, and it was only when she glanced about her that she saw the unbroken walls and noticed that no candles or flambeaux were present. Eyrik motioned her forwards and she stepped onto a floor of the same aquamarine hue as the walls and the low ceiling, feeling as if she moved into breathable water, her steps somehow slowed, graceful as the languid movements of a cruising fish. It was less disconcerting than the riot of colour that filled the rainbow room, but still confusing to the senses, tricking the eyes so that distance became hard to judge and she found herself at first holding her breath.

There was no furniture, nor any form of decoration, every surface smooth. Or so it seemed until Eyrik halted, staring down, and she saw that he stood beside a circular pool of transluscent water. This seemed to be the source of the chamber's illumination for the light was brighter about its confines and when she looked at it, it seemed to hold her gaze, the flawless surface hypnotic in its liquid purity.

It was impossible to judge the depth: there was no bottom visible despite the blue clarity, nor any darkening to suggest the abyss of a well.

Eyrik grunted wordlessly, as though he saw something there that pleased him, and turned towards Wynett.

'What do you see?'

Her eyes were fixed on the surface; it was impossible to shift her stare and she did not turn to answer him.

'What do you see?' he repeated, his tone a fraction more demanding, edged with an urgency she did not recognise, so intent was her concentration.

The pool seemed to shift, though she saw no movement on its surface or in its depths, and an image took gradual shape. At first it was unclear, more an alteration in the nature of the light than any distinct form, but then it rippled, though still no movement showed physically, and she gasped as she saw Kedryn.

He was seated on a dun horse, lathered with the effort of swift passage, galloping, his brown hair flung in streamers back from a visage planed harsh with urgency, his eyes narrowed as if in concentration, or against a wind. He wore a plain riding tunic and a sword was slung across his back, his jaw set in a determined line. She could not be certain, but it seemed two others flanked him, or pursued him, for she had the impression two other horses raced close behind. Where, on what trail, she could not tell, nor at what hour of the day they rode, but the sight filled her with surging hope, for it convinced her he lived – had survived the leviathan and the sinking of the barge both.

'What do you see?' Eyrik demanded again, his hand clutching her shoulder, his grip tightening.

'I see Kedryn,' she whispered. 'Praise the Lady! I see Kedryn!'

Eyrik's hand left her shoulder and the image faded, the pool becoming once more clear water. Wynett stared at the blue-silver disc, willing the vision to return, but it did not and she turned slowly to face her host.

'He lives,' she said slowly. 'I saw him, and that must surely mean he lives.'

A question hung on the sentence and Eyrik nodded, his lips curving in a smile. 'Aye, it means he lives. What was he doing?'

'Riding,' Wynett answered. 'Galloping. I think there were two others with him. Or chasing him – I could not be sure. I could not see where they rode.'

'Doubtless in search of you,' said Eyrik. 'If he lives, will he not seek you? I should.'

Wynett ignored the gallantry, consumed by the knowledge that her love was alive. She nodded.

'Then,' said Eyrik, his voice calm, 'we need only wait.'

'Can you not guide him?' asked Wynett.

Eyrik grew thoughtful, then smiled enigmatically. 'Mayhap,' he murmured. 'I shall do what I can.'

'Can you show me more?' Wynett gestured at the pool.

Eyrik shook his head, his expression becoming doleful. 'The pool shows what it shows – I do not command it or control it. But now you have seen it, you may come back; and if it has anything to show you, it will.'

Wynett cast a longing glance at the radiant circle, but no further images formed and she sighed.

'Let us eat,' Eyrik suggested abruptly. 'Eat and sleep, and mayhap on the morrow we shall see more.'

Reluctantly, Wynett allowed him to lead her from the strange blue-lit chamber, finding herself once again in the atrium, across which Eyrik led her to a room set ready for dinner.

# Chapter Eight

FROM the watchtower surmounting High Fort's southern gate
Barris Edon had a clear view of the Kingdomside approaches. The
glacis running up to the massive wooden portals was surrounded
on three sides by cleared ground, levelled and regularly burnt on
the standing orders of Chatelain Rycol, affording an open killing
ground for catapults and archers should the mighty fortress ever
face siegement from the south. Such was unthinkable, of course,
for the land Edon surveyed was Tamur and whatever rumours had
come north up the Idre since the defeat of the Horde, the soldier
could not conceive of his countrymen turning on the stronghold, or
allowing any hostile force access. Nonetheless, Rycol was a stern
taskmaster and maintained constant vigilance on all approaches, so
the lookout kept his eyes peeled, and when he saw the three dusty
riders quit the town that sprawled alongside the river and urge
horses obviously close to exhaustion towards the fort he shouted
a warning to his captain, alerting the bowmen patrolling the wall.

That wall loomed grey in the afternoon sun as Kedryn and his two
companions pushed their lathered horses onwards to the great stone
redoubt. The river canyon was already darkening into twilight, the
massive buttress of the western Lozins overshadowing the bastion so
that only the ramparts still caught the westering light, the waterway
spilling through the vast cleft a dark ribbon, secretive and, after the
disaster at Geffyn, menacing. Sufficient of the settlements along
the Idre road held mehdri remount stations that Kedryn, using his
authority as king, had been able to command fresh horses at regular
intervals as he hurried north. Even so, he pushed the animals to the
limits of their strength in his desperate haste, and had Tepshen Lahl
not forced him to slow their headlong pace he might have found
himself walking, a dead horse behind him. He was gripped with
fearful urgency, anxious to reach the Beltrevan as swiftly as possible
and seek out Drul's Mound, to obtain the sword that seemed his only
hope of saving Wynett, and could not think beyond that imperative,

his customary thoughtfulness lost to the goad of impatience. His damaged ribs were fully healed, as were the injuries sustained by Tepshen and Brannoc, and the physical discomfort of the long ride was ignored as they pressed towards their goal.

He allowed his weary animal to slow as the hooves clattered on the flags of the glacis and archers turned nocked bows towards him, rising in the stirrups to announce his identity and demand entrance, reining in as the sally port opened and a captain emerged, flanked by a squad of armoured warriors, to study the travel-stained trio warily.

'I am Kedryn Caitin; I want Lord Rycol.'

He ignored protocol, leaning forwards in his saddle to thrust the medallion of his office at the startled captain, who gasped, saluting, and said, 'I did not recognise you, Sire.'

'No matter.' Kedryn essayed a weary smile, heeling his mount to a walk even as the officer shouted for the gate to be opened and for a serjeant to summon Rycol.

Kedryn rode into the shadowed courtyard and halted. Dismounting seemed less a process of swinging clear of the saddle than of ungluing himself, and when his feet touched the cobbles he swayed, his legs rubbery. He shook his head, grunting as he stretched, and passed the reins to a startled soldier, requesting the exhausted horse be rubbed down and settled in the fort's stables, and without further delay began to walk unsteadily towards the inner buildings. Tepshen and Brannoc followed him, no less marked by their hours in the saddle, and they reached the door granting ingress to the citadel's living quarters before the chatelain appeared. He met them as they crossed a hall, his lean features registering shock as he hurried towards them.

'Kedryn! Sire . . . What is amiss?'

Kedryn extended a hand that Rycol took and said, 'Kedryn will suffice, Rycol. We need baths and food and fresh mounts.'

'Of course.' Rycol issued orders, studying the three with troubled eyes. 'And soft beds by the look of you.'

For a moment Kedryn contemplated pressing on without delay, but common sense prevailed and he nodded gratefully. 'And beds, my friend. For one night, at least.'

Rycol nodded and brought them across the hall to a stairway, curbing his curiosity as he led them upwards to his private chambers. Within the oak panelled room his wife, the Lady Marga, rose from her sampler, her rosy cheeks paling in concern as she saw their determined faces and the weary slump of their shoulders.

'Kedryn, what is wrong?' She motioned the two great brindle hounds grumbling beside the empty hearth to silence as she came towards the trio, taking Kedryn's hand with motherly solicitude. 'We had thought you bound for Estrevan.'

'We were.' Kedryn allowed her to lead him to a chair, easing down with a wince of discomfort, his voice bitter as he continued, 'We were attacked. Wynett is taken.'

'What?' Rycol was instantly alert, the barked question eliciting a fresh rumbling from the hounds. 'By whom?'

'Not whom – what,' Kedryn said, and told them of the leviathan's attack and the taking of his wife.

Rycol gasped at the telling, mouthing a curse as he turned to Marga and said, 'The thing I thought I saw. Do you remember?'

Marga nodded, her eyes troubled, and Rycol explained the strange floodtide they had witnessed and the shape he discerned moving south down the Idre. 'So it was long-planned,' Kedryn murmured. 'Ashar thinks ahead.'

'And will doubtless anticipate your coming,' Rycol warned. 'If only I had trusted my own eyes better and sent word.'

'You could not know and I shall not be defenceless,' Kedryn declared, explaining how Gerat had met them at Geffyn and told them of Qualle's writings, describing Brannoc's story of Drul's sword.

Rycol turned to the halfbreed, his grey eyes narrow. 'I have heard that tale, but I never gave it much credence. Do you truly believe it?'

Brannoc nodded, his grin a shadow of its former self, and eased his buttocks to a more comfortable position. 'As much as any legend. More than many. My aching bones are testament to my belief.'

'It appears to conform with Gerat's interpretation of Qualle's writings,' said Kedryn. 'And it is all I have.'

Marga shook her head, in apprehension rather than disbelief, and filled cups with evshan, distributing the liquor as her husband looked to Tepshen Lahl, a question in his eyes.

The kyo ducked his head once, grimly, and said, 'The beast was not of this world.'

'But to attempt what you plan ...' Rycol paused, stroking his grizzled moustache.

'Would you have me abandon Wynett?' Kedryn fixed the chatelain with fierce eyes and Rycol shook his head in negation. 'Then you must agree there is no other choice to it.'

Rycol studied the younger man, seeing a face grown older than the youthful demeanour he remembered, seeing the agony of loss in the tired brown eyes, and chose his words with care.

'You are the king now. As king do you deem it wise to risk your life in this way?'

Kedryn sighed and took a long draft of evshan, coughing as the fierce spirit filled his belly with fire. 'There is a council established,' he explained, outlining the measures he had instituted before quitting Andurel. 'The Kingdoms will not fall apart in my absence. *And I will not forsake Wynett!*' He modified his tone, smiling wearily as he added, 'I cannot abandon her, my friend. Further, there is the matter of Qualle's prophecy.'

Rycol frowned doubtfully. 'Can that be trusted?'

'The Paramount Sister of Estrevan believes it can,' said Kedryn. 'She broke with all precedence to bring me word – would you gainsay her?'

'No.' Rycol shook his head. 'But to venture into the Beltrevan with only two companions . . . at least take an escort.'

'No.' It was Kedryn's turn to shake his head, the movement sending sharp darts of pain down his back. 'Remember our treaties with the woodsfolk. Mayhap it is Ashar's design to foment fresh trouble by luring us into such a move. Do you think the passage of so large a body of armed men would go unnoticed? Do you think the tribes would accept it?'

'I would not see you slain by the Drott,' Rycol argued.

'And I would not see another war started,' said Kedryn.

'The Drott are scattered,' said Brannoc. 'They will not come together until the summer Gathering. We have enough time. Just.'

'Just,' murmured Rycol, his tone dubious. 'Do you think you can reach Drul's Mound and disinter this blade before they find you?'

Brannoc shrugged. Kedryn said, 'Aye, I do.'

'What if they do find you there?' Rycol insisted. 'What then?'

'Then likely they will kill us,' replied Kedryn, his voice flat.

Rycol stared at him, then turned again to Tepshen. 'Do you counsel this, old friend?'

Had he hoped to find support in that quarter he was doomed to disappointment, for the easterner's jet gaze met the chatelain's grey stare, Tepshen's features impassive as he said, 'I go where Kedryn goes.'

'I cannot dissuade you.'

It was not a question, though Kedryn answered it with a humourless smile and a dismissive movement of his head.

Rycol sighed. 'Then at least rest here a day or two.'

'A night,' Kedryn amended. 'We depart on the morrow.'

Rycol raised his hands helplessly. 'Were you not the king I should consider holding you, albeit against your will – you all three look exhausted.'

'But I *am* the king,' Kedryn responded, a hint of humour in his voice, 'and it is my wish that we enter the Beltrevan as swiftly as we may.'

'So be it,' Rycol allowed. 'There will be fresh mounts ready for you.'

'And two packhorses,' Brannoc said. 'With supplies. Food for us and grain for the animals – foraging will slow us.'

'And two packhorses,' Rycol agreed.

'And clean clothes.' Marga gestured at their stained garments. 'I shall see fresh outfits set ready for you.'

'My thanks,' said Kedryn. 'And now may we bathe?'

He did not wait for an answer, but rose stiffly, bowing awkwardly to his hostess as her husband ushered him to the door and escorted them to the bath house.

He had not realised how weary he was until he sank into the hot water, Tepshen and Brannoc slipping with grateful sighs into the pool beside him, all three resting chin-deep in the great tub as the warmth eased muscles strained by the long, hard ride, returning flexibility to joints set near-solid from the long hours in the saddle.

They lay for a long time without speaking, content merely to float there until Kedryn rose and moved to the second pool, where they scrubbed themselves and sluiced off the grime beneath a jet of cold water. Masseurs completed the restorative process, and when they emerged they found the clothing promised by Marga waiting for them together with a Sister Hospitaller who insisted on examining them and applying ointments to their sorer parts before handing them packages of herbs that she explained would revivify them along the way.

By then they were almost too sleepy to eat, and only the determination to fuel their bodies for the task ahead sat them at the table to consume the meal prepared. What little conversation took place was desultory and immediately they had satisfied their hunger they found their beds.

Kedryn's was in the chamber he had occupied on his previous visits to the fort, as familiar by now as his quarters in Caitin Hold, and he was quickly stretched on the hard mattress; even faster asleep. His last conscious thought was that the talisman he clutched, as he had clutched it every night since departing Geffyn, still vibrated with that faint, almost intangible life that assured him Wynett still survived.

He dreamt of her, a confused jumble of impressions, seeing her beloved face smiling, believing her beside him in the bed, then seeing her again plunge towards the jaws of the behemoth, almost waking then, but falling back into welcome slumber as his tired body imposed its own discipline on his troubled mind. When finally he came to wakefulness the sun limned a rectangle of brightness on the stone floor of the room and he climbed from the bed with a curse on his lips because he saw that the hour was long past dawn. Doubtless Rycol's concern had prompted the chatelain to leave him abed, and his own exhaustion had done the rest. He glanced from the window, seeing the sun some distance above the eastern rim of the river canyon and crossed to the washstand to lave himself before tugging on his gear and belting his sword about his waist. Then, inflamed once more with urgency, he hurried to the dining hall.

Rycol sat there with Tepshen at his side, the two men deep in conversation that ended as Kedryn joined them.

'I deemed it wise to let you sleep,' the chatelain explained unapologetically. 'Sister Onya suggested it.'

'Sister Onya?' Kedryn helped himself to bread.

'She replaced Wynett,' Rycol expanded. 'It was she who examined you last night, and announced you near spent.'

Kedryn began to protest, but Tepshen motioned him to silence and said, 'We were all close to exhaustion, and we shall need our wits about us for what lies ahead.'

Despite his impatience, Kedryn recognised the sense of his comrade's admonishment and mumbled an apology.

Brannoc entered the hall then, his customary cheerfulness regained with the night's sound sleep, his appetite, too, for he set to eating with a will, urging Kedryn to do the same.

'We ride hard and fast after today,' he said around a mouthful of coddled egg, 'and likely eat cold food. Make the most of this excellent fare while you can.'

Kedryn nodded his agreement, but still found his appetite diminished by fear for Wynett. What he did eat was swallowed without

164

enjoyment, taken for the pure need of physical sustenance, and he pushed his plate away before Brannoc declared himself replete.

'May we depart now?' he demanded as the halfbreed sighed his contentment, fastidiously wiping his mouth.

'Aye.' Brannoc rose unabashed by Kedryn's ill-concealed impatience and bowed in Rycol's direction. 'My thanks for your hospitality, Lord Rycol.'

The chatelain smiled thinly. Not very long ago he had advocated hanging Brannoc, and whilst the halfbreed had since proven himself a trusted companion, earning Rycol's respect, the grey-haired keeper of High Fort remained a trifle uncomfortable in the presence of the former wolfshead. 'I am honoured by your presence,' he murmured automatically, gesturing in the direction of the door. 'Your mounts await you.'

They followed him from the dining hall and through the winding corridors to the stableyard. Five horses stood ready. Three were stallions, two black, one grey, their deep chests and long legs attesting the cross-breeding of Tamurin and Keshi stock, fleet of foot and hardy, willing animals that could endure hardship without flagging, able to maintain a swift pace and then produce a burst of speed when called upon. The others were geldings, their lines more akin to the sturdy hill ponies of Tamur than the sleek chargers of Kesh. They were laden with supplies. Brannoc examined them all with a professional eye, admiration writ clear on his dark features.

'They are the best I have,' Rycol declared. 'And the packs are filled with journey fare and grain.'

'They are superb,' nodded Brannoc.

'I added bows.' Rycol gestured at the hide-wrapped packages slung beside each saddle. 'And a score of arrows apiece. Shovels and picks, also, if you are to excavate the Mound.'

'My thanks,' Kedryn said, taking the older man's hand. 'You do us proud.'

Rycol stared at him, sadness in his stern eyes, and more than a little pride. 'I do no more than my duty,' he murmured. 'Wynett was – *is* – close to my heart, and I pray that the Lady ward you and guide you that you return her safe.'

Kedryn nodded and swung astride one of the blacks. Tepshen took the second and Brannoc the grey, securing the long halter rope of the pack animals to his saddlehorn, and with Rycol pacing them they rode through High Fort to the north gate.

The Lady Marga waited for them here, resolutely concealing her anxiety as she bade them farewell and Ladyspeed.

'Send word to Andurel,' was Kedryn's last request.

'I will,' Rycol promised, raising a hand in salute as the postern was swung open and the three men rode out.

'We enter Ashar's domain,' Brannoc announced as the hooves drummed on the hard stone of the Beltrevan road, his left hand shaping the three-fingered warding gesturing.

'On the Lady's business,' Kedryn responded, his voice grim.

'I have never ridden against a god before,' said the halfbreed.

Tepshen Lahl smiled briefly and said nothing.

*

The chamber to which Eyrik escorted Wynett was intimate. Scented candles burned in sconces on the white stone walls and a spray of wild flowers occupied the centre of a table set for dinner with silver platters and exquisite crystal goblets. Two windows looked out onto the courtyard, the perspective reassuringly normal after the incongruities of the other rooms she had seen, though two more distorted spatial dimensions by overlooking the lawns, now darkening into night. Two chairs faced one another across the table and Eyrik brought Wynett to the one facing inwards, as though aware of the sensory confusion wrought by the physical impossibilities of the fabulous palace. He held her chair until she was seated and settled himself on the far side, reaching across to fill her goblet with ruby wine.

'I trust it is to your liking,' he smiled as he filled his own glass.

Wynett raised the goblet to her lips, finding the vintage excellent, drinking deep to quell the turmoil aroused by the image of Kedryn the strange pool had revealed.

'How can it be?' she murmured, almost to herself, though Eyrik answered with a smile and a shrug.

'The pool? Who knows? Different rules govern here.'

'Did I truly see him?' she wondered.

'Aye, truly,' confirmed her enigmatic host. 'The pool does not lie.'

He gestured at the roast steaming fragrantly on a gleaming platter, surrounded by succulent vegetables. 'May I help you to meat? You must surely be hungry.'

Wynett was not sure. She felt sure of hardly anything, save that she was alive – though not of how, or where – but Eyrik took her silence as agreement and proceeded to carve the meat, forking thick slices onto her plate, adding vegetables, and she began to eat more from habit than want of food. Nonetheless, it was delicious and the first mouthful aroused her appetite, eliciting a pleased smile from the brown-haired man.

'It is good, is it not?' he enquired just as she was about to press him with further questions, and she smiled faintly, nodding, 'It is very good.'

'I am delighted,' he said enthusiastically. 'I would have your sojourn here be as pleasant as possible.'

Wynett studied his face, wondering, and he smiled, dabbing at his lips with a spotless napkin before raising his goblet again and declaring, 'To your re-unification.'

It seemed a somewhat strange toast, but his expression was without guile and his smile appeared genuine: she lifted her own goblet and drank in response.

'Are there not servants?' she asked as she set the glass down.

'Do you require aught else?'

His tone was solicitous and Wynett shook her head. 'No, your fare is excellent.'

'Good,' he murmured, 'I was afraid you found some fault in my hospitality.'

'None,' she replied, and Eyrik smiled as though relieved.

'More wine?'

Before she could answer with either affirmative or negative he was pouring the rich red liquid into her glass, for all the world no more than a man intent on proving himself a good host. Wynett drank again, hardly aware that he had not answered her question, for he went on speaking, commenting on the flavour of the vegetables and the meat, asking if the sauce was to her liking, inviting her comments on the silver and the chamber, his conversation light, seeming less devious than anxious to please, concerned for her comfort.

She ate her fill and Eyrik removed the platters to a sideboard with the casual comment that they could be cleared away later, which she took to be confirmation of unseen servants. He brought a bowl of fruit to the table and when she selected an apple, insisted on peeling it for her, coring the fruit and presenting her with neatly-cut segments.

'Thank you,' she smiled, though she found his attentions a trifle overwhelming.

167

Eyrik beamed, white teeth gleaming in the candlelight, the yellow glow striking gold from his thick chestnut hair. He ate an apple, too, his incisors cleaving the fruit sharply as a knife, swallowing wine between bites. Wynett finished her portion and found herself abruptly tired, hiding a yawn behind her napkin.

'Would you retire?' Eyrik asked.

She nodded, realising that her lids drooped, heavy over eyes that were suddenly blurred with weariness. The candles seemed to waver in their sconces, their radiance hypnotic, shimmering against the pristine whiteness of the walls. She yawned again, this time making no effort to conceal it, and Eyrik was instantly on his feet, coming around the table to draw back her chair. She rose and took the arm he presented, fatigue filling her now, weighting her feet so that the few steps it took to cross the small chamber seemed ponderous, slowed by her weariness.

Eyrik opened the door and they walked out into the courtyard. A full moon hung directly above the atrium, silvering the vinous growths twining around the pillars, reflecting from the water of the fountain. The scents of magnolia and jasmine mingled in air still warm from the sun's heat, the tendrils rustled by a faint, pleasantly cool breeze. Moonlight and shadow made a latticework on the flagstones, the soft musical tinkling of the fountain an auricular counterpoint.

'Is it not lovely?' Eyrik murmured, his voice low, as if he feared that sound might disturb the scene.

Wynett nodded, for it was indeed a magical sight.

'But you are tired,' he said, a fraction louder. 'Come, I shall escort you to your chambers.'

He eased a hand beneath her arm, holding her elbow as though afraid she might falter, and took her across the yard to the winding, rose-decked stairway.

They climbed upwards, longer, it seemed to Wynett, than her original descent had taken, though she assumed that was due to fatigue, and halted before a door filigreed with the shifting patterns of moonlight shining through the overhanging trellis of roses. Eyrik turned the golden handle and pushed the door inwards, removing his hand from Wynett's arm as he bowed decorously.

'Sleep well,' he urged, making no move to enter, and Wynett murmured, 'Goodnight,' and went in, closing the door behind her.

Candles burned softly in the outer chamber and she saw that a single column was set beside her bed. She slid the bolt into its sockets and yawned hugely, noticing that the windows were shuttered. Rejecting the temptation to simply throw herself upon the bed and let sleep come, she undressed, choosing a nightgown from the selection in the wardrobes, and went into the alcove to perform her ablutions. Only then did she enter the sleeping-chamber.

Shutters were latched over the windows here, too, and because it was her habit to sleep in an aerated room she went to open them, turning them back against the walls where they fastened with small golden catches. She pushed the flawless glass open and paused a moment at the casement as the breeze she had felt in the atrium bathed her face in cool air. At first it was pleasantly refreshing, redolent of grass and the bosky odours of the woodland, and she was on the point of turning to the bed, but then some other scent intruded and she inhaled, curious to identify the fume. It was pungent, smelling of decay, as if something rotted and the breeze carried the effluvium. Her nostrils pinched as it grew stronger and she exhaled vigorously, seeking to expel the malodorous scent. Then it was gone and the night once again bore the fragrance of growing things. She leant against the embrasure, staring out into the darkness as she wondered what the reek had been. The lawns were clearly visible under the moon's silver fulgence, though the woodland bordering the stream was a solid, subfusc mass, as if it absorbed the lambency, swallowing light to return only shadow. It was as though the building from which she stared stood within a pool of light, surrounded by the umbra of the timber that stretched out to fuse with the velvet blackness of the sky. She had the impression of standing alone on some great vessel, seeing only the dark unknown all around.

Then she felt her skin chill, apprehensive pinpricks dancing like tiny needles over her bare forearms, the hairs at the nape of her neck standing upright as a howl echoed from the aphotic wood. It was akin to a lupine moon-hymn, but there was a quality to it that had no part of any wolf's wail. It was thin at first, a keening, but then it grew in volume, becoming a lament, empty of hope, filled with despair and suffering. It battered at her ears, syphoning her with dread so that she clutched instinctively at the talisman, mouthing a prayer to the Lady. It ululated into silence, quavering to a stop, and she shivered, aware of perspiration moist on her face and back. For long moments she stared over the moonlit lawns towards the darkened woodland, wondering if the awful lament would sound again, hoping it would not, but nonetheless curious as to its origin, and then drew back from the window, still holding firm to the talisman as she folded her arms across her breast and willed her involuntary trembling to cease.

She tried to tell herself that whatever made the sound was some animal – a wolf or a forest cat – but in this weird place she was not sure, thinking that if windows could admit sunlight where no windows could be and rooms extended beyond their natural, physical limits, then anything might inhabit the wood. Unthinking, propelled by insensate urgency, she unlatched the shutters and folded them again across the window before hurrying to the bed.

She had climbed beneath the covers before she remembered that the candles still burned in the outer chamber, but she lacked the will to rise and snuff them, preferring the reassurance of their light to the alternative of darkness. Still holding tight to Kyrie's stone she closed her eyes and let sleep come.

It was deep and dreamless and she woke surprised to see sunlight barring the walls, gold and white striating the stone, mundane motes of dust floating in the radiance. The candle still burned beside her bed and those in the outer chamber still shone in their sconces, none seeming reduced, their flames standing straight and true. The numbing horror that had gripped her before seemed foolish in the light of the new day, though its echoes still rang in her mind and she lay still, looking about her before she cast off the covers and rose. Outside birds sang matins and, as was her custom, she joined them in a brief prayer, then resolutely crossed to the shuttered window and threw back the screens.

Sunlight bathed her face; the air was balmy. The lawns shone verdant, the buttercups and daisies littering the grass, a patchwork of welcome normality. The brook glistened; beyond it the woods formed a green mosaic of sylvan tranquillity. A zephyr stirred her hair and she felt all the apprehension of the previous night dissolve. It was a wolf, she told herself, nothing more than a wolf; or perhaps a cat, that spread of seemingly-endless timber was large enough to contain the great predators of the forest. She chose to ignore the small, sceptical voice that muttered at the back of her mind, for to listen to it was to allow madness a foothold in this strange place.

She snubbed the candle beside her bed and entered the dressing room, performing her toilette before selecting another gown from the wardrobes, a thing of soft, green silk that fitted as well as the discarded blue robe; as though made specifically for her. Then, determined that this day she would ask all the questions she wanted, she went out onto the balcony.

The light there was pink, filtered through rose petals, the balcony seeming an ethereal creation that floated above the atrium, where she saw Eyrik lounging beside the fountain. He looked up as she studied him, as though he sensed her presence, and waved cheerily.

'Are you hungry?' he called. 'Breakfast awaits.'

Wynett descended the arboreal stairway to find a table set close to the foot. Immaculate linen draped the surface, spread with salvers containing butter and bread, fruit, cold meats and cheeses, eggs, several compotes. Porcelain cups stood beside the plates and at the centre of the table a pot exuded the aromatic odour of a tisane. Eyrik was on his feet waiting for her, dressed today in a loose shirt of dark green and snug black breeks, high boots laced upon his feet. His smile was brilliant as he bowed.

'You are lovely,' he complimented. 'I believe that colour suits you better even than the blue. Did you sleep well?'

Again, Wynett felt that sensation of being overwhelmed by his attentions as he held her chair and saw her seated, dutifully filling her cup and enquiring which of the delicacies set before her he might help her to.

'I heard something,' she remarked, firm in her determination to have answers from him.

'Something?' He presented her with bread, still warm from the oven, not quite interrupting her, but still succeeding in disrupting her concentration.

She took the bread and nodded, refusing to meet his gold-flecked gaze. 'Before I slept. I think it came from the woods.'

'From the woods?' he echoed, his smile quizzical. 'Do you prefer eggs or meat? Some cheese, perhaps?'

He would not be forestalled and Wynett allowed him to fill a plate with cold meat and a thick slice of yellow cheese. She said, 'Aye. It sounded like a wolf, but . . .'

'Mayhap it was,' he said easily. 'I trust you were not frightened?'

She was about to tell him that the wailing had filled her with dread, but thought better of it and shook her head.

'I am not sure it was a wolf.'

'There are wolves in the farther reaches; and forest cats.' He took an egg, boiled hard in its shell, and began to peel the carapace away. There was a delicacy to his movements that belied the obvious strength of his powerful hands and Wynett found the action oddly disturbing, almost mesmeric. When he was done and the fragments

171

of shell littered his plate he raised the egg to his mouth and bit down. His teeth severed the soft albumen with an almost unnatural precision, so even were they. 'Mayhap it was a cat. Hunting, I expect.'

His eyes met Wynett's and she felt her gaze captured and held, her resolve dissipating under his ingenuous smile. 'Mayhap,' she agreed.

'You need not be afraid,' he informed her. 'They do not venture close to this place. Though if you care for hunting . . .?'

Wynett shook her head in answer.

'Of course not.' His expression became instantly apologetic. 'You were of Estrevan – you would not enjoy the spilling of blood.'

'I see no reason to kill, save to eat,' she murmured, vaguely wondering why she felt any need to explain. 'The Lady teaches us that . . .' She halted, frowning. 'How is it you know so much about me?'

Eyrik shrugged. 'Do you not wear that talisman?'

'Aye.' Wynett glanced down instinctively at the stone suspended between her breasts, aware for the first time that the green gown was cut somewhat low in that area.

'May I see it?'

Eyrik leant forwards, his eyes frankly appreciative as they moved over her bust. Wynett was not sure whether modesty or some inchoate apprehension prompted her to raise her hands, the one holding a napkin that served to obscure her cleavage, the other cupping the jewel.

'I may not remove it,' she said. 'It was given in cognizance of a vow.'

Eyrik's right hand extended towards the talisman, halting a finger's width from the stone, whether from regard for her modesty or some other motivation, Wynett could not be certain. She noticed for the first time that his nails were long, very white, and almost pointed. A thought of claws crossed her mind, then was dismissed as he smiled and said, 'Never?'

'Never.' She shook her head in confirmation, and saw his eyes flash for an instant, the gold flecks seeming to spark against the brown.

'No matter,' he said softly, resuming his amiable stance.

Wynett allowed the stone to fall back against her skin. It felt cooler than usual and as it touched her again she felt it tingle, sending little prickles deep into her flesh, much like the urtication she had felt at the howling in the night.

'So,' he asked her, 'would you view the pool again? Mayhap we shall see further sign of Kedryn's approach.'

Wynett nodded eagerly. 'Do you know that he comes? Have you sought to use those powers you spoke of?'

'He comes, have no doubt of it,' Eyrik assured her. 'How long the journey may take him I cannot know for sure, but he does come. Of that I am certain.'

There was a note of anticipatory triumph in his tone that Wynett assumed stemmed from his obvious desire to please, and she smiled as he rose, offering his arm, forgetting any further questions as he escorted her across the yard to a shadowed door of dark blue wood.

It opened directly into the blue-lit chamber containing the pool and without preamble Eyrik brought her to the circle, leaning forwards with one hand resting casually at her back. Wynett scarcely noticed the touch, peering down into the argent disc with wide eyes and hope-filled heart.

'Do you see it?' Eyrik murmured, his soft question seeming faraway, whispery as water rustling over stones.

Wynett stared at the immobile surface, at first seeing only the translucent liquid, then saw it shimmer again, rippling without movement, an image forming, unclear at first, but then becoming lucid. She stifled a gasp as the oracle revealed not Kedryn, but a wagon, painted pale blue and drawn by four horses. A grizzled, grey-headed man dressed in a simple tunic of brown leather held the reins and beside him sat a woman wearing the blue robe of Estrevan, her hair a sleek black, her eyes a startling blue.

'Gerat!' Wynett mouthed.

'Gerat?' queried Eyrik.

'The Paramount Sister of Estrevan,' Wynett whispered, her gaze still fastened on the vision.

She did not hear Eyrik's sharp intake of breath because she was watching Gerat turn on the wagon seat to speak with the women riding in the box. One she did not recognise, save as an acolyte, but the other she knew instantly. That sun-golden hair, like the features, so similar to her own, belonged to no one other than her sister and she said aloud, 'It is Ashrivelle.'

The image flickered on the name, shifting and blurring so that her only other impression was of sunlight and a dusty trail, some hint of running water in the distance. It dissolved even as she willed it to remain and the pool was once more clear and fathomless.

'Your sister.' Eyrik's voice was thoughtful. 'And the Paramount Sister of Estrevan.'

Wynett nodded, confused. 'Why that?' she asked. 'Why did I see Gerat and Ashrivelle?'

Eyrik shrugged, his smile consoling. 'I do not know. The pool reveals what it will. Mayhap they ride with Kedryn.'

'I did not see Kedryn,' Wynett responded, her voice forlorn.

'But they are doubtless linked to Kedryn.'

Eyrik stared at the pool, his comment absent, as though other thoughts filled his mind. Wynett turned to face him. 'Ashrivelle was with us on the barge,' she offered.

'And so you know she, too, survived,' he said. 'Is that not good news?'

'Aye, but I had hoped to see Kedryn.' She knew that her tone was petulant and felt immediately ashamed. 'Can you not summon his image?'

'I do not control the pool,' Eyrik told her. 'Much as I would grant your every wish, I cannot summon that which it will not show. I am sorry.'

'No,' Wynett murmured, 'it is I who should apologise. You do your best to aid me, yet I behave like a child when I fail to see what I want.'

'You could never behave like a child,' he retorted gallantly. 'Your disappointment is understandable, and consequently entirely forgivable.'

'Perhaps later,' she wondered.

'Perhaps,' he agreed. 'You may come here whenever you wish – you do not need me. Simply enter the blue door and you will find the pool.'

Wynett frowned incomprehension. 'I had believed your agency was necessary,' she said.

Eyrik shook his head. 'At first, perhaps. But now the pool will respond to you alone. And if I am to aid you, I shall need to work alone at times.' He drew her towards the door, smiling reassuringly. 'There is a certain amount of . . . danger . . . in what I must do, and I would not subject you to that.'

Wynett was about to ask him exactly what was involved, but they were at the door and he was leading her through into the courtyard, beaming as he tilted his head back to stare up at the brilliant sun, suggesting that they walk beyond the walls, and before she could voice her queries he had her hand and was moving towards a far door, enthusiastically describing the glories of the gardens she had not yet seen.

*

Without chance of finding remounts in the forest country, Kedryn was forced to hold a steady pace for fear of winding the horses. His impulse was to charge headlong into the Beltrevan, but common sense prevailed and he held the black stallion to a canter that ate the miles without exhausting the animal until they turned off the canyon trail and began the arduous climb into the heights of the Lozins. They made no attempt to conceal their coming, relying on the clusters of red and white feathers, symbolic of peaceful intent, that Brannoc tied to the bridles and their scabbards, and the treaties concluded with the tribes, to guarantee their safe passage.

For the first three days they descended the scarp of the mountains, traversing bare flanks of rock where only pines caught lonely footing, moving along ravines and over slopes of treacherous scree, moving steadily northwestwards. It was a switchback trail, each vertiginous descent seeming matched by a climb, the gulleys that Brannoc assured his impatient companion were shortcuts seeming always to lead to yet another ascent, sometimes so precipitous that they needed to dismount and lead the animals, bringing them singly to the crests. Kedryn wondered if the straighter trail north along the Idre might not have been the swifter, but bowed before the halfbreed's superior knowledge of the mountains, allowing Brannoc to pick their way as he curbed his haste, fighting the temptation of impetuosity. They rode from dawn to noon to dusk, halting only to rest the animals and snatch food from the packs Rycol had provided, camping as darkness fell, too weary to do more than build a fire, eat, and roll themselves into their blankets to sleep in preparation for departure at first light.

Then, on the fourth day, the craggy terrain gentled, the stands of pine becoming thicker and more numerous, clumps of sparse grass showing where soil found purchase on the stone. Brannoc led the way along a twisting ravine that began to climb towards its northern end and they emerged onto a small plateau. The halfbreed reined in, staring ahead with his mouth curved in a smile, one hand rising to encompass the vista spread before them.

'The Beltrevan,' he said softly, almost reverentially.

Kedryn and Tepshen halted to either side, silent as they studied the panorama below. Both had seen the forest country before, but its sheer enormity still impressed, its vastness breathtaking. Before them the ground slanted down to the bend of a river, the waterway a boundary between foothills and forest. Beyond the river the timber started, an immense ocean of woodland that stretched to the far horizons, a harlequin riot of greens that dulled and faded into blue where forest met sky, merging, seeming to run on forever, endlessly. Summer brought it to its fullest flourish, obscuring all details beneath the burgeoning mass of leaf-decked branches, the river turning into the trees lost from sight as if swallowed by the woodland, the timber possessing the world with an ageless dendrological majesty.

'Where does Drul's Mound lie?' Kedryn demanded, the prospect of navigating that arboreal sea daunting.

Brannoc's hand swung to point a fraction north of northwest. 'In that direction. The river is the Alagor: we follow it.'

Kedryn grunted and drove his heels against the stallion's flanks, urging the big horse forwards over the rim of the plateau without further comment. Tepshen glanced at Brannoc and took his own mount over, the two packhorses behind. Brannoc sat for a moment, staring at the timber country, then made the warding gesture and followed his two comrades.

The slope was steep at first, but then levelled to a more gradual descent as it approached the river, grass becoming more abundant with the presence of water. It was close on noon and Brannoc suggested they halt before fording and allow the animals to forage. With only a small display of reluctance Kedryn agreed and they dismounted, hobbling the animals. The horses began to crop enthusiastically on the herbage and the three men chewed smoked meat and dried fruit.

'We are likely to encounter woodlanders ere long,' Brannoc remarked. 'Caroc, most likely, but later Drott. Should any question our presence, we are come to seek out Cord.'

'I have no *byavan*,' Kedryn returned, referring to the lingua franca of the tribes.

'No matter.' Brannoc shrugged negligently. 'I speak both Drott and Caroc. Should we be questioned I shall explain that you are the hef-Alador, and come to visit with your old friend.'

Kedryn grinned at the notion of a casual visit to the *ulan* of the fiercest tribe, but Tepshen frowned, turning a doubtful face to Brannoc.

'What if they decide to escort us?' he demanded.

'I shall endeavour to dissuade them,' Brannoc answered. 'If they will not be dissuaded ...' He shrugged, '... then we must kill them.'

Kedryn's grin froze at this casual suggestion and he shook his head. 'I would not see innocent blood spilled.'

'There is little innocent blood in the Beltrevan,' said Brannoc.

'Nonetheless,' Kedryn insisted. 'I prefer to avoid such callous action. It smacks too much of Ashar's way. We need the Lady's blessing on what we attempt and that may be withheld should we resort to Ashar's means.'

'Mayhap the Lady will bring us through unseen,' Brannoc retorted, 'but should some wandering band of Drott take it upon themselves to provide escort to Cord we shall forfeit all chance of entering Drul's Mound. No matter what regard he holds you in, he will not permit you to rummage through that tomb.'

'Pray that is not necessary,' Tepshen suggested. 'And if it is, leave the killing to Brannoc and me.'

'I would not jeopardise our mission or your souls,' Kedryn argued, 'and I believe that wanton killing may thwart the protections Gerat gave you.'

'My soul is my own,' the kyo returned calmly. 'My duty is to you. If killing aids your mission, then kill I shall.'

'I will endeavour to avoid contact,' Brannoc added. 'It may be that we can reach the Mound unseen. If not ... well, let us extemporise.'

Kedryn found himself in a quandary. Speed was of the essence if they were to reach Drul's Mound before the summer Gathering, and that speed would be greatly reduced should they need to skulk through the forests like night-come thieves. Fear for Wynett prompted him to accept the expedient measure, and he recognised the sense of Tepshen's dubiety: the company of tribesmen might well thwart his purpose. Yet he could not accept that casual killing would find favour with the Lady, and he was certain beyond any doubt that he must fail without her blessing. He gnawed on the problem, a hand moving unthinking to the talisman beneath his shirt, tugging it loose that he might enclose it in his fist. He felt its vibration and turned towards Brannoc.

'Should we encounter woodlanders, might you not tell them we travel under religious vows? That those require us to travel alone?'

Brannoc's swarthy face creased in a frown as he contemplated the notion, then he shrugged, snorting half-hearted laughter. 'It is not that far removed from the truth. Mayhap they would accept it. But mayhap also they would follow us anyway.'

'Our horses lend an advantage,' Kedryn pressed. 'How could they pace us?'

'They are of the forests,' replied the halfbreed, bluntly.

'So are you,' said Kedryn.

Brannoc nodded, dark eyes fixed on Kedryn. 'Are you sure no blood must be spilled? Even though clemency jeopardise our mission?'

'Aye,' the younger man confirmed, still holding the talisman, 'I am.'

'Then we had best travel warily,' sighed Brannoc.

'And soon,' Kedryn declared, wishing to bring the discussion to an end.

He swallowed a mouthful of water, thus missing the look Brannoc exchanged with Tepshen, and climbed to his feet. The others rose with him and they removed the hobbles, settling packs in place and mounting the rested animals.

'We must ride west a little,' said Brannoc. 'The ford lies in that direction.'

Kedryn urged his stallion to a trot, following the bank of the Alagor, his face turned towards the forest's edge looming across the water. Tepshen and Brannoc fell in behind him, riding close.

'Should it happen . . .' the kyo touched the hilt of the long eastern blade slung across his back.

'Aye,' nodded Brannoc.

They rode for half the afternoon before the halfbreed announced the river safe to cross. There was a beach of shale settled within a cup of stone, the Alagor rippling clear over the pebbles, and Brannoc took the lead, urging his grey horse down into the water. The animal snorted a protest, but forged ahead, rapidly moving chest-deep into the stream. Soon it was swimming, Brannoc slipping from the saddle to clutch the horn as the beast carried him across. He emerged dripping on the far bank and scanned the timber before waving to the others. Tepshen separated the pack animals, handing one halter line to Kedryn, who tugged the reluctant horse behind him as he heeled his black into the river. With the sight of Brannoc's grey on the opposite bank, the stallion struck out not unwillingly, towing both Kedryn and the smaller horse behind. The current was strong, and the water cold despite the summer sun shining on the surface, and Kedryn emerged some distance down from Brannoc. He walked back along the bank as Tepshen crossed, the kyo striking out at an angle that brought him level with Brannoc's position even as Kedryn reached the beach.

The bank was shadowed by the mass of trees and the three men shivered, emptying water from their boots and drying their weapons before remounting and striking into the timber. They ignored the discomfort of soaking garments for the sake of speed, and it was not until the shadows elongated, presaging night's fall that they halted again, building a fire around which they huddled, steam rising from their clothes.

The next day Kedryn was awake with the birds that chorused a greeting to the dawn, aware that he now stood in Ashar's territory, anxious to press on. He built the fire to fresh life and checked the horses, finding none of them the worse for their ducking. Soon Tepshen and Brannoc rose and they ate a hurried breakfast, then mounted, the halfbreed taking the lead again as they rode steadily deeper into the Beltrevan, steadily closer to Drul's Mound and whatever unknown hazards awaited there.

# Chapter Nine

THE wagon rumbled with agonising slowness over the dusty road that trailed the Idre northwards, its passage marked by the grey-white clouds the wheels and hooves raised. Wyxx sat stolid as ever on the seat, holding the four horses to the pace he maintained was the swiftest they could safely manage, Gerat beside him, Ashrivelle and Donella in the box behind, the Paramount Sister turning to speak with the blonde woman.

'I am not sure how I may aid them,' she said, 'but I am certain I can do it better from High Fort than Estrevan. The Sacred City is too far removed from the Beltrevan, whilst Rycol's hold sits on the very doorstep.'

'But what *can* you do?' Ashrivelle demanded. 'If they succeed in entering the netherworld then surely they will go beyond even the compass of your powers.'

'I am not sure,' Gerat repeated patiently, curbing the temptation to wonder if it had not been better to send Ashrivelle on to Estrevan from Genyff. Since departing the riverside settlement she had done little but ply Gerat with questions, each one concerned with Kedryn's welfare, and it seemed to Gerat that her interest was more than sisterly. Ashrivelle, she thought, transferred her affections, though why that should trouble her she was not clear. The princess would, after all, go on to Estrevan if she remained intent on expunging her self-imposed guilt by seeking the life of a lay Sister, and even should she choose to remit that decision, Kedryn's love for Wynett was not of a kind to be easily forgotten. He would not, Gerat was confident, turn in search of solace to Ashrivelle. If, she reminded herself, he emerged unscathed from Ashar's domain.

'Proximity may be of benefit,' she continued, 'and Rycol will send mehdri with word to my Sisters of what is attempted. Mayhap we shall be able to establish a connection with Estrevan through the agency of our Senders.'

Had she hoped that would silence Ashrivelle it was forlorn optimism, for the princess frowned and demanded, 'I had thought the Gadrizels denied such linkage.'

'They do,' Gerat answered, stifling a sigh. 'Usually, they do; but if Senders are located at the entrance to the Morfah Pass – then through it – and one travels to High Fort, the natural barrier imposed by the mountains may be overcome, and I shall be able to draw on Estrevan's power to augment my own.'

'But if you do not know *how*,' Ashrivelle began, cut off by Gerat's abrupt response.

'Guidance may be granted me, Ashrivelle. And you must learn to accept that the Lady works in her own ways – she does not always set down exactly what we must do, but leaves some work to us. By establishing contact with Estrevan – *if* I am able – then I shall at least have the resources of all the Sisterhood to draw on. Mayhap I shall then be able to extend the Lady's power into the Beltrevan, or even into the netherworld, I am not sure, but I shall do all I can think of and at present that *is* all I can think of.'

Ashrivelle nodded thoughtfully and Gerat could see fresh questions forming in her blue eyes. Enough, she thought, you have asked me enough when I have sufficient doubts of my own at a time I should have none. Seeking to forestall the blonde woman she turned away, studying the road ahead. It stretched before her like a challenge, straight and long, leading to High Fort, certainly, but oh, so slowly, so very slowly when, she *did* feel sure, time was an essential factor in the godly game.

She heard Donella murmur something to Ashrivelle and blessed the young acolyte for her perspicacity as the princess fell silent, leaving her to her own thoughts.

Did any of them, she wondered, realise what lay at stake? More than the lives of Kedryn and Wynett, Tepshen Lahl and Brannoc, though those were, without doubt, precious enough. The cold-eyed easterner and the laughing halfbreed were brave men and their lives would be sadly mourned should they fall. Wynett, still soul kin for all she had relinquished the devotions of the Sorority, was vital to Kedryn's strength, a part of him now; and Kedryn was the Chosen One. If Ashar should defeat him there would be none to oppose the god, none capable of doing more than dying in denial of his ghastly might. And should Ashar succeed in securing the talismans his might would become insuperable.

The thought chilled her, her mind moving instinctively away from its contemplation. She forced herself to concentrate upon it.

If Ashar should secure both talismans he would be able to surmount the barriers established by the Lady to hold him beyond the Lozins. He would have no further need of minions such as the Messenger or Hattim Sethiyan to work his will in the Kingdoms for he would emerge himself, an awful, godly plague upon mankind. The threat of the Horde was as nothing beside that danger. He would stalk like destruction incarnate through the Kingdoms, reaping lives as those farmers beside the road scythed the early wheat. There would be only desolation then and everything the Lady had given, everything Estrevan sought to nurture, would become ashes and annihilation.

Was that the mad god's intent, ultimately? Was that the end he worked towards? The leviathan sent not to destroy Kedryn as she had at first suspected, but to bring the talismans – or one, at least – within Ashar's grasp? Were that the case then the stone could be in no firmer hands than Wynett's, for she would surely not relinquish it willingly, and to utilise its power it must be given of Wynett's free will. And yet . . . and yet, could even Wynett stand against the blandishments of that primal being? The god of lies, of deceits, the god of duplicity, he was all of those, and the face he showed Wynett might seem fair. Might – Gerat's hands clenched into fists at the thought – seduce even Wynett into compliance.

Games within games, Gerat thought. Beside this the suborning of Hattim Sethiyan is as nothing; the threat of the Horde a clumsy ploy. It is a game that forces the players to conform to rules they know nothing of, for the rules are established by Ashar as he sees fit. Should Ashar secure both halves of the talisman all is lost, and even now Kedryn brings the one half to him. Yet Kedryn *must* enter the netherworld, for if he does not then Ashar holds Wynett and her half and the Chosen One is consequently weakened by that loss. And the only sure way to defeat the god is to believe in Qualle's words and trust in the Lady to see Kedryn through, for only by entering Ashar's domain may he obtain the means of Ashar's destruction.

'Lady, watch over him,' she said to herself. 'Watch over them all and endow them with your strength that they may succeed.'

She did not add the ugly thought that lingered at the tail of the prayer: *even though it means their deaths, let them succeed.*

She pushed that from her mind for it chilled her and she felt icy fingers play upon her spine. She shivered, feeling her flesh creep, and realised that cold gripped her, as if she sat, not upon a wagon seat warmed by the bright sun of a summer morning, but in some hibernal place where frigid vapours wreathed her in wintry rigor.

'What ails you, Sister?'

She heard Donella's voice and turned in startled surprise to find the acolyte's brown eyes studying her with nervous concern, seeing Wyxx, too, cast a curious gaze her way. She realised that her teeth chattered and clenched them against the brumal chill.

She began to say, 'Nothing,' but saw only mounting alarm in Donella's eyes as the word came out a stutter, a castanet rattling of tooth against tooth.

Then it was gone and the air was warm again, the only hint of chill the pleasant zephyr that blew off the Idre, and she said it: 'Nothing. I lost myself in contemplation.'

Donella continued to stare at her and she smiled, willing a reassurance she did not entirely share on the acolyte.

'It was nothing. The breeze blew chill for a moment and I was far away.'

But she knew it was not that, for the chill was such as strikes when the mind's inner eye discovers some hidden watcher and the body reacts. It was a chill of fear, of loathing of the concealed gaze.

Does Ashar watch me? she wondered. Can the presence of Wynett, of the talisman, within his realm allow him to spy?

Cautiously she opened her mind, sending forth wary mental feelers, but there was nothing, only Donella's concern and Wyxx's placidity and Ashrivelle's confusion. She shut those out, not wishing to invade the privacy of her companions, and found nothing else. I must be careful, she thought. More careful than I have ever been, for I must give nothing away to the god. Deliberately, she filled her mind with thoughts of the Lady, letting her gaze wander over the pleasant landscape of Tamur that stretched about her, over the fields and woods, the rolling hills in the distance and the higher wolds ahead. They basked in the sun, the sky a pure blue, white clouds like sails against the azure. Birds sang and insects buzzed, the horses made a steady drumbeat on the road, and in a little while she was calm again. Calm, but still wary.

\*

Sunlight dappled the forest trail with harlequin patterns of shadow and brightness as Brannoc led the way steadily deeper into the

183

timber. The Alagor shone silver through the trees, invisible more often than not as the halfbreed took them along the secret ways of the Beltrevan. It was so different now than when Kedryn had last seen it, the trees rimed white with frost, their boughs heavy-laden with snow, the trails vanished under winter's white mantle. Now all was green, the paths cut dark, bare earth where feet and hooves stamped out the grass that otherwise spread everywhere the brackens and brambles allowed. And it was noisy. The Alagor sounded a sussurating background melody and the wind rustled the foliage overhead, birds chorused, small, unseen animals chattered and occasionally a startled deer charged from their advance. The shod hooves of the five horses drummed against the trail, and for all the oiling and tying-down of tack and gear Kedryn could hear the creak of leather and the jingle of metal.

He studied Brannoc's back, seeing the man turn his plaited head steadily from side to side, knowing that his forester's ears were attuned to any sound that did not belong amongst the natural symphony of the timberland. Then Brannoc raised a hand in warning and curbed his mount to a halt. Behind, Kedryn heard the soft scrape of leather on linen as Tepshen unlatched his scabbard, letting the blade slide down from shoulder to hip in readiness. He turned, glancing at the kyo, who stared back with impassive gaze, and swung in his saddle to watch Brannoc again.

The halfbreed beckoned them forwards and they moved up at a walk. The trail widened where he waited, paths entering from left and right to form a crossroads at which Brannoc pointed.

'Tracks.' He gestured to the right; Kedryn saw only the hard-packed dirt. 'They move in the same direction; slowly.'

'Which tribe?' Kedryn asked.

'Caroc by my guess,' Brannoc responded, dismounting and tossing his reins to the younger man. He walked a few paces along the trail with his eyes on the ground, then knelt to examine the spoor more closely. 'A family group. Perhaps five warriors and as many women. Likely some children and oldsters.'

'Peaceful?' demanded Tepshen.

Brannoc shrugged. 'Probably.'

'What do we do?' Kedryn wondered as the halfbreed remounted.

'We can go around them and lose half a day,' said Brannoc. 'A full day if we are to be certain of avoiding any hunters they may have out. Or we can ride on and hope they will not detain us.'

'If they are peaceful why should they be a threat?'

Brannoc grinned at the question. 'The Beltrevan teaches that *everything* is a threat, my friend. Treaties or no, the Caroc may object to our wandering at will through their territory. And they may have forgotten that you slew Niloc Yarrum to become hef-Alador; I cannot tell, but you have a decision to make.'

Kedryn thought for a moment, then pointed ahead. 'We cannot afford to lose half a day – we press on.' He looked to each man in turn, adding, 'And we seek to avoid swordplay.'

Brannoc went on grinning; Tepshen nodded once, but his sword remained at the ready. Praying that he had made the right decision, Kedryn lifted his stallion to a trot. The others followed and in a short distance Brannoc passed him, assuming the lead again.

They continued along the leafy trail until the halfbreed once more raised a warning hand. Kedryn reined in alongside, aware that the woodland had fallen silent. Brannoc pointed through the trees and Kedryn saw movement.

The trail went down a shallow slope to a grassy bowl spread around a stream tributary to the Alagor. What timber had once grown there was long cleared, indicating a regular camp site. It was occupied: seven hide lodges were pitched in a circle on the far side of the stream, a cook fire burning at the centre; six women sat about it preparing food. Seven men, five burly warriors, the remaining two white-haired, lounged in the sun, and nine children splashed in the water. There were eight massive dogs sprawled close to the fire in hope of scraps, and as the watchers studied the camp one raised an ugly grey head to growl a warning.

Instantly the hounds were on their feet, closely followed by the warriors. The big grey dog barked and started towards the stream, the rest of the pack behind, hackles bristling and lips drawn back from the savage fangs.

'*Ka emblan pasa,*' Brannoc called, urging his horse out from the shelter of the timber. '*Ka vajari sul Drott. Nera balan tu drami, quero tu aldan sul para em pladijo.*'

Dark faces studied him suspiciously, but one man shouted at the dogs, stilling their forwards surge. Brannoc reached forwards to touch the red and white feathers attached to his bridle.

'*Pasa fori, chaddah. Ka pulan ni terro.*' He smiled hugely and muttered, 'Follow me.'

Kedryn and Tepshen did as they were bade, bringing their horses out from the trees and down the slope behind the halfbreed. The warrior who had ordered the dogs to a halt spoke again and the hounds, grumbling at the intrusion of strangers, slunk back amongst the tents. The warriors studied the trio warily, nocked bows in their hands, and Kedryn saw that the knives the women had been using on the food were now held in readiness of more hostile purpose. Brannoc halted at the stream and spoke again, no longer in the byavan, but in a more guttural tongue that sounded to Kedryn all clicks and grunts.

Whatever he said appeared to find favour with the woodlanders, for the bows were lowered and the women went back to the communal cookpot, the children emerging from the stream to stare in wide-eyed wonder at the newcomers.

More words were exchanged and Kedryn took the opportunity to study the Caroc. They were darker of skin than the Drott, with mostly red or auburn hair. The women wore braids wound in thick circles either side of their faces, fastened with gold pins. The men were bearded, some teased into plaits, others great bushes, and their hair was uniformly drawn into long tails woven with shells and feathers. Only the two oldsters wore shirts, patched garments of red and blue and green, while the younger warriors were bare chested, wearing only plaid breeks bound about their sturdy calves with thongs, ankle length moccasins on their feet. All wore short swords at their waists, and long hunting knives; four axes lay on the grass.

'We are invited to eat with them,' Brannoc announced. 'I have told them we travel on a mission of peace to the Drott territory. The leader is called Mykal and he says we may go with his blessing.'

Kedryn let slip a quiet sigh of relief, grateful that no opposition was offered, and followed Brannoc across the stream.

At a word from Mykal, the horses were led away from the circle of lodges and tethered in the shade of the trees, where they began to crop the luxuriant grass with only an occasional snicker of animosity directed at the dogs. Mykal gestured at the ground and Brannoc sat down, Kedryn and Tepshen to either side. The Caroc hunkered around them, the children gathering behind the men, fascinated by the strangers.

A volley of guttural questions was directed at Brannoc, who responded with the same unintelligible sounds, pausing every so often to translate for his companions.

'Mykal says that he will give us his symbol so that we may pass unquestioned,' he explained. 'He adds that the Drott are not yet gathered. This band is moving to the Caroc Gathering, which the hef-Alador is invited to attend – he says he remembers you from the battle at High Fort.'

Kedryn paled at the thought of finding himself forced to delay his journey, but Brannoc reassured him with the promise that he had explained their mission did not allow such a sojourn, but that the hef-Alador would endeavour to attend the Caroc Gathering on his return. He smiled at the red-bearded warrior, who beamed back and directed a torrent of grunts and clicks in his direction.

'He says,' Brannoc translated, 'that it is a great honour to have the hef-Alador eat in his camp, and that you are welcome to stay as long as you wish.'

'Thank him,' Kedryn asked, 'and make some reasonable excuse.'

Brannoc grinned and turned to Mykal, who shrugged eloquently, nodding vigorously.

What excuse Brannoc had offered Kedryn never discovered, for a woman called then and they moved to the fire, where wooden bowls were distributed, filled with a flavoursome stew of venison and vegetables. It was a tasty meal and when it was done Mykal brought a leather sack from his hogan and clay cups were passed around.

'We must drink with him,' Brannoc elucidated, grinning at the prospect. 'It would be an insult to refuse after taking his food.'

Kedryn nodded agreement, although he had preferred to move on, but deemed it wiser to go with the good will of the headman. He smiled as Mykal unstoppered the sack and filled the cups with dark red liquid. It tasted sweet, no more potent than watered wine, and with Brannoc pointing out that only on occasions of great importance was the brew produced, Kedryn found himself forced to swallow several cups. Mykal was enthusiastic in his hospitality, filling his guests' mugs as the day drew on and Kedryn felt impatience growing.

Finally Brannoc announced that they might leave without offering offence and Kedryn realised that the brew was far from innocuous as the circle of lodges seemed to rotate slowly as he rose to his feet. Blinking owlishly he bowed to Mykal, instantly regretting the courtesy as the movement transformed the rotation of the tents to a seesawing motion. The Caroc laughed hugely, slapping Kedryn's shoulder with an enthusiasm that threatened to pitch him face down on the grass.

'Come,' Brannoc suggested. 'Before he decides you are too drunk to ride and insists you stay.'

187

Kedryn nodded, thinking that he should express gratitude for the woodlanders' hospitality, but afraid that any words would founder on his swollen tongue. 'Thank him,' he mumbled.

Brannoc, more accustomed to the liquor than his companions, expressed their gratitude and turned towards the horses. Kedryn paced after him, concentrating on each step as the ground appeared to undulate before him. It was not until he reached his mount that he realised Tepshen was in little better condition. His own foot seemed unable to find the stirrup, and it took a helping hand from Brannoc to get him astride the stallion. Tepshen, he saw, still stood beside his mount, staring fixedly at the saddle. The kyo's face was calm as ever and his movements had shown no sign of ill-effects, but now he appeared immobilised, simply standing with his reins in one hand, the other on the pommel.

'Mount,' urged Brannoc from his own vantage point astride the grey.

Tepshen raised his head and Kedryn saw his eyes were unfocused, the pupils pinpricks in the jet irises. He felt laughter building and gritted his teeth, fighting the impulse.

'I cannot,' said the kyo.

Brannoc shook his head in exasperation and was about to dismount, but Mykal came to Tepshen's aid, shoving the wiry easterner bodily across the horse. It skittered at the movement and Tepshen clutched desperately at the horn as Mykal slotted one foot into a stirrup and another laughing Caroc set the other in place. Tepshen straightened his back with an obvious effort and looked solemnly down at the tribesmen.

'My thanks,' he declared, enunciating each word with drunken care. 'You are true friends.'

Brannoc translated, adding something that raised a gale of laughter from the Caroc, and took the lead lines of the two pack animals.

'Now follow me,' he ordered, turning along the tree line to pick up the trail where it left the bowl.

The motion of his horse threatened to bring Kedryn's stomach up to his mouth and he concentrated on the figure of Brannoc riding before him with grim determination, vowing that in future he would find out what he drank before allowing a drop to pass his lips. Then he heard Tepshen curse volubly as a branch struck the kyo's face, turning in his saddle to watch the easterner struggling to maintain his seat. For all his impatience, Kedryn could no longer hold back his mirth and began to chuckle at the sight of his friend swaying and swearing, his customary dignity lost to the powerful Caroc alcohol. He stopped when he suffered the same fate, so intent on watching Tepshen that he failed to heed Brannoc's warning and caught a branch squarely across his shoulder, finding himself suddenly sprawled full length on the trail, looking up into the kyo's glazed eyes.

He sat up, groaning, and rose on unsteady feet, not sure he was capable of reaching the saddle again.

He was about to try when Brannoc came up beside him. 'I think,' said the halfbreed, 'that we had best find the river.'

'Why?' Kedryn asked, frowning as he concentrated on the suggestion. 'We have water.'

'Lead your horse,' Brannoc said. 'Tepshen, can you stay in the saddle?'

'Of course,' replied the kyo, swaying wildly.

'Then follow me.'

Without further ado Brannoc took them off the trail, down a deer track to the waterside. He swung down and tethered the animals. Tepshen remained mounted.

'Climb down,' Brannoc said, and the kyo proceeded to slip sideways, caught by the halfbreed.

'Undress,' Brannoc ordered.

'Why?' asked Kedryn.

'Because,' said Brannoc with elaborate patience, 'the water is very cold and it will clear your heads.'

Kedryn and Tepshen nodded solemn agreement and shed their clothes.

'Now into the river,' said Brannoc, punctuating the sentence with a hearty double-handed shove that sent them both tumbling down the bank into the Alagor.

He was right: the water was cold and the shock of immersion dispelled the violent effects of the liquor. Kedryn rose spluttering, flailing against the current as he felt himself sober. Tepshen, he saw, was closer to the bank, closing his eyes as he let his feet go from under him to sink beneath the sun-sparkled surface. He rose shaking his head, his queue swinging from side to side, his features set in an expression of stoic acceptance. Kedryn swam to his side, dunking his own ringing head until he was confident the last vestiges of drunkenness were gone. Brannoc lounged on the bank, grinning.

'I should have warned you,' he remarked as the two shivering men climbed out and began to dry themselves. 'The Caroc are renowned for their liquor.'

*

The wine that Eyrik poured to accompany the fish was superb. So pale as to be almost colourless, it sat light on the palate, its bouquet delicate as the scent of the spring flowers that filled the chamber. Wynett acknowledged that she had tasted none finer, studying the play of candlelight on the crystal of the goblet as she sought to conceal the confusion that filled her mind. She sipped the vintage, but it offered no insights and she set her glass down, barely aware that Eyrik spoke.

'You seem far away,' he repeated. 'Is something amiss?'

Wynett was tempted to laugh at the mundanity of the question, knowing that it would be bitter humour.

'I am in a strange place – I know not where,' she murmured. 'You say that you seek to return me, or that Kedryn will come for me, but you cannot set a time on either thing. I am lost!'

'No!' Eyrik was on his feet in the instant, coming around the table to kneel beside her, cupping her hand in both of his. 'You must not say that.'

'Why not?' she demanded. 'It is the truth.'

She blinked, fighting the tears that threatened to well, feeling his grip tighten as he stared at her, his flecked brown eyes alight with concern. Candlelight rendered his hair glossy as ripe chestnut and the teeth that showed between his slightly parted lips were white and even. He looked very handsome, reminding her of Kedryn; which memory filled her with fresh waves of bewilderment.

'You are not lost,' he said, his voice deep and confident. 'You are here, safe. I know this appears strange, but it is merely another aspect of the world and not something that should frighten or upset you. Had I not intervened to save you from the leviathan, you would be in a far worse place than this.'

'But where *is* this?' she demanded, the turmoil that consumed her lending an edge to her voice.

'It is a place separate from all you know,' he said. 'Ashar cannot touch you here, but because the leviathan was his creature I cannot easily return you to your world. Mayhap it must take Kedryn's coming to achieve that, I am not sure. Mayhap it is necessary the two parts of that talisman you wear must be joined to return you, and for that Kedryn *must* come. I cannot give you some geographic location for such laws do not apply here, but you must trust me. Believe in me, Wynett.'

There was a tenderness in his voice that promised only safety, honest goodwill, and she forced a smile, aware that it was camouflage. 'I am poor company this night. I think perhaps I should retire.'

'You have barely eaten,' he protested, indicating the nibbled trout that sat on her platter.

'I have no appetite.' She shook her head. 'If you will excuse me, I shall find my chambers.'

'Of course, if that is your wish.' He was on his feet before she rose, courteous as ever. 'But believe that I do all I can to re-unite you with Kedryn.'

His tone was sincere and she felt churlish that the only response she could muster was a disconsolate, 'Aye,' but her mood allowed for none other and she made no further attempt at conversation as he opened the door of the dining chamber and led her into the courtyard.

The air was humid, sullen with the threat of rain, the perfume of the climbing plants that wound about the colonnades become overpowering and sickly. The splashing of the fountain seemed dulled by the oppressive weight of the air, no longer musical but somehow morbid, and the moon was hidden behind heavy rafts of menacing nimbus.

'I believe a storm approaches,' Eyrik remarked, and Wynett found herself surprised, for the weather had seemed fixed, as though this place knew only summer. It was almost reassuring that the climate did change, for it made her circumstances seem fractionally more normal.

She crossed the atrium and climbed the stairway to the balcony, Eyrik at her elbow, gallant as ever as he flung open her door and bowed.

'Shall I leave food?' he enquired, gesturing at the ante-chamber. 'Perchance you will regain your appetite.'

'Thank you, no.'

Wynett felt no desire for sustenance, wishing only for solitude and the opportunity to assess her disordered thoughts. She stepped across the threshold, halted by Eyrik's touch. He bowed, lifting her hand to his lips. His mouth was dry.

'It distresses me to see you so melancholy,' he declared, retaining his grip.

'Mayhap it is this change in the weather,' she said wanly, extricating her hand.

'Mayhap,' he nodded, accepting the tacit dismissal with grave face. 'Sleep well.'

'Thank you,' she replied, and closed the door.

For some moments she leant against the wood, hearing his footsteps retreat and fade as he descended to the lower level, then she crossed to the ornate table and filled a goblet with pale wine. She settled herself in one of the chairs, sipping the vintage as she concentrated on the events of that strange day, forcing herself to review what had transpired for all its heart-sickening unpleasantness.

She had risen and performed her toilette as usual, no longer sure how long she had been here, for one day blended into the next with a seamless regularity that leeched all sense of time, the dimensional contradictions of the palace continuing to bewilder her senses, adding their own confusion to her perceptions. She was not certain if it was merely the few days she thought, or longer since she had awoken in these rooms and found Eyrik awaiting her. He had been there again that morning, seated as usual at the breakfast table in the courtyard, greeting her with apologies that he must absent himself for most of the day and the – vague, she now realised – suggestion that it had something to do with Kedryn. Consequently she had been left, for the first time, to her own devices.

At first she had seized the opportunity to explore, attempting to seek out the servants, if such existed, who so regularly provided such excellent food, changed her bed linen, performed the sundry tasks that must be involved in the maintenance of the fabulous palace. None had appeared after Eyrik left her, although she had waited long at the table, until her patience dissolved and she rose, wandering to the nearest door. That, for all it was overhung by the balcony, opened on a chamber of glass and sunlight filled with plants. The floor had been green marble, verdant as spring grass, interspersed with trenches of rich, dark soil from which grew such a profusion of plants and flowers that the chamber was more akin to a garden than an interior room. Light filled it, shining down from a vast cupola of clear glass supported on unbelievably fine golden beams, gossamer delicate as they arched above her head. She had wandered there a while, examining the vegetation, then returned to the courtyard to find the remnants of breakfast cleared away, the table set with a decanter of wine and a single glass. She had gone in search of kitchens, but found none, nor any sign of other beings, loneliness mounting as her quest revealed only one fantastic chamber after another. Before long her mind had spun with the wonders of the place and she had found herself increasingly convinced that she was alone with her mysterious host.

She had decided to seek him out then, and entered the chamber of the oracular pool. It had been empty, but even as she determined to investigate the farther rooms, she had felt herself drawn to the silver disc at the centre. Eyrik had told her it would respond to her alone now, and she had knelt beside it, staring into the bottomless well as she willed it to show her some image of Kedryn.

She shuddered as she recalled what she had seen, her mind withdrawing from the picture presented her, then, with an effort of will, made herself study it again in memory.

The pool had remained transluscent at first, then shimmered as it had done before, seeming to shift within its depths, outlines forming to become slowly clearer until a definite manifestation became visible. Wynett had stared, scarcely able to credit what she saw, her mind rebelling even as her gaze was held, transfixed by the scene.

Kedryn had sat within a stone-walled chamber, lounging in a high-backed wooden chair, a tall window to one side revealing rocky walls that darkened towards night. She had recognised, or thought she recognised, the delineaments of High Fort, and assumed that he had reached the citadel and rested there preparatory to seeking her. He held a goblet, and a decanter sat upon a table at his side, and he had drunk deep as she watched. Then he had risen, his mouth curving in the smile she recalled so well, turning to greet whoever entered the room. He had set the goblet down and she had anticipated sight of Tepshen Lahl, or Brannoc, or Rycol. But then Kedryn had opened his arms and Wynett had gasped, a fisted hand flying to her mouth as Ashrivelle came into view, and into Kedryn's arms. She could remember clearly that she had said, 'No!' as her husband enfolded her sister in tender embrace, Ashrivelle's head tilting back to spill blonde tresses over her shoulders as her lips parted to receive Kedryn's kiss. They had remained like that for long moments as Wynett's heart drummed against her ribs and she fought panic, unable to tear her eyes away even when Ashrivelle moved out of the embrace and walked smiling into a bed chamber, Kedryn on her heels, his hands moving to the fastenings of his shirt. She had watched in horrified fascination as they disrobed, Ashrivelle standing before Kedryn in a wanton display that visibly aroused him. She had felt nausea roil in her stomach as Kedryn stepped towards her sister and they fell together onto the bed, their limbs entwined, their mouths exploring. She had closed her eyes as Kedryn pushed Ashrivelle onto her back and rolled between her legs, no longer able to watch.

When she had opened her eyes again the vision had gone and she was trembling, tears coursing her cheeks. She had crouched beside the pool, willing herself to be calm, only dimly aware that she clutched the talisman as she prayed to the Lady that what she had seen be false.

Yet, she thought now, had Eyrik not said the pool showed only the truth? So if what she had seen was false, then Eyrik lied. Or understood the pool less than he pretended. But if he *had* told the truth, then what she had seen was true: Kedryn and Ashrivelle had become lovers.

Could that be possible? Certainly, she had suspected her sister harboured an affection for Kedryn. She had seen that growing during their sojourn in Andurel, but dismissed it as meaningless. Ashrivelle had been mightily disturbed by guilt and her gratitude for Kedryn's concern had become a trivial enamouration that Kedryn himself had laughed off.

Yet what if Kedryn believed her dead?

Would he forget her so swiftly?

Or did loss propel him into Ashrivelle's arms? Did grief seek solace in passion?

Doubts swirled in a maelstrom of confusion as Wynett sought to master her bewilderment. Truth or falsehood, which did the pool show? She folded both hands about the talisman, willing herself to calm, seeking a tranquillity that would enable her to properly assess what she had seen and what it meant.

If what she had seen was the truth, then hope was lost: Kedryn assumed her dead and found consolation with her sister. He did not come in search of her, and she was doomed, presumably, to remain here for . . . for how long? Eyrik had said time had no meaning in this place, so mayhap for all eternity.

But what if those images had been untrue? Then – her mind reeled at the prospect, for it was in a way more frightening even than the alternative – perhaps Eyrik lied. And if Eyrik lied about the pool, then mayhap he lied about all else.

Did Eyrik lie?

And if he lied, to what end?

If he was not what he seemed, then what was he?

Only one answer seemed valid, and that was a thing that filled her with cold dread.

She had been taken by the leviathan, and that monstrous beast was Ashar's creature. Eyrik claimed to have rescued her from its, and Ashar's, clutches, but what if the leviathan had brought her to him?

Rank terror numbed Wynett's mind as the answer presented itself: Eyrik was of Ashar's following! She was a prisoner of the god.

Trembling, she mouthed a prayer to the Lady, the ugly knot of fear clenching tight within her suggesting that here her prayers might go unheard, that she rested in Ashar's grip and not Kedryn, not the Lady, could hear her or save her.

Her mouth was dry and she reached for the goblet, wetting lips that shuddered, the wine tasting sour now as revulsion curdled in her belly. She drank and fastened her hands tight again on the talisman. It was warm to the touch and she felt a vibration against her palms, a resonance that seemed to slowly work its way into her fingers, through her skin to the flesh and blood and bone beneath. Her trembling slowed and ceased, the dryness that, despite the wine, glued her lips, dissipated, and she felt that same calm she had experienced first on the walls of High Fort when Grania joined her mind in linkage with Kedryn's, and then again as she and Kedryn stood in opposition to the Messenger. It filled her with tranquillity and strength, and she felt her panic slough off like a shed cloak.

The talisman told her that Kedryn lived, of that she was certain beyond all doubt. And if her half of Kyrie's stone reassured her of Kedryn's life, then his must surely do the same: he must know she lived. And if he knew that, he would come seeking her. How, she was not sure, but that he would, she *knew*. Knew beyond any consideration of alternatives; knew with a certainty on which she would willingly stake her life.

And if Kedryn knew that she lived, he would not dally with Ashrivelle, and that must mean the pool had lied!

Wynett smiled, albeit grimly, at the thought. The pool had lied and therefore likely Eyrik lied. She could no more trust him than she could any longer trust the pool.

She rose, crossing to the alcove where she splashed her face with cool water, then sat again, considering her situation.

Whether Eyrik was Ashar's minion, or the god himself, it appeared that for the moment at least he intended her no harm. Mayhap the talisman deterred him; perhaps the stone circumvented his powers. She remembered the leviathan threatening from the doleful mere of the underworld, driven back when Kedryn showed it his stone, and her plunge into the creature's jaws. It had not killed her then, so perhaps it could not whilst she held the jewel. Perhaps Eyrik – or Ashar! – could not address physical force so long as she retained Kyrie's talisman. It had stood against Taws's magicks, defeating the Messenger, so mayhap it could withstand his master.

She nodded as one thought led to another, aware now of the power flowing from the stone into her, perhaps not power to overcome Eyrik, but certainly power enough to circumvent the bewilderment this place instilled, to overcome the despair that threatened.

Kedryn was the Chosen One and the talisman he held imbued him with a strength that *could* overcome Ashar. Was that what lay behind the deceptions? Did Ashar set her out as bait to lure Kedryn here? Did the god seek to entrap them both in this separate world, this place where time was meaningless, where physical dimensions had no reality?

Or did Eyrik hope with his blandishments, his courtesies, all his gallantry, to separate her from her half of the stone? Was it his intent to divide the talismans? To utilise in some way she could not know the very power that now aided her? If that was his intention, he would find it thwarted, for no matter what ploys he might use she would not willingly allow the stone to be taken from her.

Wynett sat lost in thought, determined now, not knowing what the next move in the weird game might be, but resolute in her faith. Kedryn had not deserted her – she would not believe that! – and would come seeking her. He would find her ready to aid him: she would not be seduced from that resolve.

Still more than a little frightened, but calm now, able to contain her fear, she rose and undressed, drawing on a silken nightgown before snuffing the candles and entering the sleeping chamber. She crossed to a window, looking out towards the woodland. The threatened storm was closer now, the atmosphere static, the air so warm and moist she could almost taste it, feel it crawl upon her skin as if invisible insects scuttled there. No moon or stars showed, the sky seeming closer, as if it pressed down upon the land, weighted with its burden of rain. Then lightning danced over the woodlands on white stilted legs, jagged bolts lancing the distance between sky and earth, outlining timber tossed in a gale she could not hear. Through the gagging warmth of the humid air she caught the smell of burning, scorched timber at first, but then a sweeter, nauseating odour, as though flesh roasted in the blasts. Abruptly rain fell, suddenly as if aerial floodgates opened, water falling in a near-solid curtain, shortening her field of vision as swiftly as might a blindfold flung across her eyes. She could see nothing. Not the woods or the lawns, only the pervading grey.

It should have freshened the air, but did not. Instead the humidity increased, the stench of decay mounting, and Wynett swung the window closed to shut out that reek. Better, she thought, a hot room than that stomach-turning odour, and at least the flowers set beside her bed should lend some lighter scent. But when she turned towards the bed she saw the flowers were wilted, drooping in the crystal vases, their petals fallen and rotted, brown with corruption.

Had her mood remained as it had been when she retired this might well have sunk her deeper into misery, for the all-encompassing greyness seemed to isolate her within the chamber, emphasising her loneliness, the dreary night conducive to despondency. Now, however, strengthened by contact with the talisman, she refused to give sway to that creeping hopelessness. Perhaps this was some device intended to sap her will: if so, it would fail. She gathered up the decaying blossoms and carried them to the outer chamber, tossing them into the hearth, then, fortified by the conviction that Kedryn sought her, and refusing to allow the logical conclusion of that conviction to daunt her, she climbed into bed. The sheets were no longer crisp and cool, but heavy, sticky, seeming to cling to her like cerements, and she cast them aside. Then, clutching the talisman in both hands, she composed herself for sleep.

When slumber finally came it was troubled, a kaleidoscope of images disporting in her racing mind. She dreamt of Kedryn, seeing him embrace Ashrivelle, and of her sister in the arms of Hattim Sethiyan. She saw Ashrivelle and Hattim plot to slay Darr. She dreamt of Eyrik, who pointed to the pool and said, 'It tells only the truth,' and of the Messenger, who opened his arms to her and said, 'Come to me.' She saw the leviathan rise again from the Idre, and the Horde storm against the walls of High Fort. She descended again into the netherworld, finding herself on the shore, where the grey mist parted to reveal half-seen shapes that beckoned, urging her to join them.

197

She awoke sweat-soaked, trembling as she fought the thing that clutched her and sought to drag her down until she opened her eyes to see the sheets wound about her lower limbs. She pushed them away and rose, throwing off her damp nightgown, telling herself that the dreams were no more than that – night phantoms. Nonetheless, they left a sour taint and she fell to her knees beside the bed, intoning a prayer that returned a measure of calm, the ritual driving away the lingering vestiges of nocturnal panic.

Outside, rain still drummed, a steady cacophany, the panes of the windows blurred by the downpour, opaque and grey. Wynett rose and crossed to the embrasure, seeing a landscape emptied of perspective as though thick fog concealed the prospect. She turned from it and went to the alcove in the outer chamber, where she bathed. Returning to the wardrobes she noticed that the flowers she had deposited in the hearth were now withered, sere as if struck by winter's chill. She ignored them, selecting the most modest gown available, the neck high, the sleeves long, its colour a rusty maroon. She drew it on and began to brush her hair, wondering as she did so how she should approach Eyrik.

To voice her suspicions seemed a dangerous course should they prove correct and she decided to pretend belief in his goodwill. Even now she was not absolutely sure he meant her harm, but she knew that she could no longer trust him. At least, she reminded herself, not until she could know for certain what his ultimate intentions might be; and should they prove hostile, then to reveal her doubts too early would be to forfeit what little advantage she might have gained.

Nervous, she rose from the dressing table and crossed to the door, opening the portal on a scene as miserable as that visible from the outer windows. The vinous ceiling held off the worst of the barrage that rattled upon the courtyard, transforming the atrium from its usual exotic splendour to an aqueous gloom, but heavy droplets fell with metronome regularity upon the stoa and the light was dim, depressing as she moved to the stairway and descended, one hand firm upon the talisman as she steeled herself to face Eyrik, unpleasantly aware that perhaps she dealt with a being of unimaginable power.

*

Barris Edon was intrigued by the comings and goings that enlivened the otherwise dull duty of the watch. He did not crave excitement, having had sufficient of that when he stood on the walls of High Fort as the barbarians stormed the bastion, and was generally content to dispense his duty as lookout and take his turn on guard rounds with the uncomplaining acceptance of any regular soldier. Mostly there was little more to lookout duty than studying the fishing craft putting out from the town and shouting warning of the merchants bringing supplies to the citadel, but of late he found himself speculating on the king's unexpected visit and equally unexpected departure into the Beltrevan. No explanation had been offered by Lord Rycol and none forthcoming from the officers Barris had questioned, whose knowledge, he suspected was as limited as his own.

It had been a topic of barracks conversation for a while, but without answers to the questions asked, it had lost its flavour soon enough. Kedryn went to parley with the woodlanders was the generally agreed-upon solution, and because he had won himself that barbarian title he needed no escort. Most accepted that, but to Barris it seemed a trifle thin, especially with Kedryn married to Wynett, who was not a woman Barris would leave in favour of barbarian hospitality. And now there was another odd visit. This time, he saw from his vantage point atop the tower, from three Sisters of Kyrie, one of whom bore a most remarkable resemblance to Wynett.

'A wagon approaches!' he bellowed. 'A driver and three Sisters.'

He watched the vehicle draw closer, experienced eyes recognising weariness in the four horses hauling the carriage, noting the dust that grimed the sides, and wished that he might be down at the gate to overhear what was said, perhaps even put a question or two of his own. Instead, he could only study the wagon as it came up the glacis and halted before the wall, wondering what was going on as the captain of the watch shouted for the gates to be opened and the wagon passed from his line of sight.

Wyxx halted inside the fortress and stared around, seeming unimpressed by the grandeur of the citadel. Beside him, Gerat took the hand offered by the captain and clambered from the seat, sighing as she straightened a back that after so long on the road felt more accustomed to sitting the wagon than treading firm ground.

'I would speak with Lord Rycol,' she announced as Ashrivelle and Donella were helped down. 'Inform him that Gerat, Paramount Sister of Estrevan, requests immediate audience.'

'Sister!' The captain saluted, startled that the Paramount Sister herself should come to High Fort. 'It shall be done.'

'My thanks,' Gerat responded, then to her driver, 'I am sure you can find stabling for the horses and quarters for yourself, friend Wyxx; and you have earned a rest.'

Wyxx nodded and the captain issued instructions that he be escorted to the stables.

'Donella, will you find the hospital,' Gerat suggested to the acolyte, 'and I am sure our Sisters will find you a room.'

A soldier was detailed to bring Donella to the quarters of the resident Sisters and the captain himself brought Gerat and Ashrivelle to Rycol.

The chatelain was alone, studying manifests in a wood-panelled chamber overlooking the Idre. He rose as Gerat entered, bowing.

'Sister Gerat, Princess Ashrivelle; greetings. Your presence is to do with Kedryn?'

Gerat studied the hawk-faced soldier, liking him on the instant. She said, 'It is, my Lord Rycol. He has already entered the Beltrevan?'

Rycol heard the urgency in her voice and bit off the suggestion that they bathe and rest, talk later, instead ushering them to chairs, seeing them settled and pouring wine, his stern features evincing concern as he stood before them.

'Some time past, Sister, in company of Tepshen Lahl and Brannoc. He informed me of your coming.'

Gerat nodded. 'Then by now he must be close to Drul's Mound and we have no time to waste.'

Rycol stared at her, brows raised in unspoken query.

'You know what he attempts?' asked Gerat, and when Rycol nodded, 'Then you must also know that he rides to gravest danger. Not only to himself, but to the Kingdoms. Should he fail – should Ashar succeed – then what you faced when the Messenger raised the Horde against you will be as nothing. Should Ashar suborn the power of the talismans he will be all-powerful.'

'What would you have me do?' Rycol asked, bluntly.

'I require parchment and pen,' said Gerat. 'And mehdri to carry word to my Sisters in Estrevan. Your instructions to the commander of the Morfah fortress. I would have all the strength of Estrevan stand in readiness to aid Kedryn.'

'It is done,' said Rycol, turning without preamble to the door.

# Chapter Ten

DARKNESS held dreary sway over the atrium as Wynett reached the foot of the stairs and darted swiftly beneath the cover of the overhanging balcony. The fountain was no more than a shadow in the gloom, the sound of its musically tinkling water overwhelmed by the drumming of the rain. The flagstones seemed dulled, their colour leeched by the downpour that transformed them to a single muted sheet of moisture from which splashes exploded as if the cloud-burst sought to shatter the stone. The perfumes of the flowers were gone, replaced by the warm, wet odour of the rain, and petals of magnolia and oleander and roses lay storm-battered and colourless, sad victims of the onslaught. Light showed in a doorway, the perspectives of the courtyard so altered by the storm that she was unsure whether she had entered the room beyond or not, and she turned towards it.

Eyrik waited inside, rising as she entered, his expression apologetic, as though he assumed personal responsibility for the inclemency of the day. It was a small and cheerful room, the windows shuttered against the gloom and the walls hung with gay tapestries, niches that held alabaster vases filled with fresh flowers. Candles burned, their glow cheering. The ceiling was low and plastered white, like the walls, thick beams of dark, reddish timber lending a homely air. The table at which he sat was spread with a spotless cloth of white linen, and that with silver salvers, fine china cups, and a large pot that steamed, exuding the aromatic scent of tisane.

'A foul day,' he remarked, 'I am sorry.'

'Are you responsible then?' she asked, lightly as she was able, while he held her chair and saw her seated.

He smiled, resuming his place across from her, leaning back as he shook his head. 'Had I such control I should visit nothing but sunshine upon you. Unless, of course, you desired differently.'

Wynett essayed an answering smile, buttering bread still warm from whatever unknown ovens produced it. 'I am minded of the

201

darkness Ashar's Messenger visited on High Fort when he sought to sap the will of the defenders.'

She glanced at her host – or was he more correctly her captor? – as she said it, but his face remained bland.

'I use no such magicks,' he murmured.

'What magicks do you then use?' she asked, hoping that her tone was sufficiently bantering as to allay any suspicion.

'Only those permitted me,' he smiled, reaching to extract an apple from the bowl set between them. 'Simple grammaryes. You appear in better humour.'

The abrupt reference to her mood of the previous night took her somewhat aback and she wondered if he prevaricated. It seemed too obvious to press her point, so she smiled, shrugging, and said, 'I am. Despite this doleful weather.'

'It will change in due course,' he promised. 'The seasons turn differently here. Mayhap we shall see the sun again on the morrow.'

Wynett selected an egg, hard boiled, and broke the shell. 'How did you come here, Eyrik?'

Had she asked casually enough? It seemed so, for he smiled wistfully and said, 'By mischance – like you. I was once no more than other men, but circumstances brought me here, and here I stay.'

Wynett spooned egg. Chewed, thinking, and asked, 'Why do you not leave?'

'I enjoy this place,' he answered simply, 'and I am not sure I could leave it.'

Alarm clenched her jaw for an instant and she fought it, determined to hold fast to her resolve to delve as deeply as she might into the mysteries of the place and his presence. 'If you cannot leave,' she said at last, 'then how are you able to aid me? How may I leave?'

'Circumstances differ,' came the answer, 'and as I have told you, it may be beyond my power to send you forth – it may require Kedryn's attendance.'

'Forgive my ignorance,' she used a napkin to dab her mouth, 'but why? Kedryn has no sorcerous powers.'

'He bears the other half of the talisman,' Eyrik said, evenly, his voice calm as though he explained some minor point of procedure. 'The strength of the two stones, united, is – as you know – remarkable.'

'But *how* shall he find me?' she wondered. 'If I was brought here by the leviathan, and that beast is Ashar's creation, then how may Kedryn come here? Must he be swallowed, too?'

Eyrik laughed; a musical sound. 'No. I do not believe so extreme a measure will be necessary. Do the talismans not attune you to one another?'

Wynett nodded: how did he know that? 'They do.'

'And what does yours tell you?'

'That Kedryn lives,' she responded.

'Then doubtless he is privy to the same information. He must know that you live, and so will seek you out. And the talisman will aid him; did it not before?'

'Aye,' Wynett ducked her head again; again wondering how he knew, thinking that if he controlled the images shown by the oracular pool this was an unlikely, an unexpected, statement. 'Then you believe the talisman will ward him should he venture into this netherworld?'

'I have no doubt of it,' said Eyrik. 'There will be dangers – but what quest is without hazard?'

'And the talisman will guide him here?' she pressed.

Eyrik nodded. 'The talisman and my own small efforts.'

'Even though he come through Ashar's domain?'

'There will be dangers,' Eyrik repeated, 'but whilst Kedryn holds the talisman he is protected.'

'Against the god?' asked Wynett.

'Ashar himself is not all-powerful.' For the briefest of instants his gold-flecked eyes sparked, as though the motes held within the brown whirled. 'Does your goddess not hold sway within the Kingdoms? Has she not penned Ashar behind the Lozin wall with her own puissance? Did the talisman not overcome Taws?'

'All that is true,' Wynett acknowledged, 'but if Kedryn enters the netherworld he comes into a place where Ashar is mightily powerful.'

'True,' Eyrik agreed, 'but there are powers beyond even the gods. Powers that bind even them in balance, and I believe the talismans focus that omnipotence.'

'Then Kedryn might withstand Ashar?'

She wondered if the charging of the air she felt, as though a massive electrical storm brewed, emanated from the atmosphere or the man seated across the table. She could feel hairs rise on the nape of her neck; her teeth seemed to tingle. Did the candles flicker, or was that merely a shifting of the light outside?

'He might,' said Eyrik. 'Is he not the Chosen One?'

Wynett steeled herself and said, 'Alaria's Text suggests he is Ashar's downfall.'

Eyrik showed no reaction other than a shrug, the ever-present smile. 'Mayhap he is. Mayhap he must come into the netherworld for that very reason.'

'But what,' she asked slowly, choosing her words with care, 'if he should fail?'

'In what?' Eyrik demanded. 'In his quest for you? Or his possible battle with Ashar?'

'What if Ashar should secure the talisman?' she asked.

'Then I think that he would have the means to breech the Lozin wall,' Eyrik told her quietly. 'He would have the means to overcome the grammaryes set upon that barrier and wreak his will upon the Kingdoms.'

Wynett suppressed a shudder, horrified by the magnitude of that awful thought. 'But if Ashar cannot harm Kedryn whilst he holds the talisman that is unlikely.'

Eyrik nodded.

'And what,' she continued doggedly, 'if Kedryn should find me but be unable to return? What if we should both remain trapped here?'

'Trapped?' Eyrik's expression grew instantly mournful. 'Do you feel trapped? I had hoped your sojourn was, at the least, sufficiently pleasant that you did not feel *trapped.*'

His expression, his manner, was that of a man sorely disappointed at his failure to make a guest comfortable and Wynett felt an emotion akin to embarrassment. Were her suspicions unfounded? Was he truly no more than another victim? She forced a smile and said, 'You have made me very comfortable.'

'I am glad,' said Eyrik.

'Though my question remains,' she added, resolved that he should not equivocate. Trying with all the skills imparted by Estrevan to read his expression, to determine whether it was irritation or concern that flickered in his eyes; but with little success.

'Were you both unable to return?' His smile faded, the full lips settling in a straight, solemn line. 'Then I should have two guests and the Kingdoms would lose their champion.'

'And Ashar cross the Lozin barrier?'

'Mayhap,' he shrugged. 'I do not know.'

'Are you not in danger?' She chose to take a different approach, perhaps to find some other way to the truth. 'If you work to unite us and return us, do you not stand in jeopardy?'

Eyrik gestured negligently, casual as some warrior dismissing the likelihood of battle-hurt.

'Do not disquiet yourself with that, flattered though I am by your concern. What I do, I do from choice.'

He appeared genuinely pleased, though Wynett felt his response did not exactly answer her question. Nonetheless she could see no way to rephrase it without revealing her doubts. The resolve that had descended upon her with contact with the talisman remained, but so did the apprehension: the outright confrontation that must surely come with direct questioning – should her suspicions be valid – could only, she felt certain, prove a disadvantage. If Eyrik did work to aid her, he must be insulted by such doubts; if not, then better he did not know she suspected his motives. She sipped tisane, seeking another avenue of exploration.

'Will the pool not show whether, or not, Kedryn traverses the netherworld safely?' she asked at last.

Eyrik frowned slightly. 'Mayhap not,' he said. 'The netherworld does not reveal itself easily, not even to the pool. Though we may determine how he fares on his approach.'

Wynett nodded, quelling the ugly stirring of distaste that welled at the thought of that last vision. If – as she was sure it did – the pool had lied to her, then it might well be revelatory to see what was Eyrik's reaction to a similar image. It was an unpleasant prospect, but she felt it might take her another step along the path of discovery, and knowledge must surely aid her if she did deal with an enemy.

'Might we consult it now?' she enquired.

'If that is your wish,' he agreed readily.

'It is,' she confirmed, hoping she did not pale as she said it.

'Then come.'

He rose, pushing back his chair, and moved to draw back hers. Wynett wondered if it was enthusiasm for what the oracle would show her that she read in his movements, or nothing more than the desire to please that he evinced so plausibly.

They left the breakfast chamber, moving beneath the shelter of the balcony to approach the door of blue wood. Eyrik thrust the portal open and bowed Wynett inside. Once more the strange submarine light struck her, distorting distance and space and time so that she seemed to walk slowly, swimmingly, across the tiles to the silent circle of silver liquid, simultaneously intrigued and frightened by what might be shown. Eyrik halted, seeming unaffected by the shifting patterns that filled the chamber, and positioned himself close to her side as she stared down at the well.

As before, the surface remained still, seeming to drink in her gaze, then somehow shifted within its depths, an image forming, slow as swirling smoke, then solidifying to become clear as though she looked through one of the palace's perfect windows.

She saw a walled garden filled with summer flowers, their brightness interspersed with herb beds, familiar benches set against grey stone, and murmured, 'The hospital garden in High Fort.'

'Then mayhap he has reached the Lozins,' Eyrik said softly.

Wynett saw the gate open and Kedryn enter. He wore a shirt of white linen and breeks of soft, brown hide, his dirk belted at his waist, but no sword. His hair hung loose about his tanned face and he pushed it carelessly back as he settled on a bench, an expectant expression on his handsome features. Then he rose as the gate opened again and Ashrivelle came into the garden. She wore a gown pink as the petals of the roses that clung to the wall behind the bench, the bodice tight and cut low. Her skin shone tan, like dark honey, and her blonde hair was long, bound with a simple fillet of pink silk. She smiled as she saw Kedryn and he smiled back, extending a hand that she took and drew to her breast, her eyes adoring as she looked up at him. He came a step closer and put his arms about her waist as hers moved to encircle his neck. They kissed, long and passionately. Wynett clenched her teeth, torn by roiling emotions and unsure what face to show to Eyrik.

It is not true, she told herself, I believe in the talisman and what I felt. I believe in what I feel for Kedryn and what I know he feels for me. *It is not true!*

She felt Eyrik's hand upon her arm, tight, and turned from the image to study his face.

It was grave, the gold-flecked eyes clouded, his lips pursed. 'I am sorry,' he said. 'I would that you had not seen that.'

'I do not believe it,' she answered.

'The pool does not lie,' he responded; quietly, as though he regretted the confirmation.

'No!' She shook her head, her free hand rising to clutch the talisman, seeking its reassurance. It sat warm against her palm, vibrating with its own strange life, and she felt again that calm certitude that had descended the previous night. 'Kedryn knows that I live, and knowing that he would not dally with my sister or any other woman.'

She turned again towards the pool, seeing the image fade as Eyrik said, 'Forgive my bluntness, but he is a man and men have . . . appetites.'

'I do not believe it,' she repeated. 'Kedryn would not forsake me.'

Eyrik's expression was difficult to interpret because the changing patterns of the room overlayed his features with bands of shifting light, as if she saw him through water, nebulous and indefinite. His grip upon her arm grew firmer. Was that through irritation at her rejection of the image? Or concern for her feelings? He said, 'Let us leave. I do not think we shall see more.'

Wynett allowed him to draw her away, back across the blue tiles to the door, out to the shelter of the balcony. He did not speak, nor release his hold, as he led her to the chamber where they had eaten breakfast. Inside, the table had been cleared and a decanter, two goblets, set upon the wooden surface. Eyrik brought her to a chair and seated her, then filled glasses with dark red wine. He sat and sipped; Wynett ignored hers. Finally, his face thoughtful, he murmured, 'You do not believe what you saw?'

'No.' She shook her head, staring at him.

'Are you so confident of his love?'

'Aye.' She nodded, emphasising the affirmative.

'Then mayhap there is another explanation.'

He toyed with his glass, turning the crystal between his powerful hands, a small smile that defied interpretation curving the corners of his mouth as he at last raised his face towards her.

'The pool does not lie – it cannot – but the truth is not always what we perceive.'

He paused as if lost in thought, seeking the words that would explain his meaning. Wynett said, 'That is a riddle I fail to comprehend.'

His smile grew broader, apologetically, then faded to become replaced by an expression of solemn gravity. He said, 'It is usual to think of your world, your life, in linear fashion: Kedryn loves you and you were taken by the leviathan, therefore Kedryn will seek you because he knows – thanks to the talisman he wears – that you live. He will rescue you and bring you back to the Kingdoms, where you will rule together and live in happiness thereafter. That is one truth.

207

'But as you have seen, this place we now inhabit is not governed by the natural laws appertaining to your life in the Kingdoms: the rules of linear progression do not apply. Therefore it is possible the pool showed you an alternative truth. Perhaps one in which the leviathan destroyed you, leaving Kedryn to find solace with your sister.

'You see, every event in life opens alternatives. Had Kedryn not been wounded when first he entered the Beltrevan, he might not have met you. He might have travelled to Andurel and fallen in love with Ashrivelle, perhaps become betrothed to her.

'Had you not chosen to travel with him when he was blind you might not have fallen in love, in which alternative you would not have been on the barge when the leviathan attacked, and so not come to this place.

'Do you understand, Wynett? It is as though life branches with each decision, each event, all possibilities becoming possible, alternative selves treading different paths, no one less real – less true – than another.'

He paused, lifting his glass to drink as though the speech had rendered him thirsty. His eyes studied her across the rim.

Wynett frowned, puzzled. She followed the gist of his argument and saw that it did nothing to confirm or refute her suspicions: it left her no more clear as to his intentions than before. She said, 'I understand what you say, but it surely means the pool cannot be relied upon. I am here and that is a fact, therefore I maintain that in the reality I inhabit Kedryn would not dally with Ashrivelle.'

'I admire your conviction,' Eyrik nodded, 'and likely you are right, but this place does not conform to your notions of reality, and the pool is a part of this place.'

'Surely we talk in circles,' she responded. 'If that is true, then the pool does not show what is true for me.'

'Assuming – and I ask your forgiveness for what I am about to say, but assure you I have only your welfare at heart – that you are correct in your assessment of Kedryn's devotion, then you are right. In a way, at least,' he answered. 'But being a creation of this place the pool may well show you the alternatives, mixing one reality with another. Mayhap it is even possible that you yourself now cross from one strand to another.'

'Then still the pool is a meaningless oracle,' she said. 'And I shall stand by my belief.'

Eyrik succeeded in bowing from a sitting position. 'I have nothing but admiration for you,' he applauded, 'and a suggestion that may bring some small comfort. Let us assume that what you saw is no more than a strand of possibility that does not apply to the alternative you occupy, still the pool shows truth. Mayhap it is for you to discern which strand connects to you, here.'

'How may I do that?' she asked, puzzled.

'If your heart does not tell you,' Eyrik said, shrugging, 'then mayhap the talisman can help you discern your particular truth.'

'I wore the talisman when I visited the pool,' she murmured, 'both yesterday and today.'

'Yesterday?' Eyrik leant forward, brows raised in mute query.

Wynett nodded without speaking, angry at herself for letting slip that tidbit of knowledge. Though surely, she thought, if he *does* control the pool he must know that.

'I see,' he said musingly. 'And does that account for your sad humour of last night? Did you perceive something similar?'

Again she nodded without speaking.

Eyrik made a sound that was both sigh and grunt, as if he understood and did not welcome the understanding. 'Twice,' he said softly. 'You have twice seen Kedryn in the arms of your sister.'

Wynett nodded silently a third time.

'Mayhap alternatives.' Eyrik smiled as though seeking to impart reassurance where none was valid. 'And you wore the talisman on each occasion?'

'I wear it always,' she confirmed.

'Perchance that is not enough,' he said, his voice thoughtful. 'I do not pretend to understand the full power of the stone, but perhaps it requires some greater application.'

'How?' she asked, bluntly.

Eyrik shrugged, his eyes narrowing as he frowned, the very image of a man locked in thought, his expression evincing only concern, the desire to help her.

'Mayhap closer contact with the pool,' he suggested after a while. 'Mayhap you should place the talisman in the pool.'

Alarm tugged at Wynett's heart and she shook her head. 'I should surely lose it.'

'I do not mean you to sink the stone,' Eyrik chuckled. 'Merely that you might suspend it beneath the surface – like bait for the truth that applies to you. In that way its power might cut through the alternatives offered to show only that which applies to you.'

'I would need remove it,' she said warily, not liking the suggestion.

'What harm could come?' Eyrik laughed again, louder, as though her fear was so groundless as to be amusing. 'You hold the chain – you may remove the stone at will. There is nothing in the pool, my dear. No leviathan will rise from its depths to snatch the talisman from you.'

'Still I am loath to . . .' she was about to say, take that risk, but thought better of it, amending the sentence to, 'remove it even for so short a time. When Sister Lavia presented us with the stones she was insistent that we should not remove them.'

Eyrik shrugged, his tone light as he suggested, 'Surely that was when danger threatened? Were you not then intent on a descent into the underworld?'

It was a reasonable enough presumption and Wynett found it impossible to judge whether some deeper design lay behind it. Indeed, she was more confused now than before. Eyrik's explanation of the images seemed plausible within the utterly implausible parameters of this strange place, where – her own eyes gave clear evidence – the natural laws governing the world she knew did not apply. Yet his explanation gave clear reason to distrust the pool, and her instincts told her that she should from henceforth ignore it; but were she to do that, she would be entirely dependent on Eyrik for any news of Kedryn, and it came to her that she might easily lose her sanity in this irrational place should she find herself cut off from all knowledge of Kedryn. The pool was a temptation, both alluring and forbidding; a quandary.

Further, she thought, if those suspicions she had felt were true, then likely some intent other than her peace of mind lay hidden within his suggestion. But if he told the truth . . . then by means of the talisman she might ascertain the reality that applied to her; and if the talisman had the power to protect her from the leviathan, then would it not likely have the power to overcome any threat offered by the pool?

'I must think on it,' she said.

'Certainly.' Eyrik's response was easy, devoid of pressure, save that which it aroused from her own emotions. 'But I think that may be the only way in which you can know the ultimate truth.'

Wynett stared at his face, seeing only good will, the desire to set her mind at rest. He smiled and said, 'And now a little wine? This must all be horrendously confusing.'

He appeared so genuine she found herself wondering if her doubts were unfounded, her suspicions groundless. She nodded and raised her glass, sipping the delicately flavoured wine.

'You must not be afraid, for no harm will come to you here and I have only your best interests at heart.' His tone was gentle, his expression calm, yet the words startled Wynett and she struggled to conceal her surprise for they suggested he read her better than she was able to read him, seeing past the facade she sought to present to the inner doubts, the fears. 'Confusion is a natural reaction when faced with such unknown concepts as the pool.'

'Aye,' she said, using ambiguous honesty as a screen, 'it is.'

'Consider my suggestion,' he advised, setting down his goblet and rising, 'and forgive me for leaving you alone again, but there are tasks that await my presence.'

He bowed, striding to the door, and was gone before Wynett had opportunity to ask what tasks awaited him. She turned, seeing the door swing closed and drained her own cup. The thought crossed her mind that perhaps the wine was drugged, or the excellent food, but she dismissed it as paranoia, recognising the danger inherent in such consideration. She could not go without food or drink and there seemed little purpose that she could conceive in such clandestine measures. She was, after all, entirely in Eyrik's powers and the very nature of her surroundings suggested that so mundane a device was unnecessary should he wish to distort her perceptions.

She leant forwards, elbows on the table as she cupped both hands about the talisman and called upon the teachings of Estrevan to bring that calm that might allow her to properly assess her situation.

The rituals were simple and effective: extraneous thoughts were rapidly banished, her mind clearing, blanking, then focusing on the problem in hand, what facts she had at her disposal reviewed, her impressions presented, conclusions considered, rejected, her mind become a mixing bowl in which ingredients mingled, hopefully emerging in some single form, some beacon that would guide her through this maze of incomprehension.

If Eyrik told the truth he was a valuable ally; indeed, her only ally, and his suggestion that she utilise the talisman to seek truth from the pool valid.

If he lied, then the suggestion was likely some ploy by which he hoped to part her from the stone, and if that was the case all that transpired here a mockery, some elaborate design.

But to what end? To gain control of the talisman? If that, then he must not be able to take it by force. Ergo: if Eyrik was false the talisman protected her in some measure.

If so, then would it not also protect her, and itself, from any danger offered by the pool? But if the talisman was impervious to threat from the pool then – if Eyrik lied – what was the point in his advising that move?

If, on the other hand, he spoke honestly, by using the talisman she might find a way through the alternatives shown and gain information of Kedryn.

Could she continue without such knowledge, ignore the pool? It would require fortitude, to inhabit this unreal realm in blind ignorance, unaware of any measures Kedryn took to find her. It seemed the pool was her only link with the world outside and she was not sure how long she might retain her sanity isolated in this weird, fabulous place. She had found no library, nor any other source of diversion save the woods and gardens, the exploration of the palace, which in itself served only to bewilder her further.

All hinged on the single consideration: did Eyrik lie or speak the truth?

It was a conclusion she could not yet decide and she opened eyes she had not known she closed and looked about the chamber. Impatience gripped her and she rose to her feet, going to the door uncertain of her purpose. Rain still filled the atrium with a wet, grey curtain and abruptly she determined to make a further exploration. A door stood to her right, one she had not yet opened, and she went to it, entering a chamber containing the appurtenances of a salon, as though grand entertainments might be held therein. The floor was an intricate parquet of polished wood, sprung as for dancing, and a minstrels' gallery stood high above the entrance. Small tables and chairs, two to each table, were arranged along the walls, which were plastered and washed with pale yellow. Banquettes stood at intervals between the more intimate seating arrangements, and great tapestries depicting woodland scenes stretched from the vaulted ceiling to the floor. High windows of multi-coloured glass were cut into all four walls, dulled by the rain, what little light they shed gloomy. The chandeliers suspended from the roof were unlit and the chamber had a musty air, as if little used. There were no other doors and Wynett left the place gladly, turning resolutely to the next portal.

212

This gave ingress to a chamber of grey stone, windowless and containing nothing save a stairway that rose from the flags to angle up the far wall. She began to climb, finding herself on a narrow landing that again held nothing but the continuation of the staircase, visible through an arched doorway. Intrigued, she resumed her ascent, the stone steps spiralling as though built within a tower. A second landing was reached and she opened the door there on a long gallery overlooking the salon. A portal stood at the far end but she chose to continue upwards, unwilling to lose herself again in the maze of chambers. She seemed to climb forever, her thighs and calves aching with the tension of the steady ascent, pausing to glance through the windows that were occasionally set into the various landings only to find her senses befuddled by the prospects they revealed. Some looked out over the lawns, although her senses told her they faced inwards; others oversaw the atrium, some the salon, several down into rooms she recognised from her earlier investigations, more into chambers she had not explored, and after a while she ignored them, concentrating on the climb.

Her breath grew short and her aching muscles were stabbed with painful complaint but she continued doggedly upwards, wondering how far towards the sky the winding stairway went or, indeed, if it would ever end, for it began to seem that it might rise forever, a ceaseless spiral leading nowhere.

Then a door showed, dark oak, hinged with thick metal, a heavy ring set at waist height. Before it the stairs ended on a circle of stone grey as the windowless walls. She halted, breathing hard, aware that her legs trembled with the effort of the climb, then took the metal ring and pulled the door inwards.

Rain struck her face, gusted on a wind that suggested great height, and she looked onto a colonnade open to the elements. It was fashioned of marble, pale and slick with rain, the columns glistening dully in the wan light. There was little shelter to be found beneath the roof, but she ignored the discomfort of rapidly-soaked clothing as she walked towards the cupola visible at the far end of the colonnade. It was raised by three steps above the level of the walkway, circular, with a pillared rail of black marble striated with gold. She brushed wet hair from her face, blinking against the rain that buffeted her eyes and stared out over a vista she had not seen before.

The sky was grey, the light poor, rendering judgement of distance uneasy, but her impression was that she stood higher than the levels of the palace she had counted from the ground, the cupola seeming to float beneath the lowering cloud like some aerial platform. Dizziness assailed her and she set her hands on the marble of the rail, the very loftiness of her vantage point, its aeriness, suggesting that she might let loose her grip and throw herself forwards, outwards, to sail bird-like downwards. She stepped back, peering into the gloom, resisting the insane temptation. Below, she saw lawns, dull in the rain, cut by a wide road she guessed led to the gates of the palace. To one side, beyond the angle of the roof, she recognised the woodland, the stream she had crossed winding into a river, grey-silver from this height and broad, curving in a great ox bow before the building. A bridge spanned its course where the road ran down to meet the water, and from the far bank to the misty horizon there was a profusion of trees to dwarf even the Beltrevan. They were no kin to the woodlands where she had walked with Eyrik but a vast solidity of timber, wild and dark, no meadows showing, nor any waterways other than the great river that swept before the palace, a liquid boundary between gentle lawns and primeval forest. She could not be sure, but in the distance, at the outermost limits of her sight, she thought she discerned the faint outlines of mountains, as though a range of colossal height bulked along the horizon. As far as she could see the timber spread, the building atop which she stood the only habitation, isolated in that vast grey arboreal ocean.

Abruptly she was filled with a terrible emptiness. She felt herself horribly alone, forsaken. An eremitical figure in the vast, rain-sodden landscape, helpless in this strange place. She turned away, wiping tears and rain from her eyes, shivering even though the wind that gusted her hair was warm, and a decision formed: she would trust the power of the talisman and seek knowledge, genuine knowledge, of Kedryn in the pool.

*

In Gerat's absence Lavia had, by common consent, assumed the duties of Paramount Sister and so it was that the travel-weary mehdri delivered his message to the tall woman with the grey-streaked hair. Lavia took it, recognising Gerat's seal and, after seeing the messenger settled with food and drink, retired to her own chambers to read the communication. She studied it with alarm

214

widening her eyes, then read it once more before calling an acolyte to summon those senior members of the Sorority comprising the governing council of Estrevan.

Jara, Porelle and Reena came on her bidding, the older woman grumbling that her luncheon was interrupted, the two younger Sisters intrigued, for news of the mehdri's arrival had spread rapidly through the Sacred City.

'Forgive me,' Lavia apologised, somewhat tartly, 'but I have received word from Gerat that brooks no delay in answer. It would seem that her fears were justified.'

'Qualle's writings have meaning?'

Porelle sounded doubtful and Lavia nodded gravely, her expression stilling any further interruption. 'Wynett has been taken by a creature of the netherworld,' she announced, 'and Kedryn – accompanied by Tepshen Lahl and the former outlaw, Brannoc – has gone into the Beltrevan, his purpose to enter the netherworld and save Wynett.'

'Both talismans are in the netherworld?' Reena's plain features grew stark as the import of that statement sank in.

'Wynett's, without doubt; Kedryn's, perhaps,' Lavia nodded. 'Gerat surmises that Ashar sets a trap that Qualle foresaw.'

'He should not have gone!' Porelle glanced at her Sisters. 'It is too dangerous.'

'He would not be dissuaded,' said Lavia. 'And further, Gerat believes that it is a gamble worth the taking. She considers it an opportunity to destroy the god.'

'Or grant him unimaginable powers,' said Porelle. 'Should he succeed in securing both talismans he will overcome any measures we may take to thwart him. With the talismans in his possession he will be able to breach the defences Kyrie herself placed about the Kingdoms.'

'The talismans must be given,' Jara reminded them. 'They may not be taken by force whilst the rightful owner lives.'

'Even so,' murmured Porelle, her eyes troubled. 'Ashar is a god of lies and deception, mayhap he will trick one of them, or both, into presenting him their stone.'

'Wynett will not be easily beguiled,' Reena said, 'but what of Kedryn? Lavia, you have met him – do you think he might be deceived?'

Lavia shook her head. 'Not easily.'

'The fate of the Kingdoms hangs on that,' Porelle said nervously.

'Aye,' Lavia nodded, 'what this action may unleash could turn the world on its head.'

'I had misjudged Qualle,' Jara remarked thoughtfully. 'It seems that in her madness she spoke the truth.'

Three faces turned towards her and her wrinkled features creased further in a wry smile. 'Do you not see it now? Gerat was right from the start, perchance inspired by the Lady.'

'To send Kedryn into the netherworld?' Porelle demanded, her question harsh with doubt.

'To send him there to slay Ashar,' Jara confirmed. 'I doubt, in any event, that she could have stopped him. Nor would she send him to that limbo without the protection of the talisman.'

'That Wynett is taken is misfortune enough,' Porelle argued. 'Surely to further risk the second talisman is . . . unwise.'

Jara shook her silver head. 'Mayhap not, even though the absence of the one half must inevitably weaken our defences against the god's minions; but the rest is a gamble I have no doubt Gerat has taken only after much calculation.'

'She believes it the only way to secure Wynett's stone,' Lavia said. 'Listen, I shall read you her message.'

They sat in silence as she read the words. When she had finished Jara said, 'Aye, I see it, and although I doubted her wisdom in travelling to Gennyf I now find myself in agreement.'

'As I do,' Lavia declared.

'Do we have sufficient Senders?' Porelle wondered. 'And can we channel our strength in such a way?'

'It has never been attempted,' Lavia said, 'therefore we cannot know, but it is possible.'

'In theory,' Reena said doubtfully. 'But in practice?'

'We shall find out,' said Lavia. 'Let us gather all our Senders and explain what is needed of them. Then we must arrange transport. Word is already delivered to the Morfah garrison and Chatelain Lyon stands ready to support our efforts.'

'Wait!' Porelle raised a hand in protest. 'Should we not first consider the possible consequences? If we establish linkage with Gerat in High Fort, and she is able to project the full strength of Estrevan into the netherworld, then we also create a potential channel down which Ashar may send *his* evil might. Should he secure the talismans he may use them to return our own strength against us – that very linkage we establish might well open the way for the god to strike at Estrevan itself!'

The others paused, contemplating her warning. Jara said, 'Gerat is still Paramount Sister – do you question her clear instructions?'

'Mayhap Gerat is too close to the problem,' Porelle replied. 'Mayhap she had failed to see the awful potential should her plan fail.'

'I doubt that,' said Lavia.

'But,' murmured Reena, glancing at Porelle, 'it is still possible that this is a part of Ashar's fell design. Mayhap he seeks this very channel to attack us.'

Lavia sighed, ducking her age-streaked head in reluctant agreement. 'Mayhap,' she acknowledged. 'But to do that he must first secure the talismans.'

'Therefore all our hopes rest on the integrity of Wynett and Kedryn,' Porelle responded.

'Indeed,' said Lavia, 'and it is Gerat's opinion that we may best lend aid by taking this chance.'

'It is a tremendous gamble,' Porelle protested.

'Aye,' confirmed Lavia, 'it is. This game is riddled with snares, but I see no other way than to comply with Gerat's instructions.'

'Nor I,' said Jara. 'Let us gather the Senders.'

'Can we rely on Kedryn alone to save Wynett?' asked Reena.

'We face terrible consequences should he fail,' said Lavia.

Reena nodded, smiling apologetically at the young woman beside her. 'Then I must vote in favour.'

Porelle sighed, shaking her head in resignation. 'I fear that we play into Ashar's hands, but let it be done.'

'Let us place our faith in the Lady,' Lavia suggested, 'and in Gerat's undoubted wisdom.'

She rose, allowing no further opportunity for debate, and hurried from the chamber with the others close behind. Soon all of Estrevan's Senders were gathered, their faces grave as she explained the nature of the task before them. She saw fear flicker in some eyes, excitement in others, for all there knew that what they were asked to do might well leave them mad, or destroyed by Ashar, and that no such thing had been attempted in the history of Estrevan. But none demurred, and by nightfall the wagons were lumbering across the plain carrying Sisters to the Morfah Pass and beyond.

*

Kedryn savoured the roast venison won by Brannoc's marksmanship as he stretched before the fire. Across the blaze, over which a haunch was spitted, Tepshen Lahl sat whetting his blade, his sallow face a mask of concentration. Brannoc squatted cross-legged, chewing on the succulent meat with evident pleasure.

'Did we but have a skin of wine,' he remarked, 'this would be perfection.'

Kedryn grimaced, recalling the effects of the Caroc liquor, more than content to forgo such vinous pleasures and still embarrassed by the results. Long days had passed since their encounter with the woodlanders, and they had met no others, although numerous tracks had been found, at first those of Caroc bands moving east and south, then more recently, those of Drott. They had avoided contact, aware that the time of the Drott Gathering drew steadily closer, impressing upon them an ever greater urgency as they approached Drul's Mound.

'How long?' he asked the halfbreed.

Brannoc wiped his mouth and shrugged. 'A day and a half; perhaps two. No more, unless we are delayed.'

Kedryn nodded, his thoughts on the increasing signs of tribal activity. 'Shall we be delayed?'

'If the Lady favours us and my woodscraft holds good, no.' Brannoc's face was innocent of expression, which to Kedryn indicated doubt. 'These tracks we have seen,' he began.

'They meander,' said Brannoc.

'They appear to move towards the mound,' Kedryn argued.

'If they are there, they are there.' Tepshen's sword slid into the scabbard, punctuating the sentence.

'And will oppose us,' said Kedryn.

The kyo stared at him, saying nothing, his very silence lethally eloquent. Kedryn shook his head: 'I would avoid bloodshed.'

'It may not avoid us,' the easterner said flatly, 'and so it is time to speak plainly – you seek Wynett and it would seem the only path to her lies through Drul's Mound. If Drott are there they will not permit that desecration and therefore bar our passage. Do you forbid us to slay them?'

Kedryn stared across the fire at his friend, aware for the first time of the change in their relationship. He had grown accustomed to look to Tepshen for guidance, no less than he sought and accepted the advice of his father, yet since that morning – so long ago, it seemed! – on the high roof of the White Palace he had formulated

218

his own decisions, looking not to them but inside himself for the answers. It had been so natural a process it had not occurred to him that he no longer turned to Bedyr or Tepshen, or that the kyo followed his lead with unquestioning loyalty. Until now.

He frowned, his eyes troubled, for Tepshen presented him with a quandary. 'You know my belief,' he said slowly. 'We go on the Lady's business and she does not welcome the careless shedding of blood. I would not jeopardise the success of this quest with the taint of casual killing.'

'Casual?' Tepshen asked softly, his jet eyes hooded. 'What if it is the only way to the mound?'

Kedryn sighed, shaking his head. 'I do not know. I can only trust in the Lady.'

'This is Ashar's domain,' Tepshen said gently. 'Might it not be that the god seeks to oppose your coming by the presentation of human obstacles?'

'Then to kill would be to take his path,' Kedryn responded.

'Which may prove the only path. Again I ask: do you forbid the use of blades?'

Kedryn studied the flat planes of the easterner's face. Firelight threw shadows from the high cheekbones, the dark eyes gleaming within the darkness. It was an impassive visage, intractable, and it offered no solution to his dilemma.

That came from Brannoc, who said, 'If we are lucky – if the Lady rides with us – it may not come to that.' He glanced up at the filling moon that showed through the lattice work of branches. 'The time of the Gathering is yet four, perhaps five, days distant and Drott custom has it that the ulan must come first to the mound, on the first day of the full moon. Until then none may approach. The clans come slowly, scattered, and the tracks we have seen are those wandering towards the place. If we ride by night and day we should have time – so long as we avoid all contact.'

'The digging will not be easy,' said Tepshen.

'No,' Brannoc agreed, 'but were we to forgo sleep tonight and ride throughout the morrow we should be at the mound by dusk, with time enough to force our entry.'

Tepshen nodded, then voiced a thought none had so far dared: 'And after? When the Drott come to find the hole?'

Brannoc shrugged. Kedryn said, 'Let us worry about that when the time comes. If we are successful it must surely prove a small enough problem. If we are not . . .'

219

The kyo smiled, briefly and grimly. Brannoc chuckled. 'It would be a sad end, would it not? To defeat a god and find ourselves given to the blood eagle.'

'Mayhap you should not accompany me,' said Kedryn. 'Rather, bring me to the mound and help me enter, then hide or return to the Kingdoms.'

Tepshen studied him for a moment, not deigning to speak, then rose.

'Douse the fire and let us be gone.'

'I would not . . .' Kedryn protested, interrupted by Brannoc, who grinned and finished for him, 'Leave us behind. I shall hear my name in a ballad yet.'

There was no more to be said and they saddled the horses and packed the remains of the venison. Kedryn kicked soil over the fire. 'Ware noise,' urged Brannoc, 'and take my lead – Drott hospitality is our enemy now.'

They rode out a trail so narrow one had perforce to follow the other, Brannoc first, then Kedryn, Tepshen bringing up the rear, the pack animals strung behind. The night was clear, moon and stars illuminating their path, the natural debris of the forest muffling the hoofbeats as the halfbreed picked up speed. He brought them swiftly to a widening of the trail, a round of bare earth circled by looming beeches, five paths joining, and crossed to follow a slightly wider avenue.

Before long he raised a hand in warning, halting them, then motioned to his left, cursing softly as his stallion forced a way through the encroaching thickets. Behind them a dog barked and Brannoc dismounted, clamping a hand over his horse's nostrils as he motioned for his companions to do the same. The dog barked again, joined by others, and Brannoc threw back his head, emitting a piercing screech such as a hunting cat would make. The hounds proceeded to bay and the halfbreed screamed again, as if in challenge, then mounted and urged the grey to a canter, taking them away from the unseen camp.

Thrice more they were forced to circumnavigate groups of Drott and it seemed to Kedryn that their progress towards the mound was become more evasive then direct. They left the trails, taking deer paths and whatever routes were available amongst the dense timber, riding as swiftly as caution and the undergrowth allowed, and as the sky grew pearly with the approach of dawn they halted beside a stream.

The horses drank thirstily, the stallions irritable, and as the sun broke through the early mist to spread roseate light across the eastern skyline they mounted again, Brannoc leading the way along the streambed.

They splashed through the water until the heavens were lit by the rising sun, blue arching above, and white clouds, birdsong loud about them, then Brannoc quit the stream and struck out across a meadow that revealed a small herd of the wild forest cattle. The heifers lowed protest and the bull bellowed a challenge, lowering the sabre-sweep of his horns and stamping the dew-wet grass. They were gone before he made up his mind to charge, galloping over the sward into the surrounding trees as the cattle milled behind them.

The terrain began to rise and at noon, when they topped a ridge, Brannoc called a halt to rest the animals and eat. From the crest of the chine they were able to survey the shallow valley that lay before them. The downslope was thinly wooded, though the timber grew thick across the bottomland and the farther slope; columns of smoke rose from the forest to indicate Drott camps. Kedryn counted thirteen.

'We are lucky,' Brannoc murmured. 'They favour the northern reaches, so few camp here. And Drul's Mound lies over that far rise.'

Thirteen camps – and the concomitant likelihood of wandering hunters – seemed to Kedryn to lend a euphemistic note to the statement, but the proximity of his goal inflamed his patience and he fretted to be gone.

'Soon,' Brannoc promised, 'let the sun take its toll and the camps sleep in the heat, then we shall be on our way.'

It was hard to wait out the noonday warmth, though both Tepshen and Brannoc stretched on the grass and dozed as Kedryn kept watch, unable to snatch that small opportunity to rest. He was grateful when the halfbreed woke and nudged the kyo, announcing that they might attempt the crossing.

'Should we be spotted,' he warned as they prepared to mount, 'ride for the farther slope and trust in speed to save us. Should we become separated, continue northwards: the site of the Gathering lies directly ahead.'

Without further ado he swung astride the grey stallion and urged the beast over the crest, riding hard and fast for the shelter of the lower timber. Kedryn followed, nerves tingling in anticipation of encounter, feeling unpleasantly exposed on the sparsely-wooded descent.

Luck, or the Lady, was with them, however, and they entered the denser timber unnoticed, trailing Brannoc as he veered west and then east, cutting a zig-zag route that brought them around the barbarian encampments and onto the summit of the northern chine.

The sun was westering as they topped the ridge and halted, the eastern sky already darkening into twilight, the moon, fatter now, hanging low and large above the horizon. A scarp descended before them, shadow pooling where it ended in a wide valley, vee-shaped, the mouth towards them, to Kedryn immeasurably enticing for he knew it held Drul's Mound. He studied the terrain ahead, seeing no sign of fires, and voiced silent thanks to Brannoc for the halfbreed's knowledge of the woodlanders and their ways.

'We need hide no longer,' Brannoc declared, and they went down the ridge.

The moon rose as they entered the valley, patterning the trees with silver light. A cat screamed and a bull lowed, but they met neither animals nor men as they urged the tiring horses onwards, their own fatigue ignored as excitement gripped them.

Then Brannoc halted, turning in his saddle to smile to Kedryn as he gestured at the bowl that lay before them.

It was located close to the centre of the valley, a massive indentation like some natural amphitheatre nor gargantuan proportions. Trees stood sentinel watch all around, though the lip of the bowl was bare, great stumps showing where the timber had been cut back to accommodate the lodges that would fill the hollow when the Drott gathered. Grass had made a patchy footing on the earth, though mostly denuded soil showed, blackened from countless fires and stamped hard by innumerable feet. At the nub, placed like the hub of a wheel whose spokes would be the alleyways running between the lodges, sat Drul's Mound. Its rise was dark under the moon, the circumference scorched by the fires that had ringed it over the years, its apex soot-black from the great sacrificial bonfire that would soon once more be lit. It appeared forbidding, a brooding presence that defied entry, and Kedryn felt a chill prickle down his spine as he studied it.

Without speaking, he heeled his mount forwards, going down the slope and across the floor of the bowl until he sat beneath the shadow of the monticle, staring up at its smooth surfaces. The dirt that packed the slope looked hard as rock, and for a moment he wondered how they hoped to broach its solidity, the chill becoming the icy tingling of despair. Then he touched the talisman and felt its warmth, the faint vibration against his fingertips, and flung himself from the saddle, turning to seek the pack horses and their burdens of tools.

'Eat first,' advised Tepshen, dismounting beside him. 'This will be hard labour.'

Kedryn nodded reluctantly and they set to establishing a camp.

The horses were stripped of their loads and tethered amongst the trees where they might forage for themselves and find water in a nearby stream. A small fire was built and the dwindling store of venison spitted over the flames. Brannoc filled their canteens. They ate hungrily, then, as the moon approached its zenith, took the picks and shovels Rycol had provided and surveyed the mound.

'It was built long and long ago,' Brannoc advised, 'after Drul was slain on the walls of High Fort. It is said the Drott spent a year on its construction, quarrying stone in the north and transporting dressed blocks here. My guess would be they raised a dome and they layered it with earth, so the entrance is likely to be found either at the foot or atop the hummock.'

They paced around the mound, finding no indication of any portal.

'Mayhap they built it as they do their lodges,' Kedryn surmised. 'In which case there would be something akin to a smoke-hole.'

'The apex is as good a place as any to start,' nodded Brannoc.

They scrambled up the sides to stand within the great fire-ring. 'Here,' Kedryn decided, driving a spade against the hard-packed earth, and gasping as the blow reverberated back, jarring his shoulders.

Tepshen motioned for him to stand aside and swung a pick. For all his wiry strength his effort had little impact on the rock-like soil, making no more than a pin's prick. Tepshen grunted and swung again. Kedryn tossed the spade aside and took pick in hand, Brannoc likewise, and they developed a rhythm, each striking in turn until the night was filled with the steady thudding of their labour, as if Drul's Mound was some gigantic drum on which they beat a cadence.

Soon they had shed their tunics, and despite the coolness of the night wind their shirts were damp with sweat. Shoulders and arms, unaccustomed to this labour, began to ache, and hands more used to wielding swords or holding reins to blister. But atop the mound the earth gave slow way, and as dawn broke the beginnings of a hole were formed.

They rested, chilled by the cold grey mist that filled the bowl, and fortified themselves with venison and a tea brewed from the herbs provided by High Fort's Sisters, then returned to the excavation. Shovels were needed now, to clear the rubble of broken earth and pebbles, and then the picks again, the rising sun revealing a shallow pit little more than a hand's length deep. For the numb ache that pervaded his back and shoulders, it seemed to Kedryn little enough, but he clenched his teeth and set to digging once more, unpleasantly aware that the burgeoning day brought the Drott a little closer, the movement of the sun across the sky eating remorselessly into the time he had left.

Fire and the passing years had transformed the upper layers of the mound to the consistency of hard-set mortar and it took the remainder of the day to break through that crust to the more malleable soil beneath. By then their hands were wrapped in strips of torn cloth, blisters raised and burst, but as the sun set and twilight filled the valley the dirt they shovelled out was darker, more friable, and the excavation deep enough that Kedryn stood knee-deep within it. They slept a few hours and commenced to dig, driving the shaft steadily deeper, two standing inside the hole, the third clearing dirt from the rim.

They laboured on throughout the day, knowing that the moon, when it rose, would be a little broader of girth, their time a little less. Then, when the blue-silver orb was almost to its zenith, Kedryn's pick jarred in his hands, striking something far harder than earth. He tossed it out and took the spade Brannoc handed him, scraping at the soil to reveal grey stone. He cursed, flinging the shovel from him in frustration.

'Stone! The tomb is ceilinged! There is no entrance here.'

'Calm yourself,' urged Tepshen. 'Likely a block was set in place to seal the hole.'

He began to clear the bottom of the pit. It was slow work, for now the excavation was deeper than their height and they must haul the loose soil clear in makeshift slings fashioned from saddle blankets and rope, but as the sun once more pierced the opalescence of the dawn a slab showed, a square block a pace wide, lined with dark earth where it fitted between its fellows.

Kedryn was persuaded to rest and eat, and then all three bathed in the stream before commencing the final assault.

Tepshen's advice seemed sound, for the jointures of the block with its fellows were wider than those indentations connecting its neighbours, and the dirt that filled the gaps came free easily under the application of knife points and fingers. Noon saw clear space all around the slab – and brought the revelation that it was angled to fit wedge-like into the hole.

Tepshen probed with his dirk and shook his head. 'Stone against stone. Its own weight seals it in place.'

Rank frustration plunged a swordpoint deep in Kedryn's soul. He stared wildly at the unyielding stone, then turned hopeless eyes to his comrades.

'A scaffold? We could use the horses to lift it clear.'

'No.' Tepshen shook his head sadly. 'We cannot gain purchase for the ropes.'

'The sides!' moaned Kedryn. 'We dig to the sides!'

'There is no time,' said Brannoc, his swarthy features grim. 'A tunnel would require propping, and we have no more than a day, two at the most.'

'No!' Kedryn's voice rose in a wail. 'It cannot be!'

His face was stark-planed with grief and rage and he fell to his knees, pounding the slab as though he sought to drive through it with his fists, seeking to achieve with flesh and bone what could not be accomplished with metal tools. Tears misted his vision and he moaned, 'Wynett! Oh, Wynett, I have failed you.'

Tepshen placed a helplessly consoling hand upon his shoulder and he fell forwards on all fours, weeping. The talisman hung about his throat fell loose, dangling down to touch the stone. 'Kyrie,' he implored, 'do not forsake me now.'

And the block groaned and collapsed inwards, pitching him down into the darkness of Drul's tomb.

# Chapter Eleven

KEDRYN landed heavily, so shocked by the sudden removal of that last, apparently insuperable, obstacle that he was at first unaware of the force with which he struck the floor of the tomb. The slab that had given way under him shattered at the impact with the floor and he lay on his back amongst the shards, winded, coughing as dust and dirt cascaded from the illuminated rectangle directly above. He spat earth from his mouth and blinked dust from his watering eyes, staring up at the hole, his blurred vision gradually clearing to reveal the anxious faces of Tepshen Lahl and Brannoc peering down at him.

'Kedryn?' He heard alarm in the kyo's voice. 'How fare you?'

'Well enough,' he answered, rising gingerly to a sitting position, then climbing as carefully to his feet. 'Nothing is broken, I think.'

'Wait,' urged Tepshen as Brannoc's head disappeared from view, to return moments later with torches.

The halfbreed struck flint to tinder and lit a flambeau whilst Kedryn assessed his condition and decided that nothing worse than bruises had accrued from his abrupt descent into the tomb. He caught the torch Brannoc dropped and raised it high, turning in a slow circle to examine the confines of the place. It was as he remembered and at the same time different, as though he saw through his eyes what previously he had observed in a dream. He stood upon a floor of grey stone thirty or forty paces across, great blocks arching to form a dome above him, his entry point overhead, a rectangle of brilliance against the shadowy slabs. Beside him, so close he touched it as he turned, was a dais carved from a single massive stone, waist high and surmounted with a sarcophagus carved with ancient runes thrown into stark relief by the torch's flickering glare. There was an odour of must, of stale, long-stilled air redolent of antiquity that was thankfully replaced by the fresher draught entering from above. Faded pictograms decorated the walls, and the ancient webs of long dead spiders. There was no other exit point than the hole overhead. He was about to examine the contents of the cist, remembering how before the occupant had risen to protest his intrusion, when Tepshen called again.

'Stand clear!'

Kedryn stood back as a rope uncoiled downwards, steadying the cord as Tepshen descended, limber as a squirrel. Brannoc dropped more torches and lowered three satchels packed with food, three canteens, then swung down himself.

The kyo handed Kedryn his sword and the younger man buckled the familiar weight about his waist as Brannoc ignited the flambeaux, finding niches and crevices in the surrounding walls so that the tomb was soon lit well.

'We are here,' he declared, more than a little nervously. 'What next?'

'Drul rose before,' Kedryn replied. 'But then the shamans of the Drott summoned his shade.'

He stepped towards the sarcophagus, flanked by his companions, each of them holding a torch so that the mortal remains of the first hef-Ulan were shown clear. They lay within the cist, unmoving and ancient, accoutred in the armour Drul had worn when he fell storming the walls of High Fort. The sallet was furnished with sweeping wings that curved protectively before the yellowed bone of the skull, revealing only the empty sockets and the upper jaw, descending to the metalled shoulders of a brigandine, loops and leather fused by the innumerable years, blackened like the helm by time. Vambraces girded the arms and gauntlets of link-sewn leather, cracked and husk-dry, the hands. Beneath the brigandine the legs were warded by grieves latched over boots reinforced with plates of metal. Aged bone showed through where leather had rotted, and the dessicated relics of long-dead beetles lay wasted amongst the ossifications. The gauntleted hands rested upon the chest, folded about the hilt of a massive glaive. The pommel was a globe cast in the shape of a skull held in a taloned hand, the hilt wrapped round with wire, the quillons wide, downswept and forward-curving at their outer extremities. The blade was close on a handspan across where it fused with the guards, tapering to a spear point, with a fuller running the length from ricasso almost to the tip. It was a sword of epic proportions, such as had not been seen in long ages.

'Drul's blade,' whispered Brannoc, his voice awed. 'See how it gleams? It is unaged.'

'It is what I need, if Gerat is correct,' said Kedryn, staring at the glaive.

'It is cumbersome,' Tepshen remarked.

'No matter.' Kedryn transferred his torch to his left hand. 'If all goes well it will slay a god.'

He reached towards the sword, warily, for he knew not what to expect, save that before the corpse had risen, aware that then the shamans of the Drott had been present to intercede on his behalf. He voiced a silent prayer to the Lady. And gasped as bone and leather creaked, protesting the movement that fastened one skeletal hand about his wrist. The torch he held dropped unnoticed to the floor. Tepshen and Brannoc sprang back, blades sliding from scabbards. Kedryn felt himself held in a grip strong as if sinew and muscle still girdled the dry bones that showed through the rotted gauntlet and heard Tepshen shout, 'Stand back! Afford me room to cut!'

Laughter like a winter wind rattling the stripped limbs of withered trees rustled then, gusting the noxious odour of decay against his offended nostrils, and a voice empty of human resonance said, 'Do you think to harm the dead? You are a fool.'

The grip on Kedryn's wrist was released and he staggered back as though driven by a blow, caroming against Tepshen so that both he and the kyo were flung to the far side of the chamber.

The ancient armour creaked as it was lifted by the bones within, rising from the cist to land upon the flags of the tomb. Dried beetle bodies cascaded from the brigandine, metal and leather groaning as the glaive was lifted, battle-ready, the sallet turning slowly from side to side, the empty sockets of the skull beneath staring blankly at each man in turn, fastening finally on Kedryn.

'You have disturbed my rest before, why do you come again?'

'I have need of your blade.' Kedryn disentangled himself from Tepshen, stepping in front of the kyo for fear the easterner would attack the corpse, convinced that such would prove useless action.

Laughter sent a fresh waft of putrescence through the still air.

'My sword? Why should the living steal from the dead? What do we dead have to give you, save notice of life's ending?'

'Not steal,' Kedryn said quickly, extemporising. 'I have a need of your blade, for only that may serve the purpose I pursue. Grant me its use and I shall return it; and leave my own in place the while.'

The helm cocked slightly to the side, as if Drul's remains considered the suggestion. Then: 'What is this purpose?'

'My wife is taken into the underworld and I go after her. Your blade has power there.'

'Aye,' the corpse confirmed, 'this sword has great power. Forged in Ashar's fires by the smith, Taziel, was this blade. Entrusted to me, and me alone.'

The great sword lowered slowly until the tip rested on the floor of the sepulchre and the sightless orbs of the skull swung ponderously to transfix Tepshen with their blank gaze.

'What is your part in this?'

'Where Kedryn goes, go I,' answered the kyo.

'Even into that place I guard? Death waits there.'

'Even unto death,' said Tepshen.

'And you?' The sallet moved to Brannoc. 'Are you, too, so tired of life?'

'Of life, no,' came the answer, 'but I am sworn to aid my companions. '

'Why? The woman is not yours.'

'No,' Brannoc agreed, his voice dry with tension, 'but I should be a poor friend were I to refuse my comrades help.'

'Your loyalty is commendable,' the corpse allowed, 'but foolish.'

'We are sworn,' said Tepshen, 'and we are not fools.'

'Any man who thinks to take my sword is a fool.'

'Is it foolish to seek that which renders a quest attainable?' Kedryn demanded. 'I am guided by the holy women of the Kingdoms, whose word is that I need your blade to save my wife.'

'Your wife is taken to the netherworld,' said Drul. 'She is lost.'

'No!' Kedryn drew the talisman from beneath his shirt, clutching the stone, thrusting it on its chain towards the armour. 'This tells me she lives.'

The helm lifted at sight of the jewel, the boots rustling as Drul's corpse stepped back a pace. 'You brought that token here before,' it said, 'and I told you then that should you pass me you might not return. Was it that carried you again to the domains of the living?'

'Aye, it was,' said Kedryn, seeing that the power of the stone swayed the shade. 'This talisman and the love of Kyrie.'

'The Lady's power wanes beyond these portals,' warned the corpse.

'But still it is there.' Kedryn took a pace forwards, still holding the talisman out-thrust. 'It brought me back then and it will again.'

'I think that this time you quest beyond the shore.' The bone-filled armour moved another reluctant step back. 'I think that this time you seek more than your sight.'

'I seek my wife,' Kedryn declared.

'And you would face Ashar himself to win her back?'

'Aye,' was the simple answer.

'So that is why you need my blade. You think to defend yourself against the god.'

'I think to slay him if he opposes me.'

A gale of laughter that was obscene in the reek it projected answered his declaration. 'A brave boast,' said Drul, 'but foolhardy. Ashar's smith forged his glaive: shall you use the weapon against the god himself?'

'If the Lady decrees it,' said Kedryn, venturing another step towards the awful thing, aware of the vibration of the talisman against his palm. Finding courage therein.

'She may shelter you,' the corpse acknowledged, 'but these others bear lesser protections. I sense magics about them, but weaker than that you carry.'

'Yet still we go with him,' said Tepshen. 'And we shall not be deterred by a suit of stinking armour.'

'You are brave,' allowed the corpse. 'But I think your comrade less sanguine.'

'I stand by my friends,' declared Brannoc.

'So,' hissed the skull, 'three fools would quest against Ashar himself.'

'Shall you allow me the usage of your blade?' Kedryn asked, advancing a pace closer still. 'Or must I fight you for it?'

'Fight me?' The question was the sussuration of a serpent sliding over dry leaves, menace and amusement mingling. 'Do you believe you can fight me?'

'Aye,' Kedryn said. 'With this I can.'

He stepped forwards, extending the talisman towards the relic, which vied away as might some dark-dwelling subterranean creature confronting a blazing torch. It took three slow steps back until the skirt of the brigandine grated against the stone of the cist, the sword raised defensively.

'I should rather you granted me the right,' Kedryn announced, 'but should you refuse that help you must face the talisman.'

The blade dropped ponderously, tip clattering on the stones of the floor. A sound like a sigh came from the lipless jaw and Drul said, 'It will be returned.'

'My word on it,' promised Kedryn, assuming a question was asked.

'Not by you,' declared the corpse. 'Ashar will return it to me when he destroys you.'

'Then what objection can you have?' Kedryn demanded, left hand reaching out to clasp the hilt.

This time there was no resistance. The gauntlets opened to allow him purchase and he took the blade, drawing it towards him. He let go the talisman, unsheathing his own sword that he might present it to Drul. The shade took it, the sallet lowering to study the blade, sighing again, the sibilance echoing with resignation.

'Take it then, for all the good it will do you. It will come back to me in time, by one means or another.'

'You have my word on it,' Kedryn nodded. 'Now may we pass?'

'Aye,' Drul allowed. 'Go to that place from which you shall not return.'

Kedryn clutched the great sword tight as the confines of the tomb grew indistinct, the light from the sun above and the flambeaux alike becoming dim, as though swirling mist filled the sepulchre. Tepshen and Brannoc stepped closer, moving slowly, as if through water, flanking him as a red light glowed beyond the cist, expanding like a torch approaching through fog, burning fiercer, the air growing warm, then hot, as if the mouth of a furnace opened. A charnel stench wafted through the chamber, thick and cloying, more offensive even than the reek that emanated from Drul's remains.

'If you dare,' said the corpse, right hand raised to point towards the rubescent glare, 'that is your way.'

The three men stepped around the dais, past the remains of the hef-Ulan. The glow grew brighter, a circle of flame burning in the rocky wall of the tomb, tongues licking upwards as though in anticipation of living flesh to roast, the stench worsening. Kedryn set a hand upon the talisman, the other holding Drul's sword, and took a deep breath as he steeled himself to enter that hellish portal.

'Come,' said Tepshen.

'Aye,' said Brannoc, 'before my courage deserts me utterly.'

'May the Lady ward us,' Kedryn murmured, stepping into the circle of flame.

For an instant there was a heat so intense he thought his hair must take fire, his flesh scorch on the bone. Then it was gone, the portal with it, and he stood in a low-roofed tunnel, the torches held by Tepshen and Brannoc affording poor illumination against the shadows that appeared to emanate from the rock itself, oozing like oil, swirling within the narrow confines as though animate. Tendrils extended towards the three comrades, writhing where they reached the coronas cast by the flambeaux, exuding the noisome odour of degenerate flesh and ordure. Kedryn held out the talisman and it began to glow, spreading a blue radiance that encompassed all three, driving back the oleaginous penumbra, and advanced along the dismal corridor.

Around them the surfaces of the tunnel had the appearance of decayed bone, a foul yellow-white pocked with a myriad holes from which came the shadows, like worms emerging. Tepshen and Brannoc trod close behind, anxious to remain within the nimbus of the talisman, all three aware of the sounds coming from the darkness ahead and to their backs, slow, slithery sounds, and scuttlings, chitterings, all horribly menacing so that hair prickled on necks and hands clutched sword hilts in preparation for attack.

None came, however, and they reached the egress of the shaft to look down into the enormous cavern Kedryn remembered from his previous descent into this ghastly limbo.

The talisman's glow faded here, for the hypogeum was lit with its own radiance, a strange grey illumination of no discernible source. The way ahead sloped down over slimy rocks, the walls vaulting into misty heights, the roof lost in the opalescence that seemed to rise like fetid vapour from the grey-surfaced mere filling the centre of the cave. Grey predominated, walls and floor and water merging in viscid union to defeat perspective, the descent to the shore appearing both gradual and defiantly steep. The atmosphere was humid and from the lake came a wailing as if the depths held a myriad lost souls that bemoaned their misfortune, whilst above fluttered creatures with ragged grey wings emitting piercing shrieks that stabbed painfully at ear drums. These aerial beings clustered close as the trio began to descend, proximity revealing human faces set between the tattered wings, tiny hands, and eyes that were filled with tears. 'Go back,' they fluted. 'Go back before you are lost.'

There was a mournful command on their piping voices that was hard to ignore, for their warnings held an imperative that struck deep, threatening to leech hope, leaving despair in its place, but the talisman afforded Kedryn the strength to resist their blandishments and the grammaryes laid by Gerat, combined with the power of Kyrie's stone, protected his companions: discarding their torches they made their way down the slippery descent.

The stone gave way to livid shingle that crunched beneath their boots, discernible from the doleful mere only in its immobility. The lake appeared gripped with a turgid energy, sluggish wavelets lapping against the strand that extended beyond the limits of their vision, each one leaving a scum that seethed acidically, glutinous bubbles rising farther out to burst and release acrid gases that assailed the nostrils, threatening to induce nausea. Kedryn halted, hefting Drul's sword to his shoulder as he stared across the miserable pond.

'It was here I saw the leviathan,' he announced. 'Wynett and I crossed by those stones and the creature rose from the depths.'

'But did not halt you,' said Tepshen, looking to where the glistening rocks extended into the misted distance.

Kedryn shook his head: 'No. I showed it the talisman and it allowed us passage over.'

'And mayhap will again,' said the kyo, although a trifle dubiously.

'Or not,' said Kedryn. 'The talisman did not prevent it attacking the barge.'

'Perchance we should take that boat,' Brannoc suggested.

Startled, Kedryn turned towards the halfbreed, following his pointing hand to see a dinghy beached along the shore.

'There was no boat before,' he mused.

'Mayhap the Lady provides us with the means of passage,' ventured Brannoc.

'Mayhap,' agreed Kedryn; doubtfully.

They walked, each step leaving an indentation that steamed, to where the boat rested. It was a solid, clinker built craft, two oars resting across the thwarts. Brannoc knelt to inspect the seams, pronouncing them well-caulked; Kedryn was more interested in the wood from which it was built, for that, despite the all-pervading grey of the cavern was of that shade of blue associated with Estrevan.

'It is sound enough,' announced the halfbreed. 'Do we chance its use?'

'Do you perceive the colour?' asked Kedryn. 'The colour of the Lady. I suspect she aids us.'

'Here?' Tepshen was dubious. 'We walk in Ashar's shadow here.'

'Yet Kyrie is not without power even here,' Kedryn returned. 'Drul's shade recoiled from the talisman, and I surmise from Gerat's words that a balance of some kind appertains. Mayhap the Lady is able to provide us with material aid, e'en though we traverse her enemy's domain.'

'Or it may be a trick,' suggested the kyo.

Kedryn nodded, aware that he must allow for that possibility. 'We have a choice,' he said, 'We must cross the lake, and to do that we must take either this craft or the stepping stones.'

'Should the leviathan rise it will swamp so small a vessel,' warned Tepshen.

'And if we use the stones it may swallow us whole, one by one,' said Brannoc.

'On the stones we shall be separated,' said Kedryn. 'In the boat we should be together, and likely all within the compass of the talisman's magic.'

'My vote is for the boat,' Brannoc declared.

'And mine,' nodded Kedryn.

'So be it,' Tepshen looked warily to the lake, studying the bubbling, colloidal surface.

They dragged the dinghy the few paces necessary to launching and clambered swiftly aboard, none willing to allow the liquid of the mere to touch them. Brannoc and Tepshen manned the sweeps whilst Kedryn settled on the stern thwart, Drul's blade upright between his knees, his right hand clutching the talisman.

Viscous ripples marked their passage over the mere and their nostrils pinched at the stench of the bursting bubbles, the threnody that seemed to come from the very surface growing louder as they progressed towards the farther shore, but of the leviathan there was no sign and after a while even the bat creatures were left behind.

'What lies ahead?' asked Brannoc as he plied his oar.

'Another strand,' said Kedryn, 'and a foul mist inhabited by the shades of the dead. It was there I encountered Borsus. I went no further.'

Brannoc grunted in response and asked no further questions. Kedryn, too, lapsed into silence, his eyes fixed on the mist, straining to perceive the shore even as he wondered what awaited him there.

Darr, he hoped, for it had been, in part at least, the notion of releasing the slain king from Ashar's bondage that had prompted him to take that fateful journey up the Idre, and it had seemed, when he spoke with Borsus's shade, that the inhabitants of that grim fog were imbued with some knowledge of their confines. Should that hope prove true, then Darr might well be able to advise him, and he, through the power of the talisman, to free Darr. If not, well, he knew of no other way by which he might enter the farther reaches of the underworld to save Wynett.

'The shore!' he warned as the mist thinned to reveal the line of featureless grey shingle that banded the lake.

Tepshen and Brannoc put a last effort into their rowing and the dinghy grounded on the gravel. Kedryn moved past them, leaping ashore and seizing the prow to haul the vessel landwards. His companions shipped their oars and sprang to join him.

They stood upon a strand little different to that they had left behind, save that it was warmer and devoid of the flying things, boundaried not with slime-decked stone but the shifting fog in which dark shapes moved.

'This,' Brannoc declared uncomfortably, 'is a dismal place.'

Kedryn looked towards the fog. It seemed to roll in thick banks, moving inexorably closer to the shore, as though driven forwards by the figures pacing inside its umbra. He took the talisman in his hand again and shouted, 'Darr! King Darr, it is Kedryn Caitin!'

The fog roiled as though unwilling to release its contents, but a figure stepped from it, treading with weighted feet, slow across the gravel towards them, tatters of fog trailing behind, breaking like drawn-out thread. Kedryn recognised Darr and a great melancholy swept through him, for the former king was a sorry sight, his thin hair matted about gaunt features, his shoulders slumped, the eyes he turned to Kedryn sunk deep within the sockets and ringed with black. Yet his bloodless lips twisted in a wan smile as he recognised his summoner and a voice near-hollow as Drul's said, 'Kedryn! Do you dare this sad place again?'

'I would free you,' Kedryn replied, reaching to take Darr's hand.

'Do not touch me!' The shade stepped back a pace. 'Best that the living have no truck with the dead, though my spirit lifts to see you and your companions.'

'The talisman freed Borsus from this place,' said Kedryn. 'I pray that the Lady grant you the same release.'

'Mayhap,' said Darr, listless, 'but that is not your sole purpose in venturing here.'

'Wynett is taken,' said Kedryn, 'and we come to bring her back.'

'You were ever courageous,' murmured the shade. 'As was Tepshen. And this other, do I assume him Brannoc?'

'Ay,' Kedryn confirmed. 'And we come with the knowledge of Estrevan to guide us.

Swiftly he told Darr of the events upon the Idre and his subsequent meeting with Gerat, of Qualle's prophecy, and Brannoc's tale of Drul's sword.

'Yet,' he concluded, extending the glaive for Darr's inspection, 'I see no way to join talisman and sword.'

'I know that legend,' nodded the shade, 'and there is more I have learned since Taws damned me to this limbo. Beyond the fog is a further extension of the netherworld. Beyond that, another, and more beyond until finally Ashar's stronghold is reached. Within one of those dwells Ashar's smith, who forged the glaive. He is called Taziel. How you may find him I do not know, nor expect him to aid you. I applaud your courage, but advise you to go back.'

'I shall not forsake Wynett!' Kedryn answered fiercely. 'The Lady will show me the way to this Taziel, and I shall find a means to persuade him.'

'What would you have him do?' asked Darr in a tone empty of hope.

Kedryn studied the great sword and touched the deathshead pommel. 'Remove this and replace it with the talisman. Then sword and stone shall be joined and defeat Ashar.'

'Then you will no longer carry the talisman and thus abdicate its protection,' said Darr. 'This was Ashar's plan from the moment he sent the leviathan forth. Do you not see it? His Messenger failed his purpose and was destroyed; the god himself set up this game that you should enter his domain. For all the love I bear my daughter I cannot advise you to go on lest Ashar secure both talismans.'

'A risk I must take,' said Kedryn.

'I cannot dissuade you?'

Kedryn shook his head.

'Then you must traverse that fog that binds those damned by the Messenger,' said Darr. 'Ignore any who speak with you or seek to halt you and if the Lady walks beside you, mayhap you shall emerge, though what you will find I cannot tell.'

'No matter,' said Kedryn, 'you show me a way and I thank you for it.'

Darr smiled forlornly and prepared to return into the fog. 'Wait,' urged Kedryn, 'Would you not be free of this place?'

'I have lost such hope,' said the shade, 'I am resigned.'

'I should not have sailed the Idre had I not sought the advice of Estrevan as to how I might effect your release,' declared Kedryn, 'and so Wynett would not have been taken. Whatever else I do, I would still seek that success.'

Darr's gaunt head shook sadly. 'Ashar planned this to enmesh you in his trap. Ward yourself, not me.'

'No!' Kedryn's voice was defiant.

He drove the sword into the gravel, leaving the blade quivering as he stepped towards Darr, seizing the hand the shade sought to snatch back. It was dry and frail as aged parchment, without the pulse of blood or life. Kedryn drew it to the talisman, forcing the withered fingers closed around the stone. Instantly the talisman burned with a fierce blue light, bright as a summer sky, growing to enfold both man and shade within its luminescence. Darr gasped, then sighed, and for a moment Kedryn saw him, hale, smiling. Then he was gone and the radiance faded.

Kedryn stood breathless, for he had felt a great power in that instant, a sense of love, of tranquillity, and he knew that Darr was brought to the Lady's peace. He turned slowly to his companions.

'You heard the way?'

They nodded, then Tepshen pointed, saying, 'Another approaches.'

Kedryn faced the fog, seeing a second ghost emerge, scarcely believing the evidence of his eyes, for the proud Hattim Sethiyan was a miserable vestige of his former self. Like Darr's, his hair was lank and matted, his eyes hollows in a bloodless face. He moved with slow steps, each one dislodging worms and maggots from the wound in his back where Brannoc's thrown knife had brought him down. He came tentatively, arms outspread to beseech mercy where none might be rightfully expected.

'Help me,' he implored. 'In the name of the Lady, help me.'

Kedryn felt distaste, and a measure of guilt at that emotion. 'You embraced Ashar,' he said accusingly.

'I was wrong.' The shade that was Hattim fell to its knees. 'Taws seduced me with false promises. Do not leave me here, I beg you.'

'He chose this place,' grunted Tepshen. 'Let us be gone.'

'Please, no!' Hattim wailed. 'I crave your forgiveness, Kedryn. In the name of the Lady I ask you to grant me succour.'

'Do you call on the Lady now?' Kedryn asked, torn between pity and loathing.

'I repent all I did,' nodded the shade, the movement spilling a vermicular flood from his back. 'I ask forgiveness in her name.'

'He would have slain you,' said Tepshen implacably.

'I was weak,' moaned Hattim. 'I was ambitious, and Taws deceived me.'

'Taws gave you what he promised, I think,' said Kedryn.

'As you love the Lady, grant me what I ask,' Hattim begged.

'What do you know of Ashar's smith, Taziel?' It occurred to Kedryn that Hattim might furnish him with further information to augment what Darr had imparted.

'He inhabits a cave,' said the shade. 'In a place of fire deep within the inner realms. The way to that place is hazardous. More than that I do not know.'

Kedryn nodded thoughtfully. 'That is not much.'

'It is all I know.' Tears of blood spilled from Hattim's sunken eyes. 'I swear it.'

'What do you know of Ashar's designs?' Kedryn pressed.

'Only that he sought information of you and Wynett, and of Ashrivelle,' the shade responded. 'I had no choice but to give him what he wanted. He seeks a means to broach Kyrie's barriers and to that end plots to secure the talismans, or trap you in the netherworld. I know no more than that.'

Kedryn studied the abject figure, pity overcoming the detestation he felt. He could hate Hattim Sethiyan as a man, but this sorry thing was beneath hatred: he extended the talisman again.

'It is in the hands of the Lady,' he declared. 'Let her judge.'

'I asked her forgiveness,' said Hattim, and took the jewel in both his hands.

Again the blue light flared, less bright this time, and within its radiance Kedryn saw Hattim smile briefly before he, too, vanished.

'You are too kind,' Tepshen remarked.

Kedryn shrugged, smiling fleetingly. 'Let the Lady decide. I ask her blessing on what we do – should I then deny so pitiful a thing her mercy?'

Tepshen hiked his shoulders once: a dismissive gesture. 'At least we know to look for a cave in a place of fire.'

'But first we must dare that fog,' said Brannoc. 'And it draws closer by the moment.'

All three turned to study the vaporous barrier which did, indeed, move ominously closer. The shapes within were more clearly definable as human forms and against the background of the lake's lament could be heard a dull, angry rumbling, as though a pack of hounds were waked from rest and growled their displeasure at the disturbance.

'It is the way we must go,' said Kedryn, though he felt an ineffable dread at the menace implicit in that gnarr. 'Stay close.'

'As if you were a maiden and I your suitor,' promised Brannoc, and moved to stand shoulder to shoulder with Tepshen, so close behind that Kedryn could feel their breath upon his neck.

Drul's glaive was too weighty to heft comfortably with one hand, so he rested the blade against his left shoulder, holding the talisman with his right hand, and paced resolutely towards the fog. Its advance halted as they approached, but the grumbling of the occupants grew louder, individual sounds becoming discernible. Mostly they were snarls or ululations, or such sounds as men make in the instant of their dying, but there were words, too. 'Take them,' they heard, and 'Make them one with us,' and 'Living flesh.' The threat was palpable as the heat the fog gave off, and all three felt the ugly stirring of fear as they stepped into the brume.

It reflected the light the talisman now spread around them so that they walked in a cocoon of azure radiance, pressing closer together as they saw what lived inside the fog. Ghastly faces stared at them, worms writhing from mouldered eyes and eaten mouths, ribbons of raw flesh hung from jaws, and hands flayed to bone thrust out, beckoning or clutching, the skeletal digits snatching back as they touched the perimeter of the talisman's protective glow. The shade of a woman cavorted before them, her capering an obscene parody of lustful dance, displaying bloodied breasts that crawled with grubs, her outthrust tongue licking over lips long gone into dessication. 'Stay with me,' she slurred. 'Stay and be my lovers,' but she retreated before the nimbus of the stone and eventually faded back into the mist. Others replaced her: hideously wounded men who threatened, women who wept tears of gore, some little older than children; an awful throng, embodying despair and hatred of all who knew not that hopeless despond that was the mark of their limbo.

Kedryn held the talisman high as the chain permitted and blocked his ears to threats and blandishments alike, not pausing in his advance, aware of Tepshen and Brannoc hard behind. He walked on gravel for some untold time, relying on Kyrie's stone to guide him, for he could not tell in that sightless vapour whether he walked a straight line or marked a circle that would bring him back to the shore of the lake; or worse, lose them all within the hellish brume. After a while he felt the hot crunching of the gravel replaced by the hardness of stone, and the heat diminished. His ears rang with the cries of the damned and it was some time before he realised that they faded, dropping back, and that the fog thinned. He marched on, seeing faint light ahead.

In time it strengthened, the talisman's radiance lessening in response, and they emerged from the mist, blinking and shading their eyes as brightness replaced the grey. Tendrils of fog still clung to them as if to draw them back and they paced on with downcast eyes until the last vestiges broke reluctantly loose, coiling back into the thick bank that now lay behind them.

Ahead they saw a panorama to distort the senses, simultaneously alien as the vistas of nightmare and weirdly akin to the landscapes of the world they had left.

A vermilion sky spread overhead, a viridescent disc several times larger than their own sun directly above, a line of majestic purple clouds stretching across the far horizon. The stone on which they stood was a bilious yellow, a great sweep that appeared to mark the edge of a mountain range, for when they looked back they saw tall, fulvous peaks rising above them, jagged as broken teeth, the fog roiling about the lower levels. Moving to the edge of the stone, which appeared to be a plateau, they looked down upon a plain of copper coloured grass, where strange trees grew in the distance, leprous white, with thin branches that held clusters of spikey, cyanic leaves. Across the plain meandered a carmine river, like an opened artery coursing the strange land, and here and there along its banks they saw groups of long-legged, angular beasts, too distant to identify, even were such classification possible. The perspective was awkward, for the sun cast no shadows, and at first it seemed that the plateau was inescapable, its scarp vertical, the jaundiced surfaces offering no more handholds than would a sheet of smooth-blown glass.

They patrolled the rim at last, close against the mountains' flank, found a stairway, narrow and slippery-looking. It descended at first through the rim of the plateau, the rock forming walls that rapidly rose above their heads, the steps steep and thin, forcing them to move in single file, wary of tumbling, for their boots overlapped the stairs. Then it turned abruptly to the left, leaving the declivity so that they climbed with open air on their right hands and the prospect of falling to the coppery grass far below. Whatever feet normally trod the lithic ladder were not human, for the descent between each step was more than a man would take, rendering the climb all the more treacherous, and rapidly causing their calves and thighs to ache. Down and down it went, traversing to right and left in a zig-zag pattern, with no places where they might halt to rest save the steps themselves, so that they clambered without respite as a hot, dry wind buffeted their faces, carrying a sweet, cloying odour redolent of rotting fruit.

Kedryn found Drul's glaive an encumbrance, for it was too long to sheath and heavier than his own blade, and he was forced to carry it rested on his shoulder, transferring its weight each time the stairway turned for fear it would unbalance him and send him spinning to the ground below.

That goal seemed no closer when he glanced up to see the wall of the plateau looming above than when they had commenced their descent, and he wondered if the deceptive perspectives tricked his eyes, or if the physical laws he understood no longer applied, allowing the stairway to descend without ending, condemning them to clamber its length forever. He gave up any attempt to calculate how much longer they must remain on the treacherous ladder and concentrated solely on the way ahead, trusting that eventually they would reach the plain below.

Finally they did, the stairway devolving on the coppery grass, the wall above them blocking out sight of the mountains so that only the reddish orange sky and bilious cliff were visible. They halted there, panting and easing muscles wearied by the descent, slumping against the unnaturally smooth stone as they drank from their canteens and nibbled on the provisions brought from the satchels they carried.

Before them, the plain appeared absolutely flat, the river invisible now, and the expanse of ochre grass interrupted only by the curious trees. It felt as though they had spent the better part of a day climbing down from the plateau, but the green sun still stood overhead, seemingly fixed at its zenith: it occurred to Kedryn that time was a meaningless concept here in the netherworld.

'Well,' Brannoc remarked with a somewhat forced cheerfulness, staring at the near-featureless landscape, 'we have passed by Drul and crossed the lake; we have penetrated the fog of limbo and descended a stairway I dread climbing; which direction do we take now?'

'I am not sure,' answered Kedryn.

'Does the talisman not tell you?' asked Tepshen.

Kedryn set a hand upon the stone, but it only tingled against his palm, offering that reassurance that Wynett still lived but no other guidance. He shook his head.

'Hattim's shade said Taziel occupies a cave in a place of fire,' the kyo said, thoughtfully.

'That seems of little help here,' Brannoc gestured at the flat terrain. 'Unless the cave exists in this wall.'

'He patted the yellow stone against which he rested, but Kedryn made a negative gesture, saying, 'I do not believe it can be so close. Darr spoke of the netherworld as though it were a series of overlapping territories: I suspect the cave lies farther into this strange land.'

'There are mountains of fire in my country,' Tepshen offered. 'The priests say they are the portals of hell, and to enter is to forfeit life. Others say they are holes into the heart of the world, which burns eternally. They are great peaks that spit fire and brimstone, and great clouds hang above them.'

'There was cloud along the horizon,' Kedryn said. 'If that purple stuff was cloud.'

'It wore the delineaments of cloud,' nodded Brannoc, 'if not the colour.' He grinned, tugging a handful of copper grass loose. 'But what does bear the colour of normality here?'

'Nothing,' Kedryn answered, glancing up, 'but ahead is as good a direction as any, so let us go that way.'

The others agreed and they prepared to leave, repacking their satchels. Kedryn unlatched his scabbard and used his swordbelt to fashion a carrying sling for Drul's blade that allowed him to stow the glaive across his back, where the weight was less cumbersome, the hilt projecting above his left shoulder. He settled the sword as comfortably as was possible and began to trudge in what he chose to call a northwards direction. No tracks showed in the grass, which was tough and springy beneath their boots, giving off a slightly acrid scent as it was crushed that combined with the fruity odour of the breeze to increase the sense of abnormality permeating the landscape. The huge viridescent disc remained unmoving overhead, a seemingly static beacon that allowed them to fix their direction and they marched until the trees took clear shape ahead.

Close to, the growths were even stranger than they had seemed from the vantage point of the plateau. The trunks were waxy, pale as diseased flesh, and each one was surrounded by series of absolutely horizontal branches commencing at precisely the same distance from the ground, approximately twice the height of a tall man. They grew in rings of six, alternating their positions on the perpendicular trunks so that each succeeding layer stood above the gaps left by its predecessor. The leaves grew in dense bunches at the tips of each branch, long and thin and straight as knife blades, unmoving in the breeze even though a metallic rustling emanated from each cluster. Each tree was equally distanced from its neighbour, and they thrust from the plain in groups of six, forming circles.

'I do not like them,' Brannoc said nervously as they approached the first stand. 'There is something threatening about them.'

Kedryn halted, staring at the odd growths.

'Six and six and six,' murmured Tepshen, pointing. 'Six branches in a circle and six trees also in a circle, as if they were planted thus.'

Kedryn saw that the kyo was right: their way was crossed by six rings of six trees, beyond them more, all weirdly regular, a barrier across their path. The obvious direction was to pass between the closest group, the clusters being each so wide that to detour around them would take some time. Nonetheless, he shared Brannoc's antipathy, for it seemed the trees waited, anticipating their arrival. He studied them, attempting to define exactly what quality it was that afforded that sense of menace. The trees, however, gave no clue and finally he took a step closer, motioning the others back. Nothing happened and he walked closer still. It seemed then that the trees moved, a faint rippling stirring the trunks, the branches wavering as though seen through heat haze. Guided more by instinct than any conscious warning, he threw himself back, rolling as he landed to put more distance between his body and the leprous timber.

Where he had stood blue leaves quivered in the ochre grass, driven deep as arrowheads, their edges exuding an oily, cyanic liquid that steamed faintly in the reddish light. He ran back farther still as the boughs of the nearest trees trembled visibly and turned towards him, fluid as tentacles, their leaves bristling now, flying like darts to thud into the ground closer to his position.

'Back!' he shouted, and he turned, running, as a volley of leaves whistled through the air, thrown by the whiplash motion of the branches.

It seemed there was a limit to their range, for the movement ceased as he reached his comrades and the trees stood still again, tall and unmoving.

'I think,' he remarked ruefully, 'that we must regard everything here as dangerous.'

'A sound policy,' Tepshen nodded.

'And a longer march,' muttered Brannoc, eyeing the waxen trunks resentfully.

They turned to what they defined as the east and proceeded to walk along the line of the trees, maintaining a respectful distance from the lethal blue leaves. The first row of six circles ended, revealing further plantations beyond, spreading back over the plain so that their detour became a wide-circling trek around the hostile forest.

The sun had not yet shifted as they reached the limit of the timber rings and skirted warily around the stands, finally leaving them behind. Further clusters showed ahead and they realised that their way to the horizon would be far from straight. Kedryn touched the talisman, seeking that reassurance that Wynett lived as he wondered how long it would take to reach her. That he might not, he refused to contemplate, even though the plain stretched out before him without sign of end, the line of purple cloud seeming an infinite distance away, farther now that he traversed a flat terrain than when he had studied it from the plateau.

The immobility of the green disc allowed for no judgement of time save that inherent in muscles and bellies. There was no indication of twilight nor any hint that the sun might set and it was when his hunger grew too avid to ignore and his legs began to ache afresh with the effort of walking that Kedryn called a halt. Tepshen and Brannoc agreed readily enough and they dropped their satchels on the ochre sward midway between two of the leprous copses. The air was warm so there was no call for a fire, and they spread their blankets, eating cold venison and the dwindling supply of journey cakes provided by Rycol. It was agreed that a watch should be kept and Kedryn take the first turn. He squatted on the grass, Drul's sword at his side as his companions drew their blankets over their heads to shut out the unrelenting light, and studied the landscape. That rapidly became a boring pursuit, for it was unchanging, monotonously regular. The grass and the sky were so similar in colouration that the horizon appeared oppressively close. There were no clouds save the band of purple and when he looked back towards the mountains he saw only a vague yellowish blur, overhung by the unmoving green sun. The wind blew steadily from the north, but seemed not to touch either the grass or the trees, for neither growths moved. Indeed, nothing moved. There were no signs of insect or animal life, the creatures they had marked along the riverbank too far away to see, and no birds flew in the vermilion sky. The only sounds were those made by Tepshen and Brannoc, or the rustle of his own clothing as he shifted position. It was a place, a vista, to leech the senses of reason, and it filled him with a deep loathing.

How long he sat he did not know, but in time he realised that the purple cloud seemed to have drawn closer. The effect was to suggest an impingement of the horizon, as if the sky itself closed down upon him, and he rose to his feet, staring at the rack. It had, indeed, moved, for it now covered a greater area of the sky, no longer banding the horizon but extending towards him to fill perhaps a quarter of the heavens. Its movement grew steadily more visible as he watched, the forward edge advancing remorselessly, like a massive storm front driven by howling winds. On and on it came, until it was overhead and he stood in shadow, craning his head back to watch it loom above him and possess the remainder of the heavens. Abruptly the land was dark. Not the obfuscation of natural night, in which stars and moon provide sufficient illumination for keen eyes to see, but a total blackness that denied all vision effectively as a blindfold. He turned to study the weird advance, seeing the blurred outlines of the mountains swallowed, the viridescent sun disappear, and found himself blind.

For a moment panic gripped him, memories of the darkness that had fallen when Borsus's sword took his sight returning, then he clutched the talisman and found the solace of calm in its touch. His racing heart slowed and realised that he had panted in his fear, hearing his own breathing regulate. He lowered himself to the ground, reaching about until he located the glaive, settling the blade across his knees and only then releasing his grip on Kyrie's stone.

Pale blue light shone forth, wan in that all-encompassing occultation, but immeasurably reassuring, for it showed him the slumbering forms of his comrades and, perhaps more important still, told him that the Lady's power was with him yet, even in this outer region of Ashar's domain. He could not see beyond the limitation of the radiance, but even that small benefit was welcome when the alternative was total absence of sight, and he sat listening for sounds in the darkness.

None came and his eyes grew heavy, his chin dropping to his chest. He shook himself, not sure what might happen if he fell asleep, but at last acknowledging that he could no longer remain awake and prodding Tepshen.

The kyo was instantly alert, rising with sword part-drawn to stare about as he realised that darkness had fallen. Kedryn explained the advance of the cloud and Tepshen paced beyond the aura of the talisman, fading almost instantly as though swallowed whole by the unnatural night. He returned moments later to announce that nothing was visible save the blue glow of the stone.

Kedryn stretched on his own blanket, the talisman hanging outside his tunic, and saw that the radiance persisted.

'Sleep,' Tepshen advised. 'If the light fades I shall wake you.'

Kedryn nodded and fell instantly asleep.

He woke to find Brannoc settled cross-legged a little distance away, staring at the sky with a quizzical expression. The world was once again a confusion of red and orange, the heavens livid as heated metal, the grass a burning copper, the sun again hanging massive and green to their rear.

'Tepshen told me what you saw,' announced the halfbreed wonderingly, 'and a little while ago the cloud rolled back north-wards. This is a very strange place, Kedryn.'

'Aye.' Kedryn grinned, cheered by the return of light, even of so odd a hue, and climbed to his feet.

Tepshen woke moments later and stretched, yawning, offering no comment on their surroundings. It seemed to Kedryn that the easterner's natural pragmatism allowed him to accept more easily their circumstances, for he set to rummaging in his satchel as if they woke on some Tamurin meadow after spending a night beside the trail. His apparently casual acceptance of their situation was comforting, communicating to the others so that they, too, brought out provisions and settled to eating breakfast as though commencing a normal day.

They began to march again, holding to a steady pace, detouring when fresh stands of the dangerous trees appeared, but always returning to their northwards course, the line of purple cloud enlarging as they moved inexorably closer. They halted when hunger indicated and then walked on, halting again when the cloud once more rolled towards them, judging the duration of the 'day' to be somewhat longer than that of the world outside, perhaps the length of midsummer's day. The temperature was unvarying and the wind continued to blow from the north, the odour of rotted fruit growing stronger.

After four days of the march they saw the river and the first of the creatures.

The stands of leprous timber had fallen away behind them, whilst ahead stretched the band of carmine that marked the watercourse. It wound in a great arc across their path, red as blood and glistening with an oily sheen. The creatures, a group of six, stood along the bank, watching their approach. They were the size of carthorses, their bodies segmented like an insect's, prompting Kedryn to think of giant ants. The bulbous hindpart extended four angular legs, twig thin, to the ground, while a narrower section slanted upwards, two heavier limbs that ended in serrated pincers thrusting out. The heads were oval, armoured like the other parts of the body with celadonite chitin, three round bulges of the same colour suggesting eyes, below which opened a circular orifice surrounded by thin hairy growths. They turned to face the oncoming men, the crimson surrounding their mouth parts implying they found sustenance in the red river.

'Are they hostile, I wonder?' mused Kedryn.

'If so, we are likely lost.' Tepshen indicated the groups farther down the bank, to left and right. All had ceased their activity and were turned towards the visitors, immobile as statues.

'We cannot avoid them,' Brannoc remarked, fingering the hilt of his sabre. 'Nor can we run from them.'

'Then let us approach,' Kedryn decided.

He began to walk towards the insectile beings, who remained still, the only movement the slow rotation of their eyes as they studied him. Tepshen and Brannoc came behind, ready to fight should that prove necessary.

Kedryn halted scant paces before the closest of the things, looking up at the smooth head. It lowered as though examining him, then the fronds abouts its mouth became agitated, throwing drop-lets of crimson all around. Immediately a high-pitched chittering sound, almost beyond the range of human hearing, rang out and the six creatures facing them, and those farther along the bank, began to snap their pincers. Kedryn reached for the hilt of the glaive slung across his back, prepared to sell his life dearly as he could.

Instead of attack, however, the creature he faced ducked its upper body, the limbs thrusting out and down until they touched the ground. The head drew level with Kedryn's and the chittering sound softened.

247

'Does it abase itself?' murmured Brannoc, amazement in his voice.

Kedryn stood his ground, staring at the blank bulges of the eyes and slowly released his grip on the sword. The creature extended a tentative limb. Kedryn heard Tepshen's sharp intake of breath and said, 'Do not attack! I do not believe it offers harm.'

He held himself still as the pincered limb came close to his face, reaching out to touch the hilt of the glaive. The pincers closed about the hilt and chittering sound rose again. Then the thing let go the sword and dropped its limb once more to the ground, fixing Kedryn with its unfathomable stare.

'We would cross the river,' he said, pointing to the crimson flood.

The creature rose to its full height, the ovoid head swung jerkily round, following his gesture, then turned to loom above him again. The fronds about the mouth quivered, the chittering dropping several octaves to come within an acoustic range more comprehensible to his ears.

It was a while before he understood that it spoke, the words slow and awkward.

'The sword,' it said, the sibilants drawn out, the consonants slurred. 'The bearer of the sword.'

'Aye.' He touched the hilt again. 'And I would cross the river.'

'River,' echoed the creature. 'Cross river.'

Kedryn nodded. 'Aye. Cross the river.'

The insect-like beast rose up, its chittering voice louder, and the groups to either side began to run, scuttling with amazing agility over the grass until the trio of humans were surrounded by a mass of yellow-green bodies, their ears assaulted by the high-pitched chittering, as if a discussion beyond their comprehension took place.

'Cross river danger,' said the creature.

'Still we must go there,' Kedryn answered. 'To where the cloud lies.'

'Mountains dangerous,' the creature hissed.

Kedryn shrugged, wondering if the gesture carried any meaning for the ant-like being, and said. 'We must. Is there any way to cross the river?'

The thing stared at him for a while, then raised its head and issued a burst of strident sound. Without warning, one of its companions plunged into the carmine flow, sinking until only its head stood

248

above the surface. A second sprang onto its back, and scuttled forwards, the watchers on the bank staring in amazement as it struggled against the current, the first creature reaching out its forelimbs to grasp the hindquarters of the second and brace it. A third followed, then a fourth and fifth a sixth, and more, until the last emerged on the far bank, their bodies forming a living bridge.

One – it was impossible to tell it if was that which had first spoken, for they were uniform in appearance – ducked its head in Kedryn's direction and said, 'Cross river.'

'My thanks,' Kedryn replied.

'You bear sword. Cross river.'

He nodded and stepped onto the sentient bridge. The stream was thick, turgid about his boots as he tramped the chitinous backs, taking care to avoid the heads. Tepshen and Brannoc followed him and they reached the farther side without incident, stepping onto the copper grass to shake their boots free of the viscid liquid. To their surprise three of the ant-beasts scuttled across after them, one communicating again with Kedryn.

'Bearer of sword go . . .' a pincered limb indicated the northern horizon. Kedryn nodded, 'Aye,' and the thing said, 'Take sword bearer.'

It bent its hindlimbs, lowering itself to the ground, clearly intending him to mount its back.

'Is it to be trusted?' asked Tepshen, warily.

'They have offered only help so far,' Kedryn responded. 'It seems Drul's sword grants me authority of some kind.'

'And we shall make better time,' added Brannoc.

'And save our legs,' Kedryn nodded.

Tepshen shrugged slightly, and Kedryn hauled himself astride the creature. Its back was somewhat wider than a horse's, but not uncomfortable, and he settled with his legs dangling before the creature's first pair, clutching the forelimbs to hold himself in place as it rose. Brannoc and Tepshen mounted the others and they fell into the line behind Kedryn's beast as it began to run across the plain.

The gait was smooth and it moved at a pace far swifter than any horse could attain. Kedryn found himself enjoying the sensation of speed, watching the ochre grass flash by beneath the narrow limbs, the line of purple cloud loom steadily closer, jagged hills becoming visible beneath the overcast.

Before another day had passed they reached foothills, jumbled stands of dull brown rock that angled steeply upwards towards even more craggy peaks overtopped by the cloud.

The ant-things halted and Kedryn's said, 'Not go farther.'

Kedryn dropped to the ground. 'You have my thanks,' he said.

'You bear sword,' answered the creature, and without further ado began to run back the way they had come, its companions behind.

The three men watched them disappear into the orange haze of the distance and turned towards the hills. They were the colour of fresh-baked brick, sharp and high, the cloud that hung above more malignant with proximity, like poisoned flesh. Cliffs showed, pocked with caves, and stunted shrubs thrust spikey limbs from crannies where puce soil found footing. The lower slopes were straited with gullies, a rocky maze that wound up to the more vertiginous levels.

'Let us rest,' Kedryn suggested, 'and climb tomorrow.'

'Sound advice,' agreed Tepshen.

They found a cleft surrounded on three sides by rock and spread their blankets on the sandy soil, waiting for the cloud to extend across the plain, wondering what lay ahead.

# Chapter Twelve

WHEN the cloud once again extended its light-absorbing blanket across the sky the proximity of the hills seemed to render the darkness more intense. It seemed now of an almost palpable density, as though the intangible matter of the air itself became tainted with the purple occultation. The radiance of the talisman lessened, encompassing a smaller area, and Kedryn wondered if its power decreased as he progressed deeper into the regions of the netherworld. It made little difference, for his determination burned fiercely as ever and he realised that they had come too far to contemplate turning back. The bloody river was a barrier they could not hope to cross unaided and he could not be sure that the ant-creatures would prove so helpful a second time, consequently they had no way to go save forwards, over the hills and on to whatever strangeness lay beyond. He was, anyway, more immediately concerned with what lay on this side as he stood his turn on watch, listening to the sounds that came out of the blackness like the echoes of nightmare.

The nights they had spent on the plain had been marked by a silence deep as the darkness, and he had considered that eerie, but now he thought fondly of that soundlessness as his ears were assailed by strange, indefinable noises that set his flesh to creeping and settled his hands firmly about the hilt of Drul's glaive. There were scuttlings and leathery rustlings, clicking sounds, gurglings and sucking noises that made him think of gigantic insects pouncing and draining their prey of body fluids. He would have clutched the talisman for comfort, but was afraid such action would dim its light and allow the creatures he heard moving over the higher slopes to approach, so instead he steeled himself to remain alert, struggling to ignore the apprehension that threatened to leech his courage. He was happy to relinquish his watch to Tepshen, and happier still when Brannoc shook him awake, for his sleep had been filled with ugly dreams.

The day was no different to the others, except that now when he looked up he saw the cloud directly overhead, looming above the jagged hills so that the brick red shading of the lower slopes became transformed through crimson to a dark umber where the topmost peaks seemed to touch the rack. The breeze was warmer and the odour of rotten fruit stronger, the caves that pocked the cliffs ineffably menacing.

'Perchance whatever creatures inhabit the holes emerge only by night,' Brannoc remarked, eyeing the openings with unalloyed distaste.

'We shall be up there then,' Tepshen grunted, shouldering his pack.

'Unless we find a pass,' the halfbreed said hopefully.

'Even so . . .' Tepshen shrugged and left the sentence unfinished.

'Mayhap one is occupied by Taziel,' Kedryn suggested.

'I see no fire.' Tepshen shook his head. 'I think the smith's forge must lie deeper.'

'There is but one way to find out.' Kedryn smiled grimly and began to climb.

At first they made their way along a gulley that slanted steadily upwards, wide at its opening, but then narrowing until they marched between high walls of red stone. Finally it became too narrow to permit further passage and they climbed out, finding themselves on a shelf of serrated rock confronted by a cliff that angled slightly backwards, presenting sufficient handholds for them to work their way to the top without excessive difficulty. They clambered over jumbled rock and assailed a second cliff to a narrow ledge that ran along the face of a steeper scarp, smooth and bereft of the irregularities that made climbing possible, a cleft showing to the right. Between the cleft and their position a cave opened its dark maw at head height; in the opposite direction there were three.

'One would seem the lesser of evils,' Brannoc muttered, 'and mayhap that crevice will afford us passage through.'

'Mayhap,' agreed Kedryn and, being the closest, set to edging his way along the ledge.

The shelf allowed no room to manoeuvre and he prayed that nothing should attack, for sword work was impossible in those narrow confines. He moved slowly, sliding first one foot and then the other over the rough surface, his arms spread wide, fingers seeking cracks and abrasions that might grant him purchase, his cheek close against the stone. As he drew nearer to the cave the reek of decayed fruit grew stronger, cloying in his nostrils and threatening to dizzy him with its fetid sweetness. He reached the cave, its floor level with his shoulders, and felt the breeze, hot now, ruffle his hair, the stench nauseating. Something moved within the darkness and he heard a scraping against stone, a sharp clicking sound. His senses rebelled against knowledge of the cave's occupant and he forced himself to peer into the shadowed interior even as he increased his pace along the ledge, anxious to be past the menacing orifice. He saw nothing, however, and went by without incident, calling a warning back to his comrades. Tepshen followed him, and then Brannoc, and it seemed the halfbreed's surmise of the creatures' nocturnal habits was correct, for nothing emerged to threaten them and Kedryn reached the opening of the cleft safely.

It was wedge-shaped, as though an axe had split the mountains, rending the stone to produce a long cut that thrust inwards, dark and forbidding. Little light penetrated the gash, the purple cloud obscuring the illumination of the vermilion sky, but the ledge ended there and the floor offered firm footing: Kedryn eased inside.

Tepshen and Brannoc joined him and they contemplated their situation, deciding to follow the cleft as far as they could, for it seemed to offer ingress to the heart of the mountains, and hopefully an exit point that would take them higher.

The ground beneath their feet was thick with pulverulent rubble, their steps raising clouds of russet dust that hung thick on the steadily warmer air. The reek of mouldering fruit was almost overpowering, and as they progressed they saw a profusion of caves marking the walls above. By unspoken consent they increased their speed, stumbling through the gritty debris of the floor, their inward passage taking them steadily deeper into the shadows. There was no breeze within the cleft and the dust plastered faces become sweaty with the effort of the climb, clogging in eyes and nostrils so that they blinked tears and began to cough, spitting the acrid stuff from their mouths. Urgency possessed them and they cast frequent glances upwards towards the cave mouths, momentarily anticipating the emergence of the dwellers within.

After a while the cut turned, hiding the entrance, and what little light there had been faded dramatically. They moved now in a weird twilight, dark purple above and dull red below, feeling the floor begin to angle upwards, aware that its incline must take them close past the lower of the caves they could just make out pocking the walls.

The sounds Kedryn had heard emanating from the first cave were louder, as though the obscuration of light allowed the inhabitants a greater freedom of movement, and they hurried as best they could on the uncertain surface, feeling their way with hands thrust out to the walls and lungs protesting the constant inhalation of dust-laden air. It seemed, after the length of the days on the plain, that relatively little time had passed before the light waned altogether. Directly beneath the cloud, there was no warning of its movement and they were abruptly plunged into darkness. Brannoc cursed volubly, his sentiments if not his fluency, echoed by his companions. Kedryn clutched the talisman, praying fervently that the Lady guard them as he heard the sounds of the previous night return.

'We have no choice but to halt,' Tepshen declared as the pale blue radiance glowed. Adding, as he cocked his head and stared into the blackness, 'With drawn swords.'

Kedryn and Brannoc followed his advice, Keshi sabre sliding from scabbard, Drul's great glaive from the sling on Kedryn's back. There was barely sufficient room within the cleft to swing a sword and the three comrades stood shoulder-to-shoulder, blades levelled at the ominous night, knowing that any attack must be faced head-on.

The noises grew, clickings and scrapings and rustling sounds, punctuated by strange, shrill whistles that preceded the horrible sucking noises, as if numerous many-legged things emerged from the caves above them. They could see nothing beyond the nimbus of the talisman and that, for all they felt an instinctive loathing of whatever monstrous creatures stalked the night, was somehow worse, their very real anticipation of physical danger magnified by its unknown quality.

It occurred to Kedryn that something might well descend upon them from above and he transferred the glaive to his shoulder, angling the point up that he might stab at anything offering harm from that quarter.

Then Tepshen said softly, 'One approaches.'

Kedryn turned slightly, peering past the kyo. At first he saw only the glow of the talisman, its light transforming the darkness to a watery, aquamarine glow, as if he stared into a pool, that illumination ending scant paces from their position, pitch blackness beyond it. He heard a scuttling, clattering sound, a little louder than the rest, and gasped as the maker was outlined by the talisman's effulgence.

A cold chill clenched his teeth, hair prickled at the nape of his neck, as he saw the thing. He heard Brannoc groan, 'Lady be with us now!' and felt the tension that emanated from Tepshen.

The closest approximation his mind could form was to a spider, for it was a thing of multiple limbs and many eyes. The larger part

254

of the body was a great bloated sac, rusty red save for a mottling of darker maroon like a design upon the upper part, narrowing at its farthest extremity to a wickedly curved stinger from which droplets of carmine fell to seethe upon the grit of the cleft's floor. From the forward part of the sac ten legs, each thick as a stout man's thigh extended, bristling with reddish hairs and holding the repulsive body high above the ground so that the head was level with his own. That was a shiny dark blue ovoid, set all round with huge, many-faceted eyes that glittered agate and implacable, staring in all directions at once. The ovoid ended in a maw in which thick palps were visible, four, curving and dripping a foaming, yellow saliva. Beyond the palps, extending so that the maw was distorted in an attitude of insensate voracity, were two huge mandibles that snapped hungrily together, producing the clicking sound.

It reared up on eight of its legs, the foremost pair waving as though in challenge, probing the outer perimeter of the talisman's protective glow.

'It attacks!' cried Brannoc, loathing and fear in his voice.

'Then it dies!' snapped Tepshen.

He moved as he spoke, feet shuffling through the dust in the tight, dancing steps Kedryn remembered from the practice ground. The long eastern sword was raised in a double-handed grip above his head and while the creature's two limbs still wavered about the edges of the light it swung down and across.

One hair-bristled limb was severed close to the body. Before it touched the gritty floor the blade was reversed, sweeping back to strike across the palps, then a third time, slashing back in a flat arc that sundered the other forelimb. The creature emitted a shrill whistling sound, almost unheard under the furious clattering of its mandibles. Viscous liquid spilled from the cut palps, red and malignant as the fluid oozing from the stinger. Tepshen halted barely within the talisman's light, blade upraised again. The arachnid-like creature seemed to stare at him, its remaining legs bunching as if it prepared to spring. Kedryn saw a second approach from down the cleft and held Drul's sword ready to strike, but the spidery beast turned aside, scuttling vertiginously up the chasm's wall and then leaping upon its wounded fellow.

The disabled monster forgot Tepshen as its upper eyes saw the attacking beast, and it turned, mandibles snapping defensively. It was too late: the other landed upon its back, legs gripping the bulbous sac of the body. The stinger drove down, piercing the carapace; the mandibles fastened around the head and the second monster rode the other as it began to tremble, throwing itself desperately against the walls of the cleft in a vain attempt to rid itself of its assailant. The stinger remained imbedded in its body sac and in a little while the poison took effect. The wounded creature's struggling slowed, its legs folded, no longer able to support the double weight, and it sank to the ground. The other withdrew the dagger-like appendage and jumped clear. With an awful efficiency it rolled the dead monster onto its back and sank its mandibles into the underside of the belly, tearing a gaping hole into which it thrust its palps. The sucking sounds Kedryn had heard were explained as the corpse was drained.

'Cannibals,' Tepshen muttered as the victor proceeded to sever limbs and suck them dry, leaving only husks that rapidly disintegrated into the dust that covered the floor.

He watched as the head of the fallen beast was devoured, then suddenly ran forward, sword arcing to slice deep into the side of the feeding creature. It turned towards him and he hacked through two limbs before darting back. The monster emitted the whistling sound they had heard before and within the instant a third was on it.

Another was attracted, either by the shrilling that appeared to indicate hurt or the sounds of battle, and they fought, rearing up to clack mandibles and manouevring to place stingers. A mêlée ensued as more came, spidery bodies falling, the devourers in turn attacked and eaten. Kedryn found himself facing one that charged out of the darkness, halting as it faced the talisman's light, and he swung the great sword down upon its startled head, splitting the ovoid in a great welter of pungent ichor. That one, too, was pounced upon, but whilst it was drained, Brannoc hacked legs and the feeder was devoured in turn.

In time the three comrades had no need to fight, for the cannibal spiders killed one another and the men needed only occasionally use their blades, when a beast ventured too close.

It was a respite that brought them no joy, for the spectacle of the hideous creatures eating was nauseating, the sundered bodies filling the night with the overwhelming reek of rotted fruit, and they were thankful for the advent of what passed for morning within the shadows of the cleft, for the return of the light sent the beasts scuttling up the walls to the safety of their caves. No traces of the ghastly combat remained, the bodies degenerating into dust as the ichor that gave them life was sucked out, and the three, grim-faced and hollow-eyed with lack of sleep, continued their progress into the mountains.

Farther along, the cleft opened and rose more steeply, eventually giving onto a bowl around which the jagged peaks reached narrow fingers to the purple cloud, like a hand clutching at the sky. They climbed the side of the bowl and traversed a long ridge, a perilous hogback that descended on both flanks into cave-pocked ravines, moving towards a solitary peak that appeared to mark the far scarp of the hills.

It seemed they had climbed above the kingdom of the spiders for the caves became less numerous as they approached the peak and eventually they found themselves crossing a landscape devoid of the threatening openings. The fruity stink faded and the red dust no longer filled the air, even the warm wind dropping away behind them. They saw that the cloud, too, ended, unnatural as all else in this strange land, ceasing as if it marked a boundary, the farther edge stretching across the sky above the peak neatly as though marked by a straight-drawn line. Beyond it the heavens were canescent, a pale, ashen grey.

They reached the peak and halted, fatigued by the long hours of climbing and the sleepless, horror-filled night, deciding to make camp while some semblance of flat terrain offered a measure of comfort.

The stone on which they stood was relatively smooth, scattered with large pebbles and shards of rock, as if chipped from the pinnacle that rose high above them, conical and tapering to a point just below the cloud. Beyond it lesser summits concealed whatever lay ahead, spreading in a downwards slant like wave tops on a cloudy day. The hills behind hid the green sun and the vermilion sky alike, and what light there was appeared to emanate from no particular source, though unlike the plain, shadows fell, stretching out from the jagged crests in stark, dark pools. Without the wind the temperature dropped rapidly, and without timber or any other combustible materials it was impossible to light a fire, so they ate and wrapped their blankets about them, preparing for a cold and cheerless night.

They had clearly entered another region of the netherworld, for here there was no cloud movement to mark the ending of day, merely a fractional lessening of the light that plunged the mountains into a dreary twilight. They took turns on watch, the darker hours passing without incident, and started their descent when the light brightened to a gloomy approximation of day. Still there was no sun, nor did the sky hold any evidence of cloud, and they wound their way down shadowed slopes rendered treacherous by the deceptive illumination until they reached an area of deep ravines and winding gullies that several times turned them back on their path so that they were still within the rocky mazes when the dim light faded again.

They passed a second cold night amongst the ravines and in the morning started out once more along the deep-cut pathways, working steadily downwards through a region empty of any signs of life. A third night was spent sleeping on hard, cold stone, and another day descending. The sky remained an unrelenting grey, glum as tarnished silver; no wind blew and the air was still, chilly and scented faintly with the odour of ashes.

Then, at about noon by their calculations, the ravine they traversed opened onto level ground.

Tepshen was in the lead and he halted abruptly at the mouth of the ravine, staring ahead. Kedryn and Brannoc moved to join him, pausing dumbstruck at the vista that spread before them.

It was a wasteland, grey and empty and forbidding. As far as the eye could see the ground was flat, a grey slightly darker than the hue that loomed overhead, striated with a myriad shallow cracks as if mud had baked dry and split. No trees grew, nor was there any sign of rivers. Not even boulders broke the inexorable advance of the smooth plain on which the only discernible marks were the scissures mazing its dull surface. How far it stretched was impossible to judge, land and sky melding along the horizons, featureless. No sun was visible, nor any landmarks, only the level, empty terrain.

Kedryn stepped past Tepshen and marched onto the flat. The ground was hard beneath his boots and when he approached the closest fissure he saw nothing save a shallow, smooth-sided indentation. He turned, studying the hills, but they showed no sign of the fires that might mark Taziel's dwelling and he faced his companions with dwindling spirits.

'I believe,' he said slowly, his voice dull, 'that we must cross this miserable landscape.'

Tepshen nodded without speaking. Brannoc said, 'At least it shows no sign of monsters.'

'No any other sign,' Kedryn sighed. 'If Taziel's smithy is, indeed, marked by fire it must lie beyond this place.'

'Then forward we go!'

Brannoc grinned, essaying a semblance of cheer that was somewhat belied by the look he cast about him. Kedryn shared his apprehension, for the terrain was horribly gloomy, of an aspect to rob souls of optimism, denying even the alleviation of danger, offering, it seemed, only unending boredom. He hiked Drul's great sword to a more comfortable position on his back and began to tread the dismal waste.

\*

Barris Edon studied the approaching wagon with some interest, recognising the blue of Estrevan beneath the dust that coated its boards and the robes of the woman seated beside the driver. This one, however, had an escort of six warriors, their travel-stained surcoats marked with the fist of Tamur in scarlet against a white roundel, which meant they came from the Morfah fort. Something, he assumed, to do with the Paramount Sister Gerat, who appeared to have taken up residence in High Fort.

His, he told himself reluctantly, was not to reason why, but to warn his watch-captain of their coming, so he shouted from his lookout post and promised himself he would enquire later as to what all the activity presaged. He knew that Kedryn had gone into the Beltrevan with the slant-eyed easterner who seemed never to leave his side, and the former wolfshead, Brannoc, and that rumour had it Kedryn's new wife was taken prisoner, either by barbarians or some follower of Ashar, according to who told the story. The former he dismissed, for were it true, Rycol would undoubtedly have mounted a full-scale rescue mission, so his money was on the latter, which might go some way to explaining Gerat's presence and this new visitor. He watched as the wagon came up to the gates and disappeared from view, wondering if war was to break out again.

Below his position the watch-captain greeted the newcomer and helped her from the wagon. She was very young, and her face was grave as she asked for the Paramount Sister. The officer was too disciplined to question her, and anyway assumed that Chatelain Rycol would inform him of anything he needed to know, so he curbed his own curiosity and brought the Sister to the commander.

Rycol greeted her with a face no less grave than hers, and sent word for Gerat to join them. The Paramount Sister entered the room alone and smiled at the young woman.

'Sister Jenille, is it not? I am pleased to see you.'

Jenille ducked her head in greeting, gratefully accepting the wine Rycol offered.

'I am come with all speed, Sister. Senders now wait along the way from Estrevan to High Fort.'

'The Morfah Pass?' Gerat asked. 'The Gadrizels have been ever a barrier.'

'Leah at the mouth,' nodded Jenille, 'and Meara in the fort. They are the most adept among us.'

'Excellent,' Gerat smiled, though the expression lacked its usual good humour.

'Is there word?' Jenille enquired.

Gerat shook her head. 'Not yet. By now Kedryn must have reached Drul's Mound, but we have heard nothing.'

'My spies report no unusual activity,' Rycol offered, 'and had Kedryn been captured, I believe some news would have reached me.'

'So mayhap he has succeeded in entering the netherworld,' murmured Jenille.

'Mayhap,' said Gerat. 'We must hope so, and remain ever alert.'

'For what?' asked the young woman, frowning.

'I am not sure.' Gerat sighed, her unlined features troubled. 'I ask that you hold your mind open, for I believe that when the time comes you or I will sense a stirring of powers.'

'So we must wait,' said Jenille.

'Aye,' Gerat confirmed, 'we must wait. It is all we can do.'

*

Wynett descended the stairs with considerable trepidation, torn between the certitude of her decision and the fear that it might serve only to reveal further contradictions. Nonetheless, the awful loneliness she had felt as she stood atop the palace and surveyed the grey, rain-sodden landscape spurred her on. To continue unknowing was to court the enemy despair; or worse, to flirt with madness. Her faith in the Lady was such that she felt truth must lie in Eyrik's suggestion: that the introduction of the talisman to the oracular pool must surely impose upon it a demand for veracity that would transcend its multi-layered depictions of reality to show her that which applied to her, here and now.

That was, she recognised, implicit acceptance of Eyrik's words, which in turn suggested a degree of faith in her mysterious host. A small degree, she told herself, for she was still uncertain of his motives and by no means any longer convinced that he was so solicitous of her desire to regain the natural world as he claimed. Still, if he did manipulate the pool, surely the talisman would

260

overcome even those grammaryes to show her what she sought to find.

If not . . . She quelled the thought, for it meant that she was truly alone, perhaps imprisoned by Ashar himself.

She lifted her skirts high as she hurried down the winding stairway, ignoring the windows that offered impossible views, intent on finding the chamber with the blue door and executing her intention.

She was breathless as she reached the stairway's foot, and paused in the small, stone room, composing herself, hoping that Eyrik would remain occupied with whatever mysterious business filled his time: she did not want him present, nor want him to witness her reaction should the experiment prove unsuccessful.

Her breathing once more normal, she opened the door and stepped beneath the shelter of the balconies. Rain still filled the atrium with its mournful cascade but she ignored it, hurrying beneath the protective ceiling to the chamber containing the pool. She saw no sign of Eyrik either in the courtyard or the chamber, but as she entered the room it occurred to her that he might be within the cavernous vault beyond and she crossed to the portal opening into that strange room. A brief inspection suggested that unless he hid within the shadows the place was empty. The candles still burned in their golden sconces and the great throne stood unoccupied, the hall still and silent. Her heart beating loud against her breast, she returned to the pool and knelt beside its limpid circle.

She mouthed a brief prayer to the Lady and fixed her eyes on the silvery liquid, her mind concentrated on Kedryn, anticipating now the strange shimmer, the sense of movement, that preceded the oracle's revelations. She saw the image form and her lips pursed as she recognised the interior of the White Palace, tapestries decorating walls, flambeaux casting radiant light over a host of folk who seemed to cheer, raising hands in accolade. She saw Bedyr and Yrla, smiling gravely, Jarl and Arlynne beside them, Bethany close by, all standing at the foot of the dais that carried the two chairs used to enthrone her and Kedryn. Now, however, only Kedryn occupied the seat, and he rose, smiling, to extend a hand as Ashrivelle, gowned in white and gold, walked proudly towards him. She halted at the foot of the dais and Kedryn descended to her side, taking her hand and turning to present her to the crowd, then turned again to face the dais on which Bethany now stood, her arms raised as if to encompass the couple before her.

Wynett recognised the form of the marriage ceremony and tore her gaze away, clutching the talisman as, despite her determination, she felt her heart pound afresh, despair threatening to well anew in her soul. Slowly she slid her hands to the chain suspending the stone, spreading it as she ducked her head so that she might lift the jewel clear. She held it tight for a moment, breathing deeply, then wound the chain about her wrist and clenched a fist around the metal, allowing the talisman to dangle free.

Then, with teeth clenched, she lowered the stone into the pool.

Instantly, the image dissolved. The pool's silvery light grew blue, then cleared, shimmering afresh as another image formed. Wynett stared, unaware that she held her breath, seeing only the forms that shaped before her nervous eyes.

Kedryn stood with Tepshen Lahl and Brannoc in a landscape unlike any she had seen. Above them was a blank, grey sky, beneath their feet what appeared to be baked, grey mud, cut with a multitude of cracks. On Kedryn's back was slung a massive sword. His hair was unkempt and his eyes hollow, as if he lacked sleep, or was burdened with great sorrow. His mouth was set in a grim, determined line, and even as he watched he turned to speak with his companions and all three began to trudge across the strange terrain, their movements those of men who have marched long in adversity.

She whispered, 'Kedryn!' and the image flickered, changing to show a dismal, red-lit chasm, narrow and filled with dust that rose in clouds as he stood with upraised blade, Tepshen and Brannoc at his back. She gasped as a nightmare creature scuttled on too many legs towards them, rearing up to display clashing mandibles and hideous, excessive eyes.

Then she screamed as the thing pounced forwards, ignoring the blade Kedryn swung even though it hacked deep into the creature's body as it landed upon him, the mandibles fastening about his chest, his face contorting in agony as the bulbous sac lunged a curved stinger towards him, driving the point into his thigh. Nausea filled her as she saw her beloved writhe in pain, the sword dropping from his grasp. She snatched the talisman from the pool as the mandibles began to tear out his stomach.

Shuddering, she lurched back from the silver disc, crouching on the blue-tiled floor as horror shook her, tears moistening her cheeks, her head shaking in mute denial.

It could not be!

Yet Eyrik had vowed the pool depicted only the truth, albeit in numerous alternatives.

Yet did Eyrik lie?

She could not know, save through the talisman, which he had suggested must impose a personal truth on the oracle; or had he lied about that, too?

She willed herself to calm and extended her hand once more above the pool, lowering the stone into the liquid, seeing a new manifestation take shape.

Now Kedryn lounged before a barbarian lodge, Tepshen and Brannoc to either side, beyond them a ring of grinning, laughing woodlanders who passed a leathern sack from hand to hand, each tilting it above their cup and quaffing deep of the liquid that poured out. Kedryn appeared at ease, drinking the brew and leaning back on unsteady elbows, roaring silent laughter at some sally and thrusting his cup eagerly forward to obtain more of the sack's contents. She saw his face clearly, recognising the signs of drunkenness in the glazed eyes, the slack mouth, and shook her head in disbelief.

The image promptly shifted, changing, and now Kedryn stood upon the ramparts of a hold, staring towards a forest of verdant trees. His face was lined and grey streaked his hair. Two young men, so similar they must be his sons, stood either side of him, smiling as he spoke, following his gesture as he indicated some event occurring beyond the walls.

That flickered and changed, and she looked upon a bier, Kedryn's body layed in state, draped with Tamur's standard. Tepshen and Brannoc stood close by, their heads bowed, and the two young men she had seen before, now grown to heart-rending semblance of their father.

That was replaced with yet another image, one of fire, in which he wielded that great sword against a thing of shadow and flame that darted just beyond the limits of her vision, pressing him hard, driving him back so that he passed from sight, the image shifting yet again.

Now he stood upon a tumulus she recognised as Drul's Mound. Dirt streaked his face and his hands were bound behind him, Tepshen and Brannoc, similarly held, to his right. Barbarians faced them, holding torches, their features twisted in rage, beyond them a circle of tribesmen bearing swords and axes and spears. She saw an order given and the prisoners driven roughly away from a pit at the mound's apex, towards three frameworks of wood. Their bonds were cut and their arms dragged out that their wrists might be lashed to the crosspieces. Their shirts were cut away and a woodlander she saw was Cord came forward with a long, broad-bladed knife. She snatched the talisman clear as he began to cut the blood eagle on Kedryn's back.

Her hand trembled as she forced herself to lower the stone into the pool once again, seeing Kedryn outstretched on a bed of blood-stained grass, a bird-like creature with black, leathery skin where feathers should be perched upon his chest, its hooked beak descending towards his blindly staring eyes.

That awful sight faded, replaced by another, then another, and another, and yet more, the pool growing animated as the depictions altered, Kedryn old ... Kedryn young and with Ashrivelle ... Kedryn with Tepshen Lahl and Brannoc in landscapes that belonged in nightmares ... Kedryn dying beneath the onslaught of strange beasts ... Kedryn laughing ... weeping ... fighting ... fleeing. One image overlayed the next until they passed too swiftly for her eyes to follow and she realised that the surface of the pool seethed and bubbled as if animated by some internal force.

She snatched the talisman from the turmoil, the silvery liquid no longer smooth and calm but roiled, wavering and rippling as if a spring burst forth deep below, rushing to the surface to disrupt the images. She stared at it, seeing it slowly settle, becoming once more the argent disc that promised so much and now offered only confusion, and loosed the talisman's chain from her wrist, replacing the blue jewel about her neck.

Despondency filled her, the hope that Kyrie's stone would show her the truth dashed, that disappointment opening gates through which disillusion threatened to flood. She closed her eyes, determined that she would not give way to the despair that stalked her soul, and imposed upon her troubled mind those meditative disciplines instilled by Estrevan.

There was no longer any point to consulting the oracular pool. Either because it would show, no matter what, the many strands of possibility that opened before Kedryn, or because it was manipulated by Eyrik. To what purpose she was not sure, nor even that he did create the images she had seen; but she did see, clearly, that to consult the pool again was to court a pessimism bordering on madness. Yet without the pool she could have no knowledge of Kedryn; could not know – save through faith now rendered blind – that he sought her, or how he fared; whether he lived or died.

The mind-numbing sensation of absolute loneliness that had assailed her on the roof of the palace descended again. Without the pool she was totally in Eyrik's hands, and without trust in his goodwill she was alone as she had never been. There existed only the unswerving belief that Kedryn *would* seek her, and the tenets of her faith.

She fixed her mind on those bedrocks . . . and found them shaken by the very disciplines from which she sought succour, for Estrevan taught a sometimes uncomfortable pragmatism that forced her to consider all the possibilities, regardless of her emotions. Kedryn *would* seek her, but to find her he must enter the netherworld and, presumably, surmount the hideous dangers she had seen revealed: his death was a possibility she could not ignore. If he should die questing for her she was trapped, condemned to live out her life here in this fabulous – and now menacing – palace, alone with Eyrik. The Lady was with her, of that she was confident, but less so of Kyrie's power to intervene directly. Her spirit, whilst she maintained her faith, was secure, but her flesh, too, was real, and it crept at the notion of remaining, perhaps forever, in this place. The talisman likely protected her from direct harm, but now it could not stave off that creeping tide of insidious doubt. All she had left were her faith and the flickering spark of hope that Kedryn, himself protected, should win through to save her. Unless, that coldly logical part of her mentality she had summoned told her, she placed her trust in Eyrik, and that, she felt, she could not do.

Ergo, she was alone.

She must rely on whatever guidance the Lady could give her and her own wit. It was a daunting prospect, and one that allowed her little initiative, for it seemed that she could do nothing but await whatever might develop, reacting to Eyrik's suggestions, the gambits in the strange game played by him.

She opened her eyes and rose, smoothing a gown she realised for the first time was soaked over her thighs. It did not seem that she had achieved much, other than an elimination of certain aspects, but she felt more calm, and gripped by a resolve she would not allow to be swayed. Practically, she decided that she would return to her rooms and assuage her spirits with the simple comforts of hot water and dry clothing. Without a further glance at the pool she quit the chamber and found her way through the sodden atrium to the stairs.

Inside, the chambers were all light and airy comfort. They emanated a sense of casual luxury, of security. The rain still fell beyond the windows, but the interior was dry and refreshingly cool, the withered flowers gone, replaced with fresh bouquets that imparted a delightful perfume to the air. Kindling was layed in the fireplace, with tapers and a tinderbox beside, but the thought of fire brought thoughts of Ashar and she ignored the hearth, turning to bolt the door behind her before unfastening her gown and removing her undergarments. She went to the alcove and spun the golden faucets, hot water steaming instantly into the ornate tub. She watched it fill, the rising water reminding her of the pool, and eased beneath the surface with a sigh. Stretching out, she let her head rest against the rim, concentrating on the purely physical pleasure of the bath.

Its warmth made her drowsy and she rubbed her body with smooth soap that gave off the scent of sandalwood, then sought the refreshment of cold water before rising to towel herself dry. She rubbed at her hair and, still naked, settled before the mirror to brush it, the drowsy feeling lingering, so that when she was satisfied she ignored the wardrobe and climbed instead into the tempting comfort of the bed. Closing one hand about the talisman she drifted into welcome sleep.

She woke with a start, aware of a presence in the room, panic erupting for an instant so that she gasped as her eyes focused to reveal Eyrik standing beside the bed, a tray of black lacquer in his hands.

He smiled a mixture of amusement and apology and said, 'Forgive me, I did not mean to startle you.'

Wynett stared at him, realising that she was naked, and drew the sheets demurely to her chin before easing to a sitting position against the pillows. Eyrik's gold-flecked eyes passed briefly over the contours delineated by the sheet and he set the tray across her thighs.

'You did not appear at dinner, so I presumed to bring you food.'

He gestured at the tray and Wynett saw that it held platters of meat, salvers of vegetables, a selection of fruit and cheeses, a carafe and two glasses. Her stomach registered the savoury odours but she ignored the temptation to eat, her gaze fixed on Eyrik.

His glossy hair was held back from his handsome face by a thin gold band that mirrored the flecks in his brown eyes. He wore a loose surcoat of white held at the waist by a belt of golden metal, his shirt and breeks maroon, white boots on his feet. His resemblance to Kedryn seemed increased. His smile was easy as he added, 'Are you not hungry?'

'How did you enter?' she asked.

266

'Forgive my presumption in intruding.' He ducked his head in apology. 'But I was concerned for you.'

'How did you enter?' she repeated, a hand reaching beneath the concealing sheet to clutch the talisman.

Eyrik shrugged. 'The door was unbolted. I knocked, but when there was no answer I thought to leave the tray for you – you awoke before I could depart.'

Wynett frowned. Had she not bolted the door? Aye, she was certain she had. Therefore bolts afforded him no obstacle. She thought for an instant to challenge him on it, but then thought better of it and turned her eyes to the food.

'Thank you.'

She had hoped he would leave, but he showed no sign of departing, gesturing instead at the bed and saying, 'May I sit?' Not giving her time to reply, but settling at the foot, smiling pleasantly.

'I believe the rain will cease soon. It is horribly depressing, is it not?'

Wynett nodded, conscious of his weight tugging at the sheets and of her own nudity.

'Please.' He gestured at the tray. 'Will you not eat? I would not see you starve yourself.'

'I . . .' She held the sheet firmly, 'I am undressed.'

The flecks in his eyes seemed to shift, and she read admiration in his gaze as they travelled from her face to her exposed shoulders, but then his smile became grave and he rose, apologetic again.

'May I bring you a gown? I would talk with you – I confess to feeling somewhat guilty at leaving you alone so long.'

He moved as he spoke, the words overcoming any opposition she might have offered, going to the outer chamber, to the wardrobes, from which he took a dressing gown of maroon silk that exactly matched his shirt and breeks. He returned, spreading it across the bed, and removed himself once more to the ante-chamber, closing the door behind him. Wynett saw that he would not be deterred and lifted the tray clear, jumping from the bed to swiftly don the gown. Her sense of vulnerability was mildly assuaged by the texture of the silk against her skin, though the decolletage was greater than she would have chosen and the silk was very sheer. It was a gown she might have worn for Kedryn, but not in the presence of any other man. She regained the bed, seeking the additional barrier of the sheets, as Eyrik called, 'May I enter?'

267

Feeling that she had little choice she replied in the affirmative and he entered again, resuming his seat at the bed's foot. Wynett nibbled on roasted veal, as much to conceal her nervousness as from hunger.

'Some wine?'

Eyrik lifted the carafe, filling both glasses, the movement bringing his face close to hers. Wynett forked a vegetable, disturbed by his proximity, sensing a subtle change in his attitude. She found it hard to define, but he appeared more confident, his solicitude now less diffident, more assertive. He raised the goblet, savouring the bouquet, then took a mouthful and sighed.

'Excellent. Will you not taste it?'

She raised her own glass, taking a small sip. It was, indeed, as he described it, light and mildly effervescent, tingling her palate as she swallowed.

'What drove you to retirement?' he wondered; and Wynett debated whether the question was so innocent as it appeared, or if he knew the answer. If he did manipulate the pool, then the latter.

She said, 'I was fatigued.' There seemed no point to concealing her activities, so she added, 'I went to the pool.'

Eyrik's finely arched brows rose questioningly. 'And did you apply the talisman as I suggested?'

Wynett nodded.

'Am I to assume from that doleful mien that the results were not to your liking?'

There was nothing in his tone to suggest duplicity; rather, his face assumed an expression of concern.

'Aye,' she said, 'they were not.'

'What did you see?'

'Do you not know?' She surprised herself with the question, not sure from whence it sprang, but now experiencing a degree of irritation that she sought rapidly to conceal.

'How should I?' His eyes narrowed, the gold flecks dancing against the brown, furrows marking his brow as he frowned: an expression of uncomprehending innocence. 'The pool shows what it shows. I have no control over its revelations.'

Wynett raised her glass, seeking a moment in which to order her thoughts. She had no wish to reveal her suspicions, nor to anger him. 'I thought perhaps,' she said carefully, 'that you were aware of them.'

Eyrik shook his head. 'How could I be? I was not there.'

Wynett shrugged. 'Forgive me, I am confused by what I saw.'

'Which was?' he prompted.

'Alternatives, as before.'

'The talisman did not impose a singular reality?' His frown grew deeper, his eyes thoughtful.

'It did not,' she said when she realised he waited for a response.

'Then I was wrong.' He shook his head, his tone grown mournful. One hand reached out to touch her arm in a gesture imbued with sympathy. 'I am sorry, Wynett. I was convinced the stone must work as I had thought.'

He shook his head again, removing his hand from her arm to cup it about his glass. So troubled was his gaze she wondered if her suspicions were misguided, her doubts unfounded.

'What *did* you see?' he asked.

'Many things,' she replied. 'Some horrible, some incomprehensible. Alternative overlaid alternative until there was only confusion.'

'My dear!' He clutched her arm again, radiating distressed concern. 'I am sorry – I had truly believed the talisman would show you the true reality, but obviously I was wrong.' His frown grew deeper, his grip a fraction stronger, as though he sought to impart comfort from the touch, his voice dropping to a murmur as he said, 'Mayhap its power is weakened here.'

'How should that be?' she asked nervously, reaching for the carafe, less from any desire for the wine than the need to remove his hand.

He shrugged, leaning slightly forwards as if in thought, looking first down at the glass he held, then up again at her face. 'We occupy a curious realm – as you already know. The power that imbues the talisman is great in the natural world, but here we exist surrounded by Ashar's magicks. Mayhap that power reduces the strength of the talisman. The Lady's domain is that world you know, not the realms of the netherworld, and perchance her puissance is overwhelmed by Ashar's might.'

He voiced the very fears Wynett had felt as she considered her situation and his pronouncement filled her with dread. She willed hands that threatened to tremble to stillness, the food she ate become tasteless in her mouth. She swallowed and lifted her glass to her lips, drinking deeper this time.

'But that does not mean hope is lost,' Eyrik declared, surprising her. 'It means simply that the pool must continue to show all that is possible.'

269

'I shall not consult it again,' Wynett declared firmly.

Eyrik nodded as if in sympathy: 'If it reduces you to such dolour I may only applaud that decision. And seek some other means by which you may obtain news of Kedryn.'

'Is there another way?' she asked, hope rising again despite all her doubts.

'Perhaps.' Eyrik straightened, his face solemn as he stared at her, something in his eyes that she could not read.

It occurred to her, obliquely, that the disciplines of Estrevan were of little help where he was concerned. For all that she had surrendered those gifts folk considered magical with her celibacy, she still retained many of the aptitudes instilled by the Sisterhood, amongst them that ability to read expressions, body movements, to see past words to the truth implicit in the muscles and the skin, the movement of the eyes, the sheen of sweat, but that talent was useless where Eyrik was concerned. She could not read him; she could see only the face he chose to present to her. Or did she take too complex a view? Was that face true?

'Perhaps?' she prompted when he fell silent.

He nodded again, hesitantly, apparently unsure of himself, or unwilling to reveal his thoughts.

'It may not be a means much to your liking,' he said at last.

'How can it not be if it allows me news of Kedryn?' she asked.

'Because it would involve the use of the talisman,' he said quietly.

Wynett bit back the negative that sprang to her lips, wondering if some verbal trap was laid. Eyrik appeared devoid of guile, his face serious as he studied her, troubled even, as though he feared her reaction. He wore, as ever, the semblance of a man intent only on aiding her, anxious to help and wary of giving offence. If he did prepare some snare, it was subtly layed: she craved knowledge of Kedryn, and to refuse out of hand was to both deny herself that knowledge and imply mistrust of Eyrik.

'How so?' she prevaricated. 'You suggest the talisman's strength is weakened here, so how might it be used?'

Eyrik shrugged, the motion rustling the soft material of his surcoat. 'It is a complicated thing,' he said, 'involving certain cantrips and apparatus of my own devising. If the talisman was unable to impose order on the pool then it is, undoubtedly, weaker here, but still not without power. Mayhap that power is become limited by the nature of our surroundings, but mayhap, also, I can enhance its strength.'

'To what end?' she asked, a hand curling instinctively about the jewel.

'I believe that I may establish a beacon,' he replied in an earnest tone, leaning forwards again as though to impress his words the more forcefully upon her. 'I believe that I am able to augment the magic of the stone so that it will guide Kedryn here. That is what has occupied me of late – the reason I have neglected my duties as host. I should not have left so lovely a guest alone had I not been anxious to satisfy your heart's desire! Today, however, I set the final touches to the machineries necessary to my purpose and all is ready. Only the talisman is needed to complete the cycle.'

'And it will guide Kedryn to this place?' she wondered.

'Aye, so I believe,' nodded Eyrik, grinning as though proud of what he had accomplished on her behalf. 'His part of the stone will respond to the clarion I broadcast and he will be guided through the intricate layers of the netherworld.'

'And when he comes?' Wynett felt excitement flutter, quickening her heartbeat, optimism threatening to overwhelm caution.

'Then the two halves of the talisman will be joined,' Eyrik responded eagerly, his smile prompting her to share his excitement. 'And joined, the power of the stone will be magnified. Was it not so when you faced the Messenger in the White Palace?'

Wynett nodded agreement, remembering that terrible duel, when the strength of the stone had seemed to possess her, guiding her, guiding Kedryn, that together they were able to overcome the awesome power of Ashar's minion.

'Thus enhanced it will, I am confident, open an avenue of escape,' he continued. 'We shall all be free.'

'We?' Wynett enquired. 'Would you, too, leave this place?'

Eyrik's smiled faded, his features rearranging in serious lines as he ducked his head. 'I am no less a prisoner than you, my dear. I would walk the byways of the Kingdoms freely, without hindrance. I grow tired of my confinement.'

His eyes flashed with exhilaration, as if the very thought transported him. Wynett studied him cautiously, seeing only excitement, wondering if some deeper emotion she could not read lay behind it.

'How should this be accomplished?' she asked.

His face became serious again and he said, 'I should need to employ the talisman, as I told you.'

'You ask that I remove it?'

He nodded, seeming nervous now.

'You know that such action is forsworn.'

Eyrik raised his hands palms upwards, spreading long fingers in a gesture of helplessness. 'There is no other way. I have constructed certain devices that will work in concert with my cantrips to establish the beacon. Without the talisman they are useless, yet their design is such that the stone must be removed from your neck.'

'I cannot,' she said, shaking her head. 'I am sworn.'

'Surely by vows taken without cognizance of your present fate,' he murmured.

'Taken in good faith,' Wynett returned. 'Nor am I confident the talisman would operate as you hope if separated from me.'

'If not, then not,' said Eyrik, his voice a trifle subdued, but still underlayed with enthusiasm. 'Though I believe the strength rests in the stone itself.'

It was a subtle admonishment and Wynett blushed at the unspoken suggestion that misplaced pride guided her. She felt a terrible dread and a mighty confusion, for if Eyrik spoke the truth then she denied him the means whereby he might guide Kedryn to her and denied herself the means of escape from the netherworld. Yet if he lied he doubtless sought the jewel for his own ends. And if he was Ashar, or a minion of the awful god, then to deliver the talisman into his hands was to betray all she believed in, to invest the god with frightening strength.

'There remains the matter of Kedryn,' Eyrik murmured, his tone apologetic again, as though he felt embarrassment at the implicit suggestion of disloyalty. 'If we are correct in our belief that he seeks you, then he has likely sought some means of entering the netherworld. If he succeeds, then he faces all the mazes Ashar will set before him. And they will be exceeding hazardous labyrinths! It may even be that the god seeks to ensnare him, so that he shall wander forever through the realms of limbo. The beacon I suggest would be such that his path would be the clearer.'

He paused, fixing her with his gold-flecked stare. Wynett lowered her eyes, caught in the mesh of his words, clutching the talisman, no longer defensively but in search of guidance, of inspiration.

All she felt, however, was that tingling that told her Kedryn was still alive. She raised her eyes, answering Eyrik's gaze, and said, 'Still you ask me to forget a vow freely given.'

He nodded agreement, a hint of melancholy entering his voice as he answered, 'So it must be, though I am confident those to whom you gave your word would understand. I repeat – I doubt they considered this eventuality when they entrusted you with the talisman.'

'Mayhap not,' Wynett allowed, 'but still the vow was taken.'

'You took others,' he reminded her, mildly enough. 'Did you not embrace celibacy when you donned the blue of Estrevan?'

'Aye.' Wynett ducked her head. 'So I did.'

'And you were released from that undertaking when the time came.'

She could not deny it: she nodded again.

'I am confident the Sisterhood would understand,' said Eyrik softly, his tone persuasive. 'Estrevan would surely condone your motives now, for they must surely be above reproach – you would seek only to protect the man you love from inestimable dangers.'

'Even so,' she said slowly, feeling his blandishments wind about her as must, she thought, the web of a spider wind about a butterfly, each attempt at escape serving only to affix a further sticky strand until finally all hope was gone.

'Even so,' he echoed, reaching out now to take a hand, enclosing it in both of his, 'I believe you must decide this for yourself. I can do no more – without the talisman my efforts are useless and you must likely remain here.' He smiled somewhat ruefully, 'I confess that notion has its attractions, but I know that you love Kedryn and so I would do all I can to re-unite you. Please trust me, Wynett – there is no other way.'

He stared into her eyes, retaining her hand in silence for a while, then let loose his grip, smiling as though to reassure her.

'Sleep on it and give me your answer in the morning.'

'Aye,' she agreed, glad that he rose now, frightened by the decision he forced upon her and wishing only to be alone with her disordered thoughts.

Eyrik bowed graciously and left the bed chamber. When she heard the outer door close she rose and bolted it again, then dragged a chair across the room and wedged its back against the bolt. Then she shed the dressing gown he had selected and took a garment of her own choosing from the wardrobe. She set the lacquered tray aside, its contents barely touched, and regained the bed.

'Lady,' she prayed, the talisman clutched in both hands, 'guide me, for I am lost.'

# Chapter Thirteen

THE landscape stretched uninterrupted before them, flat and featureless, the horizons lost in the gloomy grey that joined land and sky in seemless union. Only the strange cracks broke the vista, zig-zagging beneath their feet, neither deep nor wide enough to offer hindrance to their steady progress. Nothing moved, either in the sky or on the ground. There was no wind, nor any sun, the canescent light unchanging and their march leaving no footprints behind, so that it seemed almost as though they walked in place, the only measure of progress the weariness that began gradually to assail their legs. Finally, Kedryn called a halt and they spread their blankets, grateful for the chance to ease muscles protesting the endless marching.

The hills lay far behind them, lost in the leaden blur of distance, the air, now that they no longer moved, chilly.

'A fire would be welcome,' Brannoc remarked.

'Three horses, more so,' retorted Tepshen.

'But we have neither,' said Kedryn. 'Nor much chance of finding kindling or mounts here.'

Brannoc shrugged, opening his satchel, his features doleful as he examined the contents.'Supplies become short, too. And I grow weary of journey bread.'

Kedryn nodded, his own face thoughtful as he watched the dark-skinned halfbreed thrust his pack aside, the food ignored. 'How long have we walked?' he asked.

'A day?' Brannoc shrugged again, reaching down to massage his calves. 'There is no way to tell time here.'

'We have not halted,' Tepshen offered, glancing at Kedryn, his sallow features curious.

'No,' agreed the younger man, 'and that is odd, is it not? My legs tell me we have marched for leagues, yet we none of us thought to halt for food or drink.'

'I felt no hunger,' said Brannoc. 'Only boredom.'

'Nor I,' Kedryn murmured. 'I did not think of food until now.'

He looked to the kyo, who shook his head, saying, 'I am not hungry even now.'

'This is strange,' Kedryn declared. 'My muscles tell me I have worked hard, yet I feel no need of sustenance. Is this some attribute of the netherworld?'

'If so, it is to our advantage,' Brannoc declared, gesturing at his pack. 'I have supplies for no more than a day or two.'

Tepshen raised his canteen and shook it, listening to the splash of water inside. 'Nor water,' he added.

'The netherworld is the realm of the dead,' Kedryn mused, 'or of Ashar's creatures, who presumably do not require sustenance as would normal beings. Mayhap by coming here we lose these needs.'

'Or Ashar tricks us into starvation,' suggested Brannoc.

'I do not feel starved,' Kedryn said.

'Eat nonetheless,' Tepshen advised. 'If you are correct, then we need not trouble ourselves over dwindling provisions.'

'Food alleviates boredom,' said Brannoc, 'And this is, without doubt, the most boring vista it has been my misfortune to encounter.'

'Aye.' Kedryn grinned tightly, chewing food that seemed somehow as devoid of flavour as the terrain was empty of character. 'Mayhap Ashar seeks to bore us to death.'

'Would you rather he challenged us with more dagger-throwing trees?' chuckled Brannoc. 'Or perhaps another spidery attack?'

Kedryn smiled back and shook his head. 'No, my friend. I would find Wynett and bring her safely from this place.'

'But first, Taziel,' admonished Tepshen. 'I doubt Ashar will readily relinquish his prize, and if Gerat is correct, you must join your talisman to that great sword if you are to defeat the god.'

Kedryn nodded, drawing the glaive closer, studying the ornate hilt. 'And first persuade Taziel to do the work,' he said quietly.

'To which end we must find his cave,' said Brannoc, looking about. 'And it is not here, I think.'

'No.' Kedryn swallowed a little water, more to wash down the flavourless food than from thirst. 'We must cross this miserable plain before we may hope to find the smith.'

'We shall,' said Tepshen, his voice firm. 'Now sleep. I shall take first watch.'

Neither Kedryn or Brannoc offered argument, and the easterner watched as they rolled themselves into their blankets, squatting cross-legged as they slept. Although he did not show it, he felt mightily uneasy, disturbed by the unchanging light and the unrelieved tedium of their surroundings. He was a man of action and had the truth been told, he preferred the dangers of the spider-haunted ravines to this characterless vista. There was no sign of anything he might have described as a sunset and after a while he decided that there would not be, that so long as they remained on this flat plain there would be only the depressing grey light and – as both Kedryn and Brannoc had remarked – boredom. After a while he rose to his feet and walked a little distance off, drawing his sword and executing a series of exercises that had the long blade whistling through the unmoving air. He did not know how long he diverted himself thus, but in time he ceased, resuming his squatting position, forcing himself to ignore the tedium that threatened to leech his concentration.

When he could fight it no longer he woke Brannoc and fell soundly asleep.

Brannoc in turn found the same disquieting problems. He sat watching the unshifting sky for a while, then stared at the grey he assumed marked the edge of the mountains they had descended. For all he could tell they had walked a circle: they left no tracks, nor were there any landmarks by which to judge direction or distance. It occurred to him that Kedryn was better suited to withstand this absence of diversions than either he or Tepshen, for Kedryn had experienced the darkness sent against High Fort and his subsequent blindness, and both must have been akin to this unalleviated tedium. He was more accustomed to the forests of the Beltrevan than this unending featurelessness and he felt the disturbing beginnings of agoraphobia.

He climbed to his feet and stepped out twenty places. Nothing changed. Kedryn and Tepshen lay huddled in their blankets, the air was chill but not so much that he felt any great physical discomfort. He studied a scissure, seeing nothing so much as a shallow crack such as might be formed in sun-baked mud, and began to follow it for want of any other action with which to occupy his mind. It ran straight for a while, then split into two, those branches dividing in turn, then those until he could no longer trace the course, seeing only a jigsaw pattern that extended into the grey distance. He returned to his companions, hoping that the plain would end before long: whatever lay ahead must surely be preferable to this nothingness. After a while he realised that he was grown drowsy and woke Kedryn.

His surmise of Kedryn's ability to withstand the tedium was, in some measure, correct. Kedryn was, at least, able to recall the utter darkness that had gripped High Fort, and he could favourably compare even this characterless grey landscape with the awful night that had descended with Borsus's sword across his eyes, but there was a difference now. In High Fort there had been a very real enemy beyond the walls, the presence of the Horde made known by the missiles that fell, and in his blindness Wynett had been at his side. Here he could only wonder at her fate as he sat with Drul's blade across his hips, and with that wondering he felt fear grow, doubts assail him.

Before long, he, too, felt the need for movement, to do something that would impart action of some kind to the watch. He rose and began to heft the glaive, familiarising himself with its weight, swinging it in sweeping cuts, adjusting his customary style to the different balance of the weapon, working until he felt his shoulders ache, then settling again to wait.

The doubts pressed in then, fear for Wynett mingling with the creeping pessimism that they would never find a way off the plain, never locate Taziel, or if they did, would fail to persuade the smith to attach talisman to hilt. He was glad when Tepshen stirred, casting off his blanket to rise, staring disapprovingly about before nudging Brannoc to wakefulness.

The halfbreed sat up, rubbing at his eyes and yawning, then took a comb from his satchel and began to dress his plaited hair.

'You will find no maidens to admire you here,' Tepshen grunted, his voice edged with irritation.

Brannoc glanced at him and shrugged, offering no responsive comment. He continued combing, then wound his braids afresh, setting the shells and feathers that decorated them in place.

'Are we to await your toilette?' Tepshen demanded gruffly. 'Or may we commence our journey?'

Brannoc climbed to his feet, stretching, then sniffed and said, 'If we find water I feel a bath in order, for I fear I must smell as bad as you.'

Tepshen's eyes narrowed and Kedryn moved between them, raising a placatory hand.

'My friends, you grow irritable. I believe this doleful place works some spell upon us – fight it, lest Ashar set us against one another.'

'Aye, forgive me,' Brannoc essayed a tight smile as he studied Tepshen. 'I feel ill-humoured.'

'And I,' nodded the kyo. 'I believed Kedryn is right.'

'Let us march then,' Kedryn suggested. 'The sooner we quit this plain the better.'

They began to walk, forgetting that they had not eaten for none felt hungry, marching in silence for none felt like speaking, each lost in his own thoughts as they proceeded across the flat, grey terrain.

After a while Kedryn gestured at the maze of cracks indenting the ground and said, 'Are they not wider?'

The others glanced down and Tepshen ducked his head. 'Aye, and deeper.'

'I wonder what caused them,' murmured Brannoc. 'There is no sun to bake the soil and they do not seem like watercourses.'

No one offered an answer and they continued their march.

As they had done on the previous day – if such chronology could be applied – they did not halt to eat, but maintained a steady pace until their bodies told them to rest, spreading their blankets again and forcing themselves to partake of the supplies remaining in their satchels. Brannoc produced a set of dice, suggesting a game, but Tepshen shook his head, saying that he had no taste for it. The denial surprised Kedryn, for the kyo was an eager gambler, but he said nothing, taking up the cubes himself and rolling a few desultory hands before Brannoc announced that he, too, had lost his enthusiasm.

'I prefer to sleep,' he declared, 'at least then I may dream of more pleasant things.'

'Mayhap you take first watch,' Tepshen said.

'Why?' Brannoc demanded. 'There is nothing to watch for.'

'You grow lax,' snapped the kyo.

'We all grow irritable,' Kedryn said, once more playing the peace maker, for he heard anger in both voices. 'I shall take first watch.'

Brannoc stared for a moment at Tepshen, then snorted and rolled himself into his blanket, turning his back on his companions.

'This place acts upon us,' Kedryn murmured.

'It is a foul place,' Tepshen agreed. 'I find my temper rising without reason.'

'Should we fall to argument we are lost.' Kedryn clasped the talisman. 'We must hold our minds to our purpose.'

'Aye.' The kyo nodded. Then, 'Brannoc? Forgive my shortness.'

'It is nothing,' came the blanket-muffled response.

The hours of the watch were worse that 'night'. Kedryn found himself filled with a melancholy longing for Wynett that was interspersed with memories of Ashrivelle, in particular that of the kiss she had bestowed on his departure from Gennyf. Try as he might, he could not drive them from his mind, but found they grew stronger, and soon he was experiencing guilt at what he considered a betrayal of his love. Tepshen, to whom Kedryn gave the second watch, occupied himself with further exercises at first, but then settled to an unwelcome contemplation of his past, memories of his homeland in the east filling him with sorrow that threatened to curdle into resentment of the peace now enjoyed by the Three Kingdoms. Brannoc, when it came his turn, found himself wondering what he was doing on so hopeless a quest. He had been happy as an outlaw and he recalled the carefree days of trading in the Beltrevan, thinking that he had been better off then than now, committed to a cause he doubted they could win. By the time he woke his companions he was thoroughly miserable.

Indeed, neither Kedryn or Tepshen Lahl were in much better spirits and the silence that fell as they continued their trek was pregnant with pent-up dissatisfaction.

The scissures that mazed their path were wider and deeper, and when they halted again none spoke. Their watches seemed longer, each one falling into unhappy contemplation of their situation, and their departure was marked by the same sullen silence that had accompanied their halt.

The cracks were now so wide they needed to extend their strides, so deep they threatened to break ankles should an unwary step place a foot within the shadowy depths.

The next 'day' they were wider still and the three found themselves jumping across fissures like drainage dykes, half a man's height in depth.

'Blood of the Lady!' Brannoc snapped as he teetered on an edge, his jump ill-judged. 'Should this continue we shall be climbing chasms before we find an end.'

'You grow careless,' Tepshen retorted.

'I grow angry.' Brannoc glowered at the kyo. 'And I have had sufficient of your insults.'

'Do you then seek redress?'

Tepshen's hand dropped to his sword hilt. Brannoc stared at him, his mouth a narrow line. His own hand lifted to the sabre sheathed across his back.

Kedryn watched them, despondency dulling him, an ugly stirring in the nethermost depths of his mind suggesting that the spectacle of armed combat would provide a welcome diversion from the endless boredom of the march. He shook off the lassitude with effort, realising that he, like his comrades, fell into the grim trap of the awful plain and sprang between them, arms extended as though to hold them apart. 'You succumb to Ashar!' he said urgently.

'Stand aside,' Tepshen warned grimly, 'lest you come between my blade and this whiner's skull.'

'Whiner?' Brannoc's sabre hissed loose. 'Give way, Kedryn, for I would teach this braggart a lesson.'

'No!' Kedryn shouted. 'Do you not see that Ashar seeks to divide us? He sets us to odds, that we slay one another. Do not give in to his foul magicks!'

Both men stared at him, swords in hands, their bodies tensed for combat. Kedryn looked to Tepshen, then at Brannoc. 'Sheath your blades,' he urged. 'Would two friends fight? In the name of the Lady, put up your weapons and give me your hands.'

Reluctantly, Tepshen slid his blade into the scabbard. Kedryn fixed Brannoc with a demanding stare until the halfbreed followed suit.

'Now give me your hands.' He took them both and directed them to the blue stone hung about his neck. 'What do you feel?'

'Foolish,' Brannoc said. 'Tepshen, I am sorry.'

'And I,' murmured the kyo. 'Ashar put words in my mouth.'

Kedryn held their hands to the talisman a while longer, letting the jewel work its calming influence upon them. When he at last released his grip both men stood shame-faced, embarrassed smiles twitching their lips. Tepshen extended a hand, clasping Brannoc's. 'Kedryn is right,' he declared, 'Ashar would set us to fighting one another.'

'Aye,' Brannoc nodded, his smile growing wider, 'Perchance because he fears to fight us himself.'

Tepshen laughed at that and Brannoc added, 'We are, after all, formidable.'

Their march became a little more cheerful then, and when they halted again Kedryn persuaded them both to touch the talisman once more, for it appeared that the jewel had the ability to dispel the glamour that clearly possessed the desolate plain. He saw that the fissures had grown no wider and it occurred to him that the strange cracks represented a visible physical manifestation of their spiritual condition, broadening and deepening in measure of the differences between them. The next 'morning' they repeated the ritual, and again during the 'day' whenever tempers frayed, and the cracks remained static. Concomitantly they began to experience hunger and thirst again, consuming the last of their provisions when next they halted.

It was a further problem but preferable, they felt, to the sullen animosity that had festered, and they ignored it, marching resolutely across the ashen plain, where the interstices now seemed to decrease in size, the ground once more resembling the bed of a dried-out river. Their halts, however, became more frequent as hunger took its toll, bodies inevitably weakening under the constant demand of the trek.

After three 'days' they grew lightheaded, their steps slowing, their tongues furred, lips parched for want of water. The chill that pervaded the plain became noticeable, a discomfort now as they burned stored body fat, and they wrapped their blankets around their shoulders as they progressed. In time they began to stagger, supporting one another as they stumbled forwards, ignoring the scissures that cut the plain beneath their feet, growing ever smaller as hardship brought them closer together, relying on each other more than ever.

Then the plain ended as abruptly as it had begun.

At first Kedryn could not credit the evidence of his eyes, for what he saw had the aspect of a mirage, or some fantasy conjured by his hunger. He halted, swaying, and raised a hand to point ahead, his mouth at first too dry to form the words he sought, wondering if Ashar did, indeed, raise a phantasm to damn his hopes.

'Is it real?'

Brannoc's voice was harsh, the question slurred as he forced it out. Tepshen stood beside him, his slanted eyes narrowed. 'Can it be?' he husked.

Kedryn stared, almost afraid to believe the reality, so hopeful was it.

The stood at the edge of the dreary plain, the grey ground falling away before them as if cut with an adze. For twice a man's height it dropped vertically, the scissures dark cuts against the scarp, then it gentled, descending in a gradually angled slope that was at first cinereous, but then shaded into the brown of healthy soil, becoming verdant with the bushes that grew lower down. Farther still below their vantage point the bushes gave way to trees, not the lofty timberland of the Beltrevan, but gentler growths, oak and ash and beech mingling to sweep onto level ground where meadows shone green beneath a golden sun, a winding river sparkling in the light, the sky ahead blue and rafted with billows of wind-blown cumulus. Close to the slope's foot was a clearing, verdant amongst the darker shades of the woodland, and its centre stood a hold of pale sandstone, walled and turreted, smoke rising lazy from its chimneys, orchards and vegetable gardens running up to the walls, watered by the stream that spanned the clearing.

'I do not know,' Kedryn mouthed, the words barely audible. 'Let us find out.'

Tepshen and Brannoc lowered him from the plain's edge and he helped them both down, then all three stumbled and slid over the slant of the upper level, across the good, brown soil to the bushes. They halted there, stretched on the ground, panting, hope overcoming their exhaustion so that they rose and began a staggering descent to the trees.

The air was warm, balmy, a zephyr stirring the foliage as they entered the timberline and heard birds singing, looking up to see the canescent sky of the plain merge with the blue that covered this haven of normality. A thrush stared down at them, head cocked to one side, beak trilling a warning that sounded to them like a welcome. They breathed in the smells of grass and woodland, laughing now, the morbid depression of the grey plain forgotten, heady with thoughts of water and food. A squirrel chattered from the bole of an oak and Kedryn chuckled at its protest, leading the way down through the trees towards the clearing.

The stream curved along the rim of the woodlands, grass and thickets of blackberries marking its banks. The water was clear, splashing over stones that shone blue and grey and yellow in the sunlight, and they halted, staring longingly at the freshet. Then Kedryn threw himself down and began to drink.

'Have care!' cautioned Tepshen throatily. 'It may not be as it seems.'

His warning was too late, for Kedryn was already swallowing, turning to smile and say, 'It tastes as water should. And by the Lady, it is good!'

Brannoc fell beside him, dunking his head before he drank, and then Tepshen, too, knelt and slaked his thirst.

The water refreshed them, going some way also to filling their bellies, and they rose, moving to the edge of the tree line to study the hold.

It seemed innocent enough. Indeed, it seemed out of place in the netherworld, for it bore a great resemblance to the holds of Tamur, the walls foursquare and set between the four solid towers that marked the corners, the merlons cut with large embrasures, the towers roofed with wood. A postern faced them, open onto a courtyard shadowed by the walls and they moved along the line of the trees, not yet quite ready to approach the place. No guards were visible between the crenellations of the ramparts and when they looked to the frontage of the keep they saw wide gates of solid timber banded with great metal bars standing open like the postern. Through the gates the courtyard was clearly visible, a wide, flagged area where figures in colourful costumes moved.

'It seems peaceable enough,' Tepshen allowed.

'Do we approach?' Brannoc wondered.

'Without bows we have little other chance of eating,' Kedryn replied. 'I think we must venture it.'

'But wary,' cautioned Tepshen. 'Normal though it seems, we are still within the realms of the netherworld.'

Kedryn could smell the apples hanging from the well-tended trees that flanked one wall and their scent aroused pangs of hunger in his belly. 'The ant-creatures were helpful enough,' he suggested. 'Mayhap we shall find allies here, too.'

'The ant-creatures delivered us to the domain of the spiders,' Tepshen reminded him. 'Mayhap they knew what they did.'

'It seems,' said Brannoc, 'that we have a choice between seeking the hospitality of this hold and stealing apples. I say that we take the gamble.'

'Aye.' Kedryn motioned to the wide track leading to the gates. It was rutted and marked with the imprints of numerous feet. 'It would appear we have come upon some populated region, and to remain undetected must surely be difficult. Let us approach.'

'So be it,' nodded Tepshen, 'but with caution.'

'As you say.'

Kedryn stepped out from the trees, splashing across the stream with his comrades close behind. The cry of alarm he had anticipated failed to materialise and they reached the gates unchallenged, pausing within the shadow of the barbican.

The courtyard had the appearance of some Tamurin hold, save that the folk he saw wore costumes more fanciful than any of the Kingdoms, though in all other aspects they seemed ordinary enough. Women in bright gowns of exotic cut, with ornate snoods retaining even more elaborate coiffeurs, mingled with men dressed in brilliant tunics and gaily patterned breeks. None bore arms and there were no soldiers amongst them, lending the yard a semblance to some market square or gala. A hay wain stood beside a well at the centre of the yard, a minstrel perched on the seat, plucking a tune from a many-stringed instrument in accompaniment to his melodious baritone, and a knot of the brightly-dressed folk stood listening attentively. More wandered the yard in conversation, or sat on wooden benches, supping from pewter tankards that were regularly refilled by servitors in costumes only marginally less fanciful than those worn by the drinkers.

None saw the watching trio and after a while Kedryn stepped from the barbican's shadow into the sunlight of the courtyard, instinctively studying their surroundings for sign of danger or routes of escape.

The yard was a square contained by the curtains of the walls, a colonnaded walkway running around the lower level, broken in five places by the stone stairways that rose to the battlements and the postern. The walls were thick, containing the chambers of the hold, which sported balconies and windows from which more folk hung, calling to those below. None appeared to see the newcomers and Kedryn walked towards a group of four men lounging about a table, tankards in hands.

They paid him no attention until he spoke, and then it was casual, as if the appearance of three gaunt men, travel-stained and weary, was of no great moment.

'Good day,' he said, 'might three strangers find welcome here?'

The four men studied him with easy smiles, then one, pale hair flowing in long curls from beneath a scarlet cap decorated with an emerald feather, shrugged shoulders decked in yellow and black and said, 'Of course. Are we not all strangers at one time or another?'

A second, legs clad in harlequin breeks of red and white thrust out, motioned with his tankard and said, 'Sit, strangers. Join us in a flask of this good ale.'

They shifted on their benches, making room, and the three sat, still wary, as tankards brimming with foam were brought. They sipped cautiously, unwilling to let the ale take possession of their senses.

'Why do you bear arms?' enquired a man dressed in a cerulean tunic cut with slashes of jade, his breeks crimson and gold.

'It is our custom,' Kedryn replied, wondering why they laughed at his response.

'It was our custom once, Jerrold,' remarked another, his dress a riot of green, scarlet, yellow, silver and sable. 'Do you not remember?'

'That was so long ago,' smiled Jerrold, 'and it has been so long since any found their way here.'

'Where is here?' asked Kedryn

'Here?' Jerrold's smile grew broader, as though the question occasioned considerable amusement. 'Why, here is Lord Taron's hold; the finest in all Magoria.'

'Magoria?' frowned Kedryn.

'You are confused,' said the man in the scarlet cap, his feather nodding as his head moved. 'From whence do you come? Are you fallen heroes? Or was your journey otherwise?'

Kedryn was uncertain what he meant, but he smiled politely and replied, 'We have come from the Beltrevan. We found entry to the netherworld and trekked across a prairie of orange grass, through mountains filled with vicious spiders, and latterly across the grey plain that surmounts the slope above this keep.'

'The Plain of Desolation,' the man nodded, his feather wagging furiously. 'Few survive that journey. Fewer still who travel in company.'

'It was arduous,' Kedryn agreed, 'and it has left us mightily hungry.'

'Forgive us!' The feather shook as though tossed in a storm. 'You will seek sustenance.'

'And answers,' Kedryn said.

'Lord Taron will doubtless provide both,' the man declared, and clapped his hands to summon a servant. 'Take these wayfarers to Lord Taron on the instant. Inform him that Marul of Bolden Hold sends them.'

'My lords?' The servant bowed decorously. 'Will you accompany me?'

'Find us, after,' suggested Marul as they rose, 'and we shall share a tankard or two.'

'My thanks,' Kedryn nodded, and turned to follow the waiting servant.

Tepshen and Brannoc fell into step beside him and they crossed the courtyard to a wide door set beneath the colonnades. Their passage brought them close to many of the strollers and past the group listening to the minstrel, but it was as if they were invisible, for few heads turned at their passing and those that did granted them no more attention than might have been given to an insect buzzing past on the warm breeze. They paused at the door, on which the servant knocked before throwing it open to lead them into a spacious chamber with windows at both ends. 'Lord Taron,' he announced, 'Marul of Bolden Hold sends you three wayfarers.'

With that he bowed and quit the room, leaving them alone with Taron.

The chamber was sunny, the windows at the farther end spilling light over a solar partially screened by folding panels of carved red-golden wood and raised three steps above the main room.

A deep voice said, 'Come forward, wayfarers,' and they crossed the hall. It was floored with polished timber, the walls panelled and hung with tapestries, a great hearth to one side, long tables and benches set in rows as if in readiness for a banquet. They mounted the steps and found themselves in a semi-circular chamber, deep embrasures occupying most of the walls, the floor the same rich wood as the main hall, though spread with luxurious carpets. Five deep chairs, high-backed and studded with brass were arranged about a low table on which stood a silver decanter and four glasses. The fifth was held by the man seated facing them.

He was small and bald, his pate gleaming yellow in the sunlight, his round face hairless save for a short scalplock and the long moustache that trailed waxed ends far past his jaw, dressed in a gown of black on which stars and crescent moons glinted silver, drawn in at his waist by a belt of silver links that stretched it tight over the mound of his paunch. His feet, slippered in black velvet, were propped on a stool, and he made no move to rise, instead motioning them to sit.

They took the three chairs facing him, Kedryn first removing Drul's glaive from his back.

'You carry Drul's blade,' Taron remarked without preamble. 'I presume, therefore, that old ghost of war granted you entry.'

'He did,' Kedryn nodded, curbing the impulse to ply the small man with the questions that boiled on his lips.

'And you have crossed the Desolate Plain. Few succeed in that. Few even reach it! I must assume you heroes as you have obviously survived the kingdom of the arana.' He clapped his hands, beaming at them. 'And who are you, brave strangers?'

Kedryn gave introduction and Taron nodded thoughtfully.

'You are hungry?' When Kedryn replied in the affirmative he clapped his hands once, summoning a servant to whom he issued instructions that food be set out in the hall. 'Meanwhile some wine?'

he suggested. 'And questions, I imagine. Mayhap I can both answer and save time – I am Taron, Lord of this hold and overlord of Magoria.'

He paused, bending forwards to fill three goblets with a ruby vintage, sipping his own before he continued, 'Magoria is one of the many realms of the netherworld, and kinder – as you have doubtless noticed – than others.

'Perchance you thought the netherworld a place of desolation and misery, but it is not so. At least, not in all aspects. Many are, indeed, hostile, but others less so, and a few as delightful as my fair domain. Likely, you thought Ashar lord of all beyond Drul's gate, but neither is that so – rather, a balance exists, established by a power greater than Ashar or the one whose stone I see you wear about your neck, and whose cantrips I perceive protect your companions.' He raised a hand as Kedryn opened his mouth to voice a question, stilling it unasked. 'There are few in the realms of humankind who understand this, but even gods are bound by laws, by checks and balances that hold them to a measure of order incomprehensible to men. It is simpler that men believe in the basic concepts of good and evil – in Ashar and the Lady, both of whom *are* real, but themselves contained within the cosmic balance.

'Ergo, whilst Ashar's strength waxes he controls greater parts of this world you have entered, but havens still exist and Magoria is one of them. Should Ashar be slain,' small eyes that Kedryn noticed were yellow as a cat's flickered over Drul's glaive as he said this, 'then more of the netherworld must become benign. Now I see that food is ready – come, eat, and I shall talk whilst you revive yourselves.'

He rose, gathering the trailing hem of his gown and led the way from the solar to the hall, where a small feast was prepared, servants standing in readiness. Kedryn glanced at Tepshen, who shrugged slightly, and at Brannoc, who grinned quizzically, and followed the dumpy little man to the table.

The food was excellent, trout grilled with almonds and bacon, roasted lamb garnished with rosemary, a soup of leeks, succulent vegetables, rosy apples, cheese, white bread still warm from the ovens, and they ate heartily, luxuriating in the comfort after the deprivation of the Desolate Plain.

While they ate Taron resumed his discourse.

'It is, of course, Ashar's desire to rule all the netherworld, and to extend his sovereignty over your world. The Lady works to prevent this dominion, and I imagine that is at least one of the reasons you are come here. The other, of course, is to save your bride.'

'You know of Wynett?' Kedryn gasped.

Taron nodded. 'Magoria maintains a degree of contact with the other realms, and thus I learnt that Ashar had sent his creature forth and that it returned with a woman wed to the man Estrevan calls The Chosen One. Now you come, wearing that talisman and carrying Drul's sword – who else might you be?'

Kedryn wiped his mouth with a napkin of soft lawn. 'Are you able to guide us to Wynett?'

'It is possible,' smiled Taron, 'but do you think to overcome Ashar himself?'

'I must first seek out a creature called Taziel,' Kedryn admitted.

'And what would you have Taziel do?' asked Taron.

'Affix this stone I wear to the sword,' Kedryn replied, 'that I have a weapon to fight the god.'

'A lofty ambition,' Taron murmured.

'Less ambition than need,' said Kedryn. 'Ashar stole my bride and I would win her back. It appears that only through combat may I achieve that aim.'

Taron's yellow eyes hooded and he steepled his fingers against his plump lips, studying Kedryn's face. 'Taziel may not be easily persuaded,' he said at last. 'And to approach the smith you must first pass his guards.'

'Would you aid us to this?'

Kedryn in turn studied the smooth features of the bald man, not yet convinced of his amity, but neither ready to assume him hostile. Certainly he seemed to hold nothing back, and had so far offered only a friendly face.

'Perhaps not directly, for I am responsible for the folk of my realm and would not submit them to Ashar's wrath,' said Taron, 'but I shall willingly furnish you with instructions.'

'Who are these folk?' asked Tepshen, speaking for the first time.

The interruption seemed not to disturb Taron, who smiled and said, 'They are largely those who, like myself, fell in combat. Presumably we had led lives unworthy of punishment and so found ourselves here; others, though very few, came as you have come. Most consider Magoria a paradise.'

'You are dead?' Three of Brannoc's fingers passed in a sweeping gesture before his face. 'We dine with ghosts?'

'Aye and nay,' beamed Taron, apparently finding both the questions and the halfbreed's obvious discomfort vastly amusing. 'That I am dead as you term the condition, I cannot dispute. I was a chieftain of the Sandurkan and fell with a Tamurin lance in my belly.' He patted the mound reflectively, chuckling. 'But I do not consider myself a ghost. I eat, I drink, I wench – I enjoy the attributes of any man, as do all my folk. Death appears to be a state of mind, dying a matter of translation. I cannot explain it better than that.'

'But the spirits we encountered in the fog,' Brannoc protested. 'They were not like you.'

'The creatures of the lakes?' Taron shook his head. 'They are not like me. For one reason or another they find themselves condemned to that sad plight. I know only that we fought a squadron of Tamurin and I misjudged a stroke, thus finding myself struck. I felt my life flow out and woke here.'

'When was that?' asked Kedryn, intrigued by this explanation of the afterlife.

'Time is of little consequence here,' returned the bald man. 'It was Gudrun of Bessyl Hold that harried us, and Farryl who sat in Andurel.'

'Farryl?' Kedryn summoned memories of history lessons spent with Sister Lyassa. 'Farryl ruled third after Corwyn. Centuries have passed.'

'Centuries?' Taron said mildly. 'Well and well, it is of no matter; not here.'

He nodded to a servant, who served him with cheeses that he set to consuming with a most human gusto. Kedryn sipped wine, confused and fascinated. Taron swallowed a wedge of milky white cheese and dabbed his lips. 'But in this matter of Taziel,' he continued, 'I would not jeopardise the somewhat fragile safety of my people by offending Ashar, or the Lady, and so I feel I can instruct you on the means of reaching the smith, but no more than that.'

'Any aid or advice will be greatly welcome,' Kedryn said.

'Then listen carefully,' Taron advised, 'The river you doubtless noticed as you approached this hold flows into his domain. You may take a boat and follow the river down. In time you will see a line of hills that belch fire at the sky, and that is where you will find Taziel. He occupies a cave beneath the tallest peak. It is reached by a trail that climbs from the river. If you are able to surmount that trail you will come upon the smith's cave, deep within the mountains. It is not a pleasant place and Taziel will demand a price for his work. You may find the fee he asks too high, but if you cannot pay you will find yourselves entrapped, for there is no returning from that forge.

'Did I not sense that you will not be persuaded otherwise, I would counsel you to forget this quest. You would be most welcome here, and I believe you would find the sojourn pleasant.'

'I shall not be dissuaded,' smiled Kedryn, 'but I thank you for your advice.'

'So be it,' Taron murmured, 'when would you depart?'

'As soon we may,' replied Kedryn.

'Tomorrow is soon enough,' said the small man. 'Refresh yourselves with baths and sleep first, and I shall have provisions readied for you.'

'You are kind,' Kedryn said, 'and you have my gratitude.'

Taron beamed, saying nothing. He beckoned a servant and whispered in the man's ear, then turned again to his guests.

'Go with Dukai and he will show you to your chambers.'

It was a polite dismissal and Kedryn rose, Tepshen and Brannoc with him, following the servant from the hall and along the colonnaded way to a winding flight of steps that brought them to the upper levels of the hold. Dukai indicated three adjoining chambers and an arch across the corridor that he told them led to the baths. 'Permit me to take your clothes,' he suggested, eyeing their grubby outfits with some distaste, 'and I shall have them cleaned. Your rooms contain garments suitable to Lord Taron's halls.'

Kedryn felt little desire to don the popinjay garments favoured by Taron's folk, but he admitted that his gear was in dire need of cleansing and so nodded.

'Simply leave them in your chambers,' Dukai said, 'and they will be returned you.'

Kedryn ducked his head in agreement and the servant departed. The three comrades turned to the rooms, Tepshen suggesting that he and Brannoc take those either side of Kedryn's. Kedryn nodded, eager to bathe, and entered the chamber.

It was spacious, wide windows looking over the orchards, blue-shadowed now as twilight fell. A bed stood against one wall, facing a small hearth before which stood two chairs and a low table, a recessed closet holding a selection of the bright outfits that were obviously the fashion here, and a garderobe in one corner. After the food and wine Kedryn felt the need to avail himself of the garderobe and shucked out of his garments, leaving them piled carelessly on the bed. Then he donned a flowing robe of the least fanciful design he could find and made for the door. An afterthought sent him back for Drul's sword, which he carried with a degree of mild embarrassment to Tepshen's chamber.

He was reassured to find the kyo holding his own blade, wearing a robe of viridescent emerald with argent patterning about the sleeves and hem, in conversation with Brannoc. The halfbreed, too, carried his sword, though he seemed at ease in his gown of scarlet and perse.

'I believe he means well,' he was saying, 'but it is a foolish man who forsakes his blade in a stranger's keep.'

'You speak of Lord Taron?' asked Kedryn.

Brannoc nodded and Tepshen said, 'I do not trust him.'

'He has offered no harm,' Kedryn returned, 'and appears almost eager to help.'

Tepshen's mouth flattened suspiciously. 'Why should he?'

'The balance he spoke of?' Kedryn suggested. 'Mayhap he has no more wish to offend the Lady than Ashar.'

'At least his food was good,' Brannoc shrugged, 'and his baths are something I shall enjoy.'

It transpired that he enjoyed them even more than he anticipated, for when they entered the room Dukai had indicated they found three maidens waiting to serve them. One was fair, with golden hair and a lightly-tanned complexion, the second dark, her skin swarthy as the halfbreed's, whilst the third was red-headed, with pale skin and a faint dusting of freckles. All were nubile and dressed in filmy pantaloons and short, sleeveless tunics of sheer, almost transparent material. They curtsied, smiling as the three men entered, ignoring the weapons they carried. The blonde maiden said, 'Your baths are ready.'

Kedryn blushed, finding it difficult to remove his gaze from the thrust of her breasts, the skimpy tunic doing little to hide them. He cleared his throat and said, 'It is not our custom to bathe with maidens.'

Her face became a pantomime of disappointment. Brannoc said quickly, 'It is not a *Tamurin* custom. But I am not Tamurin.'

'Have care,' admonished Tepshen.

Brannoc grinned and said, 'Of three fair maidens? What harm can they do me?'

'I thought you wary of ghosts,' replied the kyo.

Brannoc's grin stretched wider as he shrugged. 'As Taron told us, it is a state of mind; and these appear fleshly enough.'

'I would bathe alone,' said Kedryn, addressing the women. 'I intend no offence, but it is my custom.'

'And mine,' said Tepshen.

'As you wish,' the fair-haired wench murmured, her grey eyes moving questioningly to Brannoc.

The halfbreed spread his arms wide. 'My dears,' he declared, 'I would not disappoint you. Nor, I hope, will you me.'

The three maidens giggled. 'You will find all you require there,' the fair one told Kedryn, pointing to a door, and took Brannoc's hand, leading him towards a separate opening as she whispered, 'And you will find nothing to disappoint you.'

Kedryn was loath to see the halfbreed separated, but had little time to produce any convincing argument as Brannoc disappeared with the maidens. He shrugged and went with Tepshen into the other chamber. It held a large tiled pool, its water steaming fragrantly, musk-scented soap and huge towels set close to hand. He set Drul's great sword down and let his robe fall, climbing gratefully into the tub, where Tepshen joined him, both men luxuriating in the welcome warmth, filled bellies and Taron's good wine combining with the heat to render them pleasantly drowsy. Kedryn decided that should the three women intend Brannoc harm, he would hear the halfbreed's shout, and when he heard laughter he allowed himself relax.

Later, scrubbed clean and greatly refreshed, he and Tepshen returned to their chambers. Kedryn wiped moisture from Drul's blade and set the sword beside the bed, noticing that night had fallen. He thought to dress and find Taron, but a knocking on the door announced Dukai with his clothes, laundered and already dry.

'Lord Taron presents his compliments,' the servant intoned, 'and would have you know that should you prefer to sleep he will understand. Should you desire company, either at table or more personally, you need but ask.'

'Give Lord Taron my thanks,' Kedryn replied, 'and inform him that I am, indeed, weary. I prefer to sleep alone.'

'As you wish,' Dukai murmured, and left.

Kedryn yawned, eyeing the bed. He could think of nothing he desired more than to stretch out beneath clean, cool sheets, save to have Wynett beside him. In time, he told himself, and shed his robe to clamber into the bed. Faint on the night air he heard the sound of laughter from Brannoc's room, the voice of the blonde maiden raised in answer to some sally of the halfbreed's, falling into silence as though muffled by Brannoc's lips.

A full moon was risen, hanging low above the woodland, pale light filling the chamber with gentle shadows. Kedryn drew up the sheets and slept on the instant, deep and dreamlessly. And woke as quickly, sitting upright as his mind struggled to identify what it was that had dragged him so urgently from slumber. The moon was higher now, no longer visible from the window, the chamber darker, and for a moment panic gripped him, his right hand reaching for the hilt of the sword propped by the bed even as he thrust the sheets aside. He rose as he identified the source of his alarm: the window was open and through it he could hear the sounds of struggle, Brannoc's voice raised in cry for aid.

Not bothering to dress he hefted the sword and crossed in swift paces to the door. Flinging it open he stepped into the dark corridor, turning to Tepshen's chamber to pound upon the door before hurrying to Brannoc's quarter. The kyo appeared, clad in his undergarments, his blade naked in his hand before Kedryn hurled himself into the halfbreed's room.

His eyes were adjusting to the darkness, but still what he saw refused for an instant to register on his mind.

Brannoc stood naked in a corner, struggling desperately with a thing no longer female but scaled and feathered and furred, some small resemblance to a human woman remaining, but more of bird and cat visible in the distorted body. Feathered legs that ended in curved talons thrust the creature remorselessly at a body already bleeding from the numerous cuts imparted by the clawed paws, whilst a head surmounted by tufted ears snapped vicious fangs at the halfbreed's throat. Yellow orbs with narrow, vertical pupils glared furiously at Kedryn as he overcame his revulsion, crossing the room with Drul's blade lifting, Tepshen close behind. For the merest blink of an eye he saw the comely maiden, her hands reaching for Brannoc as though to embrace him, then he was close enough that the radiance now emanating from the talisman encompassed the thing within its blue light and its hideous form was clearly visible. It turned as he swung the glaive, snarling and spitting, a paw upraised.

The paw flew loose as the broad blade cut bone, a shriek filled more with anger than pain bursting together with the blood that jetted from the stump of the furry wrist. Brannoc ducked, throwing himself clear, as Tepshen joined Kedryn, the long curve of the eastern sword slashing down in a cut that would have sundered the beast had it not sprung back so swiftly. Instead, a gash was carved from shoulder to groin, across the scaly chest, from which withered dugs hung in ghastly parody of femininity.

It screamed again, in rage, and the legs bunched to propel it up and forwards in a great leap, fangs bared, the remaining paw outthrust to claw at the kyo's eyes.

Kedryn caught it in mid-air, lifting Drul's sword in a great upwards swing that landed across the belly, doubling the monster over so that its feline head went down, exposed to Tepshen's blade. This time it could not escape the stroke and the long sword carved the skull, splitting it to spill the brains across the floor. Kedryn drove the glaive down again, across the small of the back, the crack of the breaking spine audible through the dying snarls. It writhed, lifting a ghastly snouted face towards him, teeth clashing as if even in the moments of its death it sought to rend and tear. Then the snarls faded, blood bubbling over the stretched lips and it lay still.

Kedryn spun towards Brannoc. The halfbreed held his sabre now, his face paled, his eyes wide with pain and shock. Ugly lacerations striated his upper body, welling blood glistening black in the moonlight, and his breath came in ragged gasps.

'Thank the Lady you came,' he panted, 'I should be dead else.'

'You are hurt,' Kedryn returned.

Brannoc grinned tightly and shook his head. 'I have survived worse. Let us worry about my wounds later.'

'He is right,' said Tepshen. 'That shrieking must alert the hold. We must flee.'

Brannoc was already tugging on his clothes, wincing as the cuts were twisted by his movements. 'Best we stay together,' Kedryn decided.

'Aye,' Tepshen stepped into the corridor, sword at the ready. 'Make haste, Brannoc.'

'I am.' Brannoc drew on his boots, lacing them, his teeth gritted against the pain. He rose and thrust his arms into his tunic, snatching his sword belt from the armoire. Blood stained the frontage of his shirt and he limped as he accompanied Kedryn to his own room. Tepshen disappeared for a moment, returning with his bundled clothes, and they dressed, moving back into the corridor, surprised that none came to oppose them as they ran for the stairs.

'The river!' Kedryn cried over his shoulder as they pelted down to the courtyard. 'Make for the river!'

'Said easier than it is done,' snapped Tepshen, pointing with his blade at the nightmare host that now appeared across the yard.

It was a ghastly multiplication of the changeling thing that had attacked Brannoc and Kedryn felt his blood chill as it began a slow advance. Lupine heads sat on scaley necks, shoulder to shoulder with lizard-like creatures with flickering forked tongues and needle fangs, beaked faces hissed, horns tossed, snouts lifted to emit snarls, paws extended talons, tusks clashed, and through it all came Taron's voice, distorted by the long, many-toothed muzzle that was now his face, but still recognisable.

'Do you then reject our hospitality?'

Braying laughter greeted his sally, coming from those throats still able to emit so human a sound, more issuing snorts, snarls, hisses.

'Aye,' Kedryn shouted, 'we do!'

'They block the gates,' Tepshen warned.

'The postern then!' Kedryn replied, and they spun about, running along the colonnaded way.

A thing with wings that ended in clawed hands and serpent head moved to oppose them, falling to Tepshen's blade. Another, horned and toothed, fell to Drul's sword; Brannoc, gasping in pain, slashed his sabre across a canine face, and they were at the entrance to the hall. The host of transformed creatures rushed like some unhuman tide to fill the corridor leading to the postern and the three men had no choice but to enter the hall.

Kedryn and Tepshen shouldered the doors closed, slamming bolts in place as claws and horns and hooves battered against the wood.

A window broke, a taloned hand on a scaley arm thrusting through. Brannoc severed it and snatched a torch from a sconce, setting the flame to a tapestry. Kedryn and Tepshen followed his cue, the ancient material burning avidly, tongues of fire licking hungrily upwards, taking hold on the veneer of the woodwork so that within moments the inner end of the hall was ablaze.

'The solar!' Kedryn shouted over the crackle of the flames and the baying of the nightmare horde. 'The windows there!'

They ran the length of the hall, hearing the clatter of claws on the stone floors of entering corridors, Taron's warped voice screaming, 'Take them!'

Kedryn and Tepshen reached the solar and Kedryn swung Drul's glaive against one window. The glass shattered, fragments cascading through the night. Tepshen lifted a chair and hurled it through the gap, enlarging the opening.

'Brannoc!' Kedryn bellowed, realising the halfbreed lingered behind.

'I come,' Brannoc shouted back. 'And with provisions.'

He limped up the steps rising to the solar, a tapestry bundled sack-like on his shoulder. Kedryn could not tell whether the grin that stretched his mouth was from triumph or pain. 'Quick!' he snapped, and Brannoc tossed his bundle outwards, then leapt through himself.

Kedryn and Tepshen paused just long enough to toss more flambeaux against the decorations on the walls and the carpets covering the floor, then launched themselves after the halfbreed.

Brannoc was already running for the moon-silvered ribbon of the river. His comrades caught up and all three reached the bank as the blaze engulfing the solar delayed Taron's changeling folk.

They ran along the bank, aware that soon the creatures of the hold must emerge from the postern and the gates to head them off, stumbling in the deceptive moonlight, the red glow of the burning hall at their backs.

'A boat,' Tepshen grated, and Kedryn saw a dory beached amongst the reeds.

Brannoc flung his bundle into the scuppers and they manhandled the craft into the water. The current was swift and they had barely sufficient time to drag themselves on board before the dory drifted clear, carried to centre of the stream, moving steadily faster as the inhuman howling of their pursuers drew closer. Kedryn peered over the high stern, seeing the host halt on the riverbank, the thing that was Taron foremost, staring after them, taloned hands upraised, his head thrown back to send a shriek of frustrated rage echoing into the night.

No further pursuit was made and he relaxed, slumping against the thwarts.

'I found food.' Brannoc indicated the bundle he had carried with him. 'The remnants of a feast.'

From the prow Tepshen said, 'There are no oars.'

'At least we escaped them,' Kedryn answered. 'Though not unscathed.'

Brannoc grinned wryly at this reference to his wounds, glancing down at his now blood-soaked shirt. 'She – it! – scratched me, no more than that.'

'Fortunate that Kedryn heard your cries,' Tepshen said. 'Take off your tunic and let me bandage those wounds.'

Brannoc stripped off his tunic and shirt, which the kyo tore into strips, winding them about the ugly claw marks ribboning the halfbreed's chest.

'By the Lady!' Brannoc muttered when Tepshen was done, essaying a smile. 'I have known hellcats before, but none like that.'

'Henceforth,' returned the kyo solemnly, 'you had best choose your bedmates with more care.'

'Until we quit this place,' Brannoc declared, no less gravely, 'I shall sleep alone. Save for my sword.'

# Chapter Fourteen

WYNETT woke to the cheerful play of sunshine on her face, opening her eyes to see the sky blue beyond the window. She rose, opening the flawless glass, and felt a breeze gentle on her skin, fresh with the scents of grass and flowers, delightful after the morbid opacity of the rain. The lawns and woodlands gleamed with the aftermath, their colours heightened by raindrops and the brilliance of the sun. Birds fluttered, darting kaleidoscopes of colour amongst the blossoms, and she felt her spirits lift despite her doubts. She went into the outer chamber, seeing the chair still firm against the door, and shed her robe, making swift toilette before selecting a demure gown of soft pink, slippers of a matching hue.

On the balcony outside her rooms the air was heady with the perfume of roses and magnolia, the atrium a glory of colour where Eyrik waited, rising politely as he caught sight of her face. He lifted a hand in greeting and she essayed a smile, her mind racing as she descended the arboreal stairs to the breakfast table. Her decision was as yet unmade, but she knew that she could not delay it and somehow, in the warm light of the welcome sun, she found it hard to doubt the sincerity of the tall, chestnut-haired man who beamed as she approached, radiating pleasure at sight of her.

'Are you cheered by this glorious day?' he asked as he saw her seated. 'Does the sun not lift your spirits?'

She nodded, accepting the cup he offered, the aromatic steam of the tisane enticing. She sipped and said, 'Aye, the sun is a wondrous cure for poor humour.'

Eyrik nibbled delicately on warm white bread spread with rich, yellow butter, his gold-flecked eyes alight as he studied her. 'I have thought,' he said, 'on our discussion and I see that I was, perhaps, a trifle precipitate. My enthusiasm was founded on alarm at your distress and the fear that the denizens of these realms might waylay Kedryn. I desire only to aid you, and that urgency in some measure rendered me abrupt.'

Wynett offered no response save a smile as she helped herself to eggs and Eyrik paused, watching her before he continued. 'I would not have you think I hurry you to a decision. More important, I would not have you think I seek to rob you of the talisman! Therefore, I suggest that you examine the apparatus I have constructed and permit me to explain it as best I may, and decide after.'

Wynett nodded. 'And Kedryn's danger? What of that?'

'It is very real.' His handsome features grew solemn, his lips pursing as though he hesitated to outline the jeopardies. Wynett made a small, impatient gesture and he said, 'As best I am able to know, the netherworld consists of numerous overlapping realms. A few are benign as this, but most are fraught with peril. Some appear tranquil but conceal deceptive hazards; others are overtly dangerous, filled with malign creatures. To steer a safe course through is no easy matter – hence my desire to establish a beacon. I believe that my creation may guide Kedryn and also in some measure protect him.'

'He wears the other half of the talisman,' she murmured, seeing only sincerity in his eyes, honesty on the planes of his face.

'Indeed,' he agreed, 'and that will doubtless afford some measure of protection, but I fear it may not be sufficient. Remember, my dear, that Ashar holds sway here and his power is mighty. He will doubtless seek to destroy Kedryn if he is able. To thwart him if not. I would circumvent such design and bring your love safely to you.'

Wynett dabbed at her lips, still unable to choose between trust and suspicion as Eyrik fell silent, clearly awaiting some response. Finally she said, 'Mayhap I should see this construction.'

He smiled hugely then, his handsome features rendered boyish, emanating the enthusiasm of a child with some new toy to display.

'When you are ready,' he said.

'Let us go now,' Wynett returned, and he rose, moving around the table to take her chair, offering his arm.

She took it and he escorted her across the courtyard to a door of beaten silvery metal, runes engraved on its surface. Beyond was a chamber tiled in dusty red, the walls black and marked with further runes, pillars of crimson marble standing in two lines to either side, dividing the room. There was no furniture and he led her through the chamber to a second door of metal, this locked unlike any others she had encountered. He produced a golden key from his tunic and turned it, swinging the door open. Wynett was surprised despite herself to find they entered the great, dark hall beyond the chamber of the pool. It was brighter now, candles and flambeaux set

299

in rows along the walls, chandeliers she had not previously noticed suspended from the vaulted ceiling, their candles giving off a sweet, somewhat cloying scent. The yellow light outlined the throne-like chair, glinting off its basalt surfaces, seeming to penetrate the dark stone to fill it with a shifting, lithic life. Set around it in a circle were high tripods of dull black metal, each holding a tall, thick candle, and within the circle stood a construction of gold filigree and crystal.

Its design was fantastic, its usage unguessable. Slender columns wound in intricate convolutions about their neighbours, shards of multi-faceted crystal exploded candle light in rainbow profusions, dazzling her eyes so that she found it difficult to follow the lines, the complicated curves. Eyrik indicated a point atop the device, where nine fine ribs joined to form a shallow cup.

'That is where your talisman will,' he smiled, correcting himself, '*should* be placed. Without it the device is no more than some fanciful sculpture.'

'And with it?' she asked softly, blinking as the light assailed her eyes.

'With it,' he said proudly, turning to face her, taking both her hands as if to impress upon her his honesty, his enthusiasm, 'I shall be able to establish a beacon that will send out a call to Kedryn, guiding him here. More than that, I believe it will open a path down which he may travel safely, the power inherent in the two halves of the stone linking to ward him against the pitfalls of Ashar's domain.'

He stared down at her, the gold flecks in his brown eyes dancing, inspired by the candles' glow, hypnotic, radiating an intensity of purpose Wynett found hard to resist. She felt the pressure of his strong hands and it was a reassuring pressure. She studied his face and found it honest. She looked into his eyes and found her doubts dissolving. It was a sensation akin to waking, finding sunlight on her face, the dismal rain ended, this weird realm again beautiful. Memories of lost hope, of the despair that had gripped her as she stood upon the roof of the palace, as she watched the multiple possibilities of the oracular pool unfold, flashed through her mind. *Trust me*, said his eyes. *I seek only to aid you*, said his hands. *Believe me*, said his smile. And she felt her suspicions falter, her doubts waver. *If he is your enemy*, said a small voice deep inside her mind, *then surely the talisman will be anathema to him. The Messenger could not stand against its power, nor can any opposed to Kyrie.* And another whisper said, *Kedryn may fall without this aid. Kedryn and Tepshen Lahl and*

*Brannoc, all of them, may go down victims of Ashar. You must aid them.*
*You must allow Eyrik to aid them. It is the only way.*

'You are sure?' she asked slowly. 'You are sure this *is* the only way?'

'I am,' said Eyrik, solemnly.

Wynett eased her hands free of his grip and felt them rise to the chain about her neck. His eyes did not leave her face as she drew the chain over her head. He stood immobile as she cupped the jewel.

'Then use it,' she said, extending her hand. 'Use it to aid Kedryn.'

'You give this willingly?' he asked, not touching the stone.

'Aye,' she nodded, 'I do.'

Eyrik held out his hand, palm upwards, and Wynett gave the talisman to him.

'My thanks,' he smiled. And laughed triumphantly as the world shifted and Wynett screamed in raw terror.

*

The leather-bound manuscript Gerat studied fell unnoticed to her feet as she gasped, eyes widening in shock. Her body shuddered, wracked by a force she dreaded to define. Her mouth opened to emit a strangled cry, part anger, more fear. Malign laughter echoed inside her skull and she shook her head, lips dried by awful apprehension mouthing words she was loath to utter.

'He has it,' she moaned. 'Lady stand by us now, for he has the talisman!'

*

Kedryn and his companions woke to a new day that revealed a landscape disconcertingly normal, for the horrors of the previous night were fresh in their memories; indeed, in Brannoc's case they were engraved upon his living flesh. The dory drifted leisurely down a broad stream banded by timber and meadows, the scene bucolic, woodlands and grass both verdant as the Tamurin highlands. Sunlight dappled the water, spreading harlequin patterns of light and shadow amongst the trees, a gentle breeze rustling the foliage, from which birdsong rang, so natural the horrendous attack of Taron's changelings seemed a nightmare left behind them in the darkness. Several times they saw gaily-clad folk along the bank, and these called to them, beckoning, urging them to beach their craft and partake of food or ale. None, however, ventured onto the river and Kedryn came to the conclusion that running water was a barrier they could not cross. Taron's folk gave no pursuit and the watchers on the banks did no more than cajole, so the journey became a respite from the travails they had so far faced. Kedryn lounged at the dory's stern whilst Tepshen sat peering ahead over the high prow and Brannoc slumped on the thwarts, dozing in the warm sun.

It was not until he began to moan that either of this companions realised he was hurt worse than he admitted.

At first Kedryn assumed him in the grip of a dream and ignored the faint sounds that escaped his lips, but then they became louder and the halfbreed began to shudder. Kedryn moved from his position in the stern to find a seat alongside the wounded man, shaking him gently to wake him. His hands, where they touched flesh, found skin slick with sweat, and when Brannoc opened his eyes they were glazed, failing at first to focus. Kedryn unstoppered a canteen and raised it to Brannoc's mouth. As he drank, Kedryn saw that his lips were dry and caked with spittle, his swarthy features drawn, a greenish hue shining beneath the tan.

'I dreamt,' Brannoc said slowly, the words ponderous as he stared about, seeming at first not to know where he was. 'I dreamt that I was taken by that . . . creature . . . and become one of them.'

'You are safe,' Kedryn assured him. 'I do not think they are able to cross water.'

Brannoc smiled his relief and abruptly lapsed back into sleep. Kedryn washed his face and looked to Tepshen. The kyo's features were grave as he moved from the prow, settling beside the halfbreed and easing him gently upright as he said softly, 'We must examine his wounds.'

Kedryn nodded and they slipped Brannoc's tunic loose, unwinding the makeshift bandages to reveal the cuts beneath. Parallel gashes latticed his torso and midriff, cut deep by the therianthrope's claws. All were inflamed, the edges swollen in pinkish-yellow ridges, pus oozing from beneath the blood that had crusted there.

'Would that we had retained our packs,' Kedryn murmured, thinking of the salves stowed therein.

'We must cleanse these as best we may,' Tepshen responded, trailing the encrusted bandages in the river's transparent flow.

He scrubbed the cloth as Kedryn swabbed the wounds, and when they were dry wrapped them once more about Brannoc.

302

The halfbreed's body was hot to the touch and by nightfall he was feverish, crying aloud and writhing with such force that they took turns holding him still for fear he might upset the dory. They forced a little food between his lips, but what he did not instantly spit out he vomited and they gave up their attempts, concentrating instead on calming him as best they could and bathing his sweat-soaked body as the sun went down and a gibbous moon shone pale over the woodlands.

They began to share Brannoc's nightmares then, for the folk they had seen along the banks became more numerous, as if called by the moon and their presence, and they no longer wore human form, become again the monstrous creatures of the hold. The night was filled with their howling; it echoed over the river as they raised wings and paws and scaled, clawed hands towards the boat, as though they sought to draw it close by the sheer power of their joint will. Kedryn clutched his wounded comrade as Brannoc moaned and trembled, seeming almost to answer the clamour. Kedryn tried to block his own ears to that awful cacophany, and saw that despite the brightness of the moon the talisman glowed brighter still, encompassing the dory in its comforting blue nimbus. A thought came to him then and he called Tepshen from his watch at the prow, urging the kyo to help him strip Brannoc.

The lacerations seemed almost to glow in the night, pulsing with a baneful life, as if they sucked out the halfbreed's vitality to stimulate their own virulence. Kedryn drew the chain of the talisman over his head and pressed the stone to Brannoc's chest, onto the topmost scratch. The halfbreed screamed shrilly, the sound seeming to come from a throat other than his own, greeted by an excited ululation from the bank.

'Hold him fast,' urged Kedryn, and Tepshen gripped the wounded man in powerful hands, immobilising him as best he could in the narrow confines of the boat.

Kedryn slid the talisman down over one long gash, repeating the action for each cut. Brannoc screamed and struggled against Tepshen's hold then, but afterwards sighed and fell supine against the kyo. His breathing, previously laboured, grew more steady, and it seemed to Kedryn that the lacerations dulled, the poisonous oozing lessening. He replaced the talisman about his neck and washed the bandages afresh, cleaning them of the purulent encrustations. Brannoc lay still, his brow cooler to the touch and the moaning of his dream-laden sleep softer; Tepshen released his grip and resumed his seat in the prow.

Morning dawned bright, the mist that spread across the river quickly burned off by the rising sun. The changelings along the banks dispersed, resuming their human form, cheerful birdsong replacing their awful yammering. Kedryn and Tepshen breakfasted on the food looted from Taron's hall and succeeded in feeding a little to Brannoc. Kedryn repeated the curative process, sun's light revealing a distinct reduction in the mephitic exudations, the wounds less angry.

Nonetheless, Brannoc remained unconscious for most of the day, his delirium heightening as night fell and the angry yammering once more rose from the banks. Again Tepshen held him as Kedryn applied the talisman, and again the stone worked its magic, quieting his struggles so that he fell into fitful sleep.

The next day he awoke and asked for water. Kedryn held the canteen to his lips and fed him small pieces of roasted meat. This time the halfbreed kept the food down.

'I feel there is something inside me,' he said hoarsely. 'Something evil. When I close my eyes I see that succuba, and she calls me to join her.'

He shuddered and Kedryn pressed his hands to the talisman. 'The stone cures you,' he declared. 'Kyrie's magic overcomes the venom of her claws.'

'I pray so,' Brannoc replied, but Kedryn heard doubt in his voice and saw that his dark eyes had a haunted look.

'It does,' he said firmly. 'See how the cuts repair.'

He eased Brannoc's tunic off and stripped away the bandages, passing them to Tepshen to wash again, then once more ran the stone over the lacerations.

Brannoc winced, gritting his teeth, but did not struggle this time, only muttering, 'Oh, by the Lady! It burns so!'

The cuts were healing visibly now, the pustulent seepage halted and the swellings reduced, the surrounding flesh no longer glistening with that angry redness, but pink as clean flesh grew over the gashes.

Brannoc sighed, staring down at the wounds, his face drawn. He reached dumbly for the canteen, drinking deep, then turned to face Kedryn.

'I was a fool,' he said contritely. 'I permitted my lust to overwhelm my judgement. I should have listened to Tepshen, and now I pay the price.'

'It is done,' Kedryn returned, 'and you have survived; do not dwell on it.'

Brannoc shook his head, fixing hollow eyes on the bank, 'I am less sure,' he murmured. 'I feel . . .' He shook his head again and Kedryn saw that his knuckles shone white where he gripped the thwarts. 'I feel . . . unclean.'

'You were poisoned,' Tepshen said from the prow. 'The venom affects your mind.'

'It is more than that,' Brannoc responded. 'I am afraid.'

This last was said low, and Kedryn saw that his jaw trembled on the words, his even teeth clenched tight, as if he fought an awful dread.

'Of what?' he asked. 'We are free of the changelings' clutches and you heal apace. We have food and water aplenty, and we ride the river to Taziel's mountains.'

'I do not know,' Brannoc answered, and lapsed into silence.

He spoke little for the remainder of the day, sleeping or staring at the forest that rolled past along the banks, and when twilight descended and the changeling creatures reappeared and set up their miserable chorus he sat huddled, shivering although the night was warm. He struggled again when Kedryn applied the talisman, requiring Tepshen's strength to hold him down as he fought the touch of the blue stone, screaming, then abruptly slumping into unconsciousness.

'This troubles me,' Tepshen murmured over the supine form. 'His wounds mend fast as any Healer might cure them, but he fights the process.'

'By night,' Kedryn amended. 'By day's light he complained only of the burning.'

The kyo nodded, his sallow features thoughtful. 'He spoke of something inside him. He said he felt unclean.'

'Surely he was delirious,' Kedryn replied. 'The poison leeched his reason – you said it yourself.'

'Aye.' Tepshen's mouth curved briefly in approximation of a smile. 'But now I wonder.'

Kedryn studied Brannoc. The halfbreed appeared to sleep sounder now, but still he twitched, moaning softly, as though held by some malign dream.

'You believe there is truth in his doubt?'

Tepshen shrugged. 'Mayhap. I know little of succubi, but I think it as well we watch our comrade.'

Kedryn stared at the easterner, not wanting to grant credence to his fears, but filled now with an ugly apprehension.

'You think him tainted? Do you say the changeling cut him deeper than his flesh?'

'I say only that we be wary,' Tepshen answered carefully. 'If he heals as I hope he will, then my thanks to the Lady. If not . . .'

He left the sentence hanging unfinished on the night air. Kedryn set a hand to the talisman, seeing its radiance shine through his flesh, outlining the bones. If not, he finished in his mind, then Ashar has tainted one of us. Would the Lady allow that? He looked to the moonlit bank, the nightmare figures standing there stark emphasis of Tepshen's fears. Can the Lady prevent it? he wondered. Here in this unearthly place is even her power great enough? He shook his head, seeking to rid himself of such ugly cobwebs of doubt, and stared at Brannoc.

Moonlight played on the dark face, flattening its planes, throwing shadows across the fever-hollowed sockets of the closed eyes. Brannoc groaned, his lips drawing back from his teeth. For an instant, as they glinted in the silvery light they seemed as fangs, bared beneath snarling jowls, and Brannoc's visage was animal. Kedryn leant closer, thrusting out the jewel, and Brannoc whimpered, turning on his side, raven hair falling across his face with a small tinkling of shells. Kedryn shook his head, dismissing that momentary impression of therianthropism, and resumed his stance in the stern.

He slept as the dory drifted on, waking when Tepshen prodded him to take his turn on watch. It was, he judged by the position of the moon, some time after midnight and they passed a section of forest too dense to permit the changelings entry, for the darkness was silent, only the gentle lapping of water against the dory's shingles disturbing the quiet. Brannoc slept, no longer moaning, and it was a tranquil scene, the river an inky blue streaked with bands of silver where moonlight struck the ripples of its passage, the woodlands ebon, merging with the velvety indigo of the sky, the dory itself encompassed by the effulgence of the talisman, drifting peacefully within its own calm nimbus. The current carried them steadily onwards, as though the river itself bent to their purpose, obviating the need for oars or rudder. He touched the hilt of the great glaive propped beside him, studying the grim deathshead shape of the pommel, seeing the curling claws that held it in place. They appeared separate from the ornamentation, and he thought that

Taziel would easily remove the round of metal and set those claws about the talisman.

With that thought in mind he stared ahead, and saw a change in the sky. The indigo hue brightened there, blue shading into a faint pink as if some unimaginably huge fire burned far off on the horizon. He blinked, not sure he could believe the evidence of his eyes, and squinted again into the darkness. Then the river turned, swinging wide around a jut of forest, and the glow was gone, the timber receding from the bank so that his attention was once more caught by the presence of the watchers, waiting along the shore, hatred redolent in their horrid chorusing. He started as Brannoc stirred, shifting where he lay, as if summoned from the depths of honest slumber by the howling. He saw the halfbreed turn, almost rising from the thwarts, then falling back, moaning again, his hair dropping clear of his face so that he seemed once more oddly lupine.

Kedryn clutched the talisman and told himself it was no more than a trick of the light and his own weariness, and did his best to ignore the unearthly stridency. It was not easy, for the therianthropes lining the banks seemed more numerous, their caterwauling more insistent, and it seemed to disturb Brannoc more. Several times Kedryn moved to still the halfbreed as he twisted on his makeshift bed, hands with hooked fingers lifting to flail at the sky, his lips drawn back from his teeth as if he fought for breath, or snarled, though only a strangled moaning emerged. Once, his eyes opened and Kedryn saw the hazel orbs yellowed, like a cat's, but they closed quickly and he could not be certain of the impression, deeming it a trick of the moonlight, for the alternative suspicion was too unpleasant to entertain. He was thankful when dawn transformed the horizon to a pearly opalescence that shaded to pink, then gold as the sun rose, night's indigo paling to azure, and Tepshen woke.

The kyo looked to Brannoc then raised his eyes to Kedryn, brows arched in unspoken question. Loath though he was to express such doubts, Kedryn told him what he had seen, and what he had thought he saw. Tepshen grunted and moved to strip the halfbreed. Brannoc groaned as the bandages were unwound, opening sleepy eyes, but offered no protest as his comrades examined his wounds. They appeared to be well on the way to healing completely, the inflammation gone and the gashes covered with healthy scabs. There was no sign of pus, and when Kedryn passed the talisman over the cuts, Brannoc did no more than stiffen, clenching his teeth. He remained silent as the strips were bound once more about

307

his chest and midriff and his tunic replaced. Then he asked for food.

It seemed a healthy sign and Kedryn rummaged through the dwindling supplies, passing the halfbreed a thick slice of roasted pork and a chunk of somewhat stale bread. Brannoc wolfed the meat and nibbled gingerly at the bread, finally handing it uneaten back to Kedryn. He smiled, a semblance of his old self returning, and said, 'I feel better.'

Tepshen said, 'You no longer feel unclean?'

Brannoc shook his head: 'No.'

Kedryn told him of the glow he had seen and Brannoc smiled again. 'We approach Taziel's fiery mountains then.'

'And you heal apace,' nodded Kedryn, 'Praise the Lady.'

'Aye,' Brannoc murmured, and closed his eyes, leaning back.

He was rapidly asleep and Kedryn grinned at Tepshen, indicating the slumbering form between them.

'It seems our doubts were groundless: he appears to recover.'

'Mayhap.' Tepshen stared sombrely at the halfbreed.

Doubt lay heavy on his luteous features and Kedryn frowned. 'You disagree?'

Tepshen shrugged. 'I do not know. The cuts heal, but I like not what you told me.'

With the sun beaming down from a sky streaked with high cirrus Kedryn was prepared to believe the night had played tricks on his eyes. 'Surely, were he tainted by some fell magick,' he argued, 'he could not bear the touch of the talisman.'

'It appears to burn him still,' Tepshen murmured.

'With a cauterizing fire,' Kedryn responded. 'It must surely leech any venom remaining.'

'Let us hope so,' Tepshen said. 'And watch him still.'

The kyo's suspicion soured the day somewhat: Kedryn recognised it as a doubt that was, given their circumstances, healthy, but nonetheless felt it was a kind of betrayal. He had shared much with the former wolfshead, both joy and sorrow, danger and hardship, and to think that Brannoc was befouled by changeling magic, a potential threat, seemed a renunciation of their comradeship. Yet he knew that Tepshen shared the bond, finding in the halfbreed a kindred spirit, and that the kyo's caution was born solely of concern for him and their quest. Still, he fell silent at the words, settling in the stern as the easterner resumed his vantage point at the prow.

The day passed much as before, save that fewer changelings appeared and Brannoc slept, waking only when roused to eat. The dory drifted onwards, held to the centre of the river by the current, the woodland unfolding tranquil along the banks, interspersed with meadows and occasional tributary streams. Dusk fell, the sun descending behind the timber to paint the horizon with crimson as the shadows lengthened across the water, the rising moon bringing a return of the therianthropes.

Brannoc roused with the first screams, sitting upright on the thwarts, his head cocked. Kedryn had dozed, waking as the ululation split the peace of twilight, and now he felt his skin crawl, a hand fastening instinctively on the hilt of his dirk as Brannoc's face turned towards him.

The halfbreed's eyes were wide, huge in the moon's silver light, glowing with an unnatural, fulvous excitement. He stared hard at Kedryn, his shoulders braced and stretched as though he strained against himself, and his lips curled slowly back to expose teeth that seemed elongated, become more canine than human. It seemed to Kedryn, in that time-stilled moment, that Brannoc's dark hair was grown more coarse, his straight nose flattened and spread, like a snout. He reached beneath his shirt with his left hand, the right still set about the dirk's hilt, and drew the talisman out. It was not yet full dark and the jewel's effulgence was consequently pale, yet still it outlined the nightmare transformation in horrid detail.

Brannoc moaned as the glow embraced him, his head arching back, tendons standing out along his neck. Behind him Tepshen slid dirk from sheath, his lean body tensed. Brannoc shook his head slowly, his shoulders trembling, and a voice that was hoarse with the effort of speaking groaned a painful warning.

'She has me! Beware, friends! I . . . cannot . . . I cannot fight it!'

He rose as the sentence ended, his body hunched, arms thrust out as if he sought to embrace Kedryn. Or to rend him, for the fingers were hooked and the nails grown long, curved and sharp as talons, and his words choked off into a savage growling.

Tepshen rose in the same instant, springing forwards with dirk raised. Horrified, Kedryn could only stare as the kyo's hand came down, once and then again, driving the pommel of the dirk hard against Brannoc's neck, where it joined the shoulder. The changed halfbreed yelped like a struck dog and slumped to his knees. The dory rocked wildy. Tepshen struck again, this time with the edge of his left hand, against the base of Brannoc's neck. The motion of

309

the boat threatened to pitch him overboard and he fell across the halfbreed, bearing the body down beneath him. Kedryn shook off his paralysis, lurching forwards, ready to strike Brannoc, but Tepshen rose, clutching at the starboard gunwale, his face grim.

'Quickly,' he snapped. 'We must bind him.'

They found cord and belts, lashing the fallen man's wrists firmly behind his back, securing his ankles.

'I thought you had killed him,' Kedryn said when they were done.

'No,' Tepshen grunted, heaving Brannoc onto his side. 'I would not – unless I must.'

They studied the unconscious man, horrified by what they saw.

Whatever foul poison the succuba had planted in Brannoc's veins had not – likely, Kedryn thought, thanks to the talisman – transformed him completely. He was not become a changeling for he retained his human form, though altered, as if he were become a were-beast, his natural shape distorted. His features were flattened, the jaw thrust forwards over lengthened, fang-like teeth, his ears grown small and pointed, his dark hair coarse as a pelt. His shoulders were spread, stretched back, his arms thickened, the hands bristling ragged fur, the nails become claws. He seemed poised at some transitional point betwixt man and animal, and Kedryn felt a great sorrow as he studied the supine form.

'He tried to warn me,' he said, his voice harsh with grief.

'Aye,' agreed Tepshen, 'and for that alone he deserves to live.'

'Perchance the talisman will effect a cure,' Kedryn offered.

'Mayhap,' Tepshen allowed. 'But the bonds remain.'

Kedryn nodded and went down on his knees beside Brannoc. He removed the talisman from his neck and held it to the wolfish face. Brannoc twitched, groaning, but there was no change in his shifted shape.

'Perchance in time,' Kedryn said sadly as he regained his seat.

'Perchance,' said Tepshen; no less miserably.

'By day's light,' Kedryn said.

Tepshen ducked his head in agreement. Or resignation, Kedryn could not decipher which.

Brannoc awoke during the night and struggled against his bonds, snarling furiously, but the cords were strong and the knots tight, and he could not free himself. His actions set the dory to rocking again and when water splashed over the gunwales he howled and fell still, confirming Kedryn's belief that running water was anathema to the changelings. As the darkness dulled into the misty grey abstraction preceding dawn he quietened, curling in a foetal ball. The hoary light brightened, the banks becoming visible again, and the sun climbed into the sky, roseate light spreading steadily upwards, driving back the night, becoming gold, and with it Brannoc resumed his human form.

He lay silent in the scuppers, then groaned, shaking his head as does a man waking from a bad dream.

'I dreamt,' he began, then halted, gasping, his voice rising to a wail as he became aware of his bonds. 'Oh, by the Lady! It was not a dream.'

'No,' Kedryn said, not knowing what else there was to say.

Brannoc ground his face against the boards of the dory, his body heaving as he wept. Kedryn moved closer, setting a hand to a shoulder. Brannoc twisted, turning his face up. 'Why did you not slay me? It would be kinder to slay me.'

'Tepshen stunned you,' Kedryn said, 'and we bound you tight. We would not kill you.'

Brannoc shook his head, in mute denial now. 'I am befouled,' he whispered. 'I would not become as Taron's creatures.'

'You shall not!' Kedryn answered fiercely, but Brannoc ignored him craning round to fix his haunted eyes on Tepshen. 'You are made of harder stuff, kyo. Will you not end this misery?'

Tepshen shook his head. 'Mayhap there is a cure. If not . . .'

'If not,' Brannoc said harshly, 'I ask you in the name of friendship to destroy me. Do you grant me that boon?'

Tepshen glanced at Kedryn and nodded. Brannoc sighed, a soul-deep sound, and let his head sink.

'It seems that by day you are safe,' Kedryn murmured, his hand still firm on the halfbreed's shoulder. 'By night you . . . change. I think that if we secure you ere the sun sets we shall be safe.'

'Better to slay me now,' Brannoc muttered; dismally.

'No,' said Kedryn, 'not whilst some chance of cure remains.'

He stooped to the fastenings about the halfbreed's wrists then, aware that Tepshen drew his dirk, ready to strike, and tugged the knots loose. Brannoc eased his arms from their cramped position and chaffed his wrists, not attempting to rise. Kedryn unloosed the bonds about his ankles and took a hand, lifting it to the talisman.

'Touch Kyrie's stone, my friend,' he suggested. 'If you *are* become one of . . . those creatures . . . I doubt you can bear that contact.'

Brannoc licked his lips, allowing Kedryn to place his hand upon the jewel. He closed his eyes, as if anticipating awful hurt, but when his fingers closed around the talisman he sighed and whispered, 'I feel . . . a calm. As when Gerat worked her magicks upon me.'

'Likely those gave you protection, too,' Kedryn smiled. 'Estrevan and the stone together ward you against the poison.'

'There is a further test,' said Tepshen. 'Look to the river and wash yourself.'

Brannoc frowned, but some little glimmer of hope sparked in his dark eyes, and he hauled himself stiffly to the thwarts, leaning over the dory's side to cup hands in the water and splash his face.

'Last night the touch of water gave you pain,' Kedryn informed him. 'We need not . . .' he bit off 'fear you', saying instead, 'worry so long as the sun is high.'

'And when night falls?' grunted Brannoc, his voice bitter again. 'What then?'

'Before sunset we bind you,' Tepshen answered.

'Will you bind me each night?' asked Brannoc mournfully. 'Will you fear me each night?'

'Mayhap the curse will lift when we depart this realm,' Kedryn said. 'Or the talisman cure you.'

'Mayhap,' Brannoc responded, his voice low. 'But if not – Tepshen, I hold you to your word.'

'My oath on it,' the kyo promised, his face solemn.

'Now eat,' suggested Kedryn.

Brannoc nodded, accepting the food handed him, his eyes sombre as he chewed. Kedryn sought to cheer him but he remained sunk in misery, slumping in his place as the dory continued its gentle passage down the river, all three eventually falling into silence as the day moved steadily towards twilight.

When the sun touched the uppermost branches of the forest Brannoc presented his wrists to Tepshen and the kyo bound him securely. Kedryn spread the folded tapestry on the scuppers and the halfbreed curled on the makeshift blanket.

'Should I break free,' he said to Tepshen.

'Aye,' said the kyo, and Brannoc nodded, clenching his teeth as he waited for night to fall.

The first cries of the therianthropes elicted an answering wail, and Kedryn found himself unable to quell the rush of horror as he saw Brannoc transformed again. Tepshen sat poised in the prow, hand on dirk as the halfbreed began to struggle against his bonds, his spine arching as he fought to burst them, his head craning back, lips stretched over snarling fangs. Kedryn wondered if the change was more marked this night, for it seemed that Brannoc's features altered more drastically, the prognathous extension of his jaw more closely resembling that of a hound or a wolf, thicker, darker hair sprouting on his arms and chest. He looked away after a while, no longer able to bear the pain of seeing so stalwart a comrade brought so low, and as he turned his head he saw again the red glow outlined against the sky.

It was stronger now, fiercer, filling all the forward horizon with a crimson light that seemed to flicker along its lower margins, as if fuelled by inconceivable fires. He pointed, raising his voice to shout over the howling of the changelings and Brannoc's furious growling.

'Do you see it? Those must surely be Taziel's mountains of fire.'

Tepshen turned, peering briefly ahead before swinging back to fix apprehensive eyes on the wriggling halfbreed.

'Aye.' Like Kedryn, he shouted. 'So do the fire mountains of my homeland look, though less fierce.'

'How long, think you, before we reach them?' Kedryn yelled.

Tepshen shrugged. 'Be they great as they seem, no more than a day or two.'

Kedryn nodded, looking once more to Brannoc, wondering if he must be bound each night of the journey, a further, uglier, doubt instilling itself in his mind. Should the halfbreed continue this metamorphosis would he be opened to Ashar's fell influence? Might it be that the closer they came to the god, the more danger the transformed halfbreed would offer? Might Brannoc become a hazard by day as well as night? If that should prove to be the case . . . His mind sheered from the thought, for it had only one logical conclusion: Tepshen must make good his promise.

He fastened a hand about the talisman, voicing a silent prayer that the Lady grant his comrade salvation, that she lift the curse imposed by the succuba's venom and return Brannoc to his normal state.

He prayed fervently, aware as he did so that an overwhelming purpose filled him. He had felt anger before, a great rage that Ashar should meddle so foully in the affairs of men, a fury that the god should steal his beloved Wynett; that and a loathing, a contempt, for the malign deity. Now those emotions became something more and he felt a pure wrath flood the very fibres of his soul, a massive outrage that Ashar should taint his comrade. It filled him, burning bright and fierce as the fires blazing along the horizon, reverberating

313

within him so that Brannoc's cries, the yammering of the changelings, all became drowned out and he stared to where the fires burned, his lips moving as he spoke aloud a vow that was equally a part of his prayer:

'I will slay him! On my life I will destroy him.'

The threnody of the changelings seemed to increase in volume at his words, and Brannoc's struggles grew fiercer. Tepshen stirred in the prow, leaning towards the halfbreed, who strained up at his approach, fangs snapping viciously. The kyo drew back, his face expressionless, and Kedryn thrust the talisman towards Brannoc, seeing the bound man recoil from the blue light, moaning at first, but then becoming still. It seemed the stone brought him some measure of peace, for his struggles decreased and he ceased his snarling, mouthing a low whimper and then falling silent.

'Sleep if you can,' urged Tepshen.

Kedryn nodded and closed his eyes.

He was not sure if he slept and dreamed, or if the talisman – or some other agency – set images in his mind, but he saw Wynett cowering in a place of darkness, threatened by a shadowy creature whose form he could not discern, but whose very presence radiated evil. He woke to the prodding of Tepshen's sheathed sword, the kyo's face frowning in the light of a new sun.

'You cried out,' the easterner said.

Kedryn nodded, the aftermath of the images still vivid in his mind, his mouth dry with fear. 'I saw Wynett,' he said slowly. 'She is in mortal peril.'

'She has the talisman,' Tepshen responded

Kedryn touched his own half of the stone and felt his fear magnified. There was a difference that he could not define. The jewel still vibrated beneath his fingers but its pulsation was somehow changed and he looked to his comrade with frightened eyes.

'We do all we can,' said Tepshen, recognising panic in Kedryn's gaze. 'Soon we shall reach Taziel's smithy. Look yonder.'

He gestured over his shoulder and Kedryn looked to the horizon, seeing the day's new sky not blue, but pink, glowing with a rubescence other than the blush of dawn. Shadow hung beneath the rubrication as if stone bulked there, and Kedryn fought the panic, his grip hard about the talisman.

'Aye,' he said, his voice ringing hollow, 'Soon.'

'Mayhap Ashar sends phantoms to confuse us,' Tepshen suggested.

'Mayhap.'

There was scant enthusiasm in the response and the kyo pointed to Brannoc, seeking to cheer Kedryn.

'At least our halfbreed friend is whole again.'

Kedryn nodded, moving to release Brannoc from his bonds. The former wolfshead grunted, raising a face become gaunt. As if to confirm he was man once more he leant over the dory's side, splashing water on his face, his enthusiasm threatening to spill them all.

'I am hungry,' he muttered, reluctant to meet their eyes.

They ate and composed themselves for another day of travel that passed without incident, fading into a twilight that again saw Brannoc bound, thrashing in the scuppers until Kedryn held the talisman close once more. The light on the horizon was brighter now, a fierce crimson that remained visible when the sun rose, no longer pink in day's light but a fiery red that coloured the sky, merging reluctantly with the blue. The woodlands thinned, the therianthropes became fewer, and the meadows along the banks grew sere. The air was warmer and acrid with the mounting scent of ash, and the ensuing dawn saw an end to the pastoral landscape.

The dory rocked precariously down a mild cascade as the current increased its pace, running between banks of naked stone that gave way not to further timberland, but to an ashen terrain reminscent of the Desolate Plain. The ground was barren, cinerous with the emanations of the peaks that were now clearly visible, no longer a dark line on the farther limits of sight, but a massive, jagged range that thrust angry pinnacles towards a no less angry sky. No blue showed there, only the furious red that shimmered, incandescent above the hills. Warmth became heat, the air heavy with ash that drifted down like rain, layering the banks, floating ugly on the water. The air was tainted with the reek of sulphur and soon they heard a sonorous booming. As the dory brought them closer they saw that the sound was accompanied by great gusts of flame that spouted heavenwards, spewing fire and ash like dragon's breath. Brannoc rose from his depression to stare at the spectacle and Kedryn began to fear for their vessel, for as night approached sparks became visible, fluttering down to scorch hair and exposed skin.

Brannoc's transformation was less vigorous that night, as if the absence of the changelings lessened his mutation, and he lay quiescent in the scuppers, whimpering like a dog terrified by a storm,

It was, indeed, a frightening night. Fire burned along the sky, a great curtain of red hanging above them, bright sparks cascading down, the river loud with the splashing of falling stone that sizzled as it struck the water when such minor sounds could be heard through the thunder of the mountains. Proximity increased the terrifying grandeur of the peaks, the rock dark under their overlay of flame, massive jets of fire roaring upwards to set the night ablaze. Several times Kedryn and Tepshen moved to stamp out small fires started by the hellish rain, or splashed water over clothing that scorched and threatened to burn, ignoring Brannoc's awful moans as the liquid touched him, and they were fatigued as the darkness brightened into day.

There was little change from night, for the sky merely became a more candescent crimson, the falling ash thicker, the heat fiercer, the river itself steaming now, the air they breathed noxious. The current grew stronger and the dory was buffeted as it rode the flow, all three clutching the gunwales as the little craft was carried relentlessly deeper into the forbidding foothills. Around noon they saw a narrow isthmus of ashy rock across their path, the stream splashing furiously against the barrier stone, a beach of fire-bleached pebbles to the side. The dory drove fast towards the promontory, spinning wild as eddies took it, striking rock that pushed them landwards. Then the force of the water flung the stern onto the strand.

Kedryn threw Drul's glaive onto the pebbles and sprang after it, snatching at the dory as it threatened to depart on the maelstrom. Tepshen caught up what little food they had left and leapt to join him, followed close by Brannoc. Kedryn let go his hold and watched the dory carried away, turning, once, twice, three times, before the flood smashed it against the isthmus and the planks cracked, the craft sinking as it was born away. Brannoc held out the cords that nightly bound him, a sad smile on his haunted features as he said, 'Do not forget these. You will need them again.'

Kedryn nodded, taking the cords and tucking them under his belt. He looked about, feeling sweat run free down his face, his shirt plastered to his back. The heat was intense and the stench of sulphur stronger, but it seemed they were sufficiently close to the fire-breathing mountains for the rain of heated stone to be spewed farther out, saving them at least one danger. The beach spread back along the line of the isthmus, a wide triangle that sloped upwards to its apex, a path showing there. For want of any other likely direction they took it.

The pebbles gave way to polished stone, black and shiny as glass, an avenue that rose between saw-edged rocks, winding up towards the ominous hills. It was smooth beneath their boots but still the going was difficult for the terrible heat seared their lungs, the acid stench of sulphur watering their eyes. They fastened cloths over mouths and nostrils, forcing legs made rubbery by the stinking atmosphere to plod the trail. Speaking was impossible for all their efforts were concentrated on the business of climbing through the miasmic fog of falling ash that now surrounded them. It grew denser as they ascended and they walked close together, fearful of becoming separated and of the dangers that might lurk with the brume.

How long they climbed Kedryn could not tell, for his world was become grey, the only light the burning sky above, his eyes so stung by the noisome emissions he could see no farther than a few paces ahead, could barely discern Tepshen and Brannoc to either side. He felt his lungs must burn within him, each breath a painful victory, each step an effort that cost him dear. To pass a night in this hellish inferno was a thought both terrifying and inconceivable, for he imagined the dawn, if dawn rose here, must see them suffocated beneath the pall of ash, roasted by the very ground he could feel burning through the sturdy soles of his boots. He clutched the talisman, seeking its reassurance, willing it to grant him strength, but the touch disturbed him now, for he felt again that strange difference in the stone's crystalline life and fear for Wynett joined the physical discomforts of the climb.

Then he grunted, raising a hand to wipe at his tear-filled eyes, staring into the grey and fiery fog. Tepshen and Brannoc looked to him as he halted and pointed, unable to speak, indicating the wall of stone that rose before them.

It was a curtain of sheer rock, dark and glossy as the trail, as if stone had melted and run, sleek and devoid of handholds, the glassy black trail ending at its foot. He felt his hope dissolve then, for there was no way around the barrier nor any way over it, and with the dory sunk they had no means of escape from this hellish place. He mouthed a curse through the cloth masking his face and paced a little closer, his hands raised in fists as if he would beat the stone. Then the curse became a hoarse cry of optimism as red light blazed within the darkness of the cliff face and he realised that a cave opened there.

He put his mouth close to Tepshen's ear, shouting over the relentless roaring of the fires above, 'Can this be Taziel's cave?'

The kyo nodded, unsheathing his sword as he moved into the looming opening. Kedryn followed him, Drul's great blade at the ready, Brannoc at his side with sabre drawn.

Flame flashed again and a searing wind rushed through the tunnel, bringing the beat of metal on metal. They moved towards it, the cave affording protection from the endless fall of ash if not from the heat, which became stronger as they paced cautiously down a corridor of gleaming ebon stone.

The corridor ended and they stood within a great cavern, lit by the flames that gouted from a molten pool at the centre. An anvil stood there and beside it a malformed, trollish creature who beat a massive hammer against the block. He turned, sensing their presence, revealing a face that seemed ill-moulded from unready clay. His pate was naked, the pink of raw flesh, domed huge, with thrusting brows that hung above tiny red eyes sunk deep in hollow pits, as if pushed there by careless thumbs. His nose was no more than an indication, a slight swelling marked by the vertical slits that flared wide open as though he savoured their scent. The mouth was lipless, a wide, flat gash that parted in ghastly approximation of a smile to display twin rows of blackened, pointed teeth. He had no neck, his head jutting forwards between enormous shoulders, his arms and chest massive and corded with muscle, the torso incongruous on a narrow waist, the legs bowed and spindly, ending in overlarge feet, the toes clawed, as were the hands that now set down his hammer.

'Human folk,' he declared, the words a slobber that sent spittle dripping over his receded chin. 'Living folk come to feed Taziel.'

Kedryn tugged the mask clear and answered the creature: 'Come to ask work of Taziel.'

'Work?' The distorted head twisted against the torso, turning first to left, then right, the glittering eyes studying each in turn. 'What task would human folk have Ashar's smith perform?'

He chuckled as he said it, spilling gobbets of saliva over his pink hide, his obscene form shaking, a long, grey tongue emerging to lick over his ragged teeth.

'I would have you set this stone as pommel to this sword.'

Kedryn indicated Drul's glaive, drew the talisman from his shirt. Taziel's laughter ended, his little eyes blinking as though in disbelief; or amazement at Kedryn's presumption. 'Drul's blade,' he croaked. 'I forged that glaive on my master's bidding that his word be carried on its edge. How came you by it?'

'Drul's shade gave it me,' Kedryn answered.

'So,' rasped Taziel, 'And what price did Drul's bones extract?'

'A fair exchange: my sword for his.'

Taziel nodded as best he could and said, 'The stone is of the other. It is a thing of my master's enemy. I feel its power and it makes me angry.'

'It is Kyrie's stone,' returned Kedryn, 'and if you will set it to the sword I shall remove it from your presence.'

'To what end?' Taziel demanded.

'Your master has my bride,' Kedryn said, 'and I would win her back.'

'You would have me forge you a weapon with which you may destroy my master,' came the hoarse response. 'How came you by the stone?'

'It was given me,' Kedryn answered. 'The Sisters of Estrevan gave me one half, my bride the other.'

'Given?' Taziel's tongue extended to probe a nostril. 'You gave nothing in exchange?'

Kedryn shook his head, struggling to conceal his disgust. 'I accepted a duty,' he said, thinking that he saw it clear for perhaps the first time. 'When I took the stone I accepted that I should defend the Kingdoms.'

Taziel grunted, the sound expressing satisfaction. 'Nothing for nothing, all has its price.'

'What is yours?' Kedryn asked.

The trollish creature stared at him and Kedryn felt that had his mouth been capable of such movement it would have curved in a smile, and that the smile would be ugly.

'A life,' said Taziel.

'No!' Kedryn had no need to consider his response.

'Then you shall not have your sword,' croaked the smith, 'and you all die here and I shall feast on your flesh.'

'Ask some other fee,' Kedryn pleaded.

Taziel's head rocked from side to side. 'There is no other. All has its price and that is mine. When I forged that blade for Drul to bear he gave nine times nine lives to the bloodeagle. Of you I ask but one.'

'It cannot be,' Kedryn said.

'Wait.' Brannoc moved past him, his face haggard in the red glow of the molten pool. 'Should you have your price, smith, you will grant this service?'

Kedryn clutched at the halfbreed's arm, saying, 'No!' Brannoc shook him off, his haunted eyes firm on Taziel's hideous features. Taziel said, 'I will.'

Brannoc said, 'And if it is done, how may he come to Ashar?'

'Easily,' said Taziel. 'Let stone be fixed to sword and the way will open there.'

He pointed to the far side of the cavern, where a dark mouth showed.

'That leads to Ashar's lair?' asked Brannoc. 'He may reach your master through that passage?'

Taziel's head bobbed in confirmation.

'Unharmed? Without hindrance or snare?'

'You ask much,' the smith complained, 'but it is long since I tasted sweet human flesh so I will answer you: aye; unharmed to Ashar he will go. But,' he chuckled horribly, 'he shall not return.'

'Then ply your forge,' Brannoc said, 'and you shall have your price.'

'No!' Kedryn shouted. 'Brannoc, I command you! We find some other way.'

'There is none other,' Brannoc turned to face Kedryn, speaking low, his tone urgent. 'You know that well as I. Without stone and sword as one you may not defeat Ashar; may not save Wynett. This foul creature is the only one who may perform this task and he will not without his price.'

'Still I forbid it,' Kedryn said.

A ghost of his old smile flickered on Brannoc's lips and he sheathed his sabre to place his hands on Kedryn's shoulders. 'I am damned,' he said gently. 'The succuba's poison flows in my veins and makes me ... what I become by night. I am a danger to you, and I have no wish to live as some were-creature, some monster that my friends must fear and bind by moon's rise. That is no life, Kedryn. I would sooner end it, and in this way I am able to further your purpose.'

Kedryn shook his head and Brannoc turned to Tepshen. 'Tell him it is the only way, my friend,' he asked. 'Do we refuse the price and we shall, as the smith says, die here. Uselessly.'

Tepshen studied the halfbreed with solemn eyes. He set a hand to Brannoc's wrist, squeezing. 'I have never doubted your courage, wolfshead, but this is more than courage.'

'Do you say aye or nay to it?' Brannoc demanded.

Sadness entered Tepshen's gaze then and he nodded. 'I say aye.'

Again Kedryn said, 'No!' and Brannoc embraced him. 'It is the only way. I have no wish to live cursed, and thus may I aid you.'

Abruptly he pushed Kedryn away and spun to face Taziel. Kedryn moved to draw him back, but Tepshen seized him and held him as the halfbreed spoke again.

'Forge stone to sword, smith. I accept your price.'

He turned, snatching the glaive from Kedryn and tossed it to the monstrous creature.

'Give him the talisman, Kedryn. In the name of the Lady I ask you to do it. For her sake grant me peace.'

Kedryn shook his head, unable to speak, and Brannoc drew the stone from round his neck as Tepshen held him still. 'Do it,' he cried, crossing the cavern's floor to hand the talisman to Taziel.

The trollish smith accepted the stone, eyeing Brannoc avidly.

'First the sword,' the halfbreed said, his voice harsh.

Taziel ducked his misshapen head and turned to his forge. Kedryn struggled in Tepshen's arms, weeping now, as the hilt of Drul's glaive was plunged into the flames. Brannoc folded his arms across his chest, watching as the smith worked the deathshead pommel loose from its embracing claws and heated the metal afresh. The fixings glowed red as he set the stone in place, tapping delicately with his hammer, securing them around the talisman. He surveyed his work, grunting in satisfaction, and blew upon the metal. It cooled under his breath and he passed the glaive to Brannoc.

'It is done.'

Brannoc hefted the sword a moment, then walked to where Tepshen held Kedryn.

'Now use it well,' the halfbreed said. 'Let Ashar pay for the misery he inflicts.'

Tepshen loosed his grip and Kedryn took the sword, staring at Brannoc. 'Let us slay him,' he murmured. 'Let us slay him and begone from here together.'

Brannoc shook his head, smiling grimly. 'That would be Ashar's way,' he said. 'The path you tread is more honest.'

'The price is too high,' moaned Kedryn.

Brannoc reached out his hands, clutching those of Kedryn and Tepshen. 'We have come a long way together, we three, but now my road is ended. I choose it this way, friends, and I ask the Lady to bless us all. Walk in her light and use the sword well.'

'Aye,' Kedryn whispered.

Brannoc turned again to Taziel. 'Let them begone, smith.'

Taziel grunted acceptance and indicated the cave mouth. Tepshen set a hand to Kedryn's arm and steered him past the leering creature. They reached the entrance and paused, looking back. Brannoc raised a hand in farewell, and for an instant his old grin returned.

'Remember to tell this to the minstrels, my friends.'

Tepshen nodded. Kedryn wiped at his eyes. 'All the Kingdoms shall sing it,' he promised.

'Go,' Brannoc urged.

They turned away, moving into the fire-lit shadows of the passage. Kedryn shouldered the glaive, feeling in its hilt the faint vibration of the stone that now glowed blue at the pommel. It seemed lighter than before, but still his shoulders slumped beneath the weight. Faint behind he heard Brannoc say, 'Now take your fee, smith.' And heard Taziel's foul chuckle, and the sound of a hammer striking bone.

# Chapter Fifteen

RYCOL studied the sun-washed expanse of timber spread below the ridge with an apprehension that etched deep lines on his weatherbeaten features and turned doubtful eyes to the blue-robed woman seated beneath the awning of the small tent.

'Is this wise, Sister?' he asked, a hand wrapping about his sword's hilt as if in anticipation of attack. 'Is it sensible that Estrevan's Paramount Sister venture so close to the Beltrevan?'

Gerat smiled wearily, mopping at her brow, for even at this height the heat was intense, and said, 'Did it not tax the powers of my Senders beyond limit I should go to Drul's Mound itself, Chatelain. This is the only place to be.'

Rycol grimaced at her placid imperturbability and eased the shoulder pieces of his leathern armour to a position less likely to chafe his broad shoulders as he glanced around the jut of stone overlooking the timberland. His men were all in place and alert. Archers stood with strung bows amongst the rocks; swordsmen squatted on the baking ground; above the main encampment and farther down the slope lookouts, each chosen for their keeness of eye, hunkered on watch. It was unlikely, with the summer Gatherings so close, that any woodlanders would wander so far south, and impossible that any sizeable force should approach unnoticed, but even so he felt uneasy. He did not like it that Gerat had decided to venture forth from High Fort, even with a full hundred in escort, and liked it less that the Paramount Sister insisted on camping out in the foothills of the Lozins. He had sufficient men that he could fight a rearguard action to see her brought safely back should the unexpected happen and knew that in military terms she was safe, but there was something else, and it was a thing he did not like at all because he could not understand it.

It was a feeling he had known only once before, when the Messenger brought the Horde against his fort, a feeling of impending doom that he could not express in words, but felt within the innermost core of his being. It was a sensation akin to the skin-prickling stillness preceding a summer storm, a feeling of power gathering, of incalculable forces massing in readiness. It threatened to render him irritable, for he felt the anticipation of battle but could see no enemy, and he turned again to Gerat, speaking less from need of explanation than the desire to fill the ominous silence with sound.

'You are certain?'

Gerat nodded, recognising his unease. 'I am certain, Rycol. One half of the talisman has been separated from its rightful owner. Which half I cannot say, but I can be certain it has fallen into Ashar's hands. With half in his possession the god is mightily strengthened. Should he secure both . . .'

Her words tailed off and Rycol was shocked to see the fear in her grey eyes. he said, 'But if Kedryn has succeeded in melding sword and stone may he not slay the god?'

'Aye,' Gerat nodded, 'he may, the Lady willing. And so we must hope it is Wynett who has surrendered her half.'

'Surely Wynett would not,' Rycol said.

'Surely Wynett would not *knowingly*,' Gerat responded. 'But Wynett was taken by Ashar's creature and so we must presume her Ashar's prisoner, and Ashar is a god of deception and betrayal. How can we know what deceits and snares he has set out to trick her? Mayhap he has deceived her into trust. We cannot know; only stand ready.'

'And should it be Kedryn's talisman?' asked Rycol.

'Then the Chosen One is lost and the Kingdoms with him,' Gerat answered bluntly. 'Only Kedryn may defeat Ashar, and if he has failed this world we know is doomed.'

Rycol grunted, swatting at a fly that buzzed about his sweating face. Gerat smiled wanly and said, 'But were Kedryn fallen or deceived I think we should know it by now.'

'How so?' Rycol demanded, staring at the trees, the foliage ethereal under the weight of the summer heat.

'We have watched here three days,' said Gerat, 'and it took us two to reach this place. I think Ashar would have struck against us ere now had he the power.'

'Then think you he now seeks Kedryn's half?' asked the chatelain.

'Aye, I do so,' Gerat confirmed. 'I suspect he has deceived poor Wynett and now seeks to inveigle Kedryn. Mayhap with Wynett the bait in his trap.'

Rycol fidgeted with his swordbelt as if he longed for some visible, mortal enemy to fight. 'Should this be the case,' he said, 'And Ashar so strengthened, were we not better placed behind the walls of High Fort?'

Gerat shook her head. 'Should Ashar prove victorious even your strong walls will be as nothing. Should he secure both halves of the talisman he will have no need of barbarian flesh to further his fell ambitions for he will no longer be bound by the grammaryes the Lady placed on these mountains – his might will be unimaginable.' She closed her eyes as though the thought was too painful to bear, then turned her calm gaze on Rycol. 'Here I shall feel the advent of battle, and when it comes I shall be able to link my mind with that of Sister Jenille in High Fort, through her to all those other Senders waiting along the road to Estrevan, and thus to the Sacred City itself. There, the strongest of my Sisters await the challenge. When they hear my call they will bend their wills that I may breach the walls of limbo and send that holy strength into the netherworld to aid Kedryn. Thus may we counter Ashar's augmented power.'

'Will it be sufficient?' Rycol asked, his voice hushed.

'I do not know,' Gerat answered him, honestly. 'We can only pray to the Lady that it will.'

Rycol felt sweat trickle down his back. The sun was hot on his face and his body seemed to seethe under the armour, but the sweat was cold. 'If it is not?' he demanded.

'Then likely I shall be destroyed,' said Gerat, her voice flat, 'and all my Sisters with me. Likely Ashar will strike directly against Estrevan itself. And fill the city with corpses.'

'It is a mighty gamble you take,' Rycol said quietly.

'Aye,' said Gerat, 'but it is one that must be taken. It is the only one.'

*

Wynett's scream choked into a horrified silence as she fought for breath and the strength of will to overcome the uncontrollable panic that threatened to rob her of reason. She felt madness beat against the walls of her mind and clenched her fists, driving nails against her palms as she gritted her teeth, hearing them clatter, feeling her body tremble with unalloyed horror, her heart thudding loud through the pounding pulse of blood in her ears. She was abruptly, weirdly, aware of her surroundings with a clarity of perception heightened by the terror that gripped her. The hall was filled with shifting shadows, the walls seeming to pulse with an impossible telluric life. The black throne swelled, becoming a vast, ornate seat on which horrid carven figures moved. The candles burned now not with honest yellow flame, but with lapping tongues the colour of blood. It would have been a boon had they consequently revealed less, but it seemed they shed more light, as though come into their own as had the thing that capered before her.

It was no longer Eyrik and had she been capable of such voluntary action she would have looked away in disgust, for the handsome human figure had become something obscene. She could not, however, remove her gaze. It seemed that her eyes were locked, hypnotised as is a rabbit by the lethal dance of a stoat, transfixed by the nightmare that cavorted in triumph before her. Goatish orbs gleamed with delight from a malformed skull, bald as bone, horned and fanged, thick lips, blubbery and raw, parting to display a snaking, forked tongue that probed salaciously towards her. Massive shoulders thick with orange hair supported man-like arms clad in grey, cracked skin from which pus oozed, ending in scaly hands, hooked talons extending from the fingers. The pulse of organs was visible beneath the leprous skin of the belly, and between bent legs covered in the same orange hair as the shoulders, ending in great black cloven hooves, a huge phallus thrust rampant.

The talisman flared as if in protest, then dulled, its blue radiance overwhelmed by the blood-red glow of the candles as the creature placed it reverentially on the cup of the intricate device. Instantly gold filigree became scarlet, glittering crystal black, and the apparatus sang with a high-pitched keening, vibrating as it drew life from the stone and turned that puissance to foul, unholy purpose.

Wynett took a step backwards and the capering thing lunged towards her, a hand fastening about her wrist, dragging her back to stand within the circle of blood-flamed candles directly before the shuddering apparatus. The stench of old sweat and excrement was noisome in her nostrils and she gagged, choking bile. 'Watch!' it ordered in a voice that boomed from the vaulted ceiling in a fetid gust, redolent of ordure and decayed flesh. 'Observe my triumph.'

She turned her head, but talons locked on her jaw, gouging her cheeks, and forced her to see as the apparatus glowed and melded, supporting limbs winding about one another, fusing, light coruscating in dazzling patterns of gold and crimson and sable, the blue of the talisman faint above. She gasped as the transformation ended and the creature laughed, reaching for the sword that now stood upright before the throne.

It was a blade of epic proportions, tall and wide, glinting crimson, the fuller deep, quillons spreading in proximation of bull's horns from a basket of web-like intricacy, black, the hilt dark and thick, ending in fascsimile of a spider, the legs wound tight about the talisman.

The thing that Eyrik had become snatched the glaive in both hands and sprang to the foot of the throne, raising the sword high, swinging it in whistling circles about his horned head, saliva drooling from the pinguid lips, capering a pantomime of swordplay.

'Is it not beautiful?' he roared, his forked tongue emerging to lick at the blade, lowering it to rub the crimson steel against the length of his phallus. 'Am I not an artist?'

Wynett stared, dumbstruck, close to madness, for she saw clearly the enormity of her mistake and could see no way to undo it. She might have welcomed death in that moment had a greater fear not overridden her terror: this thing was undoubtedly Ashar himself and he must intend to use the blade against Kedryn.

And with that knowledge came a further revelation: Ashar must *need* the blade.

She fought the despair that threatened to unhinge her sanity, fought panic and fear, willing that part of her mind still able to stand off from the nightmare unveiled before her to think rationally. If Ashar needed the glaive, then he could not overcome Kedryn unaided: even with the talisman in his hands he could not face Kedryn without this weapon. Did Kedryn then possess such strength that the god feared him? It must surely be so, and therefore an element of hope existed still. She rejected madness, clinging to faith. The sword jabbed towards her and she started back.

'Do you not think it lovely?' Foul breath wafted over her. 'Tell me, lest I test the edge on your soft flesh.'

She nodded, eyeing the wavering point, needle-sharp. 'Aye,' she said, 'but why?'

'Why?' Ashar lowered the blade, settling himself on the throne, a hand fondling his engorged member. 'You dare to ask me why?'

'What need have you of a sword?'

She thought him likely to slay her then, for he leant forwards, yellow eyes blazing, his tongue lashing as though possessed of its own angry life. Then he laughed and gestured and the world shifted again. Abruptly it was once more Eyrik who lounged upon the basalt

327

seat and that was a relief, even though it was no longer the courteous Eyrik, but a tall, prideful figure, in whose eyes arrogance shone. He settled his hands about the hilt, resting his chin on the stone. Wynett saw now that it still retained some small degree of its former blue life.

'I believe,' he said in a tone of mocking amusement, 'that mayhap I shall now tell you the truth.'

Wynett licked lips dry with fear, fighting the urge to spit out the foul memory of his breath, and waited in silence.

'Taws failed me and was duly punished,' he continued, his smile evil as he relived that memory, 'But those he sent me furnished knowledge of your world. Hattim Sethiyan was one; your own father another. I have lived too long bound by the strictures of the one you worship and it is past time I came into my own, yet still *she*,' he spat the word, unwilling or, Wynett thought, unable to voice the Lady's name, 'thwarted me. She set her hand to establishing such grammaryes as rendered the Lozin wall insurmountable, and she paved the way for the creation of the Chosen One. Thanks to her the Horde was defeated; thanks to her were you and Kedryn able to defeat Taws. And yet your feeble human weakness showed me the path to victory.

'That bitch, for all the power she commands, is vulnerable in the love she has for your kind. She should not have allowed her creation to love you, for love is weakness. Had Estrevan not entrusted you both with the two parts of the talisman, I should not have had this chance.'

He chuckled, shaking his head. Wynett said defiantly, 'Estrevan gave the stones that Kedryn might regain his sight. Thus was he able to stand against your Messenger.'

Ashar twisted his human lips in a cynical smile, dismissing her argument. 'But thus did I learn of the talismans' owners and so foment my design.'

Wynett opened her mouth to speak again but he raised a hand and a fetid wind lashed about her, leeching the words from her mouth, replacing them with the stench of decay. For an instant his image flickered, becoming the goatish thing again, then a bloated spider that clacked mandibles in threat. Wynett bit back her protest and saw him resume human form.

'It was easy then, with what I learnt, to send the leviathan into your world. I saw that if it took you Kedryn would follow, and so he has.' He chuckled, displaying white teeth. 'Much of what you saw in the pool was true. It amused me to use your own weakness against you: love renders you transparent. With your part of the talisman in my domain – and your belief that I sought to aid you! – it was not difficult to establish links. Your sister does, indeed, harbour feelings for Kedryn. Some aftermath of the love potion Taws fed her, mayhap, but still a most available lever. I created images to disturb you. And how well I succeeded! You doubted your husband, did you not? You thought him locked in Ashrivelle's arms – your love betrayed you!'

He paused, tittering. Wynett offered no response, better able now that he took human form to think clearly, not willing to tell him he was wrong – that she had not doubted Kedryn – for it seemed his pride was a potential weakness, whilst her love was a strength.

'After that,' he continued, 'it was easy to assail your hopes, to damp your spirit until I seemed your only ally. Meanwhile, Kedryn had entered the netherworld. As hef-Alador he had the right to demand Drul's glaive as, I suspect, the blue-robed whores you call Sisters told him he must. You see, that blade was forged for my purpose and thus may be used against me. Save now, I have its equal.' He spun the sword he had created between his palms, admiring the flicker of light on the crimson blade. 'I might easily have destroyed Kedryn once he entered my domain, but that did not serve my purpose so well as to lure him ever deeper. Oh, there were a few of my creatures unable to contain their hatred of living flesh that sought to slay him, but he survived them thanks to his talisman and now approaches, thinking to destroy me. *Me!*'

Wynett stared as his eyes bulged, the gold-flecks whirling. His mouth was open and saliva glistened on his lips, flecking his shirt. He shook his head in prideful disbelief. 'Why did you let him live?' she asked, glorying in this little piece of knowledge.

'Because the talisman must be freely given,' he answered, 'As you gave yours to me. That, or be taken by its match. Which I now have.'

He stroked the sword as might a lover caress his mistress. Wynett watched him, wondering how she might aid Kedryn. 'So he has the sword,' she said. 'And has joined it with the talisman.'

Ashar's smile faded, his handsome features suddenly ugly as he nodded curtly. 'He has,' he agreed. 'There was a price I did not think he would pay, for he holds his comrades too dear.'

'His comrades?' Wynett prompted, seeking to learn as much as she could, thinking that knowledge was a weapon she might use against him.

'He came with the two you saw in the pool,' came the answer; dismissive. 'The one called Tepshen Lahl and another called Brannoc. The latter paid with his life.'

Something in his tone told her that he was not pleased with this outcome and she forced down the rush of grief she felt for Brannoc as she asked, 'How so?'

'The ... enthusiasm ... of one of my followers tainted him,' Ashar grunted. 'He became a were-thing and chose death that my smith fix stone to sword.'

'Kedryn will not relinquish either,' she said.

'You think not?' the smile returned. 'Be you right, then he is not so weak as I suppose.'

His tone was malicious and Wynett felt a fresh flood of fear as he eyed her, his gaze speculative. 'He is strong,' she said, fighting the apprehension that fluttered nervously behind her self-imposed calm.

'You are his weakness,' Ashar returned. 'Do you believe he will sacrifice you?'

Wynett was neither certain of the answer nor the response she should give. Were the situation reversed could she sacrifice Kedryn, even for the sake of the Kingdoms? She did not know, and in a way was grateful that so awful a decision was Kedryn's and not hers. She forced composure on her features and a steadiness she did not feel on her voice as she answered, 'Kedryn is the Chosen One.'

Ashar bellowed reeking laughter, his form flickering, shifting, becoming wraith-like, as if coiling smoke sat upon the throne, then resumed the form of Eyrik.

'He is also a man in love.'

Gross contempt rang in his voice and it occurred to her then that victory alone was not enough for this malign deity. Conquest was his ultimate aim, but the simple assertion of his power was insufficient: his ego demanded more than fleshly dominance. It seemed he had a need to debase his foes, to force upon them the full realisation of his cunning, to grind their faces in the bitter despair of vanquishment. More than just Kedryn's defeat, he sought to undermine the very beliefs that made his enemy strong. He revelled in the notion of betrayal as eagerly as he lusted for victory.

'He loves the Kingdoms and the Lady as much,' she said.

Did doubt flash briefly in the gold-flecked eyes? She could not be sure, only that he smiled an ugly smile and said, 'We shall see.'

Abruptly, he rose from the throne, taking the great sword by its blade, seizing her wrist with his free hand. There was a strength in him she could not resist and she allowed him to drag her across the red-lit hall, out through the marbled chamber to the courtyard.

The interior of the palace was changed, as if, with the need for deception gone, he allowed it to revert to its natural condition. Now gloomy walls of green-slimed grey stone rose about her, the sky above ruddy as if lit by vast fires. Jasmine and roses and magnolia no longer climbed about colonnades, filling the atrium with their scent, but were replaced with ugly weeds, leprously verdant and emanating a sour odour. Dull black stone flagged the yard and the fountain was become a pit of fire jetting a column of incandescent flame high into the noxious air. Ashar gestured and the flame died, revealing a pillar of seared grey metal. He dragged her towards the pile and she saw that it rose from a plinth, chains dangling from its upper level. He stepped onto the plinth, hauling her behind, and forced her arm up, snapping a manacle about her wrist. He chained her other arm and she was left standing, hands upraised. Ashar stepped back, setting down the sword as he surveyed his handiwork.

'I believe,' he said, smiling lasciviously, 'that some further distraction might be amusing.'

Wynett cried out then, as he took the neckline of her gown and tore it from her. He chuckled and ripped away her undergarments so that she stood naked, her erect posture thrusting out her breasts. Ashar studied her speculatively, his form changing again so that she gazed, close to tears, at the misshapen thing that appeared the physical embodiment of his spiritual deformity. He fondled the huge phallus jutting towards her suggestively, the forked tongue lashing over his fleshy lips.

'Mayhap later,' he said softly, 'after you have seen Kedryn slain I shall offer you a choice. You may give yourself to me, or I shall take you. Think on it, Wynett – you may yet live.'

'Never,' she moaned and he chuckled, taking Eyrik's shape again, and retrieved the sword, swinging it to his broad shoulder as he turned and walked away, leaving her alone in the dismal yard.

She struggled against the chains but they were firm and she could neither tear them loose nor work her hands through the hoops of the manacles. She gave up the effort as she felt her skin chafe and blood ooze down her arms. Tears clouded her vision and she blinked them away, concentrating on the need to remain calm, to think clearly, that she might, should the Lady grant her so great a boon, aid Kedryn in some way when he came.

How she might do that she was not sure and she forced herself to review all that Ashar had said. He was not confident of victory, of that she felt certain, for why else should he prepare to offer Kedryn a choice between willing surrender of the talisman and combat? Nor, whatever Kedryn decided, did the god intend to honour any bargain. 'After you have seen Kedryn slain' he had said. Therefore, no matter what blandishments he offered, no matter what fate should befall her, Kedryn must not relinquish his sword. He must at all costs fight Ashar; and with the Lady's blessing slay him.

She could not think beyond that and she closed her eyes, murmuring a heartfelt prayer to Kyrie that Kedryn see her life did not matter, only the defeat of Ashar.

\*

Kedryn and Tepshen emerged from the tunnel to find themselves on a windswept plateau overlooking a narrow valley of dismal prospect. There was an air of miserable desolation about the vista, a sense of palpable menace that hung threateningly on the very wind that scoured the landscape. Behind them, the stone bulked grey and gloomy against the sky, that red as though underlit by the flames gouting from the farther reaches of the mountains, stretching like a great bloody curtain to the hill-pocked horizons. Below, trees thrust skeletal limbs denuded of foliage in attitudes of supplication, seeming to beg forgiveness of the draught, spreading over sere ground to a wide river that curved steel-grey about an islet of black rock. Jagged stone thrust fang-like, tortured shapes up from the jet mound, forbidding as the jaws of some massive beast, conforming at the central point to a vague approximation of a castle. It was clearly no human construct, for no windows showed in the ebon surfaces and the towers were spires of smooth rock, the walls like melted slag spewed from a molten core. One entrance was visible, a great, dark portal with opened, anticipatory gates, that faced a narrow bridge spanning the ominous stream.

Kedryn sniffed the wind, his nostrils crinkling in distaste as it brought the odours of corruption, and turned to his companion.

'I think we have found Ashar's hold.'

'Aye.' Tepshen's luteous features were grim. 'And likely he awaits our coming.'

'Then let us not disappoint him,' Kedryn declared.

Tepshen studied his face for a moment, then smiled gravely and took his hand in an unusual display of emotion.

'Whatever fate befall us now, I am proud of you. You are a true warrior.'

His sinewy hand squeezed tight and Kedryn returned the pressure, smiling no less gravely.

'You honour me, my friend. I could ask no better comrade on this quest.'

Tepshen nodded and murmured, 'Save Brannoc, perchance.'

'That is another debt we shall settle,' Kedryn answered, and they began to climb down through the jumbled stones towards the grim, grey trees.

The wind grew stronger as they descended, feculent as the stench of a midden, rattling the withered branches so that the cadaverous trees seemed to reach towards them, seeking to ensnare them. They stood gaunt, reminding Kedryn of the frameworks of the bloodeagle, that impression heightened by the charnel reek that mingled with the fecal stench as they drew closer to the river. Thorny limbs seemed to clutch at him and he drew Drul's glaive, ready to lop off any that took life and sought to steal his. The ground beneath his feet was grey and parched as mummified skin, striated with tiny cracks that seemed to sigh as he stepped upon them, the combination of clattering branches and plangent ground soul-numbingly miserable, the wind an offence that threatened to void his stomach. He fought against the sensual assault, marching resolutely onwards, Tepshen at his side, intent on reaching the weird keep that bulked ever larger before them.

They reached the river, pausing at the bridge. It seemed too fragile to sustain their weight, its span held on either bank by massy pillars of basalt, graven with indecipherable runes, the footway stretching out unsupported over the steely race that frothed against the sheer banks, lashing angrily at the desolate soil.

'There is no other way,' Tepshen remarked, and set out across the span.

Kedryn hurried to follow, aware that the bridge swayed as they crossed it, each step setting its planks to vibrating, the retaining walls shuddering under his hand. It seemed the structure must fall apart beneath them, spilling them into the flood below, and Kedryn felt vertigo assail him as he speeded his pace, trotting behind the kyo.

They halted again when they reached the farther bank, staring up at the hold that now loomed vast above them. A broad roadway of seamless jet ran up to the open gates, the portal glowing red as if fire burned within the walls, those sheer and smooth, seamless as the road, stone run as if poured from a melting pot, evil a presence tangible as the stench of the wind that Kedryn now realised wafted from that door. He set both hands about the hilt of his sword and stepped past Tepshen, taking the lead as they approached Ashar's stronghold.

The wind was fierce as they entered the keep, sighing down a long, low corridor filled with the mephitic frowst. It threatened to numb their senses as they paced the doleful tunnel, their blades held battle-ready, anticipating momentary attack in the gloomy darkness.

Then the tunnel gave way to a yard as forbidding as the hold's exterior, shadowy beneath the jut of sweeping walls, encased in a tangled spread of rank weeds from which came the fetor. Kedryn ignored it now, for at the centre of the yard stood a column surrounded by a low wall, and chained to that column was Wynett.

He was shocked to see her naked even as his heart lurched with joy as the steady rise and fall of her breasts told him she lived. He gazed upon the sweet perfection of her features and called her name as he ran to free her.

Her head turned then, her clear blue eyes opening wide as she saw him start towards her, and he saw fear writ stark, her mouth opening to cry a warning.

'Kedryn, no! Ward yourself!'

He halted, Drul's glaive raised, spinning in a circle, his eyes scanning the shadowy depths of the weed-hung yard.

And gaped as he saw a tall, brown-haired man emerge from the tangles at the far side of the court. His senses reeled as he studied the sternly handsome face, the set of the broad shoulders, for in them he saw his father as Bedyr had been in his youth, and that similarity, that recognition was weirdly disorientating. He hesitated, sword point lowering as the man stepped out onto the black flagstones. He held a sword akin to Drul's, but the blade was crimson as if soaked in blood, and he smiled.

Wynett cried, 'He is Ashar, Kedryn! Do not trust him.'

'Kill him,' murmured Tepshen, close at his back. 'I shall look to Wynett.'

Kedryn took a pace forward, matched by the brown-haired man, still smiling, each movement an echo of Kedryn's.

'So,' he called, 'you are the Chosen One. Kedryn Caitin! You have dared much to come here.'

'I will dare more,' Kedryn responded, feeling the glaive tremble in his grip, the talisman mounted on the pommel glowing brighter, its radiance gradually banishing the dull shadows, pulsating, filling him with a dreadful purpose.

'No doubt,' Ashar returned, and his voice was Bedyr's, 'but will you sacrifice your wife?'

Kedryn halted, aware that Tepshen moved a short distance away, sidling towards the column.

'I offer you a bargain,' Ashar said, and Wynett screamed, 'Do not listen to him! He intends to slay you!'

Ashar gestured and for an instant fire spurted around Wynett. Kedryn roared, 'No!' and the flames died. Ashar said, 'I will give you the woman for that sword. It is, after all, rightfully mine.'

'He lies,' Wynett cried. 'He will take the sword and slay you.'

'Would you see her die?' asked Ashar, gesturing again so that a fresh gout of fire sprang upwards.

Kedryn stared at him. From the corner of his eye he saw Tepshen halt, realising that the kyo had reached a point where the column must block him from the god's sight.

'He is afraid of you,' Wynett screamed.

Tepshen began to move cautiously towards the pillar. Kedryn said, 'You are a god of lies, why should I trust you?'

'Because you love her,' Ashar said, 'and because you will see her die horribly if you refuse.'

Kedryn paused, aghast at the alternatives. Ashar smiled, and he was Bedyr, standing beaming at his son. 'Give me the sword,' he urged, 'and you shall go free with your wife.'

Kedryn shook his head, not in refusal, but bafflement. It seemed he stood before his father and his soul rebelled at the notion of striking Bedyr, rebelled at the notion of condemning Wynett to death. Did the Lady ask this of him? Was he capable of so awful a choice?

'Give me the sword,' repeated Bedyr. 'Do you not trust me? Am I not your father?'

*

Gerat rose from the stool, stepping from beneath the awning of the tent into the sunlight. Rycol moved to join her, but she motioned him

335

back, lifting her arms as her eyes closed and her lips moved to utter a single word: 'Now.'

The chatelain halted as she gasped, her body trembling, shaking as through gripped by some terrible force. It seemed for an instant that she was wreathed in blue flame, surrounded by a corona that concentrated about her hands and flashed, driving out and away, streaking like lightning over the startled faces of his soldiery, lancing over the treetops below to strike deep into the woodlands of the Beltrevan.

*

Kedryn felt the power flood through him. It was cleansing, a cool, cauterizing fire that banished doubt. He saw the nimbus emanating from his glaive burn fiercer, felt the sword shudder in his grip, compelling him forwards. He saw Bedyr's form dissolve, replaced by that of the tall, brown-haired man, then by something else, something hideous that snarled and sprang forwards on cloven hooves, lips drawn back from lupine fangs between which a forked tongue lashed. He was possessed by that certainty that had gripped him when he faced Niloc Yarrum, by the surety that had sustained him as he faced Taws, by the implacable sense of rectitude that had filled him as he held the talisman atop the roofs of the White Palace. He saw Ashar in all the god's malignant ugliness and knew that he faced a liar, a foul thing that held only the antithesis of truth.

'For Wynett!' he roared. 'For the Lady and the Kingdoms!'

And before Ashar had time to gesture again, before the flames could lick once more, one final time, about Wynett, Kedryn gestured with the sword, not knowing from whence came the cantrip, or how he knew to work it, only that incalculable strength filled him as blue light flashed, encompassing his beloved, wreathing her in the Lady's protective light. He barked angry laughter as Ashar cursed and returned his blade to the attack stance as his feet carried him swift across the yard, the glaive swinging in a furious arc at the god's misshapen skull.

Ashar raised his own ensorcelled blade and blue steel rang loud against crimson, sparks coruscating about the combatants, both weapons glowing with magical life.

'You cannot win,' rasped the god, becoming Bedyr again, though but briefly, for it seemed the power invested in Kedryn and in Drul's glaive robbed him of that shape-shifting ability, revealing him clear to Kedryn's angry eyes.

'By the Lady,' answered the Chosen One, 'I can.'

He turned his sword as Ashar parried, the great weapon light in his hands, deflecting the god's cut, driving in again to hack at the pulsating belly. Ashar stood his ground, trading blow for blow, the yard filled with the clamour of steel on steel, cloven hooves clattering as the deity danced and sought to sunder Kedryn's chest, sever his neck, raining savage blows against the gaunt, fierce-eyed man. Each attack was turned and answered in kind, the righteous fury that possessed Kedryn lending him a physical strength to match the spiritual puissance burning within him, and Ashar was slowly driven back towards the weed-hung colonnades.

Tepshen saw his chance and sprang to the plinth, stepping into the blue nimbus that surrounded Wynett. He slid his blade between the links of the binding chain and levered, tendons bulging along his arms. The chain broke and the manacles securing Wynett's wrists fell free. Tepshen put an arm about her waist and swung her clear of the pillar, depositing her on the flagstones, neither of them, their eyes fixed on the battle raging across the yard, aware of her nudity.

'Aid him,' Wynett urged.

Tepshen shook his head. 'I cannot. This is his battle and his alone.'

He took her wrist then, holding her back as she moved to aid Kedryn, who now pressed Ashar hard, sending the god scuttling back against the leprous weeds.

The growths smouldered in the sparks cascading from the clashing blades, the acrid smell of burning joining the fetor of the stinking hold. Kedryn felt his hair scorch, was aware of tiny points of pain on his exposed skin as he moved through the fiery rain, but they were as nothing under the purpose that gripped him. He saw fear flicker in the yellow eyes and laughed again, the sound eliciting a foul curse from Ashar. He swung his blade in a great, two-handed stroke and felt it snag on burning vines. Now Ashar grinned a deathshead smile and stabbed his blade like a dagger at Kedryn's belly. Kedryn spun, all the long hours of Tepshen's training coming to his aid, sucking in his stomach as he bent, seeing the crimson steel slice the filthy linen of his shirt, the same movement freeing his weapon so that he drove the hilt down against the god's outthrust wrist.

Ashar screamed as the talisman mounted on the pommel touched him. His flesh seared and he darted back. Kedryn paced after

337

him, parrying a thrust, unable to swing the glaive in that confined space.

Then the god was backed against a door of dully burnished metal and he kicked it open, springing into the chamber behind. Kedryn followed him, raising the glaive to deflect a cut that would have split his skull had it landed, seeing that they now fought within a chamber of blood-red marble, twinned pillars forming an aisle down the centre. Ashar ducked behind the shelter of a column and they commenced a slow, zig-zagging progress through the piles, marble chipping and flaking as their blades clashed and were deflected, sparks of livid crimson flying from Ashar's, sparks of purest azure from Kedryn's, filling the room with dazzling, rainbow light. Rank sweat beaded the god's forehead, running down his hideous face to mat the orange hair that mantled his shoulders. Kedryn felt only the exhilaration of combat, uplifted by the purity of his intent, fuelled by the desire to revenge Wynett's suffering, Brannoc's death, all the suffering and the misery inflicted by this malign deity. Drul's glaive was a steel feather in his hands, his own battle-skill augmented by the power of the talisman that glowed fierce as vengeance at the hilt. He had no thought of hurt, no fear, only the compelling animus of Ashar's destruction. It drove him onwards, oblivious of Wynett and Tepshen entering the chamber behind him.

Ashar, his face towards the door, saw them and attacked with a fresh fury, screaming obscene curses as he hacked and slashed, his blade a blur of motion that now put Kedryn on the defensive. The god forced the man back, Kedryn retreating slowly, moving between the lines of pillars. He sensed the door at his back and allowed Ashar to drive him towards it, thinking to ensnare the god's blade in the vines beyond. Instead, Ashar leapt, goatishly nimble, to the side, his great sword arcing in a flat curve that smashed Tepshen's defence aside as easily as if the eastern blade were matchwood, swinging on to carve a great red gash across Wynett's naked stomach.

Kedryn saw it as though time slowed, allowing him to observe each awful detail. He saw Tepshen stagger back. Saw Wynett's flesh part, the droplets of blood arch crimson from the wound. Saw the greater flow as her life gushed out on the pulse beat of her heart. Heard her scream. Saw her eyes open wide in pain. Heard Ashar's triumphant roar and his own heart-rent bellow. Saw Wynett double, hands pressing to the dreadful wound as she fell down on her face. Saw Ashar's blade continue in a circle as the god spun, aiming a devastating cut at his own belly.

338

And blocked it with Drul's glaive, feeling the shock vibrate through his shoulders as dreadful rage consumed him, terrifying in its intensity, awesome, overwhelming him.

He became then something as inhuman as the god himself, a machine of pure destruction. The power he had felt before magnified, and Ashar recognised it, the triumph that lit his yellow eyes fading as Kedryn rasped the glaive up the length of the crimson sword, stepping inside his reach to slice the blade upwards, carving a line from chest to chin. Pus-thick gore oozed from the wound and Ashar danced backwards as Kedryn's stroke reversed, sweeping at his skull. Steel glanced from a curling horn and Ashar gasped, disbelief widening his gaze. Kedryn swung again and Ashar ducked, prancing away as the tip of one horn was sundered. He strove to turn the blows, losing chunks of grey skin as Kedryn forced him back between the pillars, his torso and shoulders becoming slick with the purulent matter that oozed from the wounds. He screamed in fury and frustration and turned on his heels, running for the farther end of the chamber.

Kedryn charged after, the glaive upraised, and saw Ashar fling open an inner door, lunging into the room beyond. He followed, finding himself now inside a great, dark hall, vaulted high, its lithic walls akin to the hold's exterior. Candles with bloody flames burned in sconces and chandeliers, and from a circle of tall stands set around a monstrous throne that loomed black from the centre. Ashar turned here, desperate now as he parried the rage-engendered strength of his foe, the hall flickering with the light coruscating from both blades. A stand toppled, its fallen candle spilling molten wax like running blood across the floor. Ashar thrust another over at Kedryn, driving in as the man ducked clear of the flame that threatened to sear his eyes. Kedryn was too fast. He turned the blow and countered with a vicious cut that propelled Ashar backwards, hooves drumming as he staggered against the dais of the throne. Kedryn lunged forwards, the glaive a weaving column of blue light in his hands, and Ashar backed up the steps of the dais.

His thighs touched the seat's edge and he realised he could retreat no farther. He roared, the sound a fetid wash about Kedryn's face, and lifted his sword high, steel catching light from the candles, burning as though he raised a blade of flame.

And Kedryn set one foot upon the lowermost step, muscles bunching as he hurled himself forwards, oblivious of the blade that descended, his own thrust out.

The point struck Ashar's belly. Drove through to imbed in the basalt of the throne, rammed home with all the strength Kedryn could muster, the power of Estrevan in his arms, the Lady's blessing guiding him, rage and grief and revenge in the stroke. He pitched face down at the foot of the throne, feeling Ashar's blade land across his back, not hard with a killing stroke, but heavy as a fallen weapon, dropped from taloned hands that now clutched at the length of blue-glowing steel pinning the god to his unholy seat.

Hooves drummed furiously before Kedryn's face and he rolled away, kicking the dropped sword across the floor. He rose on hands and knees, staring, and climbed slowly to his feet, his eyes fixed on the creature that screamed and writhed before him.

Drul's glaive was driven hilt-deep into Ashar's belly. The god whimpered as he clutched at the haft, screaming as the blue fire radiating from the talisman seared his fingers. The nimbus grew, surrounding him with its azure fulguration and his hands fell away, clawing at his chest. Bloody tears spilled from his pain-slitted eyes and his movements slowed until finally he slumped still, his arms dropping to his sides, his ghastly head drooping on his ravaged chest. Kedryn saw that he was pinned, nor sure if he was dead, and turned in search of the fallen sword, intent on severing the horned head from the slumped shoulders.

He saw the blade gleam in the blue light, plain steel now, and saw Wynett's half of the talisman fallen clear of the arachnid pommel as if, the god defeated, it sought to distance itself from his debased creation. It pulsed with a faint life and Kedryn cupped it, forgetting Ashar as the rage left him and his eyes filled with tears. He groaned, 'Wynett!' and turned his back on the vanquished god, moving on leaden feet towards the door.

The talisman glowed brighter as he quit the hall and he felt it vibrate beneath his fingers. Clutching it tight he stepped into the marbled chamber, grief like ashes in his mouth as he saw Tepshen knelt beside Wynett's body, a torn pink gown hiding her nudity, the pink dark red where cloth touched wound.

'Ashar is defeated,' he said dully, kneeling, his vision blurred by tears as he stared at the dear, dead face.

Tepshen stared at him, his own features lined with grief. Kedryn reached out, stroking Wynett's sun-golden hair, touching her lips, easing lids down over the blankly-staring blue eyes he could not bear to see. Grief filled him then and he threw back his head, wailing.

Tepshen reached to hold him, but halted the movement, his slanted eyes widening as blue radiance filled the doorway.

'Would you have her back?' asked a voice of such tranquil passion that Kedryn's keening died in his throat.

He wiped a hand over his tear-filled eyes, head turning slowly to observe the figure that entered the chamber.

She moved within a corona of light, almost too intense to permit clear vision, her form and features impressions rather than definite outlines, but nonetheless glorious, radiating love, serenity, a calm confidence that brooked no doubt of her ability to fulfil the promise implicit in her question. Kedryn stared at her, seeing a woman who was Wynett and Yrla, the Sisters of Estrevan, all one, embodying all that was good, all that was pure and honest. He nodded dumbly, unable to speak, and she smiled, that simple expression wondrous.

Gracefully she walked towards them, kneeling beside Wynett, gently removing the blood-stained gown. She extended a hand, her fingertips touching the bloody wound. Still dumb-struck, Kedryn stared as the gash sealed, flesh knitting seamlessly, no scar or trace of hurt remaining. Wynett's breasts rose and her lips parted, breath sighing as though she awoke from deep slumber. Her eyes opened, widening as she found herself looking at the woman.

'Lady?' she murmured. 'Am I then come to you? Is Kedryn . . .?'

She fell silent as Kyrie touched her lips, smiling.

'Not yet, Sister,' said the goddess. 'And Kedryn lives. I would not see you parted.'

Wynett turned her head then, seeing Kedryn, and held out her arms. He enfolded her in his embrace, tears of joy spilling now, kissing her, stroking her hair, glorying in the touch of her warm, living flesh.

'Thank you, Lady,' he wept, laughing and crying at the same time.

'I owe *you* thanks,' she returned. 'All the world owes you thanks, for without your travails – and those of your comrades – ' her radiant gaze took in Tepshen, 'Ashar should have conquered and evil reign.'

'Is he then dead?' Wynett asked.

'Not dead.' Kyrie shook her head. 'He is a god and it is no easy task to slay a god. But he is held now, thanks to Kedryn. The talisman will pin him, for none here may venture close and Ashar may not remove the sword himself. In time, perchance, there will be one who finds a way to bring him back, but that is for the far future and for now the Kingdoms shall know peace. The Beltrevan, too, for with Ashar defeated his power shall wane and brotherhood hold sway.'

'I would have taken his head,' Kedryn murmured, 'had I not seen Wynett's talisman.'

'It is not too late,' Tepshen declared, fingering his sword.

'Leave him,' smiled Kyrie. 'What is done is sufficient, and it is time you quit this place. Balance is restored to the world and you have fulfilled all that may be asked of you.'

'Brannoc,' said Kedryn, 'Might you not restore Brannoc to life?'

For an instant Kyrie's face grew sad and she shook her head. 'That may not be. I am able to restore Wynett because she died on Ashar's blade and that weapon was forged with something of mine to lend it power. In his hatred and his pride Ashar did not realise that what is good may never be totally overwhelmed, so the stolen part of my talisman enabled me to return Wynett's life. But Brannoc's was taken by Taziel's hammer and that I cannot give back.'

Kedryn sighed, holding tighter to Wynett. 'Does he then dwell in this foul place?' he asked mournfully.

'No,' said Kyrie. 'Brannoc gave his life willingly that you might succeed, and now inhabits those realms where dwell my followers. He is at peace, Kedryn – you need not mourn him.'

'I shall miss him, however,' he said.

'He was a true friend,' the goddess nodded, 'and you should not forget to name him to the balladers.'

Kedryn smiled then and promised, 'I shall not. The coffers of Andurel shall reward the finest elegy.'

'He will like that,' smiled Kyrie, 'Now, let us depart this miserable place.'

'One thing more,' Kedryn said, 'I promised Drul's shade the return of his glaive – how may I now honour that undertaking?'

'Bring him the other,' Kyrie advised. 'He will accept it.'

'I will fetch it,' said Tepshen, rising to stride into the hall.

Kedryn was glad enough to leave that task to the kyo, for he had no great desire to see Ashar's transfixed body again, and waited until Tepshen returned with the weapon.

'So,' Kyrie declared, 'It is done.'

She rose, motioning them to follow her. Kedryn helped Wynett to her feet, frowning as he realised she was naked. Kyrie saw his expression and stooped to retrieve the blood-stained gown, holding it a moment before handing it to Wynett.

'It is cleansed,' she murmured as Wynett hesitated to take the robe, 'and it will do for now.'

Wynett accepted the gown and as she took it, it became a dress of purest Estrevan blue, unsullied. 'My thanks, Lady,' she smiled, donning the garment.

Kyrie acknowledged her gratitude with a nod and led the way to the door. 'Come,' she urged, 'Change is afoot and we had best be gone.'

Her words were emphasised by a peal of sullen thunder that shook the walls of the keep. The fecal stench was gone, replaced by a sulpherous odour reminiscent of Taziel's cavern. Above, lightning roiled scarlet, the fiery sky avid, great gusting billows of black cloud racing on the growing wind. Kedryn pressed the talisman into Wynett's hand saying, 'This fell from the sword.'

Wynett studied the jewel, her eyes troubled. 'I gave it to Ashar,' she whispered. 'Do I have the right to hold it now?'

'Child,' smiled Kyrie, 'Ashar deceived you and you acted only to aid Kedryn – take it and wear it in the knowledge it carries my blessing.'

She paused beside the column that had held Wynett prisoner, taking the severed chains and passing them through her hands to form a necklace of delicate silver links that she attached to the talisman, sealing the chain about Wynett's neck.

'With my blessing,' she repeated. 'Now hurry, lest this odious place fall about our ears.'

There was an urgency in her tone that brooked no delay and they hurried through the courtyard as fresh thunder rumbled above them, the lightning striking the black towers now, ebon stone burning red, the flags trembling under their feet. They passed through the gates and walked quickly to the bridge, halting there as Kyrie beckoned them closer, raising her arms so that the effulgence surrounding her held them all within its light. Kedryn looked back, seeing Ashar's hold shudder beneath the onslaught of the storm, the towers crumbling, crashing down upon the walls, that in turn fell, sealing the place. Forever, he hoped as the vision faded and he clutched Wynett, suspended in blue light.

When that radiance faded they stood within the confines of Drul's tomb, firelight bright above, throwing stark shadows over the mouldered armour and the yellow bones. Tepshen placed Ashar's sword

343

between the gauntleted hands and Kyrie said, 'Now all is done, and done well. The woodlanders will not harm you – go out amongst them and they will bring you safely home.'

She gestured and they stood atop the mound, the great bonfire of the Gathering blazing fierce all round. Of the Lady there was no sign, but from the talisman Wynett wore there came a radiance that surrounded them and Wynett said, 'Come, the fire will not harm us.'

Kedryn set an arm about her shoulders and she linked hands with Tepshen as they walked through the flames to confront the startled faces of the Drott. Cord stepped forth, his bearded features awed as he bowed and raised his arms in greeting.

'Hef-Alador?' he said wonderingly.

'Aye,' Kedryn answered. 'And come to tell you of the world's new turning.'

*

Barris Edon felt his close-cropped hair rise beneath his leathern helm and took a firmer grip on his sword, deciding that one of the disadvantages of keen eyesight was that it placed him always on watch, and whilst that was an easy enough duty on the walls of High Fort, here in the Beltrevan it was somewhat less desirable. Especially with so vast a throng of woodlanders moving remorselessly towards him. He shaded his eyes, wondering why the horde cheered so, and why the warriors held, not swords and axes, but clusters of white and red feathers. He rose to his feet, shouting up the slope, seeing bows nocked and Chatelain Rycol come running down with an agility that belied the commander's age, Gerat close on his heels. Then he shouted again as he saw the three figures riding at the head of the barbarian column and recognised them.

'Kedryn returns!' he bellowed. 'And the Lady Wynett with him! The kyo, too!'

Rycol slithered to a stop beside him, staring in wonder at the mass of warriors. 'Peace feathers?' he asked, disbelievingly.

Barris Edon saluted the chatelain and bowed to the Paramount Sister, whose descent was, he felt, most unbecoming to one of Estrevan.

'Peace feathers!' she cried, clutching Rycol's arm, her ageless face split by a huge smile. 'They are safe! They have won!'

To the amazement of both soldiers she promptly clambered over the breastwork of rocks and, her skirts lifted high, proceeded to scamper down the slope, her laughter loud on the summer air.

'Praise the Lady!' Barris Edon heard her shout. 'Praise the Lady you are come back safe.'

Rycol bellowed orders for his archers to put up their shafts and further surprised Barris by following the Paramount Sister. The soldier could not hear what was said, but from the smiles he could see, he guessed that the news was good. Indeed, the very air felt suddenly fresher, and as he watched Kedryn embrace Wynett he thought they made a decidedly handsome couple, ideal rulers of the Three Kingdoms. He was not sure what duty had taken them into the Beltrevan, nor what caused such joy to lighten their faces, even the stern-featured kyo beaming mightily, but somehow he felt certain that a new age dawned.

Beaming himself, Barris Edon sheathed his sword and began to cheer, his cry taken up by his fellows so that soon the Lozins rang with their joyful shouts:

'Hail Kedryn! Hail Wynett!'

'And praise the Lady,' Kedryn whispered against Wynett's cheek, holding her tight to him, her arm about his waist, her lovely face radiant.

'Aye,' she answered. 'May her blessings be with us always, and we always together.'

And it seemed then that a calm voice spoke in both their minds, saying, 'So shall it be.'

Sphere now offers an exciting range of quality fiction and non-fiction by both established and new authors. All of the books in this series are available from good bookshops, or can be ordered from the following address:

Sphere Books
Cash Sales Department
P.O. Box 11
Falmouth
Cornwall TR10 9EN.

Please send cheque or postal order (no currency), and allow 60p for postage and packing for the first book plus 25p for the second book and 15p for each additional book ordered up to a maximum charge of £1.50 in U.K.

B.F.P.O. customers please allow 60p for the first book, 25p for the second book plus 15p per copy for the next 7 books, thereafter 9p per book.

Overseas customers including Eire please allow £1.25 for postage and packing for the first book, 75p for the second book and 28p for each subsequent title ordered.